# FRANCIENE

*A Novel by*

Janice Mae Robinson

*To Pat and Harvey;* 10/20/13
*Enjoy Franciene! I surely
did — Love
Jan Robinson*

This book is dedicated to my Mother, who
believed I could do anything,
And,
To my great Son, Tim, who kept his vow
to do it all for both of our boys,
And to the precious friends who gave such
support for this, my first novel.

# ACKNOWLEDGEMENT

A lovely lady, long passed away now, a teacher, an accomplished artist, and as beautiful inside and out, as I ever saw, created the pastel rendering of a road on the Island from where this novel takes its' inspiration.

I asked to purchase it at first sight, that day twenty-seven years ago, breathless from the way she had captured the little lanes we loved. She brought it to me where I worked, on the private club property she was a member of, after she had participated in a member-guest art show. It is so darn good it should have gone into print, but it remains the only one, and now graces my dining room wall. I am humbled for it, for her sweet gesture, and after trying to find a living relative to discuss using it with produced no success, decided I should still honor her memory by using it on the cover of my book, and here in this acknowledgement. I wish she could know… maybe she does.

Her name was Gretchen Ramsey, and she will be remembered by me for all the time I have left.   Thank you, Gretchen

Jan Robinson

# CONTENTS

# FOREWORD

## MARCH 14, 2013

Not long after my amazing Mother, Iris Belle Strickland Wise, died in 1998, there was a stirring in me to do something that would remain in tribute to her, and her belief, her forever belief, that I could do ANYTHING, and, so it can be said, "Yep, that was some gal, that Janice Mae... she always had something to say!"

Here it is, with whatever value may be derived from your simply getting through the whole thing... a novel! A real book! I can not believe it myself.

The story is in no way autobiographical. It is woven from hundreds of factually precise experiences, while I was fortunate enough to live in a place very much the same as Squires Island is depicted. Reading through the text, (and I have many times), it has been great to feel myself flying backward to the place and time when each memory was carved. The sights, the smells, and the sounds of, "Back then", never fail to fill me up with all sorts of reactions. This passage has been enriching for that alone.

Gratitude flows into many places, and over more heads than I can count, for the opportunity and the honor to have been there for that special time.

No apology for the ribald turns this story takes, there were many flights to saucy and dark places, and the occasional eyebrow-raising scenario adds the provocative edge I believe is necessary to paint what I want readers to see and feel, and be excited by. As an aside, it was a lot of fun to be so bad! Ladies and Gents… this ain't no "Gone with the Wind"!

None of the characters can be fingered as actually living or dead, since all of the folks in the story are products of this author's imagination, blended and seasoned with social and cultural styles and foibles observed during a life amongst 'em.

It might be fun to point out a person or two you, who are "Been heah's" believe a character might be representing… "That HAS to be good old so-and-so"! I encourage the game, while aware who, in true life, was called to mind as the characters emerged. They are all composites, and I have been most respectful and careful to leave the impression that they are some mighty fine people wherever they are now. The little piece of them you may believe you recognize won't bother anybody too much.

Other writers of fiction have told me the cast of their stories simply came and introduced themselves as they joined the tale… it is the same here. I was skeptical about the repeated revelation, until my own experience. It is hard to believe unless one has it happen to them. So help me, the people in this story simply drifted into my mind's backyard and began to play with me.

Wrapping up, I intend for this tale to emphasize my opinion that some of the finest and sweetest human beings ever, lived on the Island when I was there. Precious memories linger of those who have gone on. I miss them to this day, and always will.

"Franciene" is true fiction, I call it one hell of a tale, and know it will hold and amuse, and, yes, titillate those who want to take it on as pure reading enjoyment!

Janice Mae Robinson

# CHAPTER ONE

*Squires Island - Off the South Carolina Coast*
**LATE MAY, 1981**

There was nowhere to go from the dock... unless it would be down a dirt road appearing to wind into another dirt road... to more nowhere. The boat left them at one, the captain mumbled something about four o'clock, and if they were there to meet them that would be good. If not, not so good!

Undaunted, the man and his young friend aimed at the road to discovery without a backward glance. It was late May, prime time to be there, and our two vagabonds knew the worst encounters, other than the gnats and skeeters they dreaded, would be intolerant locals. No matter, this was going to happen, regardless.

Sporting a couple of knapsacks packed with fresh khaki, a canteen apiece, maps that were of no use here, a few packs of crackers, and some insect repellent, the lanky, yellow haired boy and the man, (middle aged, but fit and lean), attacked the discouraging expanse of sandy road with vigor. They would have liked to meet one friendly local who could orient them, eliminating the guesswork about which of the thickly foliated, deep-rutted lanes they could turn into, but no one was about... not man nor beast, so the older man gestured they might want to make the next right.

As if the dust and cloying humidity were trapped behind them by a glass wall, the white sand trail was cool, the air clear, and all that grew was a vibrant spring green... Eden-like, after the avenue of dust-coated trees and bushes before they turned. Smiles exchanged, they raised their proud chins toward the broadening beauty ahead. After a half-mile march, the horizon of a marsh vista peeked through moss-wrapped live oaks, and they topped an impressive bluff which hung out over a tightly winding, skinny salt creek. The tide was low enough to expose sand and mud banks frosted with ancient, bleached oyster shells and darting fiddler crabs. The triumph following this eye-pleasing discovery was about to be replaced by shock and disbelief, when the boy called out, "Toby! Come quick!"

The kid had slid down the bank, and was on his knees facing the water's edge, pointing to the middle of the creek. His tone and the frozen straightness of his spine said he wasn't simply pointing out an otter or a dolphin, or anything good. This boy was afraid... more than that. He was horrified.

"What is it Will?" came tumbling out while Toby Howell made his cautious way down the bluff, using tree roots and shell outcroppings as crude steps. The creek bank was still quite soupy from the tide fall, so he stepped carefully to the boy's side in order to follow the pointing finger with his eyes. Toby took a bead along Will's arm and breathed, "What do you see, Will?" The boy still pointing, jumped to his feet shouting, "Can't you see it? It was right there in the rip line! A hand and arm sticking up! I swear it was there!"

Since the tide had begun to flood moments before, the current was moving swiftly, churning through the little creek bed. Sure enough, a boil in the water produced a shoulder and an upper arm. It was quickly gone again, as if never there, but this time they both saw, and they ran, slipping and sliding down the sloping edge into the flow of deeper water. Toby shouted, "Will boy! Swim downstream! Try to trap it!" They had to know what the hell it was. The man dove and began to swim with his eyes open in the murky-green, stinging salty water, hoping the sun would outline the body for him. It was Will who caught hold of it, and he yelled for help. A few minutes passed before they wrestled the wretched thing to the bank, and they took a moment to catch their breath before taking a look at their unfortunate discovery.

It was a young woman... not quite a woman... more a girl, and she had been a beauty, dressed in a halter and shorts, barely visible the pink and white fabric through the muddy swirl, and her hair was a lovely, sun-streaked, strawberry blonde. What a damn shame to see this, to know that even in such a peaceful place, horror like this exists. Will became sick, and Toby had to turn away and shake himself to divert the dizziness that announces nausea.

Toby forced himself to focus on their situation. They knew no one here, and didn't know where to go to find help. What if they were suspected of this deed, if in fact it was a misdeed, and not just a tragic accident? He gathered himself up, became as detached and clinical as he could manage, and took a closer look at the poor girl in the mud. She had been a beauty... that was a fact. Even death could not mar the perfection of her sweet face and perfect body, obviously very alive, mere hours ago.

She had been a child of the coast, her face, shoulders, midriff, and long limbs were a grotesque, greenish gray from being in the water, but the coppery overtone of her skin resulted from a regularly upgraded tan...Her hands were well tended...the nails were short, but manicured, and painted with clear polish recently applied. There was a tiny circlet of coquina shells on links of gold around her left wrist, so delicately telling her loveliness, and to add to the poignancy of the still little body, a small gold, deeply monogrammed signet ring, obviously an heirloom, was on her left hand.

Such a surreal moment, standing in the bright sun, before a girl whose time on earth ended while so young, left Will trembling, his head turned away, so he didn't have to face the lousy truth they had pulled from the water. She wasn't much older than he, in fact they could have been the same age, and in another time, he would have been thrilled just to talk to such a beauty, making it doubly difficult for the boy to bear. Toby put his hand on Will's shoulder and they rose to their feet, steadying each other. Steering the boy to the end of the sandy spit by the creek so they could compose themselves away from the grisly sight, man pressed boy to talk about what they had found.

"What could have happened to her?" Will was trying not to cry, as his voice cracked. "I have no idea, son," Toby whispered, "But we need to figure how to deal with this, right now!" Toby searched his mind for options, while a creative Will surprised both of them with a solution of sorts.

"Let's cover her with palmetto fronds, and walk out of here like nothing happened, Toby! I don't want to get into trouble in this weird place, and neither do you!" He was losing it, Toby feared, but he worked his arm free when he was taken hold of, and turned to continue his tirade. "Anybody could have found her just like we did, or nobody, depending on pure chance, so let's go for a walk around this damned island like we meant to, get on that four o'clock boat like the captain said, and just forget it!" Toby did not reply... he wanted to think on it for a moment. Will pressed the point further.

"Forget it all and start over in the morning at the beach house. This isn't the kind of stuff you're putting in your guidebook, that's for damn sure, so let's just go... now!" He began running around among the palms gathering up dead fronds like someone gone wild. Toby thought to stop him, then looked back at the pitiful little body near the water, and he relented. He went to the girl and took her cold, tiny wrists in his two-handed grip. After dragging her across the sand above the high water mark, he reverently laid her under a cedar bough out of the sun, and went to help the boy gather covering material.

This man who had until this moment, figured he was pragmatic and clear-headed, was muttering like a fool by the time he had tugged several fan-like boughs to the body. "What in the world are we thinking? Is this how easy it is to get tangled in something so bizarre it alters your life?" He muttered to himself, then fell silent, knowing he couldn't answer his own question. It took about ten minutes, but even after they were satisfied she was hidden, to be sure they checked carefully and couldn't see her from any angle. Toby swept a muddy frond back and to across the track her body had left, and, knowing the tide would do the rest, considered the deed done. She was concealed well enough for them to get away from there.

It was thirty minutes into the afternoon... God! Would four o'clock ever get here? They got out their canteens and drank, then splashed their flushed, sweaty faces, trying to settle their nerves a bit, before walking back up the road. Neither said a word, or looked at each other. No reason to. Time can be fickle when so much takes place, willy-nilly. It had taken only a short time to arrive at that serene bower by the creek, yet the hike back to the dock seemed endless. Will, stoic and trembling, was near to a state of shock... while he was pasty-pale, his face was beaded with sweat, and he would jerk involuntarily at intervals.

His friend knew of no way to comfort him, so they walked the return in silence. Neither of them noticed before, that there was a little store to the right of the pier head. It was of weather-worn, unpainted wood, [or perhaps the paint was just gone over time], the architecture was a hip-roofed, simple cube, with an open porch that wrapped around the entire building.

There was an ancient Coke machine dominating the porch, a rusty ice storage box with an old brass lock firmly secured, and a cork bulletin board festooned with a few faded event notices, business cards, and "FOR SALE" posters. The shabby, glass-paned door was locked as well, with a sign, duct-taped in the center that announced hours of operation.

"OPEN Monday-Tuesday -10 to 12 - 2 to 4 - CLOSED WEDNESDAY - OPEN Thursday - Friday 10 to 2 - 2 to 4 - Open Saturday - 12 - 3 - CLOSED SUNDAY! " The kicker was printed at the bottom of this very well worked out schedule. "IF WE AIN'T HERE BY POSTED TIME WE JUST DIDN'T GET HERE YET—HANG ON!"

Toby peered inside and could see a beer cooler, a counter with a peeling cash register, a few racks of snacks and boat stuff. Taking up a big part of the room, was a couple of open chest freezers, holding God knows what, since one could see, even from outside, that the years of untended frost had taken them over. A pay phone on the far wall and a couple of rusty metal chairs, obviously to accommodate the locals for lying to each other, appointed the far end of the room.

There was no one around, same as when they got off the boat. Toby looked at Will, and putting his arm, father-like, around his dropped shoulders, saying, "Boy, we just have to sit here and wait for that shitty boat to come... are you okay?" He nodded, sniffed up some unshed tears, and dropped to the bench by the door. "It just doesn't seem real, Toby." The older one thought hard about how to answer him, since it was the first he had spoken about her since they left her on the beach. "It's not real, Will... we decided that when we did what we did, so until we have let a good stretch of time and distance get between then and now, let's not talk more about this, alright?"

He could have punched himself out for such a cowardly reply, but no better words came to him. The boy looked up in his mentor's face with such trust and belief in his command of their predicament, Toby wished he could disappear. Instead, he sat down beside him, lamely patting his knee. It was a moment like the protective state one puts himself in while having his teeth drilled, or his butt turned up at the doctor's... a "this will be over soon, and I won't ever have to think of it again", type situation. With the view before them, across the wide river where several small islands and hammocks pushed at the horizon, Toby let himself drift into the vista, as he had always managed to do since a youth. Will followed suit, and appeared to relax a bit. It was now one thirty-five. Were their watches working? Yes, there's the bloody second hand traveling its way around the dial without a care.

"Let's walk down the dock... want to?" Toby asked, with mock cheer. Will got to his feet in a single move, and walked off alone with his head down. He was so much taller than when Toby first took him in two years ago. Only just past sixteen then, Toby would have thought better of taking on such a young, completely untested kid, if he hadn't seemed so lost, and so dreadfully alone.

\* \* \*

They met in the Okeefenokee Swamp, while Toby was doing some recreational canoeing and nature photography. The map from the ranger in Waycross, showed a high knoll near the edge of the swamp, and a small structure where he could get water and a snack for his trip, so he was obliged to paddle to the little pier and loop his line around a crooked post. A skinny yellow dog charged toward him, barking and showing his teeth, and Toby was about to decide he didn't need anything there after all, when a boy ran to the dog with a piece of rope and tied it to his neck, softly calming him with his hands and voice. He didn't look at the canoe or the paddler until he had tied the pooch to the porch rail of the store. "Sorry, he thinks he's supposed to do that," he said. "He is, actually," Toby answered back. "Guarding his home and people is just exactly what he's about; to his mind...don't give it a thought." While walking to the porch, he offered his hand and introduced himself. "My name's Tobias Howell... Toby to my friends... What's yours?"

The boy became instantly shy, looking toward the water as if trying to think of his name for a moment, then said haltingly, "I'm William Parrish... nice to meet you." He shook hands readily... hungrily, giving the impression that not too many, if anyone, ever took the time to engage him. They went inside the tiny "store". Some would hesitate to call it so, since there was nothing more than a vinyl covered counter with a few baskets and jars of barely sale-worthy items, and a washtub with a nearly melted block of ice and some bottled soft drinks.

"I hope those drinks are still cold... the ice man is coming tomorrow. He tries to get here every other day, but I guess I'm not as important as most of his other customers," the boy admitted. It looks like this kid is the whole show, Toby told himself as he gave the room another going over. How did he come to be here alone? This place isn't fit for that old dog, much less a growing boy. It appeared stuck in the forties, with ancient wiring, and no visible plumbing... a rusted old pot-bellied wood-burning stove reigned in a corner. It all smelled of mold and wet burned wood, and of course the reeking dog didn't help.

The curious thing was, when Toby regarded the young man against this backdrop, he seemed to shine apart from the place with a fresh, unspoiled aura...as if he had been set down here one day from better times. "You here alone?" Toby asked cautiously. The kid started at the question, and his guard came up immediately. "I'm not alone! My grandpa will be back soon. He's in Waycross visiting his sister, and he let me stay and watch things. It's not hard to do, nobody much comes here this time of year. It's too hot in June for the swamp, too many bugs, and snakes, and 'gators, some say… What about you? What 'you doin' here yourself?"

The words were bitten off with a snap, as if he feared the question might seem rude. The boy was most unusual… well mannered, with sensitivities alien to such a backwater. Toby answered honestly. "It's just a pleasure trip. I'm a naturalist and a writer of sorts, and when I can, I go off to places, just for me. This is a spot I've meant to visit for years, but always pass it by on my way somewhere else. I'm here with my camera and notebook to get a feel of this swamp. How long have you been here, William?" The boy looked at the new man's face to check for sincerity, and whispered, "You can call me Will, that's what I go by, Sir. I don't know how long exactly, but Grandpa says my mama left me here one day and never came back for me. Guess I was too little to know much, 'cause I don't remember her, or anyplace else I ever lived."

He stopped talking abruptly like before, seeming to be so happy to be in conversation, he feared he'd talk it all away in one breath. The feeling of utter pity for this little fellow was consuming… painful. "It must be peaceful and beautiful too, for a boy, being in such an unspoiled place," Toby offered, trying to make him feel better about conditions he had no hand in. Will brightened a little and offered, "We've done okay, I guess. Grandpa and I have been hunting and fishing and guiding, and it's gotten us by. This old store doesn't do much, but the rangers help out with supplies a little so we can stay open to take care of the tourists when they come through, likely it keeps them from being bothered." The pleasantries were getting a little forced by now, so Toby picked up some crackers and nuts and a couple of cokes and paid. As he walked to the canoe Will ran after him, calling out, "Toby! Toby, wait!"

Turning toward him, Toby saw as desperate an expression on his face as he ever had seen. "What's wrong, boy? What's the matter?"

He was astonished to see large tears spilling down his freckled cheeks, and the poor boy slapped them away furiously as he blurted, "Don't you want a guide? I mean, can I go with you?" He was begging with his eyes...so piteously, it embarrassed Toby, who quickly said, "What about your grandpa, and the store? Can you just leave everything and go off?"

He wondered if he was wrong to question the boy's attempt to escape, when it was obvious how against the wall the child was. "He's not comin' back! He never left here! My grandpa's dead since last month! I buried him out back and haven't told anybody, 'cause they'd say I'm not of age enough to stay here alone, and I got no place else to go!" His pleading would break a monster's heart, and Toby was melting like a Popsicle in July. Please, please let me go with you! It's so frightful bad to be alone with just that ole' dog! I swear I won't be any trouble. I'll show you all the best places... even my secret ones nobody else knows about. I can leave food and water for Shine, [the dog's name was called so], and a note for the ice man and the ranger that I had a guidin' job come up. Don't say no...Please!"

Toby didn't say no... not then, and not after their canoe trip, which came to be the best exploration he had been part of, before or since... nor when Will figured they could, "Do this for keeps," and maybe even someday be a famous team, going worldwide, writing and photographing the most beautiful and remote places for folks who never could go to such places themselves. It was impulsive and spontaneous on both sides, but never once had they regretted the decision. Toby was a widower, childless, and very much alone like Will. Hand in glove, they set out together. Days later they decided between them that old Shine probably got adopted by the ranger. Better to believe that, than the gator-lunch, or panther-dinner fate he probably met.

# CHAPTER TWO

Back to the present, and to Will, moving away from him toward the end of the dock. Toby smiled a little after the recollection, but was soon right back to the thudding reality of their plight.

They stood together, leaning over a little to see into the swift current under the pier, and warmed to the sight of a dolphin, with her new calf learning the graceful moves from its mother and nearby nurse-mates, all four or five of them circling with obvious care. Such beauty was healing.

"I wonder where her folks are." Will whispered, and Toby rushed to answer him. "Right there with her, boy! Don't you see all of them swimming around?" Knowing he wasn't talking about the creatures below, Toby meant to stand by his decision not to give words to their nightmare. He properly caught himself up short, and fell silent again. The guilt from not helping Will with his pain was painful in itself, and Toby mentally swore to make it better, soon as they got away from this damned island, and began a silent plan. How stupid it was to think demons couldn't follow them to a better place.

Checking his watch for the hundredth time, and finding them with more than an hour left to fill, Toby suggested they walk down the path that followed the riverbank to the left, around the rear of the store. It was simply something to do, and Will seemed relieved to be involved in his own footsteps as they walked. Turned out, it was a pretty trail, with continuous river views and some virgin forest on the other side, consisting of live oak, hickory, sweet gum, cedar, and the ever present palmetto palm, wherever the sun gave the light they need to flourish.

The two hikers heard a sudden noise in a myrtle thicket near the edge of the woods, and were startled to see a huge buck emerge... an impressive rack of antlers flashing as he leapt away. Will turned to Toby with a look of unabashed delight, and for just a moment he forgot, and the man thanked that big deer and God for the look on the boy's face.

The trail seemed to reinvent itself as they walked, sometimes moving into the woods a little, then down a gully or through Indian shell middens, many centuries old. What a good idea this was, Toby thought, the time before the boat's arrival would slip by more easily because of the break. After a couple of turns they were once again at the river's edge. The trail seemed to incline a little, and the senior trekker decided that his forty-eight year old legs would be happy to turn around at the top of the rise to head back. Since it was already three-fifteen, he announced the plan to his young friend. Just as they were slowing to head back, Will let out such a moan Toby ran and grabbed his arm.

"What is it? What, Will?" The boy threw his arm toward the bank and fell to his knees. Toby looked, and was aghast to realize they had revisited the same damned sand-spit where they had left the covered body, by another route. There it was! The pile of brown palmetto boughs... the bier it truly had become.

"Why is this happening?" Are you trying to tell us not to leave you here alone?" shouted poor Will to the grisly pile. Toby lifted him to standing and turned around to walk swiftly back to the dock, all the while entreating him that his plan was their best choice, that they had no part in the mess, and if they had chosen another island instead of this one it would be a whole different day... all the things he could think of to say in support. Will began to breathe easier as they came in sight of the store and the dock, and it was three-forty, Thank God, Thank God!

Toby left Will on the bench and ran down the dock to see if the boat was in sight. It was just rounding the bend, about two miles away... right on schedule. He could feel escape at hand, when he looked back to the road and saw a cloud of dust indicating a vehicle approaching. The first sign that there was life on this rock, and mercifully the two friends didn't have to know a thing about them... ever. Will joined Toby, and they started down the pier for boarding. The car, a nice but very dirty Land Rover, slid to a stop and a powerfully large and handsome man got out to begin the walk they were halfway along. When he caught up with them on the floating dock, he only nodded and made a sound near to a grunt. Toby nodded back and turned to watch the boat's arrival and the docking procedure. There were a couple of middle aged black women with grocery boxes, a young boat mate who hadn't been aboard on the trip over, and the same captain, looking just as distracted as before. Guess he'd rather be most anywhere, doing most anything else, Toby observed silently.

The big man came down to help the women with their boxes, chatting them up with familiar humor. He off-loaded the parcels as fast as his two hundred-plus pound body could manage, and bending down to peer into the ports of the boat's cabin, called gently, "Franciene! Francie honey, 'you in there?" The captain came to the side of the boat, and leaning on the toe rail, drawled, "I ain't seen your girl yet, Massey, guess she missed the boat again. No big deal, I'll bring her to you next run."

The man on the dock wheeled around, stomping his well-worn weejuns down the floater and back, behaving like a petulant child. "She called over here at eleven o'clock last night... woke me up to tell me to meet this boat, I swear she did! Now what the hell am I supposed to think?" His face was as red as a tomato, and Toby could smell the brown liquor on his body and his breath, obviously from copious consumption. The stuff was part of his chemistry. His overall appearance didn't speak of a perpetual drunk, however. He was, in fact, quite a fine looking man. The captain shook his shaggy head and drawled, "Nothing we can do about it right now, Massey, I'll give you a shout from town to let you know if she's aboard." To that, the frazzled father just looked away, helpless to do anything else. The solicitous captain, obviously a friend, continued.

"You know how these kids are, Bo-Cap, the world's schedules ain't always for these kids like ours to follow. She more'n'likely hooked up with some of them townies and lost track o' time. I'd say that's just about what done happened." The agitated first mate decided to offer up.

"Pop, now you hush! You don't know nothin' 'bout what she's doin', nor with who, and that's a fact!", to put an end to the sparring. "Let's get on back so's we can look for her and bring her home!"

Will and Toby stopped moving, as if their pure presence could signal guilty association. Here they were, so close to the girl's father they could touch him, and he did not know what they had found! He was just here for his little girl, to fetch her home, while she is lying dead under palm fronds they put over her, and they couldn't say a word! Will began to shuffle his feet... spinning his wheels in frustration, so Toby took his elbow and steered him to the boarding steps. He snapped his head around as if to say, "Can we really leave like this?" Toby ignored the look and kept going up the three steps to freedom, praying for their return to innocence.

The boat was untied, they backed away from the floating dock, and the big man they called Massey walked disconsolately up to his car with the women in tow. Toby signed them into the log book, and he and Will settled into opposite corners of one of the bench seats, soon lost in personal replay of what had happened. They tried not to look at the two crew men as they began scanning the harbor, when the boat docked at Frenchport, obviously looking for Franciene. There was a bar and restaurant adjacent to the marina. The two passengers alighted and walked inside, heading for the men's room. Will bolted to the sink, running cold water to splash his face, as Toby stood nearby, concern all over him. Outside again, they sat down at the bar, and Toby ordered two long necks. At the far end, the captain was already on his second rum runner... untimely, since he had another trip to make.

The mate came in and sat by his dad and ordered a beer. Toby and Will were moments from leaving, when a girl walked through, joining the two men. She was what you would call a cute kid, obviously at ease at the bar, never mind her tender age, chewing her gum like it was chewing back, and her voice when she spoke, was quite the room filler.

"You just get back from your four o'clock run?" she chirped. The boy nodded as she continued, "I guess Franciene's home by now, wearing her old man down for more money. I swear, some people got all the luck. All she's gotta' think about is what to buy and who to go see, and come back when the money runs out, so Daddy can shell out again."

The boy shook his head slowly, saying nothing, and the captain spoke up. "She ain't home yet, Cissy. She missed the three o'clock boat, so what else is new? Massey is a fumin' mess over there, probably givin' his help holy hell about now just 'cause he can. Worse yet, I gotta' call him and tell him she ain't here to bring over even as yet, and we don't know where the damn hell she's at!"

Would somebody please explain why Toby and Will didn't get out of there? Truth be told, they were both frozen to the stools, listening to the repartee, perhaps needing to glean something about her, since they were so horribly involved. It was Cissy who spoke next.

"Now this just don't make any sense at all, y'all, since I saw her at about eight o'clock this morning." I could tell she was powerful hung over and not too happy about something, but she said she couldn't wait to leave this place behind her. I never saw her lookin' so bad, like she'd been up all night." The girl, who still had not taken a breath until now, went on.

"I asked her who she'd been out with last evenin' and she said I wouldn't know him... that's all she said. I sure figured she'd catch that boat, no matter what... wouldn't you think so? Do y'all know who she was out with? Jaime, did you see her last night?" Her question barrage was obviously irritating the bejesus out of the boy.

Jaime shook his head slowly, rolled his eyes and took a meaning-ful pull on his long neck before answering with a singsong, "No, Cissy, I didn't see her with anybody last night. When I ran up on her, she was alone, unlocking a damn nice car at the corner, and lookin' good too, in that little pink play suit she had on. I whistled at her, but she just flipped her middle finger my way and got in the car. I can't wait 'til she gets on the boat, so's I can pay her back for that bird she shot me!" Cissy gave him a look, and giggled before answering, "Wait a minute! Did you say she had on a pink play suit? You mean a halter top and sassy little tap pants... white trim on the legs and halter straps?" Jaime nodded passively.

"Lord Almighty! She was wearing the same thing when I saw her this mornin'! She must have gotten separated from her luggage overnight, since that girl never wears the same thing two days in a row, no matter what! Wonder what was goin' on with her?" There was no way the two eavesdroppers could walk out on the conversation, given the subject. Toby felt drained of strength as he listened, and his mind saw the obvious. She was still wearing that play suit when she died, but HOW did she die, and who would know what had happened?

Was it going to be impossible for them to leave without trying to get answers, and even worse, were they going to implicate themselves by staying? Toby glanced at Will in the mirror behind the bar. He was ashen. Without a word, he bolted for the door and ran out toward the boat slips, with Toby hard after him. He found Will cross legged on a dock box, rocking back and forth like a bowling pin about to fall. He was keening miserably, and chanting, "Why, Why... WHY? She was so young and beautiful and sweet, why did she die?" Frustrated by his ineptness, Toby answered. "Damn it, boy, you're going to get us in real deep here if you don't take control of yourself! We are too god-awful close to this mess being seen by so many people, and our names are on the boat's log. All that has to happen next, is that poor girl's body gets found, and a list of suspects is started by the police. We can't appear even slightly suspicious!"

The roar of what he had just said came back like a sickening echo... The boat's log! They signed their names when they boarded both times! That would be the first place the police would look for witnesses or suspects. This was beginning to stink! Toby told Will to sit right there, and not say a word to anyone while he was gone. He walked as evenly as he could down to the fuel dock where the ferry was tied up. No one was around to see, so he stepped onto the swim platform astern and climbed to the aft-deck, taking off his shoes first before stepping down. Subterfuge has begun in earnest, he thought, as he went to the wheelhouse to find the log book. It was there, hanging on a hook. He grabbed it with his shirttail, wiping it off, and opened it to the damning page. What to do...tear it out? Take the whole book?

He decided to carefully remove the pages joined together under the cord, took the pen and made a replacement entry for the day, forging the two women's names from their signatures, one, Carrie Treacle, the other, Pansy Griffin, then made up two names for Will and himself. Simple enough if the crew didn't read the names and remember they weren't the same ones they had signed earlier. It had to do, so the incriminating page was taken out of the way, and they could get the hell out of the harbor, rendered anonymous. He crumpled the offending sheet and shoved it into his pocket, intending to burn it to ashes later. As he headed back to where Will was perched, he remembered two old saws, from when he was a boy. "Every time you tell a lie, you have to lie again to cover the first one." and, "Oh what a tangled web we weave when first we practice to deceive."

Maybe they should have run immediately to the first policeman they could find and report the discovery of the body, clearing it up with complete honesty. Too late now... the deception must continue, but it must continue away from Squires Island, and the town of Frenchport. He had to get Will out of there, and quick. He is much too young to prevail under such pressure, and any further information about Franciene Thornedike could only push him more resolutely toward an irrational act, even putting their lives in potential jeopardy.

Back to the dock box, and... No Will! Toby swung in a circle, looking all around for his sun-streaked head, but he was no longer on the dock. Running back to the restaurant, he looked in the men's room...no luck there. The two crewmen were gone, but Cissy was still there, and... Was Toby hallucinating? Will was sitting at her side, leaning toward her face with a questioning look. "He's lost his mind!"...Toby said aloud. He hid around the corner behind them, just in time to hear, "I haven't known her very long... just about two years. See, I only just moved here three years ago this past August.

Francine went to school on Squires Island, but her daddy let her come to parties at his friends' homes, and things at the public school sometimes." She was obviously enjoying herself with a new boy to talk to. Toby held back, and let her go on, and on and on.

"After we got to know one another, we did some partying one night early last summer. Boy, did we party! It doesn't hurt a girl's chances to meet great looking guys when she arrives with the prettiest girl around. I will never know how she does it, but Franciene knows exactly how to play the boys to her advantage, and no girl I know would mind even taking her castoffs. How she learned all those moves while under her daddy's thumb is a mystery. I figure some girls' just got it and some don't, and baby doll, let me tell you, she's got it!"

Toby didn't wait for Will to ask another question, rounding the corner to stand between them. He clasped his shoulder, harder than it would appear, and cheerfully offered, "Will! I'm glad I found you! We need to get on the road if we want to be at the beach before dark. I hope you will forgive me for interrupting, Miss, but we do need to be going." The man all but rode the lanky boy out of the bar with his knee up in his butt, and when they got outside, Will went OFF!

"Damn you, Toby! I wasn't doin' anything wrong! I didn't even tell her my name. I just sat down by her and said it sounds like there's a lot of fun to be had in Frenchport, from her conversation about her friend, Franciene, and she took it from there. It felt right to try to find out as much about her as I could...but now I don't know what to do next!" Toby could see the kid was a wreck, and so paranoid it had taken away his ability to reason. At least he gave no opposition to their leaving on the spot. They threw their packs in the back of the jeep and drove away from the lovely little harbor for what Toby hoped would be forever.

# CHAPTER THREE

Charleston is everything a southern city should be. Just enough sophistication sprinkled over a wedding cake of a town, networked with beautifully restored, historically notable streets lined with grand old houses, gothic churches, and noble public buildings, all unique to the style the city was created with. Every edifice seemed to have been perfectly placed along each narrow avenue, (like a model town on a table), surrounded on three sides by water. The escapees began to relax as soon as they crossed the bridge over the Cooper River toward Padgetts Island, and Toby's place at the beach. His wife's family had kept a vacation cottage for generations, still shared among those tied by blood or other bonds. Each shareholder was graced with two weeks per season, but what with all the traveling, it had been necessary for Toby to pass on his weeks for many years running. When he petitioned for this particular week out of place, he was graciously accepted, and the others who loved him and Katie's memory, shuffled their schedules willingly with no notice. Today, two battered souls were going to the shore to heal.

Almost there, they relaxed enough to turn on the radio, and Will tuned in some locally preferred beach music to prepare. Maybe, just maybe, with strong effort and each other, they could get on with what they had planned since two years back, before Squires Island. Toby's plan was all about "getting on with it".

# ...... A TOBY SKETCH

His time while a boy was passed poking through forest and field, pond and creek, seashore and marshland... ever inquisitive, never satisfied with other folks's explanation for things. It was natural to him, that Toby's education followed a scientific track, more focused on the mysteries of creation than theories of men... ferreting out answers to questions not normally asked. Predictably, Toby realized his fortune wouldn't be made as a result of pursuing his passionately selfish thirst for knowledge, so he seized on a way to do both. Field guide material began to flow from his brain to his fingers... even the illustrations and photography enhancing each new book, were his own work. To Toby's and his new bride's delight, he quickly became a successfully published author of more than a dozen sought after volumes.

They lived well, though simply, as they traveled across the country with their two Boykin Spaniels in the back of a new-fangled motor home, and tried not to come off smug when they visited their more conventional friends and family. It was perfect...perfect... too perfect to remain so.

Toby's cherished wife, Kate, began to have symptoms they couldn't ignore, and by the time she let him take her for tests, the news was devastating. Their six year union would end with the prognosis of Kate's death inside of six months, after a brave struggle with ovarian cancer. God bless her, she would not let her husband leave the road, and she journeyed with him, armed for the fight with the names and numbers of medical facilities and doctors, to be called when they needed them. One morning into the second month, he found her at the bottom of a ravine, deep in the Montana wilds. The autopsy results said she had overdosed on her pain medicine and blacked out before she fell.

Toby, of course, would have never been prepared to lose her, but he believed it came about as she wished. They had been told, six to twelve months of life left. He surmised the end was by her design. He was pragmatic enough to be able to allow her that freedom, her choice, if that was how she had wanted it. In his heart, he was glad he would never truly know what happened. Anyway, she continued to delight him with her pealing laughter, and the exquisite feel of her while they made sweet love in his dreams, both while sleeping, and while he was awake.

"I'll never love another!" He had told her, and himself, over and over. It appeared to be a prophecy, for as time took him along, no one could come close to replacing the Kate who visited him in his dreams... not for now.

After weeks of stupefied, random adjustment, Toby took himself out of step for a year...bumming around alone except for the dogs, and his Katie's welcome ghost. It took every bit of that year to stop hating God and everyone who still had love, and a reason for getting up in the morning. It was a palpable depression...an illness in his head that consumed him, and then it was just gone one day. He began to smile a little... then a lot. He allowed, finally, that he was lucky to have had her, even for a little while, and he couldn't be bitter anymore.

Back to his work, and the years flew. Toby taught a few semesters at a private school in North Carolina, and gave a gaggle of lectures and nature walks as a free-lance guide. As if a mere moment had passed, he found himself paddling into the Okeefenokee. This re-born Toby was aware he was entering a soul filling time in his middle years, where there could be room for someone else. It turned out not to be a woman, but a forlorn boy he didn't know... a boy who took up the slack in the loose coils of his lifeline, and kept him afloat. Will Parrish was family, as sure as if he'd been the son Katie and Toby had hoped someday to have. The truism left to the memory of that time was every recovering person's hope in the truism that, "The Lord never closes a door, without opening a window."

## ALMOST TO PEACE AND AWAY FROM TROUBLE

It was nearly dark when the jeep turned into the lane to the beach house. A caretaker who prepared the property each time someone was due had opened the shutters, mowed around the cottage to create walking space in the wild grasses, and turned on the lights so they could see to get inside. There was enough in the refrigerator to get them through breakfast tomorrow, and best of all, the bar was stocked...even a cooler of cold beer, in case they wanted to take it with them to the beach.

Excited to be there, the pair elected to unpack later, and took to the dune path, and what they came for. It was a perfect evening to throw their shocking memories from the day into the moonlit surf, and Toby was ready for it, but couldn't say the same for the kid who instantly tore off down the beach as if his ass was on fire. He let him go without a word, and sunk to the sand cooled by the evening, thankful to be distanced from that gory reality. What else could they do but put it away? Toby hoped he could help Will with his pseudo-exorcism, to find their way back to sanity and purpose.

But the boy was just GONE! His form got smaller and finally popped off the horizon, as darkness took the view. Toby worried for a moment he wouldn't be able to find the right dune walk to the cottage, but he dismissed it, telling himself this was the same boy he had brought out of a great swamp, for Christ's sake. Tired to the bone, He dragged his toes through the sand toward the glow of the porch lights... a cold beer and a sandwich, a shower and bed, in that order. Leaving all the lights on so Will could see the house from the beach, he was soon asleep.

Even with the cleansing solace of his run, a naive young Will was unable to shoulder it all with the dismissive resolve Toby had used. He had wanted nothing more than to strike off down this beach, to outrun that dragon of doom lumbering just behind him since the discovery of the dead girl. How good it felt to dash freely down the deserted strand, and he lost time, as if it were measured out in the droplets of perspiration flying from his hair.

Ambient light in the houses gave him an even more deceptive impression of the hour, so when he slowed, perhaps as long as half an hour after he began to run, it was obvious he was way down the beach. Dropping to the sand, he breathed evenly until his body settled down. The surf was calling, so he waded through the waves as into a good dream...swimming easily, as soon as his footing slipped away.

More time lost, because when he returned to shore, the lights were turned off in the houses, one by one. It must be getting mighty late, he mused groggily, and considered for the first time that Toby might be looking for him. Trudging back in the direction of the cottage, Will felt surreal... outside his body. He had read in the books from Toby's library about things spiritual, and he determined this to be a pleasurable state, the best he had felt since early this morning when life was still clean and simple. Deciding he didn't want to share his euphoria with anyone, and fearing he would find it replaced with the dragon's hot breath, young Will found a spot in the sand in the highest part of the dune, and fell asleep in moments, dreaming of nothing at all... blessed oblivion. But not so fast! The damned dragon had curled up beside him... resting as well, for conjuring new and renewed torments tomorrow.

Sunlight in shafts from over the dune woke Will with a start. He had slept all night as if drugged. It was cool on the beach at sunrise, and there wasn't a soul in sight. The tide had washed the sand of footprints and children's bucket and shovel excavations from yesterday, making it seem even more like Will's personal world.

Hungry! After steadying himself on his abused legs, the boy trotted to the water and took a short swim to rinse off. It was long past time to find the cottage and Toby, and as he moved off up the beach he imagined what his friend's mood might be. He's probably going to be really pissed! The thought played over and over, as the boy beat his conscience, for his selfishness and disregard. Jogging along, he tried to compose some sort of apologetic speech. The run back was much longer, or seemed to be... perhaps because Will was loping instead of sprinting, and he suspected he had passed the path. He slowed to a walk and began looking around for clues. He was ready to turn and backtrack when he saw a white ball of something on the sand. Picking it up, he meant to pocket it for proper disposal in the house, but impulsively straightened and smoothed the paper out. It was the page from the logbook!

The names burned into his squinting eyes, and he dropped the sheet as if it was hot, picked it up again, glancing furtively in either direction, and shoved it into his shorts pocket where his fingers met up with about half a cup of wet sand. Another sign from "Her"... that he should tell everything... just go back to that Island, find her daddy, and get the police to come and tell them exactly how and why they had become involved. Maybe they would all sympathize and understand, and he and Toby could just post regret for running off, and leave with their consciences clear. In his young, simplistic mind, it was the only way. Will knew Toby would have none of it, more for Will's protection than his own. The piece of beach litter in his pocket was proof that Toby was serious about erasing all traces of their implication, and he decided to hang on to it.

"The truth shall set you free!" Will had read somewhere, and it became the drumbeat he marched up the path to, the repetitive punctuation to his purpose. He walked around the house to the jeep... took his pack from the back, and after gazing up at the windows for a moment with affection and a guilty soul, he turned and walked up the drive to the blacktop and beyond, as sure as he was Will Parrish, that he was doing the right thing for both of them, and for that poor girl.

\* \* \*

Sunrise on Padgett's Island was hard to get through sometimes, partly because of its beauty... its eternal effect on Toby's senses, and of course because he had counted so many of them with his Katie. It was getting easier each time, to experience other beaches without tears and a constricted gullet, so he guessed he could visit here again, given the chance... and someday, even those times here with Katie would be recalled with proper joy. After returning to the house from the color show, he peeked in to check on Will, having decided earlier to let him sleep as long as he would. Toby planned to leave a note and go to town for groceries and videos that would distract and amuse the boy. When he leaned into the dim room, there was just enough light to see that nothing had been touched... no Will-smells, not one thing to say he had returned from his run last night. Disturbed, concerned, but not yet worried, Toby went down to the beach to track the shoreline for sight of him, but there was nothing.

Now the worry kicked in. Toby mentally checked his list of options. The boy may have decided to get into nature's loving arms, as he liked to call camping outside under the stars. He is a tough-hided outdoorsman, Toby reminded himself, and Padgett's isn't exactly the wilds of Africa. His concern back down to comfort level, Toby went back in the house, showered and dressed for town. While stocking his pockets with his wallet and the rest of the stuff on the dresser, he was aware something was missing. THE PAGE FROM THE LOGBOOK!

Maybe it fell out in the jeep! He thought like a prayer. A quick check to no avail sent an unexplainable chill running through him. "Shit!" He muttered, "Why didn't I burn that page like I meant to! I haven't a clue where it is now! What if it fell out at that bar in Frenchport when I paid for the beer before we left?" That was the worst-case-scenario. That page could implicate them completely if it was discovered in that harbor town. There was a big lump choking his throat, and he knew he couldn't relax, or stop wondering until he found that page. Then he remembered lolling on the beach last night, being so tired he hadn't given a thought to how laid out he had been on the dune, while watching the sky.

With hope flowing, Toby raced down the porch stairs and dashed to the beach, looking frantically right, and then left...positive he would find the ball of paper there. After a half-hour search both to the right of the walk and down toward the lapping surf, he concluded that the tide, or someone, had taken it. Not a good way to begin the first day of their retreat, but there it was to deal with. With controlled panic, Toby turned and went back to the house, the missing logbook page filling his head, with the issue of Will's whereabouts tucked behind it.

If he had known what the boy was setting out for, how different things would be.

# CHAPTER FOUR

Throughout most of Squires Island's anglo-inhabited history, there had always been a Thornedike, or the get of a Thornedike, either on or near to the place. The signs of the times were always changing, resulting in a population fluctuation like the tides that bathed banks and beaches on the little island. There were periods during the post-oystering boom, when, "white people" numbered less than twenty-five, double that for the number of descendants of plantation-era slave families remaining staunchly through "hard times" and hurricanes.

Since those having nowhere else they would rather be were free to own their land and their destinies, a counter-culture of elegant African descendants, now true Americans was perpetuated. It was a good mix, those co-existing cultures. Friendly, but obviously separate social lives were able to flourish, since the island is several miles squared, and so sparsely peopled, folks used to declare proudly that you didn't have to see anybody you didn't want to see for quite a spell. For true, nobody came looking for you, or bothered you unless it had been circulated that nobody had seen you for a spell, when somebody was sent to check on you, in case you were sick, or worse. The oldest and wisest of the men once said, "It ain' so bad when they dead, as when they sick." It has forever been so true.

Josiah Massey Thornedike liked the entire premise of island life, especially the elective solitude and privacy. He had done a few years away from his home as a youth, for the same reasons most puberty affected boys left Squires, but had intended all the while, to return when his wild oats were satisfactorily sown. He was a welcome prodigal son, bringing the family name and resources back home, just as commerce was at a poverty bearing low.

It seemed to all that Massey was a man complete, self-sufficient, and with good purpose. He turned twenty-one in fifty-eight, young by most standards for assuming the proceeds of a family dynasty, but the road had done things to him... some good, some bad. He felt old in ways, and tired... in need of time alone to reflect. Not only was he isolated from his Island's people by choice, he was guaranteed no hindrance from the mainland. The owners of the three docks sturdy enough to tie a boat to did not allow any vessel unless it had been pre-arranged, and the passengers had to be invited by someone on the island prior to their arrival.

The phrase, "They can't get at us from there," was repeated many times over as many years, and it provided comfort for the same number of reasons as there were residents. Mind you, with those kinds of conditions, Squires attracted a goodly share of unscrupulous shady types, attempting to take up a life not tolerated on the mainland, where the law would intervene. This might have worked out well for dropouts for a little while, [in fact not a few of that genre became community "pets," and lived happily in the mode], until the fates dealt what fate eventually deals to us all. It never worked out, though, if one intended to bring his or her bad habits for continuing practice. Inevitably they weeded themselves out before very long. The scene of a patrol boat arriving, and uniforms walking up the dock with papers in hand, usually meant the population would diminish by one or two before the sun set.

As soon as the "collar was made", locals filed into the only night spot, and after settling down to a libation, would weave several spicy versions of the event, until they were all satisfied they had the straight skinny of the "who and why". It was quite entertaining stuff... for a little place happy with no bridge to the real world. Massey rarely patronized the colorful watering hole, and then only when his resolve was weakened by his dwindling bar stock at home, and he usually regretted the misstep for days after, since he was often foggy as to what went on, "that night", and how he got home.

Considering himself the solid young patriarch of Squires, he had a reputation and a duty to uphold. The entire population black and white, knew he cultivated this post, and it was tolerated, (though snorted at in private), but it was known to be beneficial if a body needed a father figure on occasion, and Massey filled the bill, signing for this, or going to court for that, when he was asked.

Old Josiah, Massey's father, long deceased, had kept the family's large tract of land, which touched both river and ocean boundaries, inside the hundred-year-old split rail fence, and Massey was still hanging onto every square foot, even when the infernal "tree-huggers," rallied for his beach front acres more than ten years back, to be condemned as public access, state park land. The good-old-boys at the state capitol closed ranks, and he prevailed, after which, all the "In-his-pocket", politicos, were shipped over to his private, hunt club hammock for a not-to-be discussed weekend of a whole lot more than shooting sports, with the warning issued afterward that, "What goes on in the river, stays in the river!" Good old Massey appeared to be bullet-proof once again, and he dug in deeper than ever, vowing to die right there on Squires Island with his snake boots on!

Loneliness sometimes visited Massey Thornedike, as it had to, since he was a young and virile man holed up in his rambling three-story, heart pine and tin-roofed castle. He married in 'fifty-nine to a debutante from Tallahassee, after spending six months away that winter on a "Mission of love," as he dubbed it. Everybody around knew it was really just an unbearable case of "the hornies." The newlyweds' arrival home in April of that year was occasion for the biggest jump-up anyone could remember... outshining no less than the wing-ding when WW2 ended, and all the husbands and sons still alive, came home on the paddle wheel boat from Savannah.

Frances Merrill Thornedike was as welcome as the proverbial flowers in spring, and she was every bit as beautiful, both inside and out. Massey was a new man, losing fifteen unneeded pounds due to Frances's watchful eye on the ham hocks and fat-back Carrie thought vital to every pot on the stove, and making him accompany her on horseback rides and beach walks at least once a day. Everyone agreed Massey turned into quite the dashing young spouse, as they watched his attitude soften and warm toward everyone, even those he had offended during the harsh, macho years before his pairing.

Frances was an angel on earth... just ask the older ladies... and the men began to take notice of their appearance. Razors and soap quickly disappeared from the store shelves, so a man could look presentable when he went callin' at the Thornedikes with a fresh-caught mess of fish, or some venison for stew. They weren't fooling Massey... not one bit, but truth be known, he was fit to bust with pride that his choice was so pleasing to everyone. Frances seemed to put the cherry right on top of life on Squires Island for him.

The news that the Thornedikes were infanticipating soon spread throughout the state. "How 'bout that' Massey!", rang out, and, "It's about time there was a whelpin' at the big house!", were some of the comments heard all around Frenchport and beyond. Frances was to deliver in October, the year being 1963. She was uncomfortable throughout her confinement, and the fact of it being a hotter than blazes summer, only made her more miserable. Massey broke a long standing vow, and had an air conditioning unit brought over and installed in her bedroom... the first one on the island. 'Tilde and Carrie were constantly up and down the stairs with iced tea, little treats and fresh fruit, taking loving turns sitting there, humming hymns beside her as the due date neared, when she took to bed around the clock.

Massey was ridiculously nervous and cloying, hanging around much too close. The two women made a plea to him to go across for some groceries and maybe a pretty surprise for Missy, just to relieve themselves and Frances of his disruptive attention. He consented, and he and Captain Dan cast off for Frenchport that Thursday morning. As soon as they tied up, it took no more than a nudge from Dan's Popeye-shaped elbow, to get Massey to settle himself down at the bar in Ruby's Place. AHHHHHHH!

Suffice it to say the tension and stress accompanying his imminent fatherhood needed washing away... just a little, mind you, by the rum punches Ruby was infamous for. Pretty soon, after Daddy-style ribbing subsided, the predictable smutty jokes began to roll, exaggerated local lore got retold, and soon a full-on party had moved to Ruby's personal table with two transient yachties and a local shrimper joining the boisterous threesome. Massey was transported! And with each round, the years of his married life got more vague and alien to him, and this place in time was the only truth he knew. Massey was having himself quite a day, by God, and he deserved it! Figuring Frances couldn't be in better hands, he let himself go full bore...for THIRTEEN AND ONE-HALF HOURS!

Ruby was the one who brought them back to sanity. She looked at her watch and dropped her forehead to her palms before drawling, "Massey, Massey, Massey, you done done it now! It's goin' on eleven o'clock and you got a piece of water to cross, back to that woman who needs you! Dan, go get the boat goin', an' I'll get this man on his feet." Thank God and King Neptune for people like Ruby. It is her ilk who takes care of old hoboes and drunks, so they can live to need help another day. She was somehow strong enough to support the large man as they tacked down the concrete pier to the waiting ferry. No worry with Captain Dan at the helm. Drunk or sober, he was on an invisible zip line to Squires after more than fifteen years of five-plus crossings a day, and everybody knew, no matter the tide or weather, he was as good as dock to dock, soon as he stepped aboard.

The boat bumped the floating dock on Squires at exactly midnight. Massey had sort of sobered up by hanging his head off the boat's port side for the trip across, all the while stupidly wishing he'd gotten another rum drink for the crossing. Dan helped him off onto the dock with a solid shove to his buttocks, and a stern, "Hold onto the rails, buddy, the tide's way low and you'd be cut to ribbons on that shell rake down there!" Massey waved at him without turning around, and moved up the steep ramp to the pier. The captain saw his friend out of sight, cast off, and disappeared from whence he came, and Massey drove home with one eye shut tight, to keep those four ruts in the road down to two. As he got close to his gate, a strange and fearsome guilt began to squeeze at his throat. "Let them all be asleep, please, God, just help me out this one time, and I'll never do it again!"...he prayed.

Not to be, his exhorted reprieve. The whole damn house was lit up. Three vehicles he recognized as belonging to the deputy sheriff, the schoolteacher, Sandy Calhoun, and the volunteer fire chief, lined the crescent drive in front of the porch. "This is bad, really bad", Massey kept repeating, over and over, moving stiffly up the steps, hating each one that brought him closer to whatever it was that was bad, really bad. Deputy Carl Stephens stood up when the door swung open, sliding his hat brim between his fingers as he began to speak the bad aloud. "Massey, uh, Mr. Thornedike, Sir, I'm afraid something bad has happened here tonight. [Here it comes, oh, damn it to hell! The bad's comin' now!]. The guilt-ridden bastard got down on one knee, [Oh, Please God…NO!], and began to stammer.

"Miz Thornedike, she, she had the baby, Sir…a little girl…but she didn't do well. You see, she had a hemorrhage, Sir, so terrible it took her life away. It took her… " And then he began to sob, and moved to the stairs to lean on the newel post, trying to still the shaking his sobs were causing. Sandy moved to Massey's side, just as it was sinking in, and caught him when his legs were of no use to keep him standing. She couldn't hold his weight, and they both crumbled on the floor. It was Massey's voice that began rolling up from his soul in a wail so very awful, all in the room covered their ears against it.

Sandy, on her knees, was holding Massey's head tight to her breast trying to stop the sound, when her threw her off and took the steps, four at a time, to the bedroom door. Inside were Hal Davis, the EMT and fire chief, poor Carrie and Clothilde, both kneeling by the big bed in tearful prayer, and the ghost of what had been Frances, covered to above her breasts, her hair brushed and arranged, with her gold Crucifix draped through her alabaster fingers.

"NNNOOOOOOOOOO!  I SAID NO-NO-NO-NO-NO-no-no-no!" Massey's protest was sure to be heard by God. But God The Almighty must have rendered it a Prayer in Requiem…. too late for Frances's little body, her spirit was now the recipient of prayers to fly her away into Eternal Peace. As if on Divine cue, a tiny sound came from the white wicker bassinet in the shadows by the armoire. It sounded to Massey, through the roaring in his ears, like a new-born lamb, perhaps a baby alligator, or a combination of the two.

The others who circled where Frances was, thought to move away, but it did not matter... he would not look at that dead thing on the bed, that waxen wraith was not the woman who had been his joy in life from the first moment he saw her. He was not going to touch her, lest he become totally insane from the reality of her cold remains.

No! She was gone, and he knew it! In his tortured head Massey began to make perfect sense for the sake of his sanity. She, his wife, was in that bassinet with her little baby! He tiptoed to the crib, and without pause, gently scooped up the infant, folding this sweetest child of his and Frances's to his heaving chest... as close to his heart as he dared press her, and the little baby girl fell instantly asleep to the comforting beat. Massey sat down in the old family rocking chair with his arms fuller than they had ever been, and began to rock and sing, "And He walks with me, and He talks with me, and He Tells me I am His Own... " She was truly his own...his little baby daughter.

* * *

The time after Frances's passing was mercifully filled, busy raising the child he christened Franciene Merrill Thornedike at her mother's graveside. To say she was exquisitely beautiful was inadequate. She was feminine perfection. Day after day, Massey would walk the big boards of the nursery floor with the baby held out before him, like he was Rhett Butler and she was his Bonnie Blue, sing-songing, "If ever there was an Angel come down from Heaven"... saying it over and over until she would fall sleep as he stared, rapt, at her little face. Carrie and 'Tilde figured they had been given a real live doll to play with, dress up, and teach how to be the perfect little southern lady. Massey was never far to the side, as the months went by, since the only world he wanted to live in spun around a tiny peach-blonde, curly head.

The only break in Massey's day-to-day devotion to his child was a time when she was going on two, and Massey was surprised by a sport fishing boat full of his old school friends, who tied up at the public dock and ordered him aboard. It was a soggy wet, bone-chilling

January that year, and when Massey was invited to join the fun for a fishing cruise to the Bahamas, he was mighty tempted. They swore they would have him back by early March, and if Carrie and 'Tilde hadn't packed for him and all but thrown him aboard, he would have missed the time of his life.

The two women were eager to have a go at un-spoiling their little charge while he was away, and they knew Massey was hungry for a break from the island and its confines. Evidently that particular boat load had themselves quite a trip, because Franciene's daddy didn't show up on Squires until May...burnt to a crisp, and packing enough quick-frozen fish to feed the whole Island. Pretty soon it was as if he'd never been gone, and life resumed as before. Daddy resumed his dotage of Francie as she grew, taking her once a week to Frenchport for her, "Treat Day." Sometimes they ventured to Beaufort or Savannah, but most times they would simply stay in the little harbor village, often visiting the fine families on outlying estates.

Massey wanted his child to know of the mainland, and have an early start in certain social graces, even though he was vaguely afraid. The training she had gotten from her Gullah-cultured nannies was precise, and to all extents more a Victorian-ethic style, rather kin to the tutelage received by young royals anticipating life at court. She never failed to say, "Yes sir," or "No thank you, ma'am," executed perfect table manners, even in the roomy old kitchen at home, and had begun instruction in embroidery and needlepoint, by way of Carrie, who was taught by Massey's mama, when Carrie herself was Franciene's age.

Invitations for Franciene to spend weekends, first in this fine home, then that one, were pondered and approved by Massey, and if approved, she went, accompanied by one or the other of the women, sometimes both, if there was any controversy about whose turn it was. Carrie was an excellent driver, taught by Massey himself, so he trusted his precious child with her completely, while still demanding a phoning up at least twice a day while they were away. The arrangement suited everyone just fine.

* * *

The unique relationship between the black and white families on Squires is possible BECAUSE it is an isolated barrier island, where no outside influence of racial intolerance on either side would be known. There had been a constant mutuality of giving and taking between and among everyone on Squires, therefore, nobody was made to feel second to another, or responsible to the other in the reverse. To a person, Squires Island folks could count on looking in each others' eyes and seeing equality and respect due to a set of unwritten, seldom spoken, but always understood by-laws.

The most regarded and vital of these was the "Pay for task" ethic. It makes perfect sense in any culture, but it only seems to work in small, inter-dependant communities. Simply put, the day's task is finished at the appointed time or when the contract is satisfied, and the worker is paid right then and there... cash money, and the exact amount earned for the task, what is due them for that day, is placed in their weary hand before the sun sets, with thanks and regard for the job well done. No check, no, "I'll catch up with you tomorrow.", not on Squires. Word of that kind of behavior spread faster than the early spring land burnoffs.

There were bound to be incidents when this good rule was scoffed at. Island-born Jasper Griffin, long known as one of the best shrimp boat strikers on the coast, would, when reminded, call back a time one season when he worked on Captain Luke Albritton's boat. They had been away for more than three weeks, having ventured as far south as the waters off Jacksonville, when Jasper announced he was bound to go home. Heeded not a whit by Captain Luke, he was kept offshore against repeated demands to be returned. His wages were to have been fifteen dollars a day for two full weeks, but the unprecedented tally of twenty-three days without a break was driving him to distraction.

Jasper tells how he was forced to wash out his clothes over the side when fresh water was low, that they had run out of coffee and grits, and still "Captain Asshole", wouldn't call off the jam. The prized May prawns were running, so greed took the helm. When finally they turned for home, and a diligent but short-patienced Jasper presented Luke with the task sheet he'd carefully prepared, the gnarly old bastard handed it back to him without a glance, sneering,

"Well, we'll see about this when we get back. I ain't sold my catch yet. Now meantime, you get yourself busy and wash the slime off this deck, or I'll see your black ass over the side!" It was a tense trip to be sure, and when at last they tied up at home, loaded down with iced shrimp, Jasper tells it he walked off the boat, and sought out the nearest deputy sheriff. "He ain't pay me, dep'a'tee, after 'most a month I strike for him!" Jasper related, out of breath, as they walked to the side of the boat. The deputy dutifully asked, "This true, Luke? Jasper here showed me a task sheet with twenty-seven marks at fifteen dollars each. You don't think you owe him for those days? If not, then, just what is it you DO think?"

Luke needed more time than he took to answer... "Cause," as Jasper said succinctly, "He words banged on 'e' tongue 'fo' dey come out, an' I di'n' know what he said right off! NO! I ain' goin' take it! It ain' right, now! He tol' dep'a'tee an' me he'd give me de rest when he sol' his ketch. Dep'a'tee say dat's fair, and he pats me on my back and he goes off. I ain' know what I can do now, knowin' he done lied 'bout that he goin' pay me, so I go in the boat cabin and t'row all Cap'n Luke's clothes and shoes and eva'ting ovah de side, right in he' face, and he ain' say a wud! It felt good doin' that, even though I never got all my pay. Sometime you get paid off in betta' ways, don' it seem?"

The indignant Captain Luke's version was that, unprovoked, Jasper went to the captain's quarters and threw out his cloth es, his shoes, the gold watch that was his daddy's, his binoculars, his radio, his engraved Zippo from the war, and a picture of his son who had been killed in Vietnam. Hardly seems worth it, when you take stock, to cheat another out of what's rightfully his. We need more Jaspers around to keep things evened up for us, no matter who we are, where we are, or what we do, was the synopsis the deputy submitted to his boss. Captain Luke Albritton, long known for his dangerous temperament, just tucked his tail and let it go, never to bring up the subject again... Cap'n Asshole until the day he died.

\* \* \*

If there were no such thing as puberty, life would have rolled on without a hitch for the Thornedikes. Franciene had been content with her lot...a happy, well molded and perfectly fulfilled child. She delighted in stories told about her sainted mother, wasn't burdened by the circumstances of her death even a particle. The way it was told to the girl made sense, just as it made sense to her daddy. Mama couldn't get as close to her little baby as she wanted to while she lived, so she became her guardian angel after she went to Heaven, and was forever inside her little heart, keeping her safe and happy, and the sweetest, the most beautiful little girl in the whole world. Her daddy was standing proudly by, admiring what a good a job her Mama-turned-Angel was doing each and every day.

Yes sir, Massey's life was just fine... that is until Franciene caught on to the fact that a woman was emerging from her child's body with a full complement of beauty queen curves, and the inevitable flood of raging hormones. Her personality shifted to that of a shrew, as if she resented the changes...even feared them, while on the other hand, on occasion, she was caught in disturbingly provocative behavior, especially around men, some as old as her father. Massey often made the joke that it was refreshing to watch her manipulating someone other than himself, for a change. It only took a couple of their trips to town after the onset of this phenomenon, however, for Massey to observe the way even his staunchest friends would stare after them, their eyes running up and down Francie's coltish little sun-tanned body, causing him deep distress and foreboding. She wore her hair long and free-flowing, like the mane on her pony at full gallop, and although she used no store bought makeup, her cheeks and lips were the color of papaya fruit, and her eyes were as green as kelp.

It isn't fair, Massey often thought, to place such a burden on a child of thirteen, much less her poor daddy, was a divine error. Sad to say, he ceased to feel pride, and turned most timorous concerning his pubescent daughter. The unnecessary trips to town stopped altogether, and she was tutored at home by Sandy Calhoun... who, though dead set against Massey incarcerating Francie in such a fashion, was devoted to the family, and did her best to add her own brand of feminism to the lessons. Sandy admired and revered

'Tilde and Carrie's successful regimen, but she knew their efforts had just about come to a dead end one early fall day, because Franciene had her first "ladies' time," as the women called it.

The old-fashioned women were reticent to attempt domination of a "lady of the house," now that she was technically a woman. The girl became an increasingly angry young lady, figuring things out for herself as she went along... her father hoping and believing she would grow out of the "phase," as he called it. Not to be, Massey's sheltering plan. He found his daughter prostrate outside the sliding oak doors to his study more than a few times, crying and pleading with him to, "Let me go to the party at Sonja's, Daddy, PLEASE!" or "Everybody's going roller skating in Savannah on Saturday but ME, Daddy, Please, Please!", or, "If you don't let me go to the pool party at Melody's, I'll get Jaime Fuller to take me to town anyway! I HATE YOU, Daddy! You don't love me or you'd LET ME GO!"...she would shriek, doing a damn good job of tearing his heart right out of his chest. Nonetheless, he stuck to his guns for the four treacherous years between her thirteenth and seventeenth birthdays. All he needed when he found himself weakening, was to take Francie to town and sit there in the restaurant, watching the human flies begin to swarm around his little honey pot.

On the way back home, he would fume and rant to Dan, "It ain't gonna' happen to MY darlin'! Oh no! I can see it all as if it was a sleazy movie. Smooth, slimy sons-a-bitches... all of 'em rushin' one another to help her off the boat... Yeah! One little feel gets copped and it's all over, 'cause I'll be done killed somebody! She's too much an innocent flower to be thrown to those slobbering hyenas! I'll lock her up 'til she's thirty, 'fore I'll see her ruined by one a' them, or anybody damn else!"

Perhaps to many, Massey was from a horribly chauvinistic place, and when observed by the likes of Franciene's friends and their families, he became infamous... archaic and tyrannical... evil-minded. It could be said they even despised him... a father who kept such a furious fist on his child's life, but he did not care. Their attitudes only spurred him to stronger stands.

\* \* \*

Early summer of 1981 proved to be the season for Franciene's epiphany. Although she was schooled at home, the district superintendent suggested she be allowed to participate in the Frenchport graduation festivities after she passed the required final exams. This was, for the girl, simply delicious. She had been pouting for weeks about missing the dances and pre-graduation parties, of course the Baccalaureate ceremony, and graduation night itself, with the formal dance afterward at Palmland.

The issue bothered Massey enough to keep him awake at night. It was too much, too soon! He was going to say no! But he was strongly challenged, when the entire Squires Island Community Association descended on him the week before exams and announced that he would be the equivalent of pond scum or the contents of a three day old, sunburned chum bag, if he didn't allow little Francie to experience the tradition of graduating from high school with her mainland class friends.

"What you gonna do, Massey honey, lock her in her room and slide her diploma under the door, just 'cause she's so pretty?" Piped Postmistress Pearl Sessoms. Massey was just about to reply, when Deputy Davis jumped to his feet. "I was there when she came into this world, Massey, and I know her Mama would a' wanted her to have special times like other kids has got!" It was plain to see Daddy would be voted down, and to tell the truth, he knew he would ultimately agree. Poor Massey had been so afraid of losing his pride, as well as his daughter's love, he had nearly created a guarantee that he would do both! The fact broke crystal clear as he looked around him. This group of well meaning friends was about to shun him, and who could blame them?"

You're right, damn it, I know you're right... My Francie... damn it… she... she can go!" They cheered and crowded around to reassure him he wouldn't regret his decision, but the doubt was too deeply rooted to be removed by a handful of neighbors. Massey sensed the end of life with Franciene as he had known it. The plan was for her to spend graduation week with the Hartsell family as their daughter Sonja's guest at their home, musically called Palmland Plantation.

Initially rice producers, the old line Hartsell family added tobacco and Indigo, and finally a hugely profitable crop of Sea Island cotton, the prized crop producing a silk-linen-like fiber with a one-third longer growing period than the ordinary seed, until the war destroyed everything the Old South had been. The Hartsell home and twenty-three hundred prime acres just north of Frenchport, bathed by the Cusabo River and Poinsett Sound, was ogled and coveted by every real estate developer from Richmond to The Keys.

Franciene wasn't the least bit impressed by all that was Palmland life, since she had grown up visiting there at least once a month, and the barns, tennis courts and heated swimming pool were well used by her as a child. When she stopped making regular visits, her daddy still arranged for her to maintain a steady form of guarded contact for propriety's sake, and the sake of Franciene's future.

There was a young man... Sonja's brother, Clifford, three years older than the girls and comfortably away at boarding school most of the time. There was just enough between the boy and girl to give spark to the dream of a love match, to culminate in the damnedest wedding the state ever would see! Massey loved to lie awake at night, watching the wedding video over and over in his head. There must be a garden ceremony, with a dinner party afterward. A big band from New York City would play all night and there would be champagne toasting and dancing under the special-order full moon. The whole county's gentry would clamor to duplicate the event for their own daughters.

Massey knew his work was still ahead of him if this was to be. He regularly sent fresh fish and game to Palmland's kitchen, and the oysters in the sparkling creeks around Squires, believed to be the best in the civilized world, were harvested before holidays, the single selects bagged and delivered for the plantation's renown oyster roasts. Christmas and birthdays never failed to be marked from Squires Island to Palmland, with clever gifts, selected by Massey's attorney's wife, who had impeccable and proper taste.

# CHAPTER FIVE

When Franciene visited Palmland as a growing girl, nannies in tow, Andrea Hartsell would sit down at her writing desk and pen a gushing note to send back home with her, praising the experience as a breath of fresh air. Massey kept every one of them, and read them many times over for bragger's rights. It was always with him, that Hartsell money would guarantee and secure Thornedike holdings, and allow for renewed speculation, mainly land-banking that had always held his interest.

Why, it could be a perfect world for EVERYBODY! Franciene and Clifford, [especially Clifford], would delight in the match, Hartsells would have a virginal daughter-in-law to be proud of, and one who could provide the most beautiful grandchildren. Moreover, every citizen of Squires Island would get trickle-down benefits, since Massey would begin to address their long standing needs in the form of creature comforts and political protections the pairing would ensure.

Yes, Massey figured a week at Palmland when Clifford would be home for his sister's graduation, and Franciene looking her very best in all those fancy clothes she was so good at choosing, would start a fire none of them could, or would want to put out. He walked around the study, arms across his chest, patting his big biceps with satisfaction. He would tell Franciene she could go, sans chaperone, that very evening. My my, she would have a hissy-fit! It was going to be fun, to make her so happy, and he could barely wait until suppertime.

Well, Francie promised to be the best, most obedient daughter in the world, while jumping up and down so high and fast her voice jiggled, along with everything else, and poor Massey fretted while watching her glee.  His heart and mind were colliding, as he prayed, "God help me, and give me the strength to get through this week without spoiling it for her. She's happier than I've seen her since she got that pony for her eighth birthday."  He had no way to know she had plans that would make his blood run cold, at the scope of her deceit.

The vain little creature penned a formidable shopping list... a smashing outfit to wear to each function through the days comprising graduation week, and when Massey scanned it and added everything up, he whistled and glared at her over the top of his reading glasses. "Now stop me if I'm wrong, Little Miss, but didn't you and 'Tilde sashay off to Charleston before Easter to dress you up for the whole damn spring and summer season to the tune of... let me see here"... he ruffled a few papers on his desk and pulled out an invoice.

"Here it is. You and your Aunt Clothilde paraded into Belle W.'s Debutante Boutique on Meeting Street, and from what I can see on this here paper were nearly stove in, tryin' to haul all the boxes and bags out of the place!"  He took on an offended creditor's expression and handed the paper to Franciene, who was getting wider-eyed, and more abashed by the second. She looked, as if she truly didn't recall, at the list that would have satisfied Imelda Marcos in her prime. "Seven hundred-eighty dollars and ninety-two cents, to put a few summer duds on that skinny little back, and I'll just bet they don't do a very good job of coverin' up nothing you got!" He moved from his desk chair to the center of the room, holding the invoice, eye level, booming, "Why can't you pack all of THIS stuff off to Sonja's? What the hell's wrong with that? The freakin' price tags are most likely still on most of it, so ain't nobody even seen you wearin' the stuff!"  The girl was blind-sided. She blanched and swallowed hard.

"Daddy!" She keened, snatching the bill from him. "These are play clothes! The parties I need outfits for next week are all either formal, or semi-formal! I never would have bought all those shorts, and tubes, and halter tops... all of them beach and backyard things, not to wear anyplace but HERE!" The "Father-Daughter Tennis Standoff", was in its' most crucial game, as Francie broke her daddy's serve.

"I have to have four party dresses, some new pool and patio things, a whole different shoe and pocketbook wardrobe, lots of matching undies and nighties, not to mention jewelry, a little light evening wrap, a few blouses and skirts and some white Levis, polo shirts... a dress for church, and... and a straw picture hat... and... there! It's all listed right there! Daddy, can't you see I really can't go to all the parties and ceremonies in my corny island rags? You must want me to be the tackiest girl of the whole week!" She sat down hard in a chair, flopped her head down to her knees, to begin a good attempt at tears. Massey conceded the match. He crossed the room, mumbling to himself.

"RAGS, she says... God, I'm glad I'm of considerable means. After all, she hasn't really asked for much all the years, and this is a "coming out" for her. It might just be the most important shopping trip she will ever make!" He stopped at his desk, sat down with a heavy sigh, and began to calculate the amount she would need. Francie moved quickly.

"Daddy... darlin', why don't you just let me have five hundred and your American Express card, and I'll keep the receipts for you... I promise!" She was tasting victory already, when Massey jumped to his feet with a roar. "Don't you EVER think you can order my wallet open with a wave of your little hand! Why, girl, if you take that tone with your daddy I'll just go over to town myself, pick out what I want you to have, and order all the shit delivered to Palmland without you even gettin' close enough to smell it, you hear me?"

He was so confused... more concerned at the thought of really spoiling her bad this time, than angry at her, and was building up a fine old Thornedike tirade. Francie had seen enough of them, even those not directed at her, to know she had to settle him down quickly or forget it. "No, Daddy, please, you know I don't want that! Just tell me how you want me to do it and that's how it's gonna' be, but I simply must choose and try on everything before I can wear it, you know that, don't you?"

Oh boy, when her voice took on that singsong lilt it made her daddy melt, and though he knew a con was in progress, he back-handedly respected her guile and gall... so much like his own. He allowed she could have the cash and the card, but she was to call him with a report of what she was choosing, and where, and must leave the credit card with Captain Dan to bring back on the next boat after her shopping was done. What a slick job she did on him! She planned to cut quite a wide path with that card, and quickly too, before he could stop her.

The morning Franciene was to go across for the week came too soon for Massey, but he had said she could go, and she was goin'! He went to the kitchen at ten past seven, dressed to drive her to the dock. As he was pouring his coffee, Carrie turned to him with a pained expression.

"Mr. Massey", she began, "It shore ain't for me to say, after you made your mind up, but I don' like this here t'ing... not one little bit!" He was shocked at her angry tone, but remained silent out of respect for her wisdom, as she took a breath for more. "It ain't that I don' want my baby to have a good time, or nuthin' that'a way... it's just she's such a pure child with no idea what those jack-leg boys are after. I ain't meanin' to worry you, but I know you're of the same mind as me. Ain't it so?" Massey could have hugged her on the spot, and later wished he had, but said instead, "Yes, Carrie, I sure do feel that'a' way, but all the same, she deserves some trust, and she needs to know we believe in the good judgment we all fought to give her. I pray her Mama is for true in her soul, to keep her safe out there when we can't."

Then he blew it... blew it big. The war in his head took a complete half-turn, and he rushed to her and grabbed her shoulders. "Carrie, this makes too damn much sense, what you're sayin'! I must have taken leave of my senses! If my girl wants to spend a week on the mainland while insistin' she not be accompanied by a chaperone, well she just better think again! Now you go call, and tell 'Tilde to pack enough things for a week. I can't spare you this time, with the freshly planted garden an' all, so she needs to go for us. I'll go call Miz' Hartsell to prepare for 'Tilde to stay with Suzanne in her cottage."

Just at that moment Francie stopped behind the swinging door to eavesdrop, and upon hearing her father's directive, wheeled and ran out the front door, beating it to 'Tilde's, cursing and kicking oyster shells as she went, like Lolita on a rampage.

\* \* \*

Clothilde had been up for hours... it was the best time of day to get her small house tidy before her work began at Massey's. The diminutive, sixty-something year old woman had been widowed since Vietnam. The only family she had left on Squires was a son, just seven years old when his father's death notice arrived. The boy's name was Aaron, and he was the center of his mother's world, just ahead of the Thornedikes.

After he reached adolescence, the devoted little Aaron became strangely distant, and seemed to be searching for direction. It was just after his sixteenth birthday when he left school and moved town-side. His mama regaled him to her friends and neighbors, since she had been told he got his high school diploma while working full-time, and he lied to her that he was a journeyman carpenter, and doing just fine, thank you. She boasted that he sent her twenty-five or thirty dollars every month to help out, but that he was so busy working he had no time to visit.

Everyone except 'Tilde knew what business Aaron was about... his nickname was "Candyman", around Frenchport, and all the name implied was sad but true. No one knew how he managed to stay alive, with the often slippery, and sometimes life-threatening drug deals he wove his way through. Add to that his poor attention to physical and emotional wellness, he often would return from the brink of self-destruction when no one gave him a chance in hell to survive. As long as the messages got over to his mama with the crumpled bills, reassuring her that he was fine, "Real busy," and that he "Sure did love her!"... well, she was content. "Young folks got to live they busy lives as they needs to, an' we back home jus' pray they're goin' to be happy!", she'd say, when asked about her boy.

Clothilde, Aaron, Carrie, and Carrie's son, Benjie, had found themselves a form of blended family after their men were killed in action in Vietnam. It was a workable situation for mothers and sons alike, since both women were permanent fixtures at the Thornedikes', and their lives paralleled. The boys were inseparable friends, and not a bother to their busy mamas with a playground of an island home to amuse them. It was a chore some evenings, to get the hot, dusty little boys to cease play and come home for supper.

Franciene was three and four years younger than the boys respectively, but just as tough and tenacious... wherever you saw Benjie and Aaron, there was little Miss Peaches and Cream, as Carrie called her, keeping right up with them. They had all been gifted a pony to ride by Francie's daddy, and it was a sight to see, when they galloped the beach road out into the surf, falling off in the waves, laughing until they nearly gagged in the brine.

The maritime forests around their homes were dotted with their handiwork, since they could build anything from a fort to a tree house with just a keyhole saw, a tack hammer, and some big-headed nails. Massey watched with guarded interest, and he was preparing a tactful speech to slow the odd trio into separation as they grew, but he needn't have worried. Benjie was moving into puberty, a sharply handsome, muscular figure of a young man, with his Mama Carrie also concerned. She didn't fall off the turnip truck, as her mama used to tell anyone trying to deceive her, and one early spring beach day, she observed her son's eyes never leaving the swimsuit clad, blossoming twelve year old vision that was his old pal, Franciene.

Later that week, she swept a strange magazine from under his bed, with the pages folded to display a blonde, nymph-like young woman in the altogether. Carrie, disturbed but undaunted, made some swift and wise plans. Benjie went to visit her brother Pratt on nearby Cattle Cay. There he was to stay... still close to mama, but far enough away from Francie for him to resume his dream of becoming a professional football player, without the consuming distraction she surely was. Carrie believed in her wise heart that bad things could happen if she didn't put space between the two children... and Massey, of like mind but too inept to figure what he should do, was struck by the insightful and painless solution she came to. He went to town the day after her announcement of Benjie's relocation, and next morning on the kitchen table, was a gift basket full of Carrie's favorite things, and just two words... "Thank you", written on a small card. The time was never mentioned, but renewed mutual admiration was ever-after present in the kitchen when Carrie and Massey were together.

For a while it was strange for Benjie to be away from home, but school was out in a few weeks, and Aaron began spending most of his time with his best friend and their Uncle Pratt on Cattle Cay. The short distance was nothing for the strong little ponies to ford the creek if the tide was dead low. There was a sandbar that reached almost from shore to shore with a swift, but negotiable current separating the two spits of land, and Pratt had pasture and shed for the ponies as their new home.

Marsh tackys are a diminishing sight in the low country, but highly prized by the traditional families who bred them to keep the strain going. They are unique in all the world... able to thrive on indigenous grasses, like the plentiful Spartina, commonly called marsh grass, and their hearts are, to capture the phrase, "Lowcountry Hearts", as Jimmy Buffet once said in a song. Fortunately, the ponies were provided with supplemental hay and grains by Massey, when supplies were transferred. Carrie sent bountiful baskets of kid-friendly goodies when Aaron went across, and to ward off predictable adolescent boredom, they even got a television set with a good antenna, and a Nintendo game for Benjie's fifteenth birthday.

It didn't take crafty old Pratt long to figure a way the youngsters could be of real benefit to him, beside the companionship he had pined for. Over nearly four decades he had been producing moonshine on Cattle Cay, for personal consumption and as enterprise, always disposing of it in Frenchport, or on Savannah's riverfront docks, and making a tidy profit. The market for his pints, quarts, and gallons had diminished over time, due to the ravages his volatile elixir could visit on an over-indulgent body, and his advanced age of late, making it necessary to reduce, then suspend the strenuous deliveries altogether. He kept in touch with loyal customers over time, and hoped for an occasional truck delivery by a friend who stopped off occasionally while fishing, but overall, Pratt suffered severe reversals of the ego and the pocketbook.

It was a simple twist of fate that the old rascal was blessed with two such able and virile young men. A few days into Aaron's first visit, the old fox put his plan before them. Nothing was mentioned about illegal activity, or the wages of sin... only how boisterous a couple of young men could get in Savannah, and how much money he would cut them for their trips. Negotiations ensued, and after the rudiments of the expeditions were worked out, including the supply shopping they must do before they returned from each trip, he swore them to secrecy, even and especially, their mothers could never know. The still began full-on production once again, with Pratt humming happy tunes from the good old days, when he was truly, "shine king".

A day in Savannah was as important to Benjie and Aaron as the prospect of becoming minor tycoons. Movies... Girls! Real Pizza... Girls! McDonald's...GIRLS, Friends with Cars, and GIRLS!! It was going to be a good summer. They were in business, and made more than a few trips down the waterway to Savannah's harbor through all seasons...summer, fall, and early winter. Pratt wasn't as prolific a still master when the cold winds blew... his old bones called for staying inside by the stove, but he managed to squeeze one more good winter batch out in late January. The trip was set for the last Saturday in the month, and it blew in with a thirty-knot, northwest wind, chilling to ten degrees and below.

Benjie and Aaron loaded the multi-coated bateau with more than twenty gallons of the pepper minted moonshine, extra line for tying the boat during a dead low tide, a cast iron bucket with white-hot lumps of coal to warm frozen fingers, and a big bag of fried chicken and biscuits. (Food was warmth out on the frigid water-way). They cast off when the sun broke through the sea fog... Pratt calling after them to, "Be sho' not to be takin' no bad money, no checks, and NO CREDIT to nobody, 'cept Miss Pearl Singleton!"... (A sentimental tradition for many years, though unrequited, he was eternally hopeful).

It was approaching noon when they turned into the Savannah River, with five more miserable miles to go. The trusty antique Evinrude hummed a steady song as usual, but God, it was cold! Aaron sat hunched over the bucket of coals, while Benjie, piloting the entire trip, squinted down-river for first sight of City Hall's gilded dome and their misery's end. He might have insisted on a change of shifts so he could warm by the bucket, but knew he was stronger against the cold. If he had seen the younger boy slip a pint from one of the boxes, he could have abridged both of their destinies.

Aaron scrunched down out of view, and began first sipping and shuddering, then slugging and gulping the throat-scalding hooch, all the way down river. When he began to sing, slurring and yelling most of the words, Benjie noticed. He flipped the control to neutral, and heading the bow into the center of the channel, stepped toward Aaron's waving arm and grabbed it in an attempt to seize the bottle. Just as the flask and the hand holding it were seized, a swell flipped the little craft to starboard forty five degrees, and Benjie swayed to balance, tipping the contents of the pint into the glowing bucket of coals.

The explosion was not witnessed, unless you count the half-dozen seagulls circling overhead, and the egret wading in the water's edge, who likely found himself in Wassaw Sound before he could blink. Aaron, being limp with drink, was thrown free, nearly to the bank of Hutchinson Island, opposite Savannah Harbor. He was up and walking in minutes, yelling Benjie's name over and over, across the creosote laden air, toward a flickering glow that had been the bateau. No one heard except those gulls, since Benjie had been incinerated by the blast and nothing of him was found to bury. Aaron walked Hutchinson Island's bank to a warehouse and pier near the big bridge. He sobbed out his story to the men, leaving out his guilty part in the tragedy, both then, and ever after.

Aaron Braswell's innocence and his joy of living ended that day, and he left his home and his mother for places she wouldn't have wanted him to go. To spare her more pain, he had the compassion to send her a bogus diploma, and news of his job. His lost brother visited him, charred and horrible, in his drugged night-dreams too many times to bear in the daylight without the help of more drugs, and thus his life continued, with no one's sake, save his mother's, to go on living for.

* * *

Gathering herself together on the approach to 'Tilde's house, the furious young girl knew she had to play her part perfectly... everything she had planned depended on going to the mainland WITHOUT a chaperone. The directive to Carrie by her father, overheard earlier in the kitchen, to have Clothilde, "Ready herself to accompany Franciene to Palmland," made her think and act quickly. With so little time until the boat was to leave at nine o'clock, the next few moments had to go perfectly. Stepping lightly up to the screen door, Francie tapped to announce herself, as she had been taught all her life to do, no matter into who's doorway she sought entry.

This was another one of those time worn rules, unwritten, seldom spoken. The island visit, unlike this particular one, would have been precipitated by a call to inquire if it was convenient to stop by for a spell, and one always took a little something for the house... usually the caller brought a treat just as nice away when goodbyes were said. It was the proper way to treat one's neighbors, whether on tiny Squires, or teeming Manhattan Island.

'Tilde, always mindful of goings on around her house, looked out the kitchen window, smiled her face-wide smile, and called out, "Come on in, chile'!" The girl looked to the right and left from the porch, and with an audible exhale, pulled open the door and went inside. The old woman was at the stove to the left end of the room. Familiar aromas revealed to Francie that she was just in time for a piece of the best blackberry dumpling ever there was anywhere. A wave of unworthiness ran over her body, but she shook it off, and pranced over to the stove to watch the sackcloth and string-wrapped bundle being lifted from its boiling bath, as she had so many hundreds of times before.

"You know what to do, baby, go over to the icebox and get the cream pot... and the sugar bowl, too, up there on the shelf. I bet you ain't had a bite o' breakfast yet this mornin', it bein' such a powerful important day as is!"

No, she hadn't. The kitchen in her own house had become a bad place for Franciene, since she overheard her daddy's orders to Carrie. She had gotten away from there as fast as she could before he had the chance to lay the morning's impossible revelation at her feet. It would have become the scene of another of her hissy-fits, and she possibly could have been refused the trip outright. It couldn't happen that way... it just couldn't, and Francie was prepared to summon the gumption to move hell and earth to take that ferryboat to freedom.

"Let me get off that boat in Frenchport, and I can make it all happen, just as we planned!"... the girl said to her whirling head as she brought the two condiments to the metal-topped kitchen table in the corner. 'Tilde dished the servings into bowls she had put out, returned the remnant of dumpling to the plate, and looked in Francie's face with those penetrating black eyes.

"What's in that sweet li'l head of yours, Honey-lamb? You been scowlin', and screwin' up your pretty face since you came in here. I'm tellin' you, you betta' stop it! Stop it right now! Carrie and me patted far too much buttermilk on that li'l face of yours to keep it smooth, for you to squinch it up like that! Stop it I say, 'fore the crows feet and furrows come for to STAY!"

Franciene could tell this wasn't just play. Tilde was serious about her little one's complexion, so she relaxed the tension in her face she hadn't known was evident, and replaced it with a demure smile, and a disarming giggle. "I don't believe I've' had even so much as a bite of your blackberry dumplin' this season, and here the blackberries are 'most gone off the vines!" Franciene sang out as she puttered about the table, putting spoons and paper napkins in place. 'Tilde was watching her like a hawk! "No you ain't! And I was figurin' to freeze some up for you to make do with, but they just ain't good like the fresh ones are." It was one of Clothilde's famously tactful remarks... like when an Island woman of questionable morals was suspected of a fresh dalliance. Carrie and Clothilde were too straight-laced and polite to come right out and supply gossipy facts they knew to be true. The only thing attributed to the two, when the rumor began to spread was, "Dey dogs don' know where dey sleep at night!"

Saying so much with such a few words, just like the dumpling reference to remind Francie how seldom she came to her house anymore, was 'Tilde's specialty. She bore no bad feelings... only hurt ones, since all her young life, the child had been at either hers or Carrie's houses at least once a day, until the last two years. It seemed to 'Tilde that it rounded out their relationship... for Francie to accept their hospitality as a regular guest in their homes, and not just as her daddy's housekeepers.

The visits gave Franciene a true impression of the women who had so lovingly brought her up, in the most personal way. At work in their own homes, cutting flowers from their own gardens for their tables, sunning their own pillows and lovingly sewn quilts, or just sitting on the porches in the evening after their work was done, rocking to the tunes they had hummed with their mothers and grandmothers, before Francie was even a gleam in their eyes. Those were red letter moments to 'Tilde, and she missed them... missed them something awful.

The delicious, tart-sweet confection went down like silk, and it seemed only a moment after her first bite, that Francie had the bowl up to her face, licking out all of the goody, like she had always done. "I do know that was the best you ever made!" She crooned, looking lovingly at her old friend. She felt the second pang of strange self-loathing, and again discarded it, knowing how vital it was to block Aunt Clothilde from getting on that boat. She didn't know that the call had already come from Carrie for her to make ready for the trip, and that her old tapestry bag was packed and waiting on the bed behind them in the shadows.

Slowly, ever so haltingly, 'Tilde was spooning tiny bites of the dumpling and cream into her mouth, with a curious look on her face. "This don't taste jus' right to me... didn't yours have a mite of a bitter tang to it? Maybe it's the cream that's turned, or maybe I didn't sweeten it jus' right." Franciene was rinsing the bowls at the sink, pretending the running water kept her from hearing the question. She went back to the table, sat down, and took Clothilde's worn little hand. "I love you so much, Aunt 'Tilde... you will just never know!" She started humming an off-key rendition of, "Swing Low, Sweet Chariot," while rocking to and fro, watching the old woman getting woozier, and more unsteady, as she sang the verses the now dying woman had taught her.

When 'Tilde pitched forward just before her face hit the table, Francie caught her, and with one arm let her gently down onto the floral patterned linoleum. Still humming the song about goin' Home to Glory, she arranged poor 'Tilde's time-wasted arms and legs into respectable repose, and kissed her silver braided head, before slipping, still humming, out the back door.

# CHAPTER SIX

Hustle and bustle was the order of that particular morning in the big house. Carrie sprinting from room to room, upstairs and down, transferring every piece of Franciene's trappings to the foyer so nothing would be forgotten. She knew sure as she knew her own name, they would be getting more than one frantic call from Palmland after Franciene was delivered, announcing that THIS was missing, or THAT didn't get put on the boat, and somebody, "Just has to get Captain Dan to bring it over on his next run!"

Massey made the call to Dan at six o'clock so he would be sure to be there at eight, in order to load a week's worth of Francie's fluff aboard, and still have time for Miss Priss-tail to be her normal fifteen to thirty minutes late. Franciene came into the kitchen from the porch, all sweaty and sporting a pair of very dirty bare feet. Carrie shrieked, "Lord, child, you better get yourse'f up them stairs and get clean, 'n' ready to go! Your daddy's done called Cap'n Dan to be over here in ten minutes to fetch you and 'Tilde to town, and jes' look at your feet and legs, and your face all smeared up with berry juice! I sure enough ain't seen the beat of you, girl"

She could have slapped her own weary face... Francie just heard from her very own lips, the news that she and Massey were going to send a chaperone for the trip. They hadn't planned to drop the bomb until they were at the dock. She did not want the news to cause a tirade here at home. If the men on the boat had to endure it, that suited Carrie fine, but she'd just as soon let the girl leave peacefully, without the stress of another tantrum. She peered at Franciene's face through her fingers, waiting for it to start, but nothing happened! Francie was, in fact, halfway up the back stairs, still humming the old spiritual from before, and closed her bedroom door behind her. Carrie tiptoed into the hallway, and heard the shower start. "Do Jesus, what does it mean?" she mused. Any other time the girl would be having a fit to end all.

"If I hadn't seen it for myself I'd never believe it! What? Tell me, was it that just happened?" Carrie wondered out loud, just as Massey filled the room with a loud, "Where did that girl get to, and where's Aunt 'Tilde?" He never reverted to calling her "Aunt" 'Tilde, unless he was angry, making him forget how time had flown. "Carrie, if I have to wait around here with my finger up my you-know-what, and all the while, Daniel's chargin' me by the minute, I'm gonna' whale on that girl, I don't care WHO's graduatin' next week!" Carrie shushed him up gently with, "She done gone upstairs, Mist'a Massey, she's gettin' ready right now, and I spec' 'Tilde'll be comin' in the door most any time!" Not trusting the wisdom of telling him about her slip of the tongue to Francie a moment ago, she turned instead to the big black range and took some loaves of pecan bread out, ready to wrap up for the Hartsells.

While Massey paced with a big cigar, Carrie decided not to tell him at all. Maybe Francie didn't even hear her, what with all the excitement. Maybe that was why she didn't explode right off. No, Carrie wouldn't mention it. She went to the wall phone and dialed 'Tilde's number. It rang seven times before she returned the receiver to the hook. "'Tilde must be on her way right now, Mr. Massey, since she ain't answered the phone when I rung her jus' now! It's only eight o'clock this minute... why don't you take Francie's things to the ferry boat, and tell Cap'n Dan to 'bide awhile."

Bless Carrie, always smoothing feathers. She stacked the breads in a basket and added, "I'll be callin' Jesse at Palmland before he leaves for fetchin' the child, not to come 'til I let him know what time's right. It ain't no more than thirty minutes from Palmland's gate to the dock, the way old Jesse drives that fine new car they got!" It all fell into place, as usual.

Massey still fretted, though...feared if he left the house alone, he would have to compensate Dan for an extra hour, but he also knew that standing around here fuming about it wasn't going to serve any purpose, except to make all of them nervous. He allowed to Carrie it was a good idea what she suggested, and they both set to loading the Rover with the luggage. Maybe Clothilde could hurry Francie along when she got to the house. Yep! He allowed it was a good plan.

Massey was chickening out too, just like Carrie... leaving the dirty work to 'Tilde to tell Francie she was to be her chaperone for the week. 'Tilde would have none of her shit, that's for sure, and the fireworks would be over when he came back for them. Oh, he thought himself so clever. He told Carrie to go to Francie's door and tell her he would be back at eight-forty-five. That was near 'bout on time, and he was thankful for that much!

* * *

Showering... even scrubbing with her sea sponge didn't take away the itchy, nervous tingle on her skin, and Franciene feared she wouldn't be able to fool anyone while she played out her part. Carrie's message from Daddy gave her a new idea for her caper, and her vixen's mind was whirling off the scale. She had only a few minutes to get dressed and haul ass on her pony, using the shortcut that feet, bicycles, and horses alone could use. It would cut precious time off the ten minute trip to the dock, and if she could leave in six minutes, she could get there while her bags were still being loaded.

It would please them, especially her daddy, that she was actually early... and she was already involved in a silent rehearsal concerning 'Tilde's absence. She slid into Levis, socks, and sneakers, and a long sleeved polo to keep the branches from scratching her as she rode, and planning to change into nicer clothes once aboard, stole down the back steps, and out to Topsy's paddock.

The dainty little mare was nibbling hay in the corner by the gate, so it was easy to take hold of her halter, slip the loop off of the gatepost, and lead her out. Clipping a lead check to her halter and throwing it over the pony's mane, she fashioned reins of a sort, needing very little more than a nudge with her knee to direct the obliging pony anywhere she wanted to go. They loped away from the house quietly at first, then the signal from Francie to take off, and Topsy's little legs seemed to blur in a headlong gallop through the woods along a trail leading straight to the dock.

Massey and the two boatmen took a break from loading everything from the cart to the aft deck of the boat, and got into a social chat, having to do with topics ranging from how well the cobia were biting in the sound, to a detailed account of Jaime's sexual triumph the night before, on his tear through Beaufort. The lad, while no heartthrob, had a sort of swarthy charm, and could outflirt just about anybody in the county. Since he resisted anything longer than a two week fling, he boasted a lot of practice playing the field.

Yeah, Boy! Jaime Fuller was a summa cum laude graduate from the Young Men's Three "F" School... you've probably heard of it... the good old, "Find 'em, Fuck 'em and Forget 'em Fraternity!" The boy and his redneck dad were puffed up and proud of this claim to fame, Dan spending many nights "alone with himself", re-running Jaime's mouth-watering tales of steamy sex in all sorts of locations, with all sorts of girls he contorted into all manner of positions. A little twisted, to live vicariously through your son's tawdry tales, but if it delivered the goods, who's to care?

Dan's all-time favorite story, the one that was sure to bring groans of abject envy and awe from the gallery of hard-tails listening, was the story of the girl Jaime met in Barbuda, while way down the chain on a charter fishing trip. She was, according to Jaime, a treetop tall... buffed up workout queen he met in a waterside bar one night. They got on well, and after procuring a barely passable bottle of champagne, Jaime went with her to her gym on the pretext of having a weight lifting contest... one of those silly dares you come up with in order to get a girl hooked, leadered, and ready for the gaff. When they got inside, Jaime noticed a set of gravity boots in a corner under a piece of equipment. They started making out... it got progressively more intense, and before long they were both buck-naked. "Here comes the best part, boys," Dan interjected, and got shushed unanimously, as Jaime continued.

There had been a lot of rum consumed, so she wasn't in the least resistant to a bizarre suggestion. Jaime opted for a session with the gravity boots, and she was strapping them on before he knew it. He lifted and swung her, tail over ta-tas, and the powerful magnets overhead connected with a "Clunk!", suspending her with her feet about sixteen inches apart, and her long hair brushing the floor.

It was something to see. A smorgasbord of luscious delights spread before him, and he in total control. She was giggling and wriggling, and asking him what was next, when he had a very clever and titillating idea.

Jaime could hardly tell his preposterous story with a smooth delivery, being so wrapped in the moment. He continued, whispering so the feminist gods couldn't hear, telling his rapt audience how he had picked up his shorts and felt around for the ever-present... yep! There it was! A single dose packet of Alka Seltzer!

"Heh, heh, heh", he chuckled nastily to himself as he moved behind her, opening the champagne. "What are you doin', Honey?" She grunted out, as he strolled around in front of her, effervescent tablets in one hand, open champagne bottle in the other.

Jaime was now approaching his story's punch line, so he kind of crouched down, as if telling an illustrious hunting or fishing tale. Not surprising, the men under his spell hunkered down the same. He held his hands out to use them as props, so they would be able to "feel" what he was doing, as he told them of placing the bottle on the floor, and bending down to her lips for a kiss. While he was kissing her, he had copped a tittie-feel or two, creating cups out of his hands for her round breasts, and then his fingers dove directly, dead center between her legs, as he deftly placed the tablets snug inside the warmly moist, sweetest part of her, in one swift and delicate move.

The topsy-turvy princess wriggled and giggled some more, Jaime remembered to them, so he gave her the grand finale... pouring wet, cold bubbly over the tablets peeking out of her crotch, exploding them into torrents of loudly fizzing, cascading foam! First, down through her pubic hair, then over her tummy, all around her navel, taking four detours, two to port, two to starboard, on the four sides of her tight breasts. Covering her neck, the fizzy torrent came to its journey's end through her voluminous hair, giving her an inverted Medusa look. The source of the foam was still spewing forth, only at that precise moment it was her body that was erupting... in ecstasy! She gave a shriek of pleasure, and was catapulted through the best external orgasm of her entire life... bar NONE!

Jaime fell silent and sat back on his haunches at that point, while his fans savored the moment... then moved to the conclusion. Begging to be taken down before it subsided, she pleaded to properly show her gratitude with a challenge of his perfect show. He told them he was prepared to allow her all night long, thank you very much, and on every piece of equipment in the gym. Damned if she didn't prevail!

He wrapped it up well, when he told the boys that he wasn't even slightly interested in a poon-tang safari for at least a week afterward... THE END! The two older men could only shuffle, shake their heads and stare at each other in wonder, their memories clanking around for anything remotely rivaling the story they'd just heard, while silently cursing time and culture warps that failed to allow them the same chance at such outrageous bliss.

The reverie broke when Massey looked at his Omega and whooped out, "Hellfire and Damnation! Where does time go! It's already eight twenty-five! We ain't done here yet, and I told Carrie I'd be back at quarter to! Y'all get the rest of this stuff loaded, and I'll be back directly with, "Her Royal Heiny", and Aunt 'Tilde in tow."

He hustled up the dock to the Rover and peeled out, leaving a dust cloud behind. As he reached the turnoff to the house, he saw Topsy through the open woods, weaving her way among the magnolias, in the direction of the barn. Massey stopped and whistled. The pony, recognizing his often used signal to bring the girl home against her wishes, changed directions and trotted to him, nickering a greeting. "Where you been, little girl? You been rode mighty hard, that's plain to see. Nobody rides you like that, 'less'n it's Francie! Where is she, Tops? Did you bring her to the boat?"

He slapped her affectionately on the rump, and the pony sashayed her cute hind-end to him as she cantered away. He pondered a moment, and then decided to go back to the dock, more inquisitive than disturbed. It was only five minutes back from where he saw Topsy, but Massey was impatient to find out what the devil was going on. Literally leaping from the car while it was still skidding to a stop, he made a few strides before he froze in disbelief. "The pissin' boat's done gone!" Turning to look down the river, he could see it silhouetted on the horizon, about to make the curve. Massey stood rooted and heaving, fists jammed into his waist, suddenly feeling great dread.

Below deck, Franciene was changing her clothes while her daddy was watching the boat disappear, after washing her hands and face in the tiny head. She chose a light cotton shirt which she tied at her waist, shades of green flowing over it like Sargasso weed, and a pair of white shorts with slightly flared cuffs, white thong sandals, and a green beaded bracelet. She brushed her ropy mane, and shook her head to let the strands fall perfectly in place, before going up top, where the boat speed would likely cause bad hair in seconds. She meant to create a sensation as usual, when the boat got to port, but she also meant to disarm Dan and Jaime to the place where they wouldn't want to present anything but a case in her defense, when her daddy questioned them.

It was a given that he would rail on them for going against his directives, and not waiting for 'Tilde, but in their defense, she had run down to them after sending her pony home with a yell, and while gasping prettily for breath, explained that she was afraid the boat might leave, so she got there as quickly as she could. As for 'Tilde, she offered that she would send Jesse back from Palmland at noon, when the boat would have made another round trip, to dispatch her chaperone, and all would be just fine!

Franciene was deftly casual when the subject of Aunt 'Tilde came up. They saw nothing amiss, and were pleased that she was early for a change, so they were underway with all systems A-OK. Now, her transformation complete, she skipped up the steps from below, and with a sweet smile across her angelic face, moved to a position close between captain and mate, making herself as irresistible as she knew how to be... which was a lot.

# THE BEACH OFFERS NO CLUE FOR TOBY

Confusion reigned as Toby Howell tumbled two concerns around in his fractured mind...first one, then the other. Where the hell was Will? Why couldn't he find the paper ball he had shoved in his shorts yesterday on the ferry at Frenchport? It leads to a touch of madness when a disappearance has no plausible explanation, and he was dealing with TWO! In the midst of his quandary, there was something not quite there, like a whisper in a library. It sort of said, "Combine the two mysteries into one, there you will find the answer to them both." FINE... just great! Now I'm supposed to go looking for my friend, and Shazzam! The ball of paper will be there, where he is... fat chance! He decided to walk the beach farther down than before. The paper most likely blew away.

Adding the truth that whatever Will was about probably wasn't rational, didn't make him any less addled, but the coffee was ready, and it smelled good, too. After pouring a stadium cup brimming nearly over, Toby set out, taking cautious steps toward the beach to spare his fingers from the hot brew. A few early risers were already setting up for their lazy beach day, and Toby enviously scanned each group as he walked by, looking for a tow head taller than the others.

Getting on toward nine o'clock, the day was warming quickly, and it was obvious Will was not on the beach. He walked back toward the house, more perplexed than ever. The next step was a drive around the island, stopping to ask after the missing boy. He had a good snapshot to show, and felt heartened by his plan. More than a mile down the paved road he realized he had not put his wallet in his back pocket. Cursing his stupidity, he decided to save time by going into Will's bag in the back of the car to gather the stash of loose money he was always tossing in. At least he could fuel up before returning for the wallet. He pulled over to the shoulder, jumped out and opened the rear door.

No backpack! Nothing belonging to Will was there. "Will's run away," Toby said out loud to the empty compartment, a finality he had up to now denied. No one would walk down that long driveway and steal a bag out of the jeep. It made perfect sense that the little shit had chosen to take his leave last night or this morning, while his guileless friend slept. There was nothing else to do but go back to the cottage. Three hours of combing Padgett's, showing Will's picture to all who could have seen him... in convenience stores, boatyards, restaurants, tackle shops, everywhere... brought no results. Suddenly famished, Toby stopped at a waterfront bar flashing a neon food sign, for a sandwich and a brew.

There were five or six people in the room, and it took some spunk to maintain an appetite, since the odor of creosote was stifling... the building appearing to be constructed from timbers coated with the stuff. He ordered a draft beer, deciding to hold off on the sandwich. When the bartender brought the beer, Toby gave her a traditional appraising glance... waiving any prurient interest.

She was about forty-five... probably a looker not long ago, but now her curves were a tad lumpy, her skin leathery from too much midday sun, and her yellow hair was arranged in a do she likely had been wearing for twenty years... a French twist or beehive sort of affair, with a bright pink clip-on bow just over her forehead, ridiculously matching the jersey, V-neck pullover she wore. The ensemble was bottomed off by a painfully tight pair of ragged white cutoffs that would not have restrained her dimpled butt-cheeks, even if they had been four inches longer. The whole effect was pretty hard to handle, even for one who has seen a bunch of "Pretty bad", as he went about, so he began looking elsewhere in the dark room for diversion. It was quiet, no one talking much. Perhaps they were mesmerized by the strains of, "Me and Bobby McGee", with Kris Kristofferson growling out his ancient hit.

An impatient and agitated Toby was getting over the scene fast, when the vision behind the bar sat a huge plate of boiled shrimp, potato salad, and sweet, onion smelling hushpuppies, in front of him. "I think this goes to someone else!" he called to her as she sauntered away, those two-toned cheeks undulating in tandem. She turned back with a big smile and stepped closer, leaning with her elbows on the bar.

"Thursday's free lunch day in Neville's, Honey. We don't adver-tise it... be up to our asses in Yankees if we did. Truth is, we kind'a like givin' back a little to the locals for helpin' me out when my husband passed away. The folks around here gathered up enough money to pay off the mortgage on the place, so's I could stay in busi-ness." She was actually quite nice, and Toby felt much less turned off, so he accepted the great looking lunch with thanks. "When did he die?", was his next question, since he knew enough about the food business to know you can't stay in the black, giving this kind of meal away on a regular basis. "Oh, he passed in nineteen seventy-seven... November it was... why you ask?" Relating the reason for the ques-tion, Toby watched her break up as she couldn't hold it in any longer. With a slap on the bar and a new peal of laughter, she looked him up and down with what seemed to be genuine affection.

"Boy, you really fell for it! I'm sorry for the put on, but I couldn't resist. I gave you the plate because I like the way you look, right-off, that's all. I guess I can treat a cute guy to lunch if I want to! Truth is, my hubby really did die awhile back, but the rest was just funnin'! What you doin' way out here? You' visitin' somebody, or just vaca-tionin'?" Toby took the joke in the same good humor with which he was enjoying the meal, and between bites, answered her inquiries. "I'm out at the Boykin cottage for the week. My wife was a Boykin, and I still have a share of the use of the place." She looked quickly into his eyes.

"You divorced? No, you're a widower, aren't you? I didn't mean to answer my own question, but the way you changed up when you spoke of her... your wife, I mean. Well, it was kind a' like you was in church or somethin'... that's what made me know." He found him-self liking this tacky woman, and was ashamed of his shallow first impression. She was obviously flirting, but more than that, she was a kind, sensitive human. Toby felt much better after the food, so he ordered another beer, and chatted on with Shirley Neville... that was her name. Finally, in desperation, he showed her the picture of Will as he was preparing to leave. She held the snapshot close to her face and said, "Yeah! He was by here about two hours back, with old George Potter. George said he picked him up on the road, and since he needed a ride, an' George, he's goin' down to Savannah to pick up his prop from the machine shop, he'd just take the kid along, kind'a like a good deed, you know? Said the little guy sorta' got under his skin, first look he got of him. (Toby knew the feeling). "The boy said he was mighty hungry, and was about to order a burger, when I went out back and made him up a to-go box of what you had just now."

What a proper coincidence. That meal would have suited Will just fine. Toby knew this after watching him devour shrimp, any style, enough to make shrimp salad to feed the whole population of Padgett's Island in high season, over a two week trip to the Louisiana bayou. It was a relief to know he was okay as late as this morning, and his friend was grateful to God that he had happened to stop there, since his passing the place by would have been a huge dead-ender. Funny, how he was beginning to feel like help was coming along with him.

Where was he going now? What kind of whacked-out thinking would give the boy a quest? With an abstract idea, Toby even wondered if he would, in his pained state, want to go where he thought his mother might be, hoping for her long overdue comfort. How could he leave without a word like that? The two comrades had been as close as blood, each commited for two years running, to consider the other as carefully as they would themselves. It was frightening to imagine what a mixed up state Will was in. He was vulnerable out there... too naive... too trusting! "I've got to find him!," Toby shouted in his head. The only thing to do was go to Waycross and start there. If Will intended to find his mom, he could stay long enough for Toby to find him. He already knew how small a place it was. Before Waycross, though, he wanted to check out Savannah, following George Potter's tracks.

Shirley was forthcoming, including a description of George's truck, and he got the name of the machine shop from one of the men shooting pool in the corner. It was a good lead, and Toby thanked the whole room fervently as he left. Driving once more, he took the access road to Interstate-95, propelling the jeep toward Savannah like a crazy man. The speedometer reached eighty miles an hour in seconds, before Toby remembered his things were still back at the beach house. Screaming out loud in frustration, he got off at the next exit and changed direction, going just as fast. If he was going to go off on this kind of trek, he would sure as shit need his stuff! Please God, let me find that boy before he loses himself completely and takes my sanity with him!"

## THE BOY HAS HIS OWN MISSION

Never since he could remember, had Will Parrish been through so many changes so quickly. Still salt encrusted from his night on the beach, he thought back, organizing events, as they tooled along state route seventeen toward Savannah. This boy... and the living, breathing cartoon at the wheel.

On reflection, as he jostled along, the first impression Will had of Toby the day they met in the swamp had been strongly positive. Sort of, "cool at first sight!" When he saw him stepping out of the canoe, Will thought, "That is the way I want to look when I'm old!" He told Toby of his observation not long after they began traveling together, and it had created an ambivalent reaction in the man. Glad to know he was cool, but that "old" reference was just wrong! They laughed over the moment many times.

Will was serious... Toby truly was his ideal for a man grown... a signature specimen. He was big... strong and tall, without an ounce of fat on his haughty frame, and his face was a mirror of his life... furrowed, tanned brow, eyebrows that would come together in a kind of bow when he pondered something, large, spheres of hazel-colored liquid for eyes, centered with black onyx pupils that seemed bottomless... and so wise. His eyelashes were incredible... almost black, sweeping toward his temples like marsh grass in a gale. His nose was aquiline, rather long but elegantly shaped, with slightly flaring nostrils, and his ample mouth appeared always about to speak.

He wore his multi-hued, wavy hair in a thick, careless ponytail. Will had only seen it flowing free once, when they were sitting on top of a peak in the Great Smokies, where the wind was blowing up a storm, and Toby decided to let it loose. It was quite a sight. Will didn't want to grow his own hair long, but he allowed the look was just right on his friend. Toby told him he hadn't cut his hair except to trim the ends since Kate died. It was a piece of his grief resolution not to let anyone else cut it, as she had been his personal barber from the first week they were together, and then forever.

\* \* \*

Will's random musings were cleansing to the unspeakable shock put there yesterday, and he began to relax, taking jovial, silent appraisal of this new angel. The man was a dead-on cutout of a salt water fisherman. If one looked up the term "Redneck," you can bet George Potter's picture would be right there on the page! Nearly six foot, having the same thirty-four inch measurements around his waist and butt as around his chest, all supported tediously on two of the shortest, most bowed legs young Will had ever seen, George was quite a sight, especially in motion.

He was gotten-up in the fishing man's uniform of the day... a pair of stained and wash-worn khaki shorts, a sun-bleached tee shirt from some long ago kingfish tournament, a web belt with a severely scratched brass buckle barely holding his pants up over his butt crack, accessorized by a Leatherman tool in its sheath, and salty, fish-gut-encrusted America's Cup Topsiders on his burnt-brown, hairy feet. He had in times past considered himself quite the stud-muffin, and except for a poorly healed broken nose and markedly receding silver- blonde hair, he was still attractive... or, "cute in the face" as the girls say in the south.

The most surprising aspect of all was that when he spoke, his words were frosted with a grand Aussie brogue. To Will's young mind, there was no more fascinating and enviable a bunch, than those from "down-under", and to spend hours listening to this man chattering away was a treat. George told Will he was from Tasmania, intriguing the boy all the more, since the area invoked exotica, and produced the chest-beaters he had seen on those croc-hunting and endurance sporting challenges on the tube.

It was an entertaining trip, with first this tale, then that legend or true adventure, each more raucous than the last. The boy haltingly told George about his own past life in Okeefenokee, feeling pride when the man admitted he'd been planning to check out the swamp park since coming to the south coast. Will wolfed down the box lunch as soon as they were underway, and with a full stomach for the first time in more than a day, as well as a break in the stress, he was able to fall deeply asleep.

His chauffer smiled as he glanced at the boy every once and again, savoring the memories his tale-telling had invoked, and finding similarities, face and figure, between Will and himself at the same age. Humming a long forgotten tune, he returned his attention to the road as they approached the bridge to the city of Savannah.

# CHAPTER SEVEN

The big barn of a house was going to echo from emptiness for the next week, Carrie was sure. She had just finished the final kitchen wipe down, and walked from room to room on her daily inspection after the house was all hers for a little while, seeing that everything was in order, upstairs and down. The schedule for graduation week was daunting, if not for her, for the girl and her daddy, who was not going to relax a moment until his daughter came home safe. "Let's see... today is Thursday, and Missy's gone to the other side with 'Tilde, 'and they've gone to Palmland so Missy can get settled in, then they goin' to town, her and Miss Sonja, to frock her up for the fancy parties to come." Her eyes toward the ceiling, Carrie watched it all play out for her.

Mr. Massey ain't gonna' get to see what she buys, and I ain't even wantin' to myself, cause I know that child ain't gonna get no lady-like fidaments," she began to speak aloud with much trepidation, pacing the floor. "No, no, she wants to be a little floozy gal, to make the young boys pant and whine, just to make 'em want to get close on by her." She drew up short from such thoughts... it would serve no purpose, except to give her palpitations, so she resumed tracking the events for the week.

Counting off the days in her head, Carrie had gotten to the supper dance at Poinsett Park in Frenchport on Saturday night, and went on to Sunday's Baccalaureate service at the old Episcopal Church in town, the party at the Country Club on Monday, the graduation ceremony itself on Tuesday, Palmland's dinner dance on the big night, Wednesday to themselves, and the trip to a Grateful Dead concert in Charleston by bus for those with tickets on Thursday, a properly chaperoned sleepover at the Mills House Hotel, then home again on Friday morning. Whew! It made Carrie tired out just to think of it! She was sure 'Tilde would have trouble keeping up and it worried her some, but she also knew her friend could place a spiritual tether on Franciene's ankle if she felt the need, thus saving herself a lot of energy.

As soon as Carrie had satisfied herself with the house's condition, she felt a gnawing in her belly. "It's goin' on nine-thirty! No wonder I'm hungry!" She allowed to herself with a comical whisper. Her appetite conjured up a treat she knew was waiting. "Those blackberries are wrapped up, and in 'Tilde's dumplin' pot, I just know it!" Carrie was still talking aloud to herself, her most attentive ear. She had long known it makes mind-workings more valid if they're recited... gives them something extra. That's why you could always hear Carrie and the rest of her friends mumbling fervently to themselves about most everything. It gave a person a chance to hear how the law to be laid-down would be heard by the party of the second part. All that aside, it was back to Aunt 'Tilde's dumplin' pot.

Carrie put on a clean apron, smoothed her work-tousled hair, and traded her scuffies for the pair of worn old espadrilles by the back door. Down the steps to the back yard, and in a moment she was on the pine needle path to a cabin as familiar to her as her own. She and Clothilde probably knew every pin, spoon, and pillowcase in each others' houses, and so it had been throughout their lives. She was on the back stoop in minutes, pushing open the hain't blue-washed door. Light spilling on the kitchen floor illuminated a sorrowful sight, causing Carrie to fall to her knees, gathering the by now almost cold body of her best friend and sister into her arms. Rocking her and moaning an inaudible chant from the deepest place in her ancestry, she sang a form of last rite, part the teachings the old folks had brought from the West Indies, and as much from her own broken heart.

The chant was working, and even though Clothilde Braswell slipped her earthly bonds over an hour ago, Carrie felt a gentle shudder, as the last thread tying her to her human host, that had waited until she got there, snapped in two forever. Carrie sighed as if somehow released as well from the pain at the moment of discovery. She laid the body back down to the floor, cleared off the kitchen table, and fetched a clean, snowy white sheet from the bed linens in the cedar chest. Humming sadly, she began a time-worn ritual. After locking the doors and windows and drawing down the shades, she shook out the sheet over the table, and a focused and composed Carrie, respectfully disrobed her charge and laid her out on the white table. Then, her friend ministered to her sister's tiny body as she had seen it done through her life, as others had done before her... the preparing of a loved one by those mothers, wives, and daughters, bade by custom to see that it was right.

It had been done like this for Miz Frances the night Franciene came... she reminisced, as she fetched the pan with tepid water and sweet oil soap, arranged the tiny, stiffening limbs lovingly... bathed and clothed her in a white batiste cotton night dress, then lit the oil lamp beside the bier of her beloved friend. The humming of the hymn continued until she, after a kiss on the still and cold cheek, was finished to her satisfaction. Without turning from the table, Carrie slipped from the dim room, and out the back door.

* * *

Over at the big house, the tall clock marked ten, and "Daddy" was fit to be tied. He had returned from the dock, found no one around, and instead of making a prudent search, poured a heavy crystal highball glass half full of brown whiskey and begun to fume. Massey Thornedike simply had to be in control of a situation, be it simple or complex, but he decided this was too much even for him. He left the dock in a daze after finding Topsy running loose, and watching the ferry grow tiny in the distance with his daughter, and WITHOUT her chaperone. How had it all come about? Why did Dan take her, and not wait for 'Tilde... and why was it that he felt so inexplicably terrified for his daughter?

He was still in a state of confusion when Carrie appeared in the doorway of the front room. Massey turned to face her and recoiled at the sight. Carrie seemed not of this world! She was literally glowing from her mission of a few minutes ago, and she couldn't manage a word to him. Massey walked to her with his hands outstretched. "Carrie! Aunt Carrie! In the name of Heaven, what's wrong?"

She was still without words, and Massey stood in fear of the reason. "Woman! Tell me what this is about!" With his shouted entreaty, and a finger-snap of a release from the spell she had been bound with, Carrie collapsed. Massey was able to catch her before she fell on the floor. She was consumed by the self-imposed trance, but Massey didn't understand. How could he? Her spiritual practices were not his provenance. The stricken man hoisted her into his arms, "Carrie, girl, you let ol' Massey help you," he crooned. The usually robust woman was limp and pale, her enraptured face now a dusky taupe. She was moving as if trying to shake free of whatever had taken her up, and for a moment, Massey suspected a stroke, or a heart attack. "Are you sick, Carrie?" he begged. "Tell ol' Massey what it is?"

The woman struggled to return... she MUST help this fearful man to get through such a bad thing, the thing he didn't even know yet. Her innate goodness overpowered her personal grief and physical state, and she, with all her powers, willed herself to a half-sitting position. Then she spoke. "OOOH, Mist'a Massey... Aunt 'Tilde, she's done gone across to the other side, DO JESUS MASTER, she did!"

He couldn't figure. His mind was whirling. With great care he said, "You mean, she's already taken the boat over? Tell me! Is that what you mean?" He knew what she meant... he had heard the term, "Done gone across!" all his life, but now he couldn't get his arms around its' truth... not if it meant what he feared. Carrie shot a look through his eyes. "No, Mister Massey, No!" Carrie pleaded, wanting so much to spare him the truth, even for a moment, but it could not be. "It's that she's done passed, Honey, she's already gone and died, just now!" Massey's ears began to ring, with an accelerating howl. This wasn't real! Not sweet Aunt 'Tilde! "You're sure, Carrie? You truly saw her dead? Where is she? Take me to her. Please take me, and right now!"

Hearing what he up to now had tried not to hear, he ran to take Carrie by her arms. "Oh, Lord, Carrie, I'm so sorry! 'Course you wouldn't tell me such if it wasn't so! Is she at her house? What happened to her? Please tell me you could be mistaken!" He was babbling away, asking too much for Carrie to answer, when to his own amazement, he started to cry. Wracking, ragged sobs shed for the realization of such a loss, for him and his family, for everyone who knew her.

He stood up, wiped his nose on his sleeve, and took a throw from the divan to put over Carrie, who had begun shivering as if it were January instead of late May. He lovingly tucked it around her and asked, "Will you be alright here without me, darlin', while I go see? I'll come right back, I promise!" His heart ached from the torment in her face, but without another word he adjusted her cover, and quickly went out back, sprinting to 'Tilde's house. The dash took only a minute, before he leapt to her back porch.

Through the window he could see the glow of the oil lamp, and his heart began thudding in his chest as he went inside. Such a familiar room, transformed from the busy, cheerful center of the home, to what felt like a funeral parlor in a bad dream, causing Massey to doubt the reality of the moment. He tiptoed to 'Tilde's side, not believing his eyes. She was gone... his lifelong friend, and his own daughter's dear companion. The best thing he could have had for a mother, most of his forty-six years, was truly dead. The sadness of her being taken was all there was in the world. The loss emptied him out so terribly, it felt as if he would crumble to the floor.

"Oh FRANCIENE... where ARE you? God, I nearly forgot my baby!" His head spun, and silently asked, "How can I tell that child her Aunt 'Tilde's gone?" He knelt on the floor beside the table, and holding his pounding head in his palms he wept, and wept, until he could not make any more tears. It must have been no more than five minutes, but it seemed to Massey that he knelt there for hours, remembering, telling himself over and over, "If ever there was an angel on earth, it was this sweet lady, right here!"

Time was fickle at that point. When he returned to the house it was nearly eleven. He managed a cup of tea with a jigger of brandy in it for Carrie, a slug for himself, and made her stay on the divan until he was satisfied that her normal color had returned. The issue of his daughter was crowding his head, and he had to call across to Dan right away, or he could no longer function. Dan was summoned to the phone at the marina by Miss Ruby. He greeted his friend haltingly, fearing a tirade. Instead, the voice he heard was weak, stuttering words that asked, "Dan, where's my little girl?"

Dan was instantly relieved not to hear his buddy's usual bellowing, and he began re-telling the events since he last saw Massey on the dock, before nine o'clock. Massey was coming around by then, and he inhaled and exhaled while the captain wrapped up his timeline. At the pause, Massey began to speak. "I want to know," he breathed, trying to get it said before he exploded, "Why you-all took my girl over there without her chaperone! I TOLD you I was goin' back to the house for Franciene and Aunt 'Tilde, (saying her name made fresh tears sting his eyes, and he swallowed them quickly to continue). "And I meant that thing, Dan, one was NOT to leave without the other!" He was trembling, but forged ahead.

"You hear this! I won't say any more to you right now, but this ain't done yet. Just you let me speak to Francie! Bring my daughter to the phone right NOW!" Poor Dan, relieved when lecturing ceased, mumbled, "Sure Buddy, I'll go get her right this minute, I shore will!" It had been a while since they docked in Frenchport, and Dan had not a clue where the girl got off to, but he knew he had to tell Massey something quick. A rapid scan of the shops and the boat docks, and confirmation that Francie's bags were gone, with no one in the harbormaster's office offering anything, he heartened a little, deciding that Jesse had surely come and fetched her to Palmland, as was planned. He ran back to the dangling receiver, grabbed it up to his ear and blurted, "She's done gone to Palmland, Massey! I seen her get in the car myself just now!"

"OOPS! Not good, Dan", his overworked old conscience whispered, "That's what we call a bald faced lie! You're going to pay for that one Up Here, boy, but not as bad as down there, when your friend Massey figures it out!" The admonition faded, with Dan so anxious to end the conversation he would have said anything.

"So... Francie is at Palmland, safe and sound." Massey didn't say a word, he simply hung up the phone, and sat down at his desk. He could have raised more hell with the rascal than he did, but it took too much energy, and Massey had practical matters surrounding a proper burial to deal with... he refused to allow his anger to mar the mournful dignity of celebrating 'Tilde's going home. The weary man went back into his front room, found Carrie not there, along with the throw cover... a check of the house produced nothing.

"She must have gone to be at 'Tilde's side," he reasoned, trudging out the door again. When he got to the back stoop, there she was, still wrapped in the afghan Frances had crocheted when they were first married, and she was reading something. "What have you got, Carrie?", he asked gently, sitting down beside her. "Tell me how you' feelin'?" Carrie regarded the latter question first, nodding slowly. "I'm alright, Mister Massey, it's gonna' be just fine now... you'll see." Ever the comfort-giver, she continued, "This is 'Tilde's wrote-out wishes, honey, she told me where to find the paper, back when she was sick with the influenza last year, an' she says this is how she wants things to be, say she should pass 'fore me." She handed the paper to him, looking right into his eyes with a look in no way a request that he consider the terms. This was how it was to be, so Massey read the little woman's last will and testament aloud, from her all too familiar hand. It was impossible to do without choking up.

\* \* \*

"This here is my wrote-down word, to tell my son and our friends what I want to happen when I go to my Lord Jesus in Glory. Don't cry and be sad, this is my reward for being a good woman, at least for trying to be." Massey sniffed and chuckled at the humor. He resumed reading.

72

"So I am, at last, truly happy and peaceful. It's nice here in this place, waiting for the arms of my Jesus to lift me up to the throne of our Father God to be in the Rapture forever. Don't weep, little Aaron. I always loved you so dear, and more than my own life. Sister Carrie, Mister Massey, and of course, most of all, my little Francie, you all are my real family, the ones who will be with me here in the Promised Land someday. I have three things to ask of you. Please save my things for Aaron. He will come back someday for them. And, I ask that you bury me beside my Mama and Daddy, between them and my dear husband's memorial cross we put up when we found out he was killed. I will rest there real GOOD. This is the last big favor for this old woman. Don't let them take my poor bones over to land-side, and put them in that refrigerator drawer, to cut me all up before I am laid to rest. I don't know how you can do it but please, Carrie, and Mister Massey, I swear if it was you asking, I would do just the same for you. Get me a nice pine wood box from Jasper. He's got two or three he keeps, in case the Island folks might need one, like I do now. He always said there'd be one for me, anytime." Massey was amazed at her attention to detail, and how strongly she got it all said. There was a little more.

"The boxes are in the shed behind his house. Dress me in my new pansy purple Easter frock, and lay me on my own pillow in my box. I will rest so nice you won't ever be bothered in the night by me ever! This I promise. I know y'all are going to be all right, babies, 'cause Jesus loves you. I love you all too." She had signed it, "Clothilde Poinsett Braswell... Aunt 'Tilde".

\* \* \*

Massey lowered the paper, his eyes blurring anew. Carrie patted his hand and nodded. Then she looked so deep in his eyes, he knew she needed the answer to her question right now. "What we goin' to do, Mister Massey? Can we let 'Tilde rest like she wants?" She wasn't going to cry again. Strength of purpose kept her stable, but intrepid tears from her eyes and nostrils, met and ran to her chin, as her eyes bored into his soul. He spoke softly to her. "Let me think,

Carrie, darlin'. Just let me think about this." A pure moment passed before Massey stood up with restored calm. He felt better because he had something he could do. It would be a privilege to carry out Aunt 'Tilde's last wishes. They went inside together, to keep their promise to their friend.

# CHAPTER EIGHT

Somewhere, away from the place where sadness and loss were so heavy, a girl was guessing that the death had been discovered by now. She hoped they wouldn't be too sad... after all, the old woman was getting on up there, and would have been dead soon anyhow. She also guessed that Aunt Carrie had given her daddy that paper. One day when she was being nosy, Franciene found it in that trunk with some other yellowed-up stuff old people like to keep. She knew that they would do it all just like she asked. Heck no! They won't be able to go against that will! No one would be getting an autopsy report on Aunt 'Tilde! The wicked girl smiled and patted her knees in triumph. Think of it! What if Aunt 'Tilde had died while they were at Palmland next week? It COULD have happened... The police, the coroner, and the funeral parlor people would have come for her, and it would have been too late to do what she wanted, written years before. It was best for all, how it happened! This girl was adept in justifying her actions...always.

No one would ever know what she did. That tin in the shed with the skull and crossbones was back in its place, like it had not been touched in years. When she took the lid off and spooned out the dose, using her headband to wrap around her fingers, even the dust and cobwebs were undisturbed, because the tin had been stored so far back under the shelf. She continued her rationalization. Aunt 'Tilde had simply fallen asleep! The way she went most likely spared her a lingering illness. "Why, I'll just bet they would all thank me if they knew what I did!", she insisted to herself. Everything was going to be fine... she would stay away, and it would be forgotten.

Francie figured it out while speeding along I-95, heading south in Clifford's Austin Healey roadster, her long hair flowing back into the slack face of a sky high young Aaron, snoring in the jump seat behind them. "Turn that up, Cliff, that's my favorite song! Hurry!", she yelled into the wind. The lad at the wheel dutifully complied, and she began to scream the ironic, chilling lyrics to, "Don't Fear the Reaper".

## TOBY MARCHES TO GEORGIA

"How very predictable," Toby groused to himself as he negotiated several state and county roads that detoured him to Savannah. He hadn't known, or didn't recall, the interstate was not complete across the river into Georgia, and it was one big pain in the ass. He chided himself for being such a baby, and resolved to take things more in stride. A search effort like the one he was making would call for a clear and precise mind. In reality the boy was most likely okay... that kind of thinking relieved Toby so much it made his knees weak. When Shirley Neville told him about Will showing up at her place, Toby smelled success.

There would be a reunion, he was sure, but just how much he had to wade through before he could get to the boy, who could know? He turned onto route 17-A, the connector that would take him over the Talmadge Bridge into Savannah, while hard at work on his plan. Timing was the key. It was possible, if this George character liked to fart around in machine shops, he could suddenly walk in on them in a few minutes. The time since Toby had last seen Will when he ran down the beach and away, seemed to be twice the actual eighteen hours. What a mess!

Crossing the bridge, he had no idea how to find Coastal Engine and Machine Shop on Jefferson Street. He hadn't gotten very far into the traffic maelstrom before he realized, against gender rules, the time to stop and ask was now!

Savannah, the first planned city in the United States, is a post-card everywhere one looks. English in flavor, sprinkled with huge, moss hung live oaks, and magnolias in full bloom, it has been the mother of all antebellum movie sets. One could easily become distracted here no matter what the mission, and find himself rubbernecking to the right and left, going "OOOH—AAAHH!", in spite of himself. Each of the more than twenty verdant, centrally placed squares, boasted at least one mansion presiding. In fact, John Wesley, who founded the Methodist Church in America, was a resident of Savannah, and his gothic gift to the city's devout still stands. The Girl Scouts were founded there as well, and Juliet Gordon Low's family home honors her memory with Georgian grace.

Toby mused that it would be fine to return in better times with Will, and dig into this visual treasure box of a Southern Belle, which, by the way, is what they call the telephone company that serves the area. There was a meter maid ahead, doing her dirty duty, and Toby slowed to a stop beside her. She turned and reflected his smile... so he inquired about Jefferson Street. She indicated he was quite near, but warned that the street switches from two-way to one-way, and that only the locals possess this knowledge. Toby agreed to be watchful, and followed her white gloved finger. It wasn't long before he was backing away from the angry grill of an approaching automobile on the offending street, flashing its' headlights to signal his error. Cursing his stupidity, he backed past the sign, now visible behind a tree.

It took about twenty minutes to proceed five blocks to the address of the shop, but he succeeded, sitting two doors from the entrance. Looking around as he locked the jeep, Toby was disheartened not to see the old green Dodge truck, this "George", was said to be driving. Undaunted, he entered the shop, wincing at the pitch of the machinery grinding away inside. A middle-aged man approached him, removing his goggles and ear plugs. "Can I do something for you, sir?" Toby got right to the point... asking if George Potter had been there.

"Yeah, he picked up his prop about twenty minutes ago. He and a tow-headed kid hung around for a minute or two, then took off." Twenty minutes! The coincidence that he had looked for this place exactly that many minutes, torqued him. One green light, and Will would be standing in front of him! "I don't guess you overheard where they were going next." he said with hesitation. The helpful fellow looked at him as if he were drooling, so Toby thanked him without waiting for an answer, and fast-walked out the door. Knowing nothing about the restaurant district in Savannah, or even if there WAS such, he swallowed his male pride and did the unthinkable... again. Back to the same meter maid, the poor guy inquired where one might look for lunch. She giggled this time, but gave him the answer.

"Most everybody who comes to town ends up on River Street at least for a drink, or to pick up some goodies they sell there... Try River Street." Soon Toby was bumping down a seriously descending cobblestone ramp, toward the below riverfront, wondering what "goodies" consisted of. It was a quaint, colorful, and busy strip of shops and bistros served by a hundreds of years old ballast-stone street, with parking expanses across on the river side. Toby was lucky to find a space, and hustled across the walking street in front of the storefronts, looking for that truck as he went. It would be of sufficient age so as to flash its rounded roof over the other cars with inches to spare.

Hurrah! There it was, beckoning like an old friend. Toby sprinted to it, looked in the windows and in back for a sign of Will... nothing there, but the boy usually took his pack, even for a pee stop, in a strange place. Whirling in a complete three-sixty, Toby chose the closest pub to the truck, remembering Shirley's description of George's radically bowed legs. There was a moment of blindness, as he entered the tastily scented room. Combined aromas of fried seafood, grilled onions, good burgers, and sauerkraut nearly knocked him back out the door, and he was hungry on the spot... such a distracting passion.

First things first, he demanded of himself, and went to the thickly glazed cedar bar. As his sight normalized, he looked left, then right, for someone who could be George. Disappointed not to see Will in the room, he swept a look down the bar. There he was! It had to be George Potter! Shirley said he was wearing a tee-shirt with a jumping fish on the back, that he was grayish-blonde, and brown-skinned... that's him! Toby moved from his stool before the bartender could ask what he'd have, and approached the sight for sore eyes, sitting five stools down. He was noshing on fish and chips, alternately shaking salt and malt vinegar, in liberal doses.

"George? George Potter? I'm Toby Howell, from Elizabeth City... you know... North Carolina?" George wiped his mouth, turned on the stool, and shook the proffered hand. "How' do, mate!" Yep, Toby thought, this is he... Shirley had offered up about the accent as well. He returned verbal service. "I've been tracking you from Padgett's Island." At the word, "tracking", the burly man jumped off of the stool, with a menacing scowl. Toby's palms waved at George's chest, and he said quickly. "Wait! No trouble's coming to you," he quickly added. George sat back down, with a raised, sun bleached eyebrow in suspicious regard. Toby pressed on, more quickly now. "I'm a close friend of young Will Parrish, and was told he has traveled here to Savannah with you. It was good of you to offer him a lift, but I really need to find him."

It occurred to Toby that he could, given the suspicious trend these days, be treading in dark places, that the old guy might think just about anything of his motives, from kidnapper to sexual deviate! He attempted clarification with a brief narrative of their relationship. George began to settle down, and Toby guessed Will had told him a little about himself... it might corroborate his tale. The weathered face softened, produced a smile, and said, "Sure is a nice boy, Toby. Sit down and let me buy you a beer. I called Shirley a little while ago, and she told me about you. I thought I might take her to a picture show or somethin' tonight." He was mumbling, almost inaudibly, "But she said no... again! Don't quite know how to figure." It sounded like unrequited love, and Toby wasn't interested. He blurted out, "Captain, I need to find the boy! He's had a hell of a shock in the last thirty-six hours, and he may come to harm by making some impulsive choices. Do you know where he is now?" His gaze was still panning the room.

George shook his head. "No, he ain't here now. I told him I would take him where he needed to go, since I could tell he was stewin' over somethin' serious, but he insisted he didn't want to put me out. He said he could get another ride." Then there was the big question. "Did you call Shirley before Will left you, or after?" A chill ran over him at the thought that Will could actually be running from HIM, not just the crisis of a few hours ago. "Oh, I called Shirley from Coastal, where I picked up my prop. It must'a been thirty minutes or so ago." Toby had instant dry mouth, as he pressed on. "Did you tell Will somebody was trying to find him?" (God, please let him say NO!)... "Sure I did! 'E's got a right to know, wouldn't ya think? I mean, the lad might'a been stalked by a faggot, good lookin' as he is, an' all!"

There it was... the stigma that threatens the credibility of well-intentioned people like Toby. He was prepared for it, and let the remark hang in the air. His next words were from his heart. "Please, sir, where did he go? I'm worried shitless over him, and he needs help!" He seemed to believe this, and offered, "He didn't know where he wanted to go, I'll wager. Seems to me, he must have family or friends someplace near here, maybe near to Okeefenokee. You know anything about his family?" Toby was touched but not surprised at his concern, since it was Will they were concerned with. "Not much. It appears the boy hasn't got too much to tell about by way of family ties. His grandfather died just before I met him, and his mother had left him with the grandfather when Will was quite small. I have no other information, and don't think Will does either. He seems to have always kept his own counsel, so to speak. I don't even know if his mother is in the area, or even still alive."

They were silent for a moment, when George said, "He slipped out from here not more 'n fifteen minutes or so ago. I was washin' up and didn't see which away he took out for, I'm sorry to say. He had his pack with him when we came in, so's I guess I should'a been expectin' that he was gonna' take off. I just didn' think of it. I'm real sorry 'bout that, mate." Without ordering the beer, Toby got up, thanked the man, and left the pub. Guess it's Waycross next, he sighed to himself. Will, let's hope you have the same plan.

By the time Toby had finished with George, Will was watching the Savannah skyline disappear over the ferryboat's churning green, foam-capped wake, ETA Frenchport... two o'clock.

# PRACTICAL MATTERS TAKE
# PRIORITY OVER GRIEF

When he was steady again, Massey backed the pickup from the shed, waved goodbye to Carrie at 'Tilde's back door, and bounced down the lane to the Griffin's. He would follow, word for word, how the woman wanted it to be, so she could rest easy. He knew it was his place to see to everything for her. Jasper's square back was gone, as was Miss Pansy's Corvair. They must have gone to town, Massey mused, never finding it queer that they took separate cars to the dock. Separate missions, was the rule, on Squires or Townside. Pansy would unload the groceries and start supper, while Jasper delivered the strange mix of goods they picked up for everyone who didn't, or couldn't go shopping for themselves. Depending on his affection and empathy for each, some he charged for the service, some he didn't. Not one of his benefactors ever ratted on him to the folks he charged... anywhere from a dollar to ten... he had his own mystical criteria about that.

Massey, already a mushy mess over Aunt 'Tilde, felt renewed warmth for the island people, as he thought how lucky he was to live among them. This coffin thing, for example, was proof of his belief in their intrinsic goodness. It wasn't Jasper's obligation provide them... but when, seven years ago, a good friend of his was drowned while fishing, and his body was brought home, there was no box to lay him out in. Like now, that fellow had asked his family never to take his remains over for any reason when he passed. Jasper worked straight through that night to have a coffin ready for the sittin' up time. Since it made everyone most timorous, concerned it wouldn't be ready for the service, and since things are taxing enough when someone dies, Jasper kept right on making those coffins that winter, until he had six... two for big men, two for medium men and ladies, and two for children. It was a sad chore to do on gloomy winter days, and he was thankful nobody needed one of them for almost two years after. Anyway, it remained his self-imposed duty, and he still kept three or four in the shed in their backyard, to the day Clothilde, God rest her, needed one for herself.

Massey backed the truck up to the door of the shed and let the tailgate down. When he went into the shed, there, second from the end, was the one. It was of medium size... a bit large for her, but would suffice, and it had a beautiful grain to the wood. The lid was all-over satin striped, like amber ribbons tossed across the surface, and Jasper had varnished and rubbed this one with many more than the two standard coats. As soon as his eyes adjusted, Massey was certain with no doubt, that this was the one Jasper would want for her. The older people had grown up together, all of them here, and now, one by one, they were departing. He was crying again as he loaded the coffin into his truck, but from beauty... and love... and tribute, more than sadness or grief. The time was growing short before they were to go across, and Massey drove the rutted road as carefully as he could, so not to scratch 'Tilde's pretty pine box.

# CHAPTER NINE

Even as a child, Will knew he was a son of the sea, when he found joy at the beach, on the dock, or in the swamp, more than anywhere else. The wake behind the ferry boat hypnotized him as he stared into its' boil... it was a comfortable, relaxing trance... allowing new thoughts to float up. If he didn't go see the girl's father, his guilty conscience would probably die of its own weight in time. No! That would be such a coward's way, and maybe he would never be free of her, no matter where he might run.

Will half believed that Franciene Thornedike may be his permanent haint, following him into the most intimate, unrelated places for the rest of his life, and if so, he needed to rearrange the present so his future could be his own! As soon as he absolved himself with her daddy, he could go back to Padgett's and Toby, free from the curse. Frenchport Harbour was dead ahead, and the crew began preparations for docking the big-bellied paddle boat. Will and the dozen other passengers disembarking, shuffled aside, Southern manners in place, for the ladies, children, and older people to go first. The long established pecking order put Will dead last, but he was fine with it. He strode up the concrete pier, and the first familiar face he saw was Cissy's!

She saw him too, and skipped over to his side, falling into step as best she could, her little legs no match for his long stride. "Remember me?" she asked, looking into his face with the kind of look a puppy has when all the others got a treat but her. He stared dispassionately at her, and spouted, "Do I look completely stupid to you?"

Whoa! Where did THAT come from? He hadn't been able to stop the rude question, but repaired his ugliness with, "What I meant to say, was that it's only been twenty-four hours since we saw each other last, but I'd remember you even if it had been a month!" He made a mental note to ask himself why he had put her down that way.

The gullible girl only cooed in reply. "What you doin' back here anyway? Weren't you and your daddy goin' to Charleston or some-place?" He was enjoying his emerging suave side, testing a swagger as he answered her. "Yes, we were headed that way, but seem to have lost something, and need to go to Squires Island this afternoon if I can, to look for it." He waited for her to answer, wanting to watch her mouth work, not knowing why. "The boat's comin' in now. They usually eat lunch, an' then go back at three. The captain tries to keep to a schedule of odd hours from here, and even hours from Squires, but sometimes it doesn't work, that is, if somebody's late, or there's a special need for a crossing. I usually come down to sit with Jaime for his lunch break." They were at the marina restaurant, and Will motioned her to a table on the weathered deck.

He seated her with a flourish, and went to order drinks. When he returned with two iced teas, Jaime and his father were standing by the table. "Hey Bo!" The younger man called out, "You back again? We don't get return visits much here, 'cept for them Yankee tourists. Where's your Dad?" Will found the last question to be most relieving... if they had looked in the log book, they would have seen that neither of the pairs of names Toby signed was that of a father and son. At any rate, he let the question hang in the air.

"I was hoping I could hop a ride with you guys back to Squires at three. I lost something, and I think it might be over there, 'cause I can't find it anyplace else I've looked." Let's see if he's as interested as he seems, Will quickly said to himself. Does he ask me what I lost, or does he not care? He grabbed the moment to figure what he could use as the "lost" item... thought of it...and, sure enough... "What'd you lose?" It was Captain Dan who asked, and Will was almost glad, so he could work his story for a little more credibility. He was relaxing for another reason, figuring it would already be the talk of the harbor if the body had been found.

He sat Cissy's tea in front of her, and sat down himself. The girl was visibly a-twitter, and Will wondered if she was nervous about Jaime finding them together. No harm in putting out the fire before it flared up. "I asked Cissy to keep me company while I wait for you. She's been telling me how your schedule works." He could actually see her relax, as she gazed at him appreciatively. Dan, still waiting for an answer, pushed on. "You lose your wallet or somethin'? We charge for every trip, you know." This guy is careful, alright. "No, I've got my wallet. What I lost is a knife. A real old, yellowed, bone-handled buck knife my granddaddy gave me before he died. I guess it didn't turn up on your boat, right?" He was playing it to the hilt.

"Naw", Jaime drawled, "we ain't seen no knife, but we'll take you over for a look. Boat leaves at three, sharp. We can hang for you to look before leavin' for the four o'clock run, but you got to be back by four-twenty, and no later! Even so, it'll press us hard to get back here by five. We got a shark fishin' trip planned for this afternoon, an' I ain't gonna' miss that good money. You're the last sign-on we' got today." Will was intent on good dealings with the two men, and he nodded hastily his understanding. They went to order burgers, and Will, nervously drumming his fingers, tried to predict how the rest of the day would play out. Cissy had been waiting for a chance to speak to him alone.

"Thank you, boy... I forgot your name, but thank you for bein' so nice to me. Jaime ain't never acted like he was jealous or nothin'. I don't know... maybe he don't really care much." Will was sorry for the poor little mess beside him. "Are you two going out? I mean, is he your boyfriend?" She began to twist her fingers together, trying to give the best answer. "Well, we hang around together some when he's not workin', and I kind of help him with cleanin' the boat when it's done for the day. You got a girlfriend yourself? What's your name again?" Will was stymied... should he give his true name, or the one Toby supplied him with? He went for the truth. "First, my name is Will, and no, I don't presently have a girl, but I'm definitely looking!" With that in the box, Cissy giggled delightedly, and rubbed her shoulder against his, stopping as Jaime returned.

They were already halfway through the monstrous burgers when Will stood up and announced he would meet them at the boat. He approached the pier, collecting more mental muscle for later. There was no way to predict the outcome of his trip across, so he planned to let destiny take him. He had no clue about how to seek out, let alone approach Mr.Thornedike anyway, so that was all he could do. All he held out as a guidon was the fact that he HAD to do something. The crew was aboard right on time, and the old boat maneuvered out of Frenchport at three o'clock sharp. Will took the log, signing his own name without a pause. When he looked up, Jaime was staring out to the horizon, deep in the imaginary throes of his shark charter, probably surmising whether he would be hooking bonnets, spinners, or if he was blessed, a huge, trophy tiger or bull. He replaced the logbook, and straightaway began rigging his baits for later.

\* \* \*

On Squires, Carrie and Massey spoke little as they readied 'Tildie's cabin for the sittin' up time to begin that evening. There were no words to match the moment. When they did speak, Carrie's thoughts were of Franciene. "It seems to me, that child' needs to come back here to be with her family for the sittin' up, an' for the service, Mista' Massey... what's your feelin'? We need a few things from town, like more lamp oil, an' some candles, an' some ice, an' coffee, an' tea, and"... She was getting agitated, running over her mental list... stacking her brain with too much at one time. Massey stopped her with a hand on her shoulder, softly saying, "Carrie, we do need to go to town... you're right. But most of all, I believe like you, we have to find Aaron, AND fetch Franciene." Her eyes sought his, and he continued.

"The boy needs to be here today to sit beside his mama, when everybody comes. Next thing, I can have Jesse bring Francie straight to the boat, and we can meet up after you shop and I fetch Aaron." Massey continued. "We can make a list on the trip across, I can leave you at the store, and you can take my credit card and get everything you want. Now, you know this will be alright, if we just stay cooled out. I'm gonna' call the flower shop right now, to order the coffin blanket, if you tell me what flowers Aunt 'Tilde liked best."

He stood waiting while Carrie pondered the request. She looked like herself for the first time since she came into the house from 'Tilde's, as she sang out, "I believe she'd like to be restin' under roses, Mista' Massey, all colors of roses, and tell them to put some of that sweet baby's breath all in with 'em, and some 'sparagus fern!" Her eyes were sparkling as she raised them to the ceiling, envisioning the beauty of it. "God Bless this woman, she is so damn good!" Massey said in his mind. Seeing it through Carrie's eyes was all he needed to know. He called Rosie's Posies in Frenchport for them to get started right now, on a blanket using every rose she could find with all the extras, and he'd pick it up at a quarter to six. When he got back to Carrie, she was in a sweet place he longed for... her face was hazy and detached from the moment.

Massey was sure she was spiritually in a field of roses and baby's breath herself. He let her be for a bit. She was so wise and had such command she was back to the present in seconds. They struggled to put 'Tilde's coffin properly in place on a bench in her parlor, and after Carrie dressed her in the shades-of-purple voile Easter dress, Massey tenderly laid her out, her head resting on her bed pillow, and Carrie took her worn prayer book from the bedside and put it between her crossed hands. Carrie then cut dozens of big, plumbago-purple hydrangea blooms from the flower garden, and divided them between two ornate pickle jars at each end of the bier. One more thing left to do... she trimmed a grapevine wreath with gardenia, magnolia, privet branches, and ivy, and hung it on the door with a notice that the time for visiting was seven o'clock in the evening, just time enough for the four of them to get back from town.

Massey plotted as he had so many times, to make best use of the brief span between the four and the six o'clock boats. He had a moment to marvel how ordinary it was to budget time in town, and how extraordinary this mission was. The difference was that this schedule had to be kept! They would go directly to the market so Carrie could do her shopping while he went after Aaron. He would call Palmland for Jesse to fetch Francie at ten minutes to six, pick up the flowers, and finally, Carrie, just in time for the 6:00 departure. It was going to be tight, but nothing Massey couldn't handle. His one surety was that Dan would wait if they ran overtime, but the Island people would not. They would begin to gather promptly at seven, at 'Tilde's house. They simply must be back there to open the door! Francie would have to be told by the Hartsells, much to her daddy's distress, after they heard the sad news from Jesse. It was all terribly touchy, Massey fretted, but things about dying usually are. His plan made, he went to his study, took a drink straight from the bottle of Jack Black, and fell on the divan, for a few minutes of nothing at all.

The ferryboat got word by radio, (without explanation or divulging the sad news to avoid a premature rush to the harbor), of the extended day while en route with Will, and Jaime went ballistic! "This is a turnaround trip, Daddy! I got a three hour shark trip goin' off at five-thirty, and Massey's mess means the boat won't be mine 'til eight!" The boy could fuss and raise hell until the cows came, but, since the boat was funded for their use, Island folks got priority. He stomped down below to call around for a boat captain who could do the charter with him. Dan wasn't happy about the extra run either, but if he could appease Massey, especially now, it was a good thing. When they got to the Island, Will jumped from the boat to the floating dock before Jaime could grab the lines. The mate told him where to find the dock cart to speed his search, and warned him the boat would leave him if he wasn't back, knife or no knife, at quarter-past four.

He checked watches with them, and they agreed he had a half hour. Will figured he could retrace to where the body was well within the time, and when he returned to the boat, he would tell them to leave him there, asking directions to Thornedike's place. The little gas powered cart crunched purposefully away from the shed, with Will's foot jammed to the floor. He left the cart at the head of the lane, and ran toward the bluff, sliding down to the creek bed. The tide was at the same level as yesterday, so he could easily find the sand spit where she would be. Will walked stiffly toward the place... he couldn't believe it! She was not there! Scattered palmetto boughs... yes, but no footprints, and no sign that a body had been there. In futility, he sank to his knees and swept his hands across the sand, asking for clues, but there were none. He was helpless, and stuck in a mystery of such scope, it made him dizzy. What to do now?

"I know we put her right here yesterday!" he said aloud. If she had been found, everyone would have known in town... that nosey girl, Cissy, would have been chattering away. No! She was just gone! The bewildered boy ran back to the cart, wanting only to be gone as well. As he was turning around, a light came on in his head... the tide must have taken her out! There had been a full moon last night while he was on Padgett's beach, and that meant the tide had been higher than yesterday, by three feet or more! He jumped back off of the cart and ran to see. YES! The brown mass of dead marsh grass had been carried all the way up to the highest line, and Franciene's body had washed away with the tide

On the way back to the dock with fifteen minutes to spare, Will was idling along, trying to sort through it. If he went to Mr.Thornedike with his story, it would be miserably weak. How could he tell the man that he had left his daughter's dead body on the creek bank so it could be reclaimed by the very creek he pulled her out of? No, he couldn't do it! It was out of his and Toby's hands now. A bit of relief came over him, and he decided to call Toby on Padgett's from the first phone he got to, and tell him to relax. Then he breathed silently, with a change of plan. "I'll get back to Padgett's as fast as I can, and forget this, because it's over!" Will had never done much praying other than grace and bedtime, but Thanks to God went up at that moment. He rounded the bend in the road, and there, at the pier head, was the Land Rover!

Will was slammed stupid by the sight of the car he knew to be Mister Thornedike's. He left the cart and began a tormented walk to the boat. There were two forms standing in the boat's aft-deck. As he neared the ramp, the boy's brain began to burn white-hot. "What's happening? Why am I feeling so funny... like I'm part of a weird dream?" The big man was talking to the captain, and beside him was his companion... a powerful looking black woman. As he approached the boat, Will could see the woman's eyes clearly, as if he were right in front of her, and they burned into his with such intensity even from so far, he could feel the purpose of her. Such purpose... an unworldly purpose. Will knew without doubt, the reason he was here was soon to be revealed.

## THE QUEST FOR WILL
## TAKES A NEW TURN

There was nothing else for Toby to do but get into the Jeep on River Street and put his weary ass on the road toward Waycross. He was so tired, angry, and frustrated, it seemed he couldn't do anything right. Relieving his hunger would keep him from passing out at the wheel, so the next eatery he came to, a feeding trough buffet, took care of that problem. Once back on the highway, he adjusted his thoughts and settled into the drive. It was a dreary trip, and boring, because he had picked the identical route apart two years ago, when he had first met Will. God! Toby tried to shake off the fury rising in him. "He should have trusted me!" Toby swore silently... I was there too! I was as rudely thrust into the nightmare as he... perhaps in deeper straits, because I was the responsible adult!" He knew he was coming unhinged. Will's defection and Toby's fear for him made him a stranger to his own soul, and he couldn't figure a way back. "When I finally find him" He stopped the anger cold, and truth took over as he finished the vow... "I'm going to hug him... that's all I'm going to do!" That felt better, and he laughed out loud. Within two hours, the jeep was exiting the interstate for Waycross.

Once in town, Toby began looking at store fronts, seeking a newspaper office or phone company. Finding neither, and getting more impatient by the minute, he pulled in at a convenience store and asked for the use of a phonebook. When he got to the"P's", he slid his finger down until it rested on the first Parrish, and went to a pay phone. Seven Parrishes down the line, he dialed the number of an L.S. Parrish. It was the door... and it was about to open. A soft, girlish voice answered, and Toby felt a sensation of success. "Hi, I'm Toby Howell, and I'm looking for someone you may know. He and I are friends. First off... if you need to check me out, I can give you any information right now with this call. I have no idea where you live, since the telephone book only gave a name." The voice again, like Christmas bells.

"It's Linda... Linda Sue Parrish. That's my name." She couldn't have been more than twenty or so by the sound of her voice, he thought. This couldn't be Will's mother, but he followed his intuition, and asked to see her. "What does this concern, Mr.Howell?"... she asked. Her voice was bubbling in his brain, as he blurted. "I'm sorry to intrude, but I'm trying to locate a young man, name of William Parrish." She gasped, and he heard her drop, then pick up the receiver, as she said, "Why did you call ME? I don't know anything about him! I can't tell you where he is! He's not here, that's all I can say!" She hung up, and Toby was positive he had found a member of Will's family.

He furiously dialed her again, and persuaded her to direct him to her house. Soon he was guiding the jeep to a stop in front of a nice little bungalow with a vegetable garden to one side, and a climbing red rose that took up the entire end of the porch, covering a trellis with velvety, black-red blooms. When he stepped up on the porch there she was, swinging back and to under the roses. "Miz Parrish... Linda Sue?" She stood, all five feet, nine inches of her, and stepped toward the suddenly weak-kneed man with her hand out. "That's me, Mr. Howell... Toby?" As soon as this mature woman spoke he was stunned, because it was the voice on the phone... those tiny bells. The rest of her was nothing less than Will in female form, and he breathed, "You're his mother, aren't you?" No answer... she stood, frozen, as the questions she had dreaded for years, flew at her.

"Why didn't his grandpa ever tell him you were here, so close by? He told him all his little life that he didn't know where you were! How come he had no idea of you at all?" She got through the questions with difficulty, and then sat back down in the swing. Motioning for Toby to sit in a nearby rocker, she calmly asked if he would like some iced tea. His eyes couldn't move from her face, and the words wouldn't come, so he just shook his head. "I wanted it that way," she finally answered.

"There was no other choice. I had to be away. If the boy had known I was close by, when he got older he'd have come to find me. My daddy wasn't the best parent material, but he was blood, and since I was desperate to fix my baby up with a safe home, I needed to believe he would rise to the need. It was all I could do. Where is Willie? Can YOU tell ME, Toby… Where is my Son?"

It got tougher and tougher to look at her. The same feeling Toby had when he first saw Will was flooding over him. She was different… there was a too-good-to-be-true, quality about her. Pretty would fall short of describing her face, while beautiful, she wasn't either. The entire package was in a word, lovely. "I know where he was as recently as noon today, and he was safe." he answered finally. She didn't need to know his foreboding or the reason for it. He was puzzled by her attitude of outrage directed at him. Then he got mad. What was he thinking about? She had been right here in this podunk town… this close, and didn't give a damn enough, even to have a park ranger report to her now and then about her child! She didn't even know her father was dead!

Will's mother was rapidly losing her aura, as Toby's first take was overruled by the plummeting impression. He went on, and told her that he and the boy had differences Wednesday, and this morning when he woke up on Padgett's Island, he was gone. That would have to do for a story. He went through the George Potter part, finishing up on the porch where they were. "There is no reason to believe he would come here to find ME!" She offered. Then she stood up, and began to pace the porch in front of Toby's chair.

The man was, to put it mildly, dismantled… trying not to leer at her heart-shaped derriere, moving up and back under the faded sun dress she was wearing. It was disturbing… the return of feeling something about a woman. He had considered those kinds of feelings thrown to the wind along with Kate's ashes. Shaking off the moment, Toby called back her last comment, and forged ahead. "You and I agree on that point, Linda, but there is nothing I won't call on to help me locate the boy. I'm devoted to him, and he to me. You need to know as his mother, that he is a fine young man, and will only get better as he matures. The fact has been obvious to everyone he meets. I believe he'll come back, but it's not in my nature to sit on my hands and wait." She stared straight into Toby's eyes for a moment, and he felt the conversation ended, or at least suspended. The woman he thought could only visit a man in his dreams, went into her house without another word, and he left, more confused than ever.

The stubborn man Toby was decided to give it a few days to see if Will would show. He might be dawdling, possibly for fear of being rejected by a mother who had discarded him years before. His friend longed to know what was in the boy's head, but was confident that he would be at the end of the journey, whether today, or a month from today. Toby was stopped dead-still for the first time in years because of a tow-headed boy and his intractable, gorgeous mother. He found the town's strip of motels, checked in at the good old Holiday Inn, and decided he would call her with his room number, in case Will appeared. He took room near the lobby, and once inside, he splashed his tired looking face, called Linda Sue's house, but got no answer. Disappointed, he left his room number on her answering machine.

It was five o'clock somewhere, and after such a day, a man was bound to have a powerful thirst. The lounge was adjacent to the dining room, where a few late-lunching folks still cooled off. No one was about to serve him, so Toby was targeting the front desk to plead for a bartender, when Linda came in, dressed for work. She flushed when she saw him, and laughed nervously. Toby followed her into the dim lounge and sat on a stool, watching while she set up the bar. She was so damn easy to watch.

# CHAPTER TEN

They had been traveling, top-down, for better than four hours. Aaron was asleep, more passed out, in the cramped jump seat of Cliff's Healey. This morning, when Francie went to the shack on Turtletail Creek that Aaron called home, she expected to find him packed and ready. He was ready alright... ready to turn over for another hour or two of sleep! It was more than she bargained for, this clever girl, manipulating the two of them to strike out for a week of freedom. The only way she could do it was to treat each of them with a different set of rules. With Aaron, their childhood together made it easy... she had always been boss. It was just that way, with both Aaron AND Benjie. No difference here, she simply told Aaron what she wanted and he made it happen.

## THE TOUGH ONE WAS CLIFF.

She had no history with him, except on **HIS** turf, and that didn't count. Although he seemed to want nothing more than to please her, she was not sure her every whim would be blindly allowed. No, she believed he was most vulnerable when his libido was involved, so she would use it against him. A soft giggle said she was confident it would go perfectly, and it did... Cliff was right on time, meeting Francie and Aaron at the corner by the Piggly Wiggly, behind the azalea hedge, so nobody could see him putting her bags in the car and helping her into the seat next to him, her head wrapped in a scarf, and Jackie-O sunglasses as a disguise.

This was "Agent 007" stuff to the sheltered preppie! He had only one thing on his mind, and it was something soft and secret, and he was sure it was going to be all his, on this trip! He imagined making up a story every one, even the girl's daddy would accept when they returned. Their overall plan hadn't jelled yet, but being twenty years old and still a virgin, (unless the hasty blow job he got from his cousin in Rockville counted), and having a fantasy come to him wrapped up so sweetly, offering herself up so she could escape her daddy's cage, really tweaked his loins.

The sensation felt like prep school graduation night, when he stood across the street from the whorehouse in Richmond. He had cowered there, unable to join in, lamely watching, as his fellow class-men went up on the porch to disappear, to emerge with flushed and goofy faces, their shirttails half-out, and their neckties wadded up in their fists. He wasn't to be calm again for days after that, no matter how he tried not to think about it. Whatever the consequences, a week with the tasty Miss Thornedike would deliver Clifford Augustus Hartsell from the clutches of humiliating innocence and ignorance, and it would be worth whatever might come after.

He and Franciene had shared a joint she had slipped from Aaron's pocket when she saw him in the harbor before she went to Palmland's Christmas party last winter. She coaxed the startled boy into the kitchen, and he could not resist. She was a vision in bottle green velvet that night... her hair tied high on top of her head with a black ribbon, spilling down over her shoulders, the entire package smelling of the exotic fragrance called Khus-Khus, ceremoniously opened for the occasion by Carrie and 'Tilde from her dear departed Mama's perfume collection. Before they could be interrupted by servants, she had taken his face to hers and kissed him with the sweetest, juiciest little mouth he had ever touched, whispering and breathing in his burning ear, "We are gonna have fun soon, Cliffie, I swear." He had dedicated quite a few washings to that moment since, promising his untested manhood good things to come.

The idea to include Aaron in the adventure came to her when she decided she would not be able to stomach Cliff one-on-one for the entire trip, and she knew Aaron's savvy would be valuable to both of the sheltered white kids. Aaron was in instant agreement, and asked nothing but a day or two of notice to be ready to go. It was a genius idea, and she was proud of herself. When they were walking to the rendezvous point, she was full of chatter. Aaron was amused at her, as he walked along, pulling the dock cart full of her bags along behind.

"I was thinking, Aaron... if we can talk Cliff into it, I'd like to go to Fort Lauderdale and get on one of those cruise ships... maybe go to Nassau, or someplace like that. How would you like to go to the Bahamas, boy?"   Aaron didn't know how he would like anything right then, except maybe another hit. When discussing their getaway, and each one's part in it, they had agreed for the sake of drawing less attention to themselves, for Aaron to leave the crack pipe at home. He could melt into the pack while merely stoned, but if he was strung out on crack... too high to be cool, he could get them all busted, with far reaching conclusions.

He had managed to squirrel away a big bag of weed to finance himself for the next couple of weeks, and figured as soon as he could lose the two white children, he could make some easy contacts all over Florida. Aaron had an advantage over most young black men his age. Being a child of Squires Island had imprinted him with a strong sense of himself, and the confidence borne of the first-class citizenship they all had enjoyed on their island home. Most times when things went sour for his mainland friends, it was because of some sort of cultural misdirection, or the stigmatization of an entire group, owing to the misdeeds of a few.

Profiling of such unfair nature had never been a part of Aaron's life, and even when the tragedy with Benjie occurred, he had received unanimous support from everyone, and his story was never, never in question. The hardest person on him was himself. [It has been said by wise men, that forgiving ones' self is the hardest thing to do.] He was pummeled by night with the most horrific of nightmares, and during the day and evening he found it impossible to endure waking hours without ingesting something. No, Aaron wasn't okay, but he did a bang up job of faking his wellness to everyone around him... all except for the girl. Franciene knew what Aaron's life was like... and his secret reason why, but she kept it to herself... promising him his mother would never know. She kept up with him when she could, considering herself to be more sophisticated for the covertness of it all.

Jaime was a customer of Aaron's, but only for the marijuana, and even then, only the primo, Okeechobee Skunk Weed Aaron dealt exclusively when it was procurable. No one had to tell either Jaime or Franciene how important their vows of secrecy were to Aaron. They lived in a small place, with a population more aware of each other's activities than was comfortable for the unscrupulous among them. The bond between the two youths was tight, and they had kept their childhood secrets close. Franciene and Aaron, born and hand-raised like brother and sister, often called themselves "Ebony and Ivory", out of her daddy's earshot, of course. Their bond would remain, unless... no, she had covered her tracks that morning... covered them perfectly. Aaron would never learn what she had done to his mama.

The shakiest leg of the tripod was Clifford. He had wanted to break from his family for most of the year... and now, when he was to be spending so much time with this, "Belle of Beaufort County," as she had so sworn, no third person, even Aaron, was going to foil his plans. The peacock of a girl knew she had Cliff firmly by a significant part of his body, but the specter of him drawing up short, mid-flight, and wimping out, was chillingly possible. The only choice she had was to keep the entertainment rolling, and watch Clifford like a hawk.

Young Clifford hadn't compiled much of a dossier, since his world had been set to spin on the axis called Palmland-by-Hartsell, from the day of his birth. There weren't any bygone Hartsells with precedence for changing the spin, and actually, until Franciene got tits, he hadn't considered abdication on any level. His life, while plodding and staid, was envied by many of the other boys, and the passing on to him of arguably the finest piece of real estate in three counties, could cause a young fellow perpetual superiority.

Clifford's little sister, the lovely Sonja Satilla, had no feministic plan to challenge the first-born-son thing, either. She had long ago figured on continuing as her mother and grandmothers before her. Sonja would finish college, marry well, blending her husband's blue-blood with hers into a fine family, and spend her days in typical southern contentment. She would choose a diversion such as breeding show horses, or contracting as agent to some newly renown local artist, and then amuse herself prancing around the region in pursuit of her social interests.

Sonja had, over the years, watched her mother turn her head while her father pranced around the world, not always on Palmland business, pacifying his wife by letting her oversee the plantation, "for the children's' sake." She was proud, as his wife, to be trusted with the duty, and did it well. Even as a child, Sonja believed in her heart that her mother had wasted her woman's life, and she was having none of it for herself. Clifford often mused in private that their chromosomes had been switched, and his little sister would have made a much better male heir than he, to see Palmland into the new millennium.

Truth was, Sonja was quite in demand. With the exotic, European beauty of her mother, she had beaux calling from all over the southeast, and after she was presented to society later in the season, the die would be cast, and her family would begin the weeding-out process. It should be noted that Sonja would never be subjected to an arranged marriage. Rather, her choice of a husband would be quite the pleasurable experience for everyone, and before long the engagement announcements would be on their way to a large portion of the states of the Confederacy. What more could Sonja wish for? It was like shooting fish in a barrel, with a whole lot more than a hell of a fish fry as the prize.

The corresponding pedestal where Clifford was placed, wasn't quite as pat. When a boy is in his position, the task is bigger than the taskmaster. Research might begin while a boy is still sliding down the banister, for the perfect wife and mother. Cliff wasn't there yet, even at the doddering age of twenty. He longed hungrily for the sexual rite of passage, less encumbered boys his age were enjoying to the tune of several new converts a day, and he had about decided that he would have to arrive by proxy. At least until there, standing prettily in velvet by the butcher block in his family's kitchen on Christmas Eve, was his ticket to paradise, just waiting to be stamped.

Franceine plotted their adventure ever since she got on the boat with Dan and Jaime that morning, and she did not intend to lose control. Aaron could sleep his crack high off in the backseat, and that would be it! No more! That was going to be the rule, or Aaron would have to find his own way around to lose the black kid would suit 'Cliff just fine, since his quarry was Franciene, with no hitches. It was unsettling for him to have Aaron along. Why, what if he got between them? He could imagine the boy seeing himself as her chaperone, or even worse! Yes, the baggage in the jump seat could complicate things all right.

God! What an obsessive-compulsive quest losing one's innocence can be! The best thing he could do was stay out of the exchanges between those two, and concentrate on what went on between himself and Francie. If having Aaron along amused his quarry, he figured to play the game.

It was nearly dinner time. Cliff figured most young couples found their way to bed in short order after dinner. His blood raced as he considered the next few hours, and what they would mean. Francie, who was oblivious to his thoughts, seemed to be napping in the sunshine. He smiled a secret smile as he enjoyed the view. She appeared to be, but was not asleep... Francie was too busy conniving to relax, wary of Cliff's long silences. A quiet person is a thinking person, something she had heard from Daddy, as he would quiet her for the millionth time. He was usually just wanting peace and quiet, but he turned the "shush", into a life lesson for her. A carefully brought up boy like this one was, could be having pangs of doubt... even fear that could change her plans.

Francie stretched luxuriantly, turning for his full view as she thrust her pointy little bosoms skyward, and parting her legs ever so slightly, making the peek he could sneak more covert and triumphant, as she exaggerated the waking up process. Cliff had driven off onto the shoulder, and was fighting the car back to the highway with a couple of downshifts, before he could take his eyes from the spectacle playing out beside him. She pretended not to notice, and curled back up into a little ball in the seat, cooing, "Cliffie, would you let me drive? My daddy taught me good in the old truck, so I can shift gears, and I never drove a cute little sporty-car like this before!"

The hapless boy was already braking to pull off the road, drawling, "You can drive, honey, but just for a little while, and I"ll do the shifting! This old girl has four forward gears with electric overdrive, and she likes an experienced hand." He had lowered his voice to accompany the pomposity of his words. The vixen was playing him like a violin, and it was fun. Crawling under his jutting chin so she could gaze up at him in mock homage, she nodded obediently... and promised to do everything just right. When they got out of the car to change places, and since Aaron hadn't stirred, Francie playfully lifted one of his eyelids. "Come on. Aaron," Cliff barked, "It's time to join the living!" Aaron's shaved head lolled first this way, then that, and as he opened his eyes, a smile traveled across his face like a drapery drawn aside.

"All right!... Cliff Mon!... Wha's happenin'?" Where you been? What ya'll been doin, an' where's li'l Francie? Don't you tell me I done missed me some fun!" He was trying valiantly to extricate his body from the jump seat, while stringing patent phrases and other foolishness together as a smokescreen against his foggy recall. "I got to make water like a racehorse, man!" He moaned. Francie opened the door and helped him negotiate his way out. "Thanks, girl, I'll be right back." He disappeared into the edge of the pine woods, and reappeared, still jabbering away. "Hey! I just thought of somethin'! We ain' outta' gas, are we? God, don't tell me this little piss-ass rich boy car has done run dry! Where 'we at, anyhow?" He was having great sport with Cliff, exaggerating his dialect and watching Franciene enjoying it to the hilt. "No, Aaron, we're not out of gas," Cliff breathed wearily, "Francie just wanted to drive a little, is all. You okay? Man, when we left Jacksonville, you were about as high as you could be and still breathin'! We figured you could sleep it down while we traveled. Why don't you get back there and nap some more, so you can get straight before we stop again?"

Cliff was intent on resuming his seduction of Franciene without an audience. She was sitting prettily behind the wheel, as Aaron stood up to his full height, straight enough to protest. "Hey... you! Boy, I ain't never been told to get in the back of nuthin', and never sat in the back of nuthin', except Wendell's ox cart, lessen' I wanted to! Now, lets us share that front seat some... okay?" It was Francie's turn to speak. "Okay, okay, y'all. I'll sit in back, and Aaron, you can drive in my place. You'll turn some heads drivin' THIS car! I can't wait to see the looks on all the old fart's faces!" She liked making Aaron feel like a big shot, and he nodded, approving of the arrangement. After they played musical seats to suit Aaron, and bowing to Francie's wishes, they were off. Cliff was only mildly in favor of such a fool taking the wheel of his fine ride.

# CHAPTER ELEVEN

A search for the perfect Austin Healey-3000, when he neared driving age, caused flurries of activity among classic buggy brokers from Richmond to Palm Beach, with Hemmings' Motor News the A-1periodical, religiously placed to the left of his father's plate at the breakfast table, while still hot off the express truck. Strahan and Andrea Hartsell did everything right. Strahan was given a British roadster when he came of age back in the fifties, and tradition had ruled Hartsell for generations. When the carrier came to the house on Cliff's sixteenth birthday, father-to-son had squared. Watching as the splashy truck made the circle to the front portico, the soft-sided boy hadn't known such a feeling of power. It was naïve, to be sure, but Cliff believed he had been delivered to manhood by way of a driver's license and a little red sports car. What a thrill! To arrive at school in Virginia that September with such a symbol, and although many of the boys had nice wheels, there was none to compare with his Healey. One-ups-manship was a daily game for the boys at school, and Cliff scored record-breaking points with his slick little ride. His father was adamant about proper care of the car, congratulating himself for having shown the way to his son that learning to be responsible for something fine would bring lifelong rewards.

An hour after Aaron took the wheel, Cliff relaxed, realizing he wasn't going to run them off a bridge or into a tree, and turned his thoughts to the girl in the backseat. "This could be very good indeed," he mused to himself. "This trip can take me to the top of the stud scene. I can go back this fall with a chest full of medals, and pictures to prove it". He had wickedly packed his camera with that in mind, since nobody would believe him when he told them how fine she was. This way they could see for themselves. Daydreams of posing her in all stages of undress, and even setting the camera's timer so he could get in the shots, sent his mind reeling with lust. He looked at Aaron, singing some jazzy tune under his breath, eyes locked on the road.

It was playtime! Cliff's hand stole down between the seats, found Francie's bare knee, and crept up between her thighs, ever so lightly. She didn't stir, although she wasn't asleep, and Cliff got bolder. He was too ignorant know the girl was allowing the fondling, poised to stop him when she wanted to, and he fancied himself as smooth as velvet. When his fingertips slipped under the edge of her shorts, he became so aroused he was afraid Aaron might see the evidence from the corner of his eye. Reluctantly withdrawing his hand, he quickly conjured memory of a painfully fought squash match to settle himself down. He leaned back and closed his eyes a moment, while Francie, disgusted near to nausea, rubbed his touch off her creamy legs, smiling a secret smug little smile.

\* \* \*

Two days and nights had elapsed since Toby arrived in Waycross and fell under the sweet spell of Will's mother. Dealing with his long-dead, but now raging libido was difficult, but he was sure that if she even suspected a crush he would lose important ground with her. Toby had only to flash on what Will would think of him and his impure thoughts, to quickly shift gears. In reality, the focus was much broader... more in Will's interest, and he knew when he found the boy he would show him. It could be the healing factor that would brush the events of the last few days away from his mind and his life. Toby wished like hell he could shake off the nagging fear that something life-altering was happening where Will was, something pertaining to that damnable place and time, that he was powerless

against. Foreboding aside, he intended to follow his narrow track...
keep trying to find Will, and make some kind of sense of Linda's
effect on him.

It was obvious that this was an industrious woman, evidence
being she worked two full-time jobs. Days, as manager of a gift and
card shop in the small downtown shopping district, and five nights
a week in the Holiday Inn lounge, and somehow she never lost her
spark. Toby wondered if the need to stay busy was borne of her
wish for a kind of shallow oblivion... simply no time for anything
other than work but sleep. Toby wanted to think that of her, to wipe
away the possibility that she didn't care about Will out there in that
swamp. The bar became Toby's world since coming to town, and
he was pleased to have time with Linda Sue when she wasn't busy.
They found a lot of common ground for conversation other than her
son, and it seemed to Toby she was beginning to kind of like him. He
knew it was sappy and desperate, to find himself hanging over the
bar in her face every night, but since no one in town had even nodded a greeting at him except her, and he wasn't disposed to hiding
out in his room after dinner, he considered it being sociable.

She came off wistfully sad and lonely, so Toby was surprised to
see her tough side one night in the lounge, when a rowdy redneck
got still rowdier. The outsider that he was, Toby witnessed the trans-
gression from down the bar, and was about to spring from his stool,
when, with just a sentence or two, she had the jerk bowing, hands
up in surrender, and begging forgiveness. Then, to Toby's astonish-
ment, she smiled at him, waved the moment away, and drew him a
draft on the house. The woman was a paradox all right, and Toby
decided she had more layers than a prize winning Vidalia onion.

Part of the search for Will was the ranger station at the edge of
the swamp on Saturday. Toby didn't know what he expected to find,
maybe re-visiting the place he rescued the boy from would soothe
the soul if nothing more. There had been a changing of the guard
at the station house... anticipated, since two years had elapsed, but
it was the same drill... suspicion and guarded body language at first,
then as he listened to Toby and Will's story, (what Toby saw fit to tell
him), he was more forthcoming. Naturally he knew about the place

where the store was, and that a boy and his grandpa had been there until a couple of years ago. Toby asked if he could paddle a canoe back there, and for whatever reason, the ranger offered to take him in his johnboat. Since it would be a quicker trip, Toby accepted with thanks. As they tied up, the ranger said there hadn't been anyone else on the place since Will left, and that he knew nothing of the old dog. (Gator banquet for sure!) There was pitifully little there to look over, nothing but a trash bag full of moldy comic books, a few pieces of tangled fishing gear, and a horribly rusted, pump action twenty-two rifle leaning on the porch. Toby silently thanked himself for taking the boy away from so backward a place. No matter what happened now, it was better than this fate.

As they prepared to leave, the ranger allowed he wanted to look around inside for a minute. They went in the rotting mess of a building, both their mouths set in a grimace. "This won't take long," he said, speeding up the inspection. Toby stepped behind the counter and spied a wooden box, resembling a cigar humidor. It was, as everything else in the place, covered with mold, and thick, dampish dust, but he rubbed it sort of clean, and worked the catch until it opened. Inside was a grouping of what had to be little Will's favorite things. A yellowed, ivory handled folding knife, a few arrowheads, two or three fishing lures, a leather wristband, a tiny reptile skull, and a nearly pulverized old snapshot, completed the inventory. Toby closed the box and stealthily slipped it into his backpack.

When he got back to the motel, he sat down with the picture, turning it over and over in his fingers. He noticed there was some smudged penciling on the back. Toby stared at it for at least a minute, but the name was indecipherable. Under that smear was another line that appeared to read, "St. Marys, Georgia," and a date... "March, 1964." The photo appeared to have been one of those disappointing passport-type shots, but Toby could make out a handsome, deeply tanned face, with a blonde beard and mustache, topped off with a shock of sun-bleached hair. Feeling like a snoop, he guiltily replaced the picture, deciding not to go through the contents any further, and hand it over to the boy, hoping he would tell who the man was of his own volition.

It was already four o'clock, and Toby was hot and thirsty, so he showered and lay down for a few minutes… or so he thought. His next awareness was sitting straight up in a dark room. His watch screamed, "It's nine-thirty, stupid!" causing him to grab for a shirt, rake through his half-dry hair, and head for the lounge. He couldn't believe how late it was. You know what "they" say about that kind of deep sleep… it must have been badly needed, and "they" would be right. Toby was anxious to tell Linda Sue about the day, but decided not to mention the box or the photo. Suspicion nagged him that she would know who the man was… for now it seemed too personal. Maybe Toby didn't want to know he might have been someone important to Linda…that particular someone. He was falling fast, and the silly jealousy was palpable. At that moment, Toby wished to God he had never met her OR Will! Oh, why couldn't Katie have just gotten well?

The lounge was crowded… A typical Saturday night… spring in the south. Weekend nights must be ugly times to work behind the bar, because the hicks flock to town to trade wages for permission to be obnoxious. Toby sat as near to the end of the bar as he could, and waited for her to notice him. When she finally regarded him, ten minutes had passed. He dismissed the lapse because she was in the weeds, but when a lull came and she was icy as she took his order, avoiding his eyes when she brought his cocktail, he was certain she was upset. After three rounds with no word, Toby caught her hand, and with a flourish, glided down the bar, while still holding on to her. He moved her out into the room to face him, close up. "What is this?" He asked, teasingly "Why am I such an object of indifference all of a sudden?"

She looked up at the ceiling as if asking for Divine help with her answer. Tilting her gaze back to his face, she began, "This is testing my sanity, Toby. You bring back to me the single most important place in my past, a part of my life I fear the most. I am a flawed woman who has made a fresh start after leaving behind sadness you do not want to know. I knew you were going to Pa's Point today. You told me you might go while you were here, but I didn't want to know just when, to recall all the wrong things I've done, and those awful choices I made. Now you are here, and they're all back in a big looming pile, tearing my heart out."

She was trembling, and Toby felt like shit. He led her to a table, and went to the desk to get someone to tend the bar in her stead for a little time alone with her. They sat quietly while she composed herself, and Toby knew he had to wait for her to find her voice again. While he was still enchanted by the woman she was, he had to admit she had done nothing to encourage him. On the contrary, she was outwardly trying her damnedest to drive him away! They had been sitting there for a time, when he noticed her eyes were brimming with huge tears. It was achingly hard to watch, so Toby spoke first.

"Linda, honey, I wouldn't hurt you for anything. Please don't cry. I'm as lost as you are in this, in some ways. The boy means the world to me... we got so close, and I feel kin to him, responsible for him. She frowned and stomped her foot in frustration. "That's exactly what's gotten to me!" Her sweet face was so full of pain it was like a mask. She had more to say, so he allowed her to continue. "You have everything of him I always wanted, and was never able to have! He was my heart, and I gave him to my father, for his peace and safety. It was the best thing at the time, but now it just hurts!"

Her sobs were uncontrolled as she went on. "I want to have what you have had! I want the memories you will have, the adventures and the laughter you, a complete stranger, are enjoying. I have hate for you, for having all that! We can't continue to be together and talk about him, Toby, because it hurts too much! Willie isn't mine anymore! I won't put him in danger by claiming him... and I sure as hell won't listen anymore to what I've missed... I can't!" He was weak with sadness and regret for hurting her, but let her go on with his whipping. The people behind them in the bar had begun to notice, so they moved down the hall from the lobby, and into an empty event room. She let him lead her like a child, but once they were alone she took a turn.

"I want you to go find him, but don't bring him to me. It's better for us to stay apart as long as he is young enough to be ruined by the wrong people. I would rather never see him again than have his life affected by my mistakes. I know you can't understand, and you

most likely think I'm either crazy or have no mother's love in me."
Poor, poor little thing", Toby kept hearing in his head. She had to
finish. "Neither is the case, I swear. Just go. I will be at home until
eight-thirty in the morning, if you want to call before you leave. Please
help me by going away." She turned and walked out of the room and
back behind the noisy bar. He watched her until he couldn't anymore,
wiped his drowning eyes and went to his room to pack.

# CHAPTER TWELVE

Standing on the dock, Will could not shake the woman's eyes from his, and he couldn't make his feet move a step closer to the boat where the two were standing with sorrowful, grieving faces. Carrie was taking him with her, with that gaze, to a place that was neither here, nor where she was. It was a place not of the earth, and yet he was aware that it was about the earth, and people, and what he must do. They were blending their two souls, and becoming of the same mind, or something he still couldn't grasp. With no less than indescribable profundity, some kind of light and power had replaced their separate entities. Carrie was speaking as if they were harmonizing a song.

"You will not remember any of this when you go back there, boy, but what you learn will stay with you to use when you need it. There are ones down there among us who are most timorous, most timorous indeed. You and I can do things for them that will ease their hurts, and help them get back to the right way to go. We need to put to right some wrongs done, and give lessons to the evil doers. You have no say about this, and you must follow. Do not fear, William, you are in a Circle of Blessing, and no harm shall come to you. There will be times you will ask to have this lifted from you, because it will give you sadness to see the wages of evil being dealt. Let the good win over the bad, my son... be glad that you are part of it. Those demons standing in the way of right hearts must be banished."

The state he was in had progressed to where, as if he were a trusting child, Will had become accepting... wanting to get closer to her, pressing his mind to expand in order to embrace higher enlightenment. It was as if there was no "He," or "She," just androgyny. It felt so good... like swimming naked, or free-falling. All mores gone, having no encumbrances or inhibitions from one's earthly existence. He had not tried to speak. The need for words from him was absent, and since he was sure they would have poured out in an inane tumble, he was relieved. The spiritual mechanism that Carrie was using had intercepted his thoughts, and spoke to him again, as if they were conversing aloud, in a normal way. "You may speak words to me, but I know what you will say. William, it will help you to be calm now, to communicate as you are accustomed to. Ask me anything you wish. You can begin now."

Will could only spout short, pointed questions. "What is this about? Where are we? Who are you? What does Franciene Thornedike have to do with it? Please, if you know... where is her body?" The woman was patiently waiting for him to stop speaking. "You are so young, and you have such a small piece of the knowledge you will need, or you would already have all the answers you seek. This is about salvation, little boy, sweet salvation borne from Grace." He was riding her words like a surfboard now, toward a reality he already embraced.

"We are sending spiritually, just us two at this time, but soon we will be back with them so we can get the work done. I am no more than Carrie Treacle from Squires Island, and you are no more than William Parrish from the edge of the swamp, but our mission takes us out of the ordinary." She was sending more rapid-fire now, as she realized he was devouring her words. "You are fearful because of what has just happened. It is simply that you have been taken out of time and place... and for a little while put in another time. It has to be done this way so we can change the course of what will be. I will not answer the question about Franciene. This has much to do with her, but you cannot know why just yet. Obedience is all you need to learn now. That, and trust! You will know where she is soon enough."

He almost spoke again, but she boomed out with maternal and divine power. "Yes, this has to be, child! Too much depends on what we accomplish now! You are not volunteering for this... rather, you were chosen long ago, to turn your earthly experience into one that will help others, instead of one who just watches and waits for his turn. Nothing worth doing or worth having, will come without effort and sacrifice, William, or it wouldn't count for anything." She paused to let that sink in. "All right, Son... now you follow my lead, and do not be troubled in your head, or in your heart when you leave this plane... I will always be here, and there, inside you, and you will know."

The next thing that happened was a sensation not unlike being sucked through a vacuum hose. He was suddenly back on the dock, still looking at the two people in the boat, with nothing in his head of what had happened, as hard as he tried to reach it. It was still there, because she said it would be and it was enough, since she was the source, and he trusted her. "Hi, folks, I'm Will Parrish." He shuffled his feet as he waited for Massey to extend a hand, but Massey Thornedike was as distracted as he'd ever been, and surely didn't need to press the flesh with a kid he would likely never see again. All the same, to his surprise, his hand reached out to Will, as if someone had pushed it. "Massey Thornedike's the name, and this here's Miz' Carrie Treacle." The lady only nodded at him, a couple of slow appraising nods, with the tiniest of a smile playing at first one, then the other corner of her generous mouth. Massey turned quickly to the captain. "Let's us get going, Dan... We're already late as is, and we've got a mighty lot to do, to be back on the six boat!"

Lines were cast off, and everyone sat down while Dan powered up. The engines drowned whatever chance there was at conversation, so Will kept his own counsel, figuring what to do... his emotions strangely in better shape than they had been since yesterday. Using conditioned sea legs, Jaime edged over to his side. "Did you find your knife?" He yelled in his ear. Will had completely forgotten his excuse for revisiting the island, and had to collect himself before he yelled back, "No, damn it! I guess it's probably in the river somewhere, or on the side of some highway where I stopped to pee. I should have been more careful." Jaime, obviously unconcerned, shrugged his shoulders, and went below. When he returned, he had that log book again... and after the other two passengers signed in, he laid it in Will's lap. When he took the pen, Will looked at the page and froze! Looking around, he let his eyes fall on Carrie's face. She merely blinked, and continued staring across the water. His signature from the first half of the trip was now the alias Toby had substituted!

This was more than just strange, but what could the explanation be? Will's hands became clammy, when the thought that Jaime or Dan had made the change after looking back to yesterday's page. But for God's sake, the handwriting was his! Somehow his alias had replaced his name and it wasn't his doing... Will hadn't even known how to spell it! The boy followed the suggestion, signing in kind, and it looked identical. He handed the book to Jaime, the scene unfolding just like before, and the book once again hung on the hook. Will's mind flashed on the wadded page in his backpack... the one he had found on the beach, and wondered what he should do with it.

His initial reaction was to get to a place alone and burn the damn thing. Then he turned around inside of his head, when it seemed someone said, "It doesn't matter anymore!" at him. When he looked around for an answer, there was none. The fifty minute trip to Frenchport was uneventful. They disembarked, and Will remembered his vow to call Toby with his plans to get back to Padgett's Island on the first ride he could hitch, but once he got to the harbor the plan was lost. All he could bring up was that he had to tell that girl's daddy what they had found, regardless of the outcome. He dashed to the edge of the parking lot just in time to see a maroon Seville turning out on to the street, with Miss Carrie in the front seat, looking back over her shoulder at him with those eyes. Will knew he couldn't catch them, so he went back to the restaurant, and had settled on a bar stool when he saw Jaime down about three stools.

The young man looked straight at the boat mate, smiled crookedly, and blurted, "Know of anyplace near here I can crash in for tonight? this feels like a place I can hang out in." The formerly petulant Jaime was already nodding enthusiastically. "They got a couple of sleepin' rooms up over the bar here, and I bet Miss Ruby would let you have one of them. I'll go in back and ask her right now." He rushed away, with Will shaking his head in disbelief. The "other" Jaime would have wasted nothing of himself, being so helpful.

What is happening here? The boy was totally vexed, but hung onto his instincts. He let it roll, and hoped to God he wasn't alone... wishing to get a sign... and quick! He kept the Carrie factor close, believing it all aligned. Jaime returned, smiling broadly, "You' all set, bubba!" He swung onto the next stool, slapping Will's back soundly. "Hey! You eat yet? The catfish mull here is the best there is, and I saw a big pot of it on the stove just now! How 'bout a brew?" As friendly a guy as you would want to meet.

"SURE! I know!" Will's swirling head allowed. "Jaime's just gone and got himself good and stoned!" That would explain a lot... the light-hearted attitude, the generosity, could all be explained by his having smoked a joint since he got off the boat. They enjoyed a few more minutes of fellowship... Will satisfied he'd figured it out.

* * *

A speeding Cadillac turned into Harris Teeter's parking lot, and stopped in front of the entrance. Massey hopped out and escorted Carrie to the door. He got her a cart and handed her his credit card, saying he'd be back in thirty minutes, and for her to wait right there for him after shopping. He was so pressed for time, and so worried about every little thing, he began to have a choking feeling from the stress. The next chore was to go by Aaron's house, since it was on the way back to the harbor. He hoped to snag the boy right off so they could save time, and Aaron could be a help to him with Franciene.

He expected she was going to go all to pieces when they told her the sad news. Down the lane to Aaron's place, and, sure enough, dammit to hell... he wasn't there! He left a note for him to be at the dock before six, without divulging the reason, and rushed to call Jesse at Palmland. Since the Hartsells had their telephones rigged to ring first in the kitchen, then to the servants' quarters over the garage, so they could field the calls, and when his extension rang sharply, Jesse picked up the receiver.

113

"Yes, Suh, Mista' Thornedike, this' Jesse. What's that you say? No, no Suh, I ain't got any call for me to fetch yo' chile! What's that? No SUH! Miss Franciene, she ain't here, Suh! No, no, ain't none of the family here neither, Suh, dey been gone mos' the afternoon. Yes SUH, I sure will, SUH! Bye now." The receiver dangling from its metal cord, a billow of gravel and dust, and two black tire tracks were hastily left by a frantic father who'd just been told that his beautiful, virginal, only child, was inexplicably out of place… and to Massey's utter rage, he realized he'd been lied to by a friend, the man who was responsible for her safe transport! In a scant three minutes, he had rocked the car to a stop at the dock, and was sprinting down the pier as fast as his body would allow. "DAN! DAN! DAN FULLER!" Massey bellowed between cupped hands as he ran.

No Dan, but no matter. He had lied to save his skin, because he didn't know where Franciene was, Massey deduced, between gasps for air. He stopped by the boat and held on to it for a moment, trying not to pass out from the exertion and the oppressive heat. Then it began… the squeezing pain in his chest, the unbearable weight, and the blackness closing around his eyes. How could it be, when he needed his body so bad, that it would betray him? He tried to keep standing, but gravity won out, and he thudded to the concrete. His chest was heaving with desperate gasps, knowing that this was it! He was dying on this dock! The last thing he saw through pain-seared eyes, was the face of the young man whose hand he had clasped on the boat earlier.

"Mister Thornedike! MISTER THORNEDIKE! Please, please don't die!" Will lifted Massey's head off the pavement, watching him as he fought for breath, his facial color going from red, to gray… then to a ghastly bluish purple. The boy yelled for help, his eyes sweeping the harbor as he called out. He'd gone to the boat looking for the man, to try and tell him what he knew, and now it may be too late! He wanted to make him see that people like him and Toby don't make trouble for folks… just the opposite. He meant to tell him everything, and offer their help. Now the man was about to die in his arms.

Will started CPR, and was doing pretty well when two fishermen who had heard him came running. They radioed for an ambulance, and the paramedics were all over them in minutes. The shocked boy watched as Massey was loaded for the trip to the emergency room, and when they were out of sight, he calmly got in the Seville... driving without pause for reason to the supermarket. "I have to do this," Will said out loud as he turned in at the store... and there she was! The Reason... standing there beside her loaded cart.

"I was about to roll this buggy down the street to the dock myself if somebody hadn't come for me purty quick!" Carrie sang to him as he loaded the bags. "Did Mista' Massey evah find Aaron? Lawd, I shore do hope he's done found him! That child better be fast home for his mama, or she'll never let him rest, and that's for sho'! You're the boy on the boat today, ain't you? I thank you for the help. 'Guess Mista' Massey's done got his child to the dock, and he's got his hands full with her! She a mess, that gal is!" She chuckled, shaking her head. Will had been enjoying the musical dialect so much he almost missed the message of the words, realizing she said a lot he needed to process quickly. "Miz' Treacle," he began, but she shushed him with, "My name's Carrie to my friends. You've done me a turn, so you can call me Carrie!"

Will nodded and continued. "Carrie, Ma'am, there's something I need to tell you. Mr.Thornedike has... well, he's had an attack of some sort, a few minutes ago on the dock." Her arms shot up and she began to keen an unworldly sound. Will took her shoulders to try and quiet her. "Wait! Let me finish. The ambulance took him to the hospital just now, and since he couldn't come for you, here I am. As for his daughter, well, I didn't see her today." Not a lie... he saw her dead yesterday, but he knew the lady could only take so much at one time, and he had to get her to the hospital without a scene.

The receptionist told them Mister Thornedike was in CICU. Will figured that meant he had a heart attack. He took Carrie to a chair vowing to get information on the man's condition, knowing even with his lack of exposure to such, that patient information for other than family would be the patent and terse, "stable at the moment." Will also knew his persuasive gifts even at his tender age, were ready to meet the challenge. Carrie sat stiffly, rummaging for a handkerchief, while Will went to the nurse, his face reflecting angelic intent.

"What can you tell us about Mister Thornedike, ma'am? See, this lady with me just about raised him, and there's no one else closer by him than she is. She needs a kind word of encouragement from somebody... a doctor, or maybe you? I know it is against policy to speak to other than a relative, but I did the CPR on him, and..." The nurse's eyes snapped to meet his, and she smiled, and spoke to him with odd tenderness.

"You know something? You may have saved his life! Keeping him alive, just alive, was crucial. Many people have died simply because someone with them wasn't able, or was too squeamish, to go mouth to mouth. I'll speak to your friend for you, I surely will." The nurse patted his hand and went to Carrie. As she sat down, she took the worn old hand in the lady's lap, and began, "Missus?" Carrie whispered, "No, it's jus' Carrie, honey, that's all you ought call me." The sadness in her voice did it. She continued softly, "All right, Carrie, I know you are worried about your friend, and it may help you to know that he is being tended to by the best team of heart specialists he could have, and when I have news from them, I will come and tell you right away." She bent to look in Carrie's downcast eyes, and asked, "Does Mister Thornedike have any relations close by? They should be here for signing treatment forms and the like. The young man here says that there's no one. Is that the case?"

Carrie's eyes were closed, but when the nurse squeezed her hand slightly, there came from her a huge sigh. "No, that ain't so." Will was on the verge of speaking up with what he knew about the girl, but the words wouldn't come. The news would be the woman's undoing. Carrie looked from the nurse to Will... then, reading his mind, she grabbed his hand, speaking with purpose. "You don't know WHAT you know! I need to call her at the place where she's stayin' at, right now! Show me where the phone is, and I'll call her to come quick! Will had a feeling akin to passing out, but he sat still, breathing deeply, while the nurse led Carrie to the phone on the desk.

When she returned, she sat down in the chair with such a great weight the chair groaned. "Lord God, Jesse's sayin' that child ain't showed her face at Palmland yet! And that ain't all, he told me that Mista' Massey knows 'bout it, since he tol' him de same t'ing when he called there this afternoon! The girl's missin'! She ain't a place to be found! Dear Jesus, no wonder my sweet Massey is prostrate in there! What we gonna' do now?" "Ask me something I can answer", thought Will, his head aching. Time was running out for him to talk to somebody, before it was exposed in a cruel, cold way. His fear he and Toby could be brought in as prime suspects if they weren't the first to talk, was growing. He swallowed a lump that had been blocking the words, stood up and faced Carrie, then began what he knew must be said.

"This is going to be hard for me to do, and harder for you to take, Miz. Carrie, but I must tell you, and I am so sorry to tell you, that she is dead." Oh! That felt like nothing he'd felt before. The woman's haggard face raised to his and their eyes met, renewing the dance that began when he first saw her. She spoke silently to his mind as before. "Don't tell your secret yet and I won't tell mine, William. The time we share for now will not abide these truths, I promise you. I will take this moment... and your nearly spilled secret, and fix it. You meet me halfway, then go along with me. It is very easy, when you are doing the right thing... it comes to you so soft and sweet, it's like you created the way yourself." After sending the words, she closed her eyes and bent over her hands, locked together in her lap.

The feeling Will experienced then was of being filled up to the top... a great well of satisfaction and purposefulness encircled and warmed his body and his spirit. He recalled the first time he hoisted a kite... caught the biggest bluegill Grandpa ever saw, and multiplied the spiritual boost a thousand times. He told himself, exultantly, "This is going to be a journey we will take together, this great woman and me." Carrie and Will were still facing each other, and the moment of their awareness had been only as long as a dream, so it felt like nothing more than the seconds between comments, as one waits for the other to finish, allowing a response. Without missing a beat, Carrie spoke to him aloud.

"How did you know that, chile? I swear, if that Jasper's found her and done gone and blabbed his mouth into de phone, I'm gonna box his ears! I know it ain't Mista' Massey what told, cause we swore, least 'til we got back home from fetchin' Aaron, to keep the sad news a secret. If everybody knows now, that little house is gonna fill up, and ain't anybody gonna be there to greet 'em, 'cept old 'Tilde herself, all laid out in the parlor! Who's told you, boy? How you come to know this?" She trained on Will a look that made him want to answer her more than anything he could think of, but silence hung like a sodden quilt between them. She was saying that someone on Squires was dead... and it had happened today. He, while thoroughly perplexed, trusted her and stayed quiet, giving in to her words. He had to trust that Carrie was on the job, and it would come out right.

"The lady's name is Clothilde Poinsett Braswell," she said testily, "and she's gone across only just this mornin', we figure. Now, you know her name, I trust you won't flap yo' mout' anymore. Next we got to make this right by gettin' a'hold of her boy, Aaron, before the whole Island's filled up with the sitters an' no kin there to greet 'em. 'Tilde's gonna' be set to spinnin' in that box she's in, if this don't go right! We got to find Aaron Braswell right now, so his mama can rest. I can come back here after dat's done, and I can sit for Mista' Massey, while Aaron sits for his mama's repose." Miss Carrie had spoken, and that was how it was to be. Okay, pondered Will, a dead lady whose name is whatever she just said. There was no mention of how she died... likely she just died.

Now what? Carrie had covered his attempt to come clean about Franciene, so she must know what he had meant to say! Why was this feeling like fiction... weirder than fiction? Carrie had said her say and returned her gaze to the doors of the pavilion, when two doctors emerged, studying the chart between them. She rose without a word and went to them. They stopped, looked into those deep-as-the-sea eyes, and answered the questions in them. No, he wasn't in immediate danger, truth be told, he was stable and comfortable. They assured her his sedation was good for at least three hours, and that she should go home, or get some food and relax, then return, or call for an update. Carrie thanked them humbly and paraded back to Will, who had heard enough to know she had accomplished her task. "Did you hear all a'that?" She crowed. Will nodded as she went on. "I expect they knew I wasn't about to take no for an answer!"

The lady was something else! "That's an understatement!" Will said, "What's next? Do we find Aaron now, since we have an hour? If you'll direct me I'll drive us around to places he might be." Without a yea or nay, she went to the chair, picked up her things, and bee-lined to the elevators. Guess she's ready to go, Will laughed, as he trotted off behind her.

# CHAPTER THIRTEEN

As soon as the elevator carrying Will and Carrie closed, the one next to it opened, letting off a distressed trio. The Hartsells, given the news by Jesse when they arrived home, were on a dual mission of search and succor. Strahan waved seating at Andrea and Sonja, and rushed the desk to harass the doctors. "I must see Massey Thornedike immediately!" His first words hung a moment waiting to be obeyed. When no one spoke, he nearly jumped the counter, yelling, "He has to tell me, right now, where MY son and HIS daughter have gone off to! Now! Which way do I go?"

The two young residents stood, regarding him as if he belonged in a contaminated waste receptacle. They nodded to each other, and motioned the nurse to come deal with his pompous rudeness. Although directed to a chair, Strahan jumped back to his feet, trumpeting, "I need to speak with Mister Thornedike on a most urgent matter that cannot wait, Miss..." The nurse was ready for him. "My name is Mattie Bell, sir. I'm terribly sorry, but we cannot permit Mister Thornedike's friends to visit just now. This is an intensive care pavilion, indicating the seriousness of the condition of the patients inside. The staff charged with their care will not compromise it, not at all! I assume you care something for that man, and would never intentionally interfere with his treatment. He is under sedation and resting, while the doctors confer. As for you, sir, if you are having some sort of crisis, perhaps I should call the hospital chaplin for you." She stood firm and silent then, waiting for his reply with her most professional posture. Strahan Hartsell was unaccustomed to being snapped up in such a way, and he sank to the chair behind him without speaking. As Nurse Bell retreated, Sonja began to cry on her mother's arm. Strange, even the Hartsells faded into obscurity in this place of life and death.

"Does anybody hear me?" Massey was regaining a sort of awareness, but he could barely push the thoughts together in his medicated, pain jostled brain. Worse than the pain, he felt overwhelmingly alone. It was not coming clear about what had happened. He couldn't remember anything. Time was suspended, and if not sedated he would have sprung from the bed. He couldn't know how close he came, and that his heart had nearly exploded due to three severely blocked valves. Stabilized and temporarily out of danger, he seemed to float above himself. The poor man was sure there was something very important he needed to be tending to, but what?

As he turned disjointed thoughts over and over, the nurse came to his side to check his fluids. She checked his pulse, and realizing he was semi-conscious, leaned to his ear and spoke softly, "There are people outside who are mighty concerned about you. I want you to relax, and let us take care of you now. I am Mattie, your nurse, and you have the very best doctors. Don't be alarmed, this will get better. You just had a spell, and we can fix you right up. I will tell the people out there that you are coming out of it a little, and are improving, so they won't worry. Now you rest easy, and I'll be back soon." She could only hope he got it.

Massey absorbed his nurse's words, and they salved his tortured mind. Never in his life had he been really ill, much less in a hospital, and the nurse had just given him the comfort of knowing he wasn't going to die here, without anyone. Wait! She said someone who loves him is out there waiting to hear how he is! That would have to be Franciene, wouldn't it? He swore to himself he wouldn't care where she had been all day if she was safe out there, waiting to see him. As his body relaxed to slip back into sleep, he saw a scene behind his eyelids. It was the dock where he fell, and the boy who was there over him, just as the nurse had been, giving him comfort and peace. He slept.

In Frenchport Harbor Will and Carrie were running out of places to look for Aaron, and it was already after six, two more hours before dark. Carrie didn't want to stop searching. "I swear 'fore Jesus, if I have to, I'll drag him 'cross by the ear!" Will played the scene in his head, and knew he could have the same treatment if he didn't follow her every word. Carrie was agitated and losing patience, showing it by twisting her purse straps first this way, then that, with jerky force, and switching about on the car seat as if sitting on a corn flake.

It was almost eight o'clock when she looked at Will, exhaled a moan, and asked to go to the boat for home. She was worrying after her friend, laid out over there with no one to stand by her to greet the mourners. Another worry... if they couldn't raise Dan or Jaime she would be stranded, since Jaime's shark charter wouldn't come in until nine or after... Not good! Will parked near the docks and told her to wait a moment. When he ran down to the slip, he was relieved to find the boat rocking on her cleats. The boy was turning to go tell Carrie, when he was grabbed by Captain Dan.

"Hey, Boy Hero! Where you been? Son, we all been wantin' to shake your hand and buy you a brew! Mighty good work you did, an' we're much obliged you were there to help Massey. How's he doin'? You hear anything yet? Sheeeit! All 'us boys ought to cut back on the bad stuff. I been tellin' him to stop with the cigars and lard, and I know we both could do with less hooch, but we ain't never been blessed with much self control. Old Massey took all the punishment for the rest of us, looks like. Where's Miz' Carrie? 'You seen her?" Will explained the last couple of hours to Dan, and asked about taking the lady across. "I guess Jaime got done with the shark trip early...."

He was drowning in all this chit-chat, and wanted to get on with it. Dan was quick to answer. "Well, soon as we got the news about Massey, I got on the horn and told him to bring the boat back and explain to the folks. He said they will go out another day... he knew we needed the boat standin' by. The boy surprises me with his smarts sometime." We'll get the lady home in no time." The night was coming on fast, and Will wanted Carrie home before dark. As he passed the deck at Ruby's he noticed Cissy sitting at the end of the bar, and lookin' good, with her corn-yellow curls piled on top of her head, tied with a ribbon the same color as her robin's egg sun dress... you know, the kind of nightie-looking thing with little bows tying the straps alluringly on the crests of her golden shoulders. Will had dreamed of pulling and untying bows like those, to let a dress kind of fall to the floor leaving the girl standing there in the altogether for him. He was hooked! Impulsively he called to Cissy, "Wait! Wait for me to come back. I'll only be a minute... don't leave!"

She stood and watched him run to the parking lot, wondering what he wanted. No matter, she didn't care...without a single word from Jaime all day why shouldn't a girl take advantage of an opportunity, if such a boy as that wanted to keep time with her? Will was back in two minutes, breathing hard from running all the way. "Thanks for waiting, Cissy, I didn't know if you had a date or something, I mean, with you looking so pretty and all." He finally took his first breath, and waited for her to speak. "Well, boy, I don't know you at all, but I sure do like the sweet way you talk. No, I don't have any date, and even if I did, it wouldn't matter a'tall, 'cause you just got my attention for the evenin'...how's that sound?"

Oh Boy! Will could see Heaven peeking over the horizon along with that yellow moon. Besides, maybe she could provide a little of the puzzle that was his and Carrie's to put together. Cissy had the kind of looks a guy remembers, and even if he had only seen her for the first time yesterday, he knew it was going to be that way for him. Today there was a fresh-ness to her he hadn't noticed before, and a kind of innocence. He pressed on with rising anticipation. "I saw you earlier and asked a guy on the fuel dock your name. My name's Will Parrish, and I'm real pleased to meet you. He told me your name is Cissy, and that's enough for now. If I want to know more, I'll ask later."

Where did all his new charisma come from, and where had it been hiding? He was really pumped at his smooth delivery. "How about we share a pizza, and then take some beer to the beach for a walk. Does that sound like fun to you, darlin'?" (Will, you're doin' just fine!). Did it sound like fun? Was he kidding? Cissy never met a boy like Will before. Jaime had been her focus for almost a year, but their dates were largely her idea, and dismally predictable. First, a rum-spiked coke right out of the can, half of Jaime's hamburger and fries if he wasn't too hungry, then HE got the dessert, usually in the vee berth of that smelly old ferry boat, where he wolfed her down like he did everything, always in five minutes or less.

Cissy cared a lot for Jaime, but hadn't heard the love word yet and didn't really expect to. This charming new boy and their dreamy plans would fill her thoughts for awhile. She sidled up to him and chirped, "I'd be dee-lighted to be your date tonight, Will. Let's get the evenin' started." They strolled down Shell Road to the pizza parlor, while Will was trying not to appear as excited as he was. He needed this special night in the worst way, just to be a boy out on a date in May, with a pretty girl. If nothing else happened than what they had planned, he would enjoy it... and if he hit the jackpot, then, "Whoopee!"

## HEY, CLIFFIE! HAVING FUN YET?

Poor Cliff had endured no less than a dozen moments of arousal since the trio left South Carolina. He was too ignorant to know Franciene had not only been aware of his distress, she had deliberately brought on each one of the episodes. Aaron had been at the wheel for almost two hours, driving the Healey like Mario Andretti, while piping out Stevie Wonder hits... the uneventful road trip was getting to be a bore for a bad girl, who was conjuring things that would have caused the two boys to make an instant U-turn back to their own version of sanity.

Francie stayed lost in thought, going back over her escape from Squires, 'Tilde's fate, her slick getaway in the boat, and finally, her plans for tonight. He didn't know, the boy she was cruelly seducing, that it would be HER first sex as well. A little imagination and the smutty books from her daddy's library were more than enough to manage a torrid tumble with her cute but nerdy traveling companion. Clifford was unable to nap with his anticipation growing. After years of mental rehearsal, he figured it would come easily to him, but when he pondered the actual moment they would be alone, and in a bed together, he had no idea what to do. How does a guy actually DO the real thing? He had done okay in a few backseat episodes at school, but only to a point. Conveniently, the girls had put the brakes on before he would have shown his ignorance. Francie just couldn't laugh at him! It would be the worst thing he could imagine.

What could he do? All those wisecracks, like "Man you'll take to it like a duck to water!" and, "Just put your tongue down her throat, and before you know, you'll be pumpin' away like crazy!" Sure! That sounded easy, but he couldn't see himself French-kissing this girl, then... Presto! There it goes again, Cliff thought miserably, looking down at his lap. It won't leave me alone! I'm getting Aaron to stop for fuel, and whack off in the restroom... that'll fix the damn thing for a while! He tapped the crooning driver on the shoulder and motioned him to stop at the next plaza. "We need gas, and I'm sure everybody needs to relieve themselves. After that I'll drive until we stop for the night, how's that sound?" He was laughing to himself about getting "relief"... Aaron didn't need to know what kind he meant! Franciene heard the plan to make a stop, and began her primping ritual as the car roared into the service plaza. Holding his driving cap in front of himself, Cliff raced for the latrine. In less time than a pee would have taken, he reappeared.

It was Aaron to the restroom next, and Franciene saw her chance to get things started. Using her most practiced moves she took Cliff's hand to lead him behind a tree. "Well, Baby," she breathed, "I think it might be time to find a place to stay the night. Besides, we didn't eat a thing since those burgers and fries back in Georgia, and my li'l ol' tummy is just a' growlin'!" She slid her hips laterally across his, first one way, then back, stopping in the middle to give him a little grind. "Me 'n' you ain't gonna get much sleep tonight, are we boy? Yessiree... you're in big trouble now!" So much for relief!

They walked further down the street, and Cliff stood, stone-like... halted by the sight. Not moving... just feeling thankful they were out of there in time. He returned to their rooms, and saw that she was on the sofa bed. "No!" he thought, "Not like this! I'm not a COMPLETE asshole!" There are rules about things like helpless girls, even bad ones. Besides, it wouldn't work right now, as bad as he wanted her! He covered her with the sheet and went into the bedroom to try again to get some sleep.

When she woke up Francie was furious to find she was alone. She had deliberately gotten into bed with Cliff to create her alibi. Her plan was to make him think they had made love while Cliff was too drunk to remember, and threaten him with her daddy's wrath if he didn't behave exactly as she ordered. In the bedroom Cliff was sitting up, rubbing his face in his hands. Francie stood outside the door, and made herself look molested by breaking her nightie strap and smearing her lip gloss before entering. She was ready to put on quite a show. "Well, now! What did I ever do to you, Mister high and mighty Hartsell! After what we did, you decide to jump up and run in here! Don't you go an' tell me you didn't like it! I know for a fact you did, 'cause you wanted to turn right around and do it again! Why did you leave me alone in there? I woke up in a strange room, all alone! After all you made me do to you, at least you could have really slept with me!"

"Now what the hell is this?" The boy was pleading silently to the ceiling. He had been roused by the ruckus down the street, and if he recalled that, he knew damn well, that if he'd gotten his first piece of ass he would remember it, chapter and verse! He got out of bed, thankful at least he was still in his shorts. "Francie, I didn't screw you last night! I would know if I had, don't you think? I only had a few beers! You and Aaron were throwing down the whole top shelf! I had to take care of you all night. No way! No way, sweetheart, are you going to lay this on me!" He strode past her with his nastiest smirk, headed for the shower. Not even slightly discouraged, Francie pranced to the bathroom door, leaned in, and harped, "Oh yes sir! And I've got the proof!" She went to the couch and stripped the sheet off, came back waving it at his face. He gaped at the mess in the center of the sheet... obviously stains from sex. It didn't take an expert to distinguish what he had seen proudly displayed after parties in the dorm.

"You want to mess with me now, Cliffie?" She sneered. "You want to snub me and make me feel like nothing now? I'll take this li'l ole sheet right home to my daddy, and tell him you went and forced me while I was sleeping on the couch, because I was afraid of you. You don't remember, because I put one of Aaron's pills in your beer at that place. You only THINK you were taking care of me!" He was horrified at her nasty, evil countenance. She wasn't finished. "Yeah, you took care of me all right. I'm underage, and you know what that means! When my daddy gets finished with your daddy! OoooWEEEE! Go on, you take your little old shower and think about it, Mister Hartsell, then I'll take mine!"

She closed the door to the bathroom in the shocked boy's face, and quickly disposed of the suntan lotion and empty ketchup packet that had created the illusion on the sheet. With that, she stripped the short nightie off her shoulders, opened the door again and posed there, letting him take a good look at what he wished he could remember from last night. He looked as long as he dared at her nubile perfection, and closed the shower door. "It's true," he said out loud, forgetting his ardor. "I've got to handle this some way or other. She and her daddy could ruin us! I'll play her game until I can get a plan. Why did I ever agree to run away with this crazy chick? Starting right now, I'm staying six feet away from her, and I'm going to call my dad for help. I guess it's my good luck the res- taurant burned. Now my credit card record is gone, and I paid cash for our rooms here. Thank You God," he whispered fervently, "I'll never be stupid like this again, if you just keep on helping me." As he was rinsing off, the door to the shower slid open, and she slipped in with him, pressing her luscious delights hard against his instantly re-excited body.

It was no use. He was powerless and vulnerable to her, even though she had tricked him last night. He would never learn the truth, could prove or disprove nothing, and he, figuring it was too late now, was lost to her at that moment. He sank to his knees, and with the water coursing over them, took his very first sample of the lovely Franciene, first with his mouth, and then in the most tradi- tional sense. As stoic as while submitting to her daddy's half-hearted switchings, she stared at the tile pattern without a hint of emotion, as Cliff spiraled to paradise behind her.

# CHAPTER FOURTEEN

It was a hard thing for the man to do... leaving in the early morning without a word to Linda. Toby had always prided himself on good manners and Golden Rule treatment of people, especially the ladies. He could only imagine her fury when she discovered his furtive flight, leaving no forwarding address or plan to inform her when he caught up with her son. He reasoned the sudden departure was to separate himself from something he couldn't handle, and wasn't going to try... not at this time. After the numbness without Katie, it was disturbing to discover sensations and emotions long buried. Maybe it was a good thing, maybe not... but for now he wanted miles between Linda and himself. For now, it was Will, poor Will. He was out there calling to him to be found. Toby turned the radio up loud, and while distancing himself from his fears, sang to the country tune, "If I could hold you tonight, I might never let go," at the top of his lungs, trying to drown out the memory of the little bells in her voice when she spoke, and staring at the highway, wishing he couldn't still see her, how her soft sun dress would catch on that impossible, heart-shaped bottom, as she walked away.

It was good to get back to the beach again. The cottage looked welcoming and peaceful... like an infirmary for the soul. Toby stopped at Neville's, but Shirley had no news for him. It was just an outside chance that she had heard from Will, thanking her for his lunch that day... he was that kind of kid. As soon as he got everything inside, Toby turned on the air and grabbed a cold one. Just beginning to relax, he thought of it. Stupid! Of course! Considering his reaction to finding the girl's body, it might be that he'd gone back to Frenchport, and could be on Squires Island up to his ass in alligators with her family by now! Not sure of anything anymore, but after checking the time, he grabbed a baloney and mayo fold over, left a note in case the boy showed up and tore out of the drive, headed south.

Now that Carrie was back on the Island, and Massey was in good hands at the hospital, Will was feeling relaxed and loose like the kid he was for the first time in days, or was it years? With everything that had happened, he had no clue which it was these days. The important thing was that for the moment, he was keeping company with a girl who seemed crazy about him, and the pizza and six pack they'd consumed had done wondrous things to their libidos. Cissy wanted to go to his room, but Miss Ruby was regarding them from behind the bar, so Will nixed the option. The anxious girl led him out on the dock to the ferryboat. It was the end of May and humid...but a breeze from the sound was playing a tune in the masts and shrouds of the sailboats, music enough to inspire romance. These two didn't need inspiration, and since the boat slip was in the shadows when clothes started coming off, no one could know or would care.

Will was delighted! He could never have dreamed up such a well put together, firecracker-hot girl wrapped in one package. His half-dozen scores had been with clumsy, bashful girls... or bimbos who could have been painting their nails while doing it, and although the worst he had ever had was wonderful, this was measuring up to be right off the scale After many tangled times with Jaime, Cissy knew how to keep control of an ardent boy, and she used all her best moves... holding him close to her while they kissed, then slipping down low, then lower, covering his body with kisses, as she guided his fingers to where she wanted pleasure. She set the rhythm to the music of her little gasps and sighs and breathless love talk, to keep him just at the boiling point, taking him expertly back down to the simmer, long enough to look deep into his asking eyes, silently saying, yes, this is really happening, and it's not a dream. She could have had anything he owned, he would have gotten her anything, believed of her anything, as long as she just, Please God, didn't stop. Her whispered words of praise, his lovemaking was perfect, how good he was, she had never been so excited, all took him on a skyward spin, and when they finally did couple, the boat rocked in helpful cadence with the roll of their bodies.

It was much too soon for him, but too intense and lovely to postpone, when, announcing it with moaning he was done, to the sweetness of her happy sobs. She hung onto him, fearing she might fall over the side as he arched his back to be able to look into her eyes at the end. It couldn't have been that good, but it was, it truly was. All spent, he lay back down on her, his lips in her neck, and they slept the deep sleep of passion and peace.

Some time later two naked young people were rudely kicked off of the boat, landing in the water between the port side and the floater. They resurfaced in time to see Jaime's slouched shoulders retreating up the ramp, staggering and cursing while shaking his fist to the sky.

"Oh! God! What have I done?" Cissy wailed, treading water while trying to grab the boat's bow line. "I love that boy goin' there, and now look! I intend to marry him someday! JAIME!" she wailed, "Jaime, I didn't mean it! You come back here!" Will lifted her up on the dock, while she grabbed for her soggy dress. He dazedly pulled himself up beside her, so sorry, and wanting to help. She was furious at herself, but thrust an accusing pout in his face. "I wish you'd never come around!"

Will wasn't having it. "Hey! You were all for this as much as me! If I'd a' known about all this Jaime stuff, you wouldn't have been able to make me to do it at gunpoint! One thing's for sure, I'm not an asshole who poaches pussy!" She knew that, but since SHE was the cheating jerk, she wanted somebody else to blame. "I've got to find him and tell him it didn't mean anything!" Thanks a lot, thought Will, but he let her go, her arms waving behind her as if to shoo him back to a place called, "Before it happened."

The boy was still naked... still sitting on the edge of the dock with a hangover already kicking in, when he felt a familiar figure sitting down beside him. Without looking or speaking, the reunited pals put their arms around each other and cried together, for joy of a craved reunion.

# GETTING READY FOR GLORY

'Tilde's little house was glowing in the twilight as if sending a beacon to God, to "Come by Here," to pick up this woman's soul for the trip home to Glory. No one was there when Carrie and Jasper pulled up to the door. Bless Jasper and Pansy, they had found 'Tilde after shopping in town, so they were waiting for the late boat. When Carrie saw them they were fishing off the dock as if it were any evening, but they put down their cane poles and were quickly beside her. Pansy, being the better communicator, set off to go from house to house to spread the word, and Jasper stayed with Carrie so she wouldn't be alone with her sad loss. The couple was shocked to hear about Mister Massey's attack, and when Carrie told them Massey himself had fetched the coffin from their shed for 'Tilde this morning, Jasper wiped grateful tears, regretting that he had been away and couldn't help.

They took the bags into the kitchen, and while Carrie unpacked, Jasper went to the parlor to light the oil lamps on the table behind the coffin. He was briefly overcome at the sight of her, so tiny and still, but he recovered, put a kiss on his fingers for her forehead, tiptoeing clumsily backward, and went to help Carrie. It was almost nine-thirty when Pansy got back from her rounds, and within minutes the little house swayed with the spirit and reverence attending all the past sittin' up times. It was a version of the death watch practiced in the Old Country, across the British Isles as well as Africa, and throughout the Caribbean. Anyone wishing to come and sit with the remains and family on shifts around the clock would be welcome, provided there was no bad blood among the living. Those who aren't received know who they are, and they stay away. A gift of food is in order, since there are a lot of folks spending time in the house.

No inappropriate sound is made in the room with the departed. An occasional, impromptu tribute or sweet story softly related, a prayer, or a hymn either sung or hummed, is acceptable. Elsewhere in the house, and on the porches, normal social discourse goes on in subdued tones. It will last all night, every night until interment. No one tipples openly, though on the fringes, a pint might be discreetly turned up. The ladies continuously cook and serve, tidying and minding children, while the men stand in groups, mostly in the yard, clumsy in their attempts to cope or comfort, but displaying their devotion by being present for each other.

At eleven thirty, about the end of Carrie's endurance, the telephone in the kitchen rang sharply. She answered it, and her eyes became as large as her dropped open mouth.

It was Aaron. "Lord Jesus has done answered my prayers! Where are you, baby? Your mama's done crossed over, chile! I'm so sorry to tell you this thing over the phone, but it can't be helped... Yes, it happened just today... this mornin'. Can you get here fast, lamb? Lord, God! I sho' need you now, and your mama needs you too, before she goes on to Jesus Land. Yes, baby, we'll be right here when you come, and Jasper and Pansy be here too!" She wiped her tear soaked face as she walked into Pansy's big welcome arms, weak with relief. "He didn't say where he's at, but he's comin' tomorrow. Now we can go on an' plan the funeral, proper." They went into the parlor, to tell everyone that 'Tilde's boy would be home the next day, to nods of approval all 'round.

Aaron hung up the pay phone, turned around to look at the throng of spring travelers in Lauderdale Airport through swimming eyes. He was crying bitterly now, forgetting the crack deal he had begun in the lounge. It was mystical, when he had abruptly risen from his stool, excused himself, and found the phone to call his mother's house. A strange compulsion that scared him, but it was so strong his fear couldn't stop him. He went into the men's room after leaving the pay phone, entered a stall, and emptied every particle from his sample bag into the toilet, staring at the whirlpool it made as he flushed it down. When it was gone, he looked up to a sky he couldn't see. He told his mama, and then he told Benjie, it was all over and he was going home. In less than an hour, he was watching the terminal lights growing smaller below him as he flew off to Carolina, and a peace only God can dispatch.

# CHAPTER FIFTEEN

No words passed between the two self-consumed young people as they sped toward Fort Lauderdale that Saturday morning. Clifford knew he was likely in dire straits, but there was no second-guessing Francie, so what could he do? He thought about the stained sheet and her threats to tell their daddies about his abuse of her innocence. Franciene, on the other hand, was not quite so rational. While riding in silence, she kept a mental mantra going to stay focused. He wasn't going to do THAT again, she vowed to herself, and since he fell for her ruse that they had made complete, lusty love the night before, he would just have to accept her rebuffs. When she replayed that tub scene in her mind, she had to stifle laughter. If THAT was all the fuss sex was about, she had no interest in accommodating him further. Boys were nasty and weird, and all she wanted this morning was to find Aaron and ditch the nerd.

With the time nearing ten o'clock, Franciene pronounced to the boy they had not had breakfast, beginning to whine her standard tune. Clifford, bred to be a gentleman, offered, "Why don't we stop for some egg and bacon sandwiches and orange juice, and have a little picnic?" The idea was appealing even to Franciene, and she turned on her knees in the seat, pleading for Cliff to stop soon. He admitted he was hungry, so the next place, no matter how rickety and whatever the bill of fare, would be it. IT turned out to be a gas-up shack, sufficiently stocked just to make do. They found a turnoff a mile from the store, and drove to a pretty spot overlooking the canal.

As they unwrapped the pimento cheese sandwiches, Francie began to cry. What NOW? Cliff was really over it!

"What is it, Francie? Why can't you think about something besides your own selfish, spoiled little ass? Look around at how pretty it is here! Come on, let's walk down to the canal and see if there really are alligators in here... it'll be fun." She put down the stale sandwich and obediently followed him. He was scanning the surface of the water for a pair of protruding dinosaur eyes, when Franciene spoke.

"You are such a fool, Clifford! Such a stupid, boring, dorky Fool! Let me tell you, Hartsell! I didn't poison my Aunt 'Tilde, run away from my daddy with you and Aaron, and burn down that fucking snooty restaurant, just to sit on a weed patch by this sewer hole passing as a wetland, and eat that stale, goopy shit NOT passing as a sandwich!" Her shoulders were hunched toward her ears in disgust, and she was shaking violently. Cliff barely had time for a half turn when she spun around with unnatural strength, slamming a snatched up cedar log at his neck. It connected well... causing his head to list forty-five degrees, as he fell to the gravel... a surprised look frozen on his face.

The aftermath went without a hitch. After ridding Cliff's pockets of cash and his wallet, she got in the car and started the engine. Then, with manic power, the girl wrestled her boyfriend into the driver's seat. At the last moment she pulled out the bottle of Jose Gold, Aaron had left in the backseat, and poured a couple of slugs of tequila in and around his mouth, for a final offense those fancy Hartsells would seek to cover up. She leaned gingerly over his slack face, put the shift into its low gear, and watched, gasping for breath, as the grand little car drove itself into the canal. It quickly slipped below the surface, the brilliant chartreuse duckweed painting the spot over in seconds. Even Franciene, as unaffected as she was by nature, was awed by the reclaiming of the site after such intrusion, and considered her toil quite clever. She slung her backpack over her shoulder, rejecting retribution, and sauntered to the edge of the highway.

The sizzling road was deserted. There were a couple of bikers who passed... a station wagon packed with itinerant workers, then no one for twenty minutes. It appeared Franciene had no choice but to be patient. Not easy for a girl who never cared for the "patience" word, or its' meaning. She could only hope that the next car along would bear someone who would swallow her story. While she stared down the straight, searing strip, Franciene put her best imaginative juices to work and up jumped her alibi, just in time. She sat down on the shoulder about to swallow some of Aaron's tequila when a vast Lincoln pulled over and stopped. She quickly stashed her bottle, as a stylish woman beckoned her over. Francie scrambled to her feet, orderiing up her best tricks. The bottom lip quivered just so, and her hands nervously twisted the strap of her bag. She looked helpless and needy.

"If somebody hadn't come by here soon, I just don't know what would have become of me! I've been waiting and waiting for that boy to send somebody back like he said he would, but he's been gone since before eight o'clock, and it's already past ten!" At that point she began to cry, convincingly... piteously. Camille couldn't have tuned up like that. Whatever... it had the desired effect on the genteel couple in the big silver car. She spun her tale about being left on the road by a man who she believed had come to her rescue. He was going ahead to meet his wife at a rest stop near the interchange and told her he would get a trooper to come back for her because he would get in trouble with the little woman, since she was mighty jealous. This story was so good Franciene believed it herself. The saga continued without a pause.

"He called his wife, "The little woman," more than once, and I didn't like it! It was, you know... gross!" She feigned a disgusted shiver for effect. Franciene then explained she had been riding with her cousin and he had gotten uncommonly fresh, just as the nice man passed them and saw her struggling. He waved them down, and invited Francie into his truck. The story was straight off the top of her head... so full of details and nuances anyone would have believed it too spontaneous to be contrived. "I hope this isn't too much bother," she said in her most disarming drawl. "If my daddy ever gets hold of Cousin Randy that boy won't know where his behind's at 'til he has to go to the potty!" Resting on that clever quip she clammed right up lest she overplay her role. The couple was hopelessly swept along with her story and insisted she come home with them to clean up and have a meal before they figured out what she should do. Francie carefully avoided being pinned down about where home was, only saying she was from "Up in Georgia"... changing the subject when questioned further, so they didn't press.

Franciene learned they lived outside of Fort Lauderdale, and she brightened, requesting to be taken to the airport. She was sill thinking to reunite with Aaron, but the couple laughed her off, not wanting to release their entertaining new indulgence so quickly. The woman squeezed her shoulder and crooned, "No, no darling, you simply must come home with us for a little brunch and a shower", the lady insisted. "Our daughter leaves her things with us while she travels, and they should fit you nicely. We've been on the West Coast near Naples for the last two days with friends, but our maid will have everything ready. You simply can't refuse us this pleasure." Franciene could see she was stuck, so she sat back for the ride, and congratulated herself on yet another clean getaway. All she wanted was the next one, and soon, so this page could turn.

# PALMLAND IS MISSING AN HEIR

The Hartsell family was close to apoplexy. They left the hospital after getting nowhere with the staff, and stood in the parking lot staring at each other. "I want you and Sonja to go home, Andee dear, and I'm going to talk to the sheriff. There's no explanation other than those two are together somewhere. If Franciene never made it to Palmland, and Clifford left with no word to the servants at noon, it follows they must have met up somewhere. The sheriff can begin to question around town tonight before it gets too late to trace them." Sonja was beside herself. "Daddy, I can't believe Cliff would do something like that! There has to be another answer to where he went! He and Francie didn't even like each other much! She would have told me if she was interested in him that way, don't you think so, Mama? I mean, we ARE best friends!"

Andrea held her daughter next to her with a firm grasp, while waggling her head in agreement. "No, baby, you are right! You and I would have noticed something, like last Christmas, when they both were at the house the night of our Christmas Eve drop in. I only saw Cliff speak to her once, then he was with Daphne Cooper for a couple of hours, dancing and laughing like they had something going on. No Strahan, there has to be another answer."

She seemed to want anything but what her husband suspected, to be true. She spoke again, this time pleading for a cool head to prevail. "Maybe Cliff went to Savannah, or got tied up with some of the other kids from school. If you think the sheriff could help, like calling the State Patrol to be looking out for his little car, that's a good idea. Why don't we call the Governor? Our families are certainly cordial enough to ask a favor, don't you think?" She was never above the pretension bred into her for generations, and would put aside even motherly concern to think warmly of the first family in the state rallying around them in a crisis. "It's probably too soon to go that far, darlin'", her husband cajoled, not missing her purpose, "I'll just go to Town Hall and get something started there. 'Don't you worry, I'll get a deputy to drive me home when I'm done."

He patted Sonja's face, kissed in the direction of his wife, and walked toward the sheriff's office across the street. "I know, sure as I know my name, that boy is with Franciene Thornedike right now!"... he said between his teeth, mentally noting that he would have been tempted too, if he were Clifford. "And if she gets pregnant, it's her problem, not ours! She will not spawn an heir to Palmland, so help me! Massey Thornedike can't pull this caper on a Hartsell, no matter how slick he thinks he is. He'd better get out of that bed soon, because his little chippy of a daughter is going to need him, AND his team of attorneys, when I get through with them!"

Carrie hadn't intended to stay with 'Tilde all night, but time had slipped away, hour by hour, until dawn began crawling across the marsh. She hadn't slept, and what with the trials of the past few days there was no reserve strength left. She was worried to distraction about Mister Massey, and whatever could be happening with young Will. Of course, Francie was hellishly torturing her mind to top it all. The girl was going more and more wrong, but as much as she wanted to wade into that crisis, Carrie's powers were much too weakened with grief and worry for clear vision. She opted to settle down and try anyway, and focused on conjuring up Franciene's movements since 'Tilde's death.

The images, collage-like and blurred, found the tired woman unable to set them apart and upright. She had spent many years worrying after that sweet child, now, as Francie's aura was becoming darker and more difficult to read, Carrie was hard put to be enlightened. She was getting flashes of Franciene in places where she was doing bad things, and try as she might, there was no way to pin her down, get a fix on her so she could help. It wasn't happening... nothing would come clear!

Carrie jumped up and ran out the door of 'Tilde's cottage, then down the path toward the big house. She knew what to do. Upstairs, she went to Franciene's room, and frantically searched over her dresser. Her eye fell on a bracelet... a silver bangle the girl wore a lot. She tucked it in her breast pocket and went down to the roomy country kitchen for a cup of tea. While she was brewing, she wiped imaginary crumbs from the table, and went to the window to straighten the ruffled curtains. Her heart leapt! Aaron was walking slowly up the drive, his head bowed in sadness. Carrie ran to the door and called to him as he stepped up to the porch.

"My Lord, I'm so glad to see you, boy! Come in here for a cup of tea, but give old Carrie a hug first'!" She was crying with him as they embraced. "Oh, Aunt Carrie, I got so much to answer for," he sobbed into her shoulder. "I can't stand that she died alone! She was an angel on earth, and she died with no one to hold her hand, not even her own child! It's too late for me to tell her what I've done, but I'm gonna' tell you. I've quit my ways of sin, and I want to come home for a spell, to stay near you and get well, and try to atone." While Aaron slipped into a chair at the table, Carrie wiped her eyes on her apron before pouring the tea. Smiling through her tears, she set his cup down.

"It's mighty good to see, when a boy finds his manhood away from sinfulness and shame. Aaron, don' you worry none... your mama knows, 'cause she's still bidin' a spell, so's to look out over you... Why, I bet she's the cause you come home... she mos' likely called you! This ain't no happenstance, honey chile, it's high time you quit your sorry ways. She never gave up on you, not ever! I'm so proud you heard her callin'." He nodded slowly and profoundly with every word she spoke. It was good to be home, even with such a sorrow. They couldn't avoid going to the cottage to be with 'Tilde any longer. Aaron became more and more tense, dreading the shock of seeing his mother in death.

They went in by the kitchen door, and he walked into the parlor alone. His mother's face lit by lamplight was beautiful to him, and he sank to his knees beside her, weeping out his love... asking forgiveness. The scene was heartbreaking, and Carrie left the house to go back to the kitchen where the rising sun was shining through the windows. It was to be a beautiful dawn. Aaron returned in ten minutes with a look of stern purpose on his face. "What happened to her, Aunt Carrie? How did she die? She wasn't sick or nothin', 'cause I had Captain Dan's promise to let me know if she ever got to ailin', and I'd have come runnin'! What did the doctor say?"

Carrie should have figured on Aaron bringing questions. As she had done for Massey, she went to fetch 'Tilde's paper of words. Aaron held the wrinkled page close to his heart with both hands, looked deep into Carrie's eyes, and then read it aloud. When finished he was quiet for a moment, then spoke with a peace his old friend understood. "My mama was right you know... the newer ways are not hers. She wanted to be done like the old ones before, and I thank you and Mista' Massey for honorin' her so." They brightened a little, and with the orange sun spilling over them, 'Tilde's family began to made final plans to lay her to rest.

## FRIENDS UNITED BUT STILL IN TURMOIL

Toby was realizing he needn't have worried about the boy after all. He seemed quite himself, though a bit the worse for wear from his evening's activity. After the naked reunion, he had gathered his clothes from the dock and dressed... babbling apologies for running away with no word. He felt the need to come forth with the entire story, Carrie Treacle and all, but when they went to Ruby's for a beer, Will found himself unwilling, or strangely unable to expose the spiritual relationship he and Carrie were keeping close between them. He didn't know if Toby would even believe him, but that wasn't the issue. He was somehow sure, that if he exposed such untold powers before they could complete, or at least begin their task, the strength to prevail could be forever lost. He could find enough exciting news to give up this night without betraying secrets before he was free to. (He had passed the first test without knowing it.)

The bar was empty except for two sun scorched-fishermen telling Miss Ruby tall tales and spicy jokes, as they took a table. Will got two beers from the bar and the two sat silently smiling at each other for a full minute. Toby spoke first, and since Will was still a little drunk, his friend kept it light, teasing about finding him on the dock. "What were you two doing out there, skinny dipping in bilge water? Moon tide's making the creeks so nice right now, I'd' a'trotted the girl down any one of those shell paths for a clean swim! Soon as we get to the beach you can try again, how's that?" He watched Will's face for a hint of his lazy grin, but it wasn't there. Instead, the boy groaned as he spoke. "God Toby, that was bad! We would have still been asleep down there, except Jaime, her damn boyfriend, came on us and rolled us into the water!" He slumped even lower... nose to bar in mock shame. He wasn't fooling his old friend.

His old friend's response was to roar with laughter, causing the barflies to stare curiously down at them, as Toby reacted to Will's plight. "So you went fishing in another guy's well! No matter, it's been done and will be done right on. Who was the girl, or do you even know?" Will was still stifling laughter, but he did volunteer the girl's name in a whisper. "We'll never see these folks again, so it doesn't really matter, I guess. I'm sorry if Jaime's pissed at me, but she said he hadn't declared his intentions for almost a year, so it seemed okay to both of us. She's really a babe, I'll say that. Anyway, there's more exciting stuff to tell you."

He sobered up before Toby's eyes in seconds... the magic of youth. His eyes got wide and clear just as he spoke. "You know the daddy of that girl we found? He had a heart attack out there on the dock this afternoon! I was alone with him when he fell... did the CPR we learned in Annapolis, and the nurse at the hospital said I saved his life!" He was babbling... bursting with pride and Toby let him bask for a bit before asking about the dead girl. Such a stricken look!

"She wasn't on the creek bank when I went back, Toby!" As if he thought he needed to, he began to rationalize the disappearance of her body. "I know what happened, though... can't you figure it too? There have been huge tides the last three or four days, what with the moon... it being spring and all... Toby! She had to be taken out on the next flood after we left her! She's probably down river somewhere. I bet if they were to drag up and down that creek they'd find her!"

Touched by the boy's pure intentions, Toby was nevertheless poised for him to take a breath. He needed to give him good advice for a reasonable conclusion. "Will, son," Toby began tenuously, "Don't you get it? The Good Lord has given us a chance to crawl out from under this mess. Next thing you and I should do is send up Thanks, and go on our way. Didn't it occur to you that our prayers were answered when you found her gone, I mean just like she was never there? God's sake, boy, take it as a gift, and let's get the hell out of here. Further away we get, the faster we'll forget this happened... I swear! Soon as you realize there's NOTHING we can do for that poor girl, but plenty we can do for our own asses, we'll be cool again."

Will looked deeply into Toby's anxious eyes and tried to explain. "Toby, listen to me... why do you think I ran off like that? No, don't answer, because you CAN'T know why. I don't know either, but this comes through. I owe that man something basic, and that is to tell him what we found. He's a nice, simple, down to earth guy, and while I was breathing in and out of him this afternoon, it felt like I was put there to save his life. If we go off and leave this hanging, it'll never leave me, I know it!" Toby had to admit to being impressed by how maturely Will was dealing with his dilemma. "What next then, Bo? Do we sit around here and wait for the man to get well enough to tell him the bad news, or do we go to the police with it and hope we don't get locking bracelets and funked up cells as a thank you for our honesty?" His warning HAD to sink in! Of course, Will took in every word Toby said... he had ever since they left the swamp. This was different... he figured this was HIS crisis, and he was going to follow it to conclusion."

He put a hand on Toby's shoulder and offered, "Let's just get some sleep tonight, and start fresh in the morning. I'd like to go over to the Island and see Miss Carrie, but first I want to visit the hospital so I can take her fresh news about her boss. On top of it all, she's burying her best friend either today or tomorrow, so she sure could use some support. Toby, you might not believe it but we hit it off instantly. It's weird... I can't get it, how she affects me. I just have to see her tomorrow! Do you understand?"

No, Toby didn't understand how Will could have gotten so close to two such people in so impossibly short a time, but it had enough mystery for his interest, and the boy deserved the chance to see the thing through. He shoved back a bit of dread, and slapped Wills shoulder with affection. "You got it, sport, we stay at least through tomorrow, and if you swear to me you won't run off at the mouth, or with the feet, I'll be all the help you want. Where we sleep tonight is another problem. Do you have any ideas?" Will was ready for that one, leading Toby upstairs to his room... more an efficiency apartment than a room, complete with a day bed on the screened porch... perfect for him. The two tired friends, with no more words needed, shared a smile, and fell into their beds, both snoring peacefully in moments. Their dreams were quite another matter.

# CHAPTER SIXTEEN

Even before first light could smear the surface of the sound's glassy canvas with peach pink and orangey red strokes of dawn, they were way, way out there... the shrimp boats, steaming off... their haughty bows rocking and bobbing... pointing the way to the dragging grounds. As those before them, craft and crew were going in seek of the season's prize catch... May's giant roe shrimp. The season had already been a good one, but they couldn't let even one of the last days slip by. The glory of the haul, when it spilled out on deck... those amazing prawns, the large and luscious "Queen Bee" of the species... plentiful in the low country for about six weeks, weather and conditions allowing. Taking advantage of prime season makes for long days in the sun, and long nights aboard, waiting for first light, and as many drags as time allows to achieve maximum yield. All hands are prepared for the work, looking forward to the sight of the nine to ten inch prawns flipping around on deck.

Generations teach the tricks to coming home with a full catch. There is even a knack to choosing the crew... everyone should be fit, savvy, affable, and at the same time, jovially competitive, making the process an intramural sport. Handling the big doors, the long nets, operating the winches, while the captain guides the boat's trawl precisely to, and over the grounds, gives the crew an extreme workout. Then, when the nets are swung to the deck, and a half ton of wiggling, jumping, slimy creatures of every sort is spilled out before the strikers, they cull and size, aiming to throw back the unusable "trash", within minutes. The crew men, (and some hearty women), know the quicker they handle and dispose of the fragile variety of sea life, the better for their pockets, and for the critters! Before long, their prime product is layered with shaved ice below in the hold, and they start again, as enthusiastically as if it were the first drag of the day. A repeat performance begins... set the nets, lower and drag, until the nets are full. Then haul and dump, cull and ice down, until the hold can take no more. The morning of June one, nineteen eighty one, was no different, except for what the last trawling would yield.

Deep pride reposes within the shrimping industry. Generations of shrimp boat captains and crew hold high their craft, their respect for each other, and most of all, they honor the reputation of the boats, many of them lovingly hand-built and tended by the grandfathers, fathers, and sons who serve on them. These boats... behemoths slathered every season in brilliant white over decades of extreme weather, abuse and urgent repair... trimmed out in traditional colors like "Haint blue", to keep evil spirits away, Charleston green, or gloss black... like their predecessors, become the captain's best girls, often named for a love... a mother, wife, or daughter, sometimes called after a muse from another time.

Come the new season, most shrimping communities mark with a ceremony called "The Blessing of the Fleet"... a colorful water parade of festooned boats precedes and follows a blessing by local clergy, then the real fun begins and continues throughout the day and evening, the revelers making fun out of everything from a pig roast, low country boil, or a fish fry, and every possible game, degenerating into just plain mischief, very late... very late indeed. They work hard and play just as hard, as often as possible.

This year on the first of June, the big shrimp were the party, and the vessel, "Tomochichi," was steaming to the fun. The crew readied for the first drag, knowing it would set the tone for the day. A lot of factors could affect how good a haul could be... the weather, the tides, their location, of course, but the captain has known where they are most likely to find the bounty under the choppy sound surface for many years, so it's on to the spot to begin their dance. The boat,

"Old Tom", as the men warmly call her, growls along, rocking and waddling over their track, her nets straining against the resistance of the bottom and the increasing load. As they see it filled, they put the winches to work, and the big doors began to creep toward the transom, a grinding squawk setting teeth on edge.

The men were poised to tend the spill when it came, and rejoiced at the uniform, monster-size of the prawns. They culled, tossed trash, and iced the shrimp in the hold, all with fine precision. When the toss-over hit the water, an immediate gaggle of seagulls, plovers, and comical pelicans began to feast off the stern. It was quite a banquet for the winged scavengers, and they soon rose, circling, full to bursting. The rest of the cull had been regarded by a comely pod of bottle-nosed dolphins, creating a water rodeo in the wake, with a couple of mating threesomes, cavorting to the delight of the crew. "Old Tom's" captain was in his glory when his men were happy, and they looked forward to a banner day. At the point when the hold's cache was to its' limit, and the crew had held back enough pan sized fish for a fry at sundown, the last vestiges of the nets' load slid over the deck toward a pair of young strikers, who hadn't cried uncle yet.

The boys were making quick work of the last haul when one of them let loose a groan, one that shaped into, "OHHH, SHIT!"… peaking in a chilling wail. He was backing toward the gape of the hold, and would have fallen in if not grabbed by his mates. The kid was hysterical, pointing toward a squirming cluster of squid, jellies, and unidentifiable sea slime. Captain was watching, and swung down from the wheelhouse to see what was going on. The men had begun advancing on the wriggling pile, expecting most anything… except what they saw.

The first to see it recoiled at the sight of a little arm, more a piece of one… all-over blue, and at the same time kind of greenish gray… picked at and chewed on from the ripped half-bicep, to its' partially devoured fingers. Lying there, it seemed some kind of sculpture, wrought from alabaster, or even pale, smoky jade. No one spoke for a minute… no one could find words. Finally the boy who saw it first said tremulously, "It's the arm of a mermaid, that's what it is! Look at the shells around its wrist, and that little ring! Oh God, what does it mean, Cap'n?"

"What should we do? Can't we just toss it back?" He was wringing his hands, the sobs he had been choking back winning their battle. The captain patted his shoulder, and after awkwardly attempting comfort, went to radio the Coast Guard. Alert coasties on the single-sideband requested they quickly bag the limb in sterile, sealable plastic, and pack it in ice for the trip back to port. They told him the sheriff and a coast guard officer would meet them at the dock. After giving coordinates, and "Tomochichi's" ETA, they powered up for Frenchport's commercial docks.

By the time "Old Tom" tied up, waiting for them was not just the law... two reporters and a few curious yachties had formed a minor crowd. The bag had been placed in the best and cleanest of the crew's personal coolers, covered up with ice the grisly thing would provide no sideshow on the pier. When the sheriff raced off with the cooler a parade followed. Big doin's in so small a place. There hadn't been a story like this one since Miss Ruby's daughter "accidentally" shoved her husband's latest dalliance off the stern of their sloop in the sound during a gale. She never surfaced so anyone knew, but that was five years back and the woman had been a robust, Cuban exotic dancer, so no one was putting the two events together... no one at all.

It was necessary for the crew to be detained to relate details to investigators before they were dismissed to deal with their fragile catch. While at the hospital, reporters followed officers everywhere they went... even into the restroom. When it became irritating to the sheriff, he waved them away with a word of advice. "You all better just hold your horses 'til the tests are done and I review the results for my own purposes. I'm not gonna' stand here and speculate on what this means, and you better not write one word or publish one picture relating to this matter 'til I give the go ahead, you hear? This ain't no laughing matter, nor is it something to jump the gun on. I'd say that limb hasn't been separated from its' body more'n a day or two, so there's somebody freshly missin' around here. I'll notify you soon as I know somethin' myself, so ya'll just cool your jets!" The anxious story mongers had to back off, so they moved into pairs and walked away to entertain each other with past scoops and tall tales.

A full blown mystery had taken root, and the few who were privy to the sketchy facts knew this could put the area into a panic, what with the usual shark attacks and sea monster stories always lurking. Morgue attendants conjecturing over the find, offered first this theory, then that, but after a close exam of the pitiful appendage, the forensics chief determined that the arm was from a caucasian female, between thirteen and twenty, probably between five-four and five-ten, slender, sun-tanned, with fair hair, denoting anglo-ethnicity. Further testing would establish whether the arm was separated at the time of, or after death occurred, with the examiner's preliminary belief it was after. The finger trauma was what sea life does to any food source, and that was about all they could offer to police at first look. No one was leaving, it was obvious when somebody sent out for sandwiches and coffee, and chairs close to the doors to the morgue were claimed for the vigil. It had been a long time between big stories in the tiny town of Frenchport.

Upstairs in Miss Ruby's rented room early Sunday morning, and Will was first up... to his surprise, since Toby usually had to pull him from his bed by the foot, especially if there had been beer consumption the night before. Toby had been consistently concerned about allowing an eighteen year old to imbibe in distilled beverage, but the truth was, they'd never seen each other drunk, and Toby had judiciously refused the boy's requests to drive when he had a couple. Their relationship was akin to the man and boy in the novel, "Captains Courageous," friends to a point, then it was mentor and pupil.

There was always so much trust between them, and the boy was being prepared for his adulthood by one of the best. He regarded their pairing as the best thing he could have ever been given... a parent he never had. Will looked down at his snoring friend with true affection, and he found himself praying a silent prayer that he will always be taken good care of, this chosen dad of his. He dressed with no sound, and slipped from the room after leaving a note saying not to worry, that he would be back soon, and they could leave for the beach with free minds and hearts.

Miss Ruby was already sweeping the deck when Will came down the steps. "She must just about live at this job", he mused as he waved to her. "You sleep good, honey? I' got some coffee over there... go help yourself, and there's some banana muffins under the net cover right by the coffee maker. Made 'em fresh this mornin'. I get up and out real early, 'cause I feel so good every day when I wake up." She was leaning on the broom as she stared off and continued, "See, what none of you guys ever notice is, I only watch people drink every night... don't touch it no more, not since my son died from drinkin' and tryin' to shoot himself to the moon on his Harley one night. I ain't sayin' he'd 'a' lived to be a ripe old age if he hadn't been a drinker, but it sure didn't do nothin' to help him."

Still leaning on the push broom, looking out to the sound with squinty eyes, Ruby was a long way from where she'd been a moment before. The boy obediently set himself up with coffee and muffin, and climbed onto a stool near her. Ruby jumped back to the present and came over to him holding out a piece of paper. "How' you know Aunt Carrie? You know her friend who died, Aunt Clothilde? I swear, I don't know which of those two's the sweetest. Oh well, now 'Tilde's gone, I guess it don't need to be figured on no more." Her naturally nosey nature bade her continue.

"So... son. You met her on Squires, or here on this side? All that note said was that she wants you to come over and help her today. I think that's just fine, for a young man to be such a gentleman, when there ain't too many around. Anyways, it would be a good idea to call her 'fore you get on the boat. Folks over there are a mite peculiar about manners and bein' thoughtey of one another... not a bad thing I'm sure. How's that muffin?  Good thing I could use those bananas for somethin'. They were just about to be coon feed. Anyways, the boat leaves on its run at ten." She sniffed, scratched her hip thoroughly, and resumed her sweeping. Will was rather surprised that there was to be no eight or nine o'clock trip... maybe Sundays are slower. "Will Jaime be aboard?" He called to her, "I'd like to talk with him about something that happened."

The buxom woman waved her arm around like a whirlwind. "Who knows? He may or may not be aboard this mornin'. His

Saturday night carousin' is famous 'round town, an' his poor daddy never knows if he'll have a mate for Sunday runs or not. Why, a few times he's called for Dan to pick him up as far away as Savannah or Beaufort, after he woke up without knowin' how he came to be there. That's a mess of a young man right there, I'll tell you that. He needs somebody to put a halter and lead on him someday soon."

"Oh!" She said sharply, with Will observing how revved up she was, "There's another thing under the bar for you. Lord, boy, you are a popular one, to only be 'round here a day or two. This was on the bar last night when I came down to set up. I hate to lie in bed thinkin' about all that work tomorrow mornin'. Anyway, I guess this is a love note or somethin'." He took the envelope and slipped out a fluffy little card depicting a dolphin on a surfboard on the front. It was from Cissy! She had printed it... dotting the "I's" with circles... cutesy-like. "I guess we were meant to make each other happy for a little while, so it's okay, as long as you forgive me for saying that it didn't mean anything to me. I'm going to stay with Jaime. You must have already figured that out. He's what I know, and what I want. I'll settle down for him soon, and he will for me. Let's me and you promise to remember last night forever... except the last part. It was Cold! Love, Cissy"

She didn't have to worry about that one, he said, shaking his head and smiling for a moment. It was nice of her to wrap things up like she did. Will knew he would always remember that about her. He suddenly got a clear flash of the two of them, she and Jaime, down the line sharing their lives, and it was a good vision. He was almost sure there would be a long life together for them... not always smooth, but full of fun and love. Will had never experienced second sight or prophetic awareness, but it had just happened about Cissy and Jaime, and he knew where it was coming from. More and more, Carrie's gifts were revealing themselves to Will, like the vignette of Cissy and her future, giving him a sense of peace for them. He was humbled by the honor and responsibility. Toby must be told about it soon, and they could use the power together, to carry on the work Carrie had foretold.

Will didn't know a thing about how he was to find who to help first, or what he could do for them. The great time last night already seemed obscure, but he was relieved to have Cissy's note. Her "Angel of the Morning", expectations could have been tedious, since the sex had been so good… and the afterglow so bad. When he had finished his second cup of coffee, Will walked to the ferry dock to tell Dan he'd be aboard for the first run, but the captain wasn't receiving. Will could hear loud snoring down below, and when he read Dan's note on the windshield asking that he not be disturbed until quarter to ten, he put his name below the scrawled message and left.

He decided to use the nearly two hour interim to go to the hospital for news of Massey to take to Carrie. The key to the Seville must still be on the tire where he left it, and he figured he could pick up some flowers for Carrie at the gift shop, making his wait productive. There had been two shifts since he and Carrie had visited ICU, and Will was sure he wouldn't see anyone they had talked with last evening, so he began concocting a new story to allow forthcoming information from a doctor or nurse. The nurse was on the phone, but rang off soon as she saw him approaching. It was Mattie Bell again, arguably the hardest working nurse on the planet. He began… trying not to look her over as completely as he would like to. "I'm anxious to learn something of Mr. Thornedike's condition as of this morning. The lady with me last night will want to know what has happened since we were here, and if the doctors think there is still a chance he may need surgery."

He hoped that if he could recap that much, it might merit an update. The nurse raised her palm and flipped the chart as she said in a sing song, superior voice, "I'm in charge of this area for the morning shift. If you are listed here as a relation, I can discuss the patient's condition with you… otherwise, I'm sorry. No, I see no names here." It was Will's turn to raise his hand, this time in surrender. "I'm not a relative, but I did perform that resuscitation procedure on him until the EMTs arrived, as you know, and besides", he arranged his eyebrows in their most piteous slants, "There is a sweet little lady on Squires Island, who is as much of a relative as anyone could be. His daughter might be missing, and Mr. Thornedike discovered this just before he had the attack. The lady, who I'm told raised his daughter, has just lost her best friend this week on top of everything, and desperately needs to know he is all right, or will be soon. I'm going to visit her later this morning, and that's why I'm here."

He dropped his hand, and let out a breath he'd been holding almost since he saw her. Will thought she had a look today that wasn't there last evening, and he was getting new emissions from her... familiar ones. This was not flirting... it was different. She was about twenty, a healthy girl with short bobbed chestnut hair, ice blue eyes, and she had the body of an athlete... lean, with toned muscles, but more gamin than feminine. She looked like one of those sassy French, sail-racing girls... like she doesn't know or care how spectacular she is, making her even lovelier. Add in her lofty career... her dedication to her patients, the iridescent gleam in her eye, and to Will's mind, a force of nature filled the room. He felt a sinking spell coming on when he saw that gleam, but he rallied and stayed his course. She looked at him for about ten seconds, before fumbling a pen and pad to her desktop.

She began scribbling, as she admonished in a firm voice, "I'm sorry, Mr. Parrish, but it would be remiss of me to betray the confidentiality of my patients' records." She turned the pad so he could read along... it was a clever note she had written! "He is awake off and on, but we are keeping him still and calm. There will be another EKG later this morning, and if you will give me a name and number, I can inform the lady about the possible treatment plan." She was writing furiously now, trying to get it all down before she was noticed. The last word was written, and Mattie handed the paper and the pen to Will. He wrote Carrie's name, and copied Mr. Thornedike's home number from his pocket, and said he would have Carrie by the phone at noon. They exchanged slips of paper, read them and looked knowingly.... warmly, into each other's eyes. Watching the approach of a doctor and nurse, they broke the spell.

"Thank you for explaining procedure to me, Miss Bell. Will said stoically, "I will tell the lady we just need to wait and pray." They shook hands, and as their hands slipped apart, their fingers curled at the tips and caught for a moment longer. He felt his breath catch, as if breathing might distort the sight of her walking away from him, to disappear behind the swinging doors. Shaking it off, he checked his watch and saw there were still thirty minutes before the boat... just time enough to get the flowers and be back at ten to ten.

While he was going out through the emergency entrance, Will noticed a clutch of people nearby. There were two policemen, a photographer with his camera at his hip, and a "gray suit," as he referred to detectives, in the huddle, buzzing excitedly. He was almost out of earshot when he heard, "The pathologist was positive it's a teenage girl's arm." Whoa! Will was interested now! He edged closer, but feigned normal nosiness, keeping a blank face. The group was oblivious to him, in its' frenzy to retain the information it had received. The buzz continued. "It must have been in the water for only a short time, or it would have been picked clean. Who knows, maybe it was hidden somehow, or gobbled up, then spit out later. I've heard of that happening with a large mouthed fish. He can't manage a whole body, so things get left behind," one reporter was saying. "Oh, God, that's enough!" the lady cop groaned. "We don't need to do this! I'm interested in identifying this thing from the jewelry, and getting on with finding out about the girl's family, for shit's sake, not all this ghoulish speculation. Did anyone hear what initials were on the signet ring? They said the engraving is so elaborate you can't tell what it is."

"It's a large T in the center, with an F, and an M, taking up the sides!" thought Will. He had gotten a clear look when the sun had hit the deepest cuts and made the monogram jump out, as her dead hand rested on her hip in the mud that day. There it was! The proof that Franciene was truly dead! Will was hardly able to contain himself until he could get to Carrie and thrash it out. How was she going to explain that dead arm, with Franciene's jewelry still on it, only a short boat ride from where they had found her? Carrie wanted the knowledge of her being dead to be suppressed, while she tried to stall the reality and wipe it away for good. There was a lot he needed to know, all right, but he and Carrie had to share it, just the two of them, until the time was right, or mercifully, things could return to life in its proper order. So much was happening so fast... Will had just enough time to choose a purple hydrangea plant wrapped in pretty pink foil, for Carrie to plant in her yard, and he made it just in time to board the ferry.

When he got to the boat it was idling and ready... and getting full! "Well, Hero, you ready to shove off?" Dan was still praising his first aid to Massey. "This trip's on me, since you saved my buddy yesterday. He and I don't always hug and kiss when we meet up, but I call him my best friend, and we'd do most anything to help one another out." With that, he put out a hand to help him aboard, patted his back, and pointed to a seat. Will turned and blurted, "Is Jaime going on the trip this morning, Cap'n? I have to apologize to him... about something that happened last night." He was hoping for redemption, and didn't elaborate... this one he would keep close to his chest. Dan went for the log book, and drawled, "I reckon he'll be here soon, but he'd better hurry along. The boy has a tough time on Sunday mornin's, that's a fact." He was chuckling as he walked back to the wheel, rubbing his neck while mulling it over with relish. Will was touched by the love between the father and his son, and his heart lurched for a moment with a touch of envy. They are lucky to have each other, he thought wistfully.

# CHAPTER SEVENTEEN

Toby was incensed... No, he was pissed! "Oh... No Sir! Not this time, Buddy!" He growled as he stalked through the strange room looking for his clothes and shoes. Oh yeah, Will left a note this time... just saying that he would call, or be back in the afternoon, with no real accounting of his intentions. How long had it been now? Twelve or fourteen hours since Toby almost tripped over his bare ass on the dock? He had heard the boy shuffling around earlier in the morning just before dawn, but sleep had enveloped him again so quickly, he did not wonder what he was doing. Now here it was, nine-fifteen, and he was at a loss what to do, except go down and scratch around for him... Deja-vu all over again!

It was plain to see that the kid was deeply involved here, more than Toby could figure alone. He wanted reasons to come from Will himself, and last night would have been the right time, but the decision had been made to enjoy each other without any pressure until he was ready to talk. Toby had been about to burst to get into the issue of Will's mom, the man in the photo, and his version of the last few days' events. He knew how important it was for everybody's sake, to get the facts sorted out before they were spun any deeper into the mess they were sinking into. Will wasn't as thrashed about finding the girl's body anymore, that was plain, and a relief to Toby. It was a bit eerie come to think of it, how dismissive he had been about her, after being so obsessed. It was good to know him to be mature enough to rise above a crisis, but only if he wasn't shoving away from the table and its pile of issues in search of a superficial peace.

Toby needed to get close to him that morning to see how he was put together, so they could deal with his new-found family history. There was a suspicion growing…. the photo had to be Will's biological father… there was no other reason to preserve such a tattered likeness of someone, especially for a small boy. These realities swirled in Toby's brain as he dressed and went downstairs. The coffee smelled great, even on such a steamy morning. Miss Ruby began pouring Toby's mug full as soon as she heard him on the stairs. It flickered in his head, how come it was that women like Miss Ruby were reduced to pampering strangers, when she should have been the matriarch of a big, beautiful family, making their lives richer with her love and care. Maybe she was supposed to take the job of caring for wayward souls like him… and like Will, who until now had no family themselves.

The sad truth of his oneness was troubling for Toby after Kate was gone, with no inspiration to fix it, until he came to believe Will could be the answer to the question, when in truth he was the reason there had never been a question, before the answer came with him. Back to the coffee and Miss Ruby, who stood, hands on her ample hips while she waited for the taste test. "Very good coffee, ma'am. I have always wondered why some folks can barely manage potable sludge, while others,"… and he toasted her with his mug, "create java perfection with ease. This is coffee's coffee!"

It felt good to give her kudos, although he knew she likely got plenty from her gaggle of ne'er do wells. Toby hoped she could give him more than coffee, as he asked lightly. "Where did that boy get off to so early… did he say? I was sleeping so hard I never heard a sound." She liked him, he could tell, and she trusted his relationship with Will… that he wasn't anything but a positive in his life, so she smiled and sat down on a stool, ready for a chat. "I know he was all stacked with plans of some sort, but the main thing he mentioned was that he was goin' over to see Aunt Carrie on Squires this mornin', on Dan's ten o'clock run. From what I could tell he's mighty anxious to talk with her about somethin' pressin'. What in the world could it be? That woman's in the throes of grief about her friend Clothilde's passin' this week gone. Maybe she needs some help about that. You got any idea what he's goin' for?"

Toby wasn't about to get into their problems with anyone, so he just shrugged and finished his coffee. After a refill and some small talk, he walked down to the dock to check on the ferry. There were ten passengers already aboard when Toby got there. Dan was taking friends and family across for the funeral tomorrow, so they could help prepare for the near thirty-six hour long event, that day, night, and early morning, before getting all done up for the twelve o'clock church service. Ruby was in her glory, standing with him, greeting old friends and former Island dwellers, coming home for Aunt 'Tilde's going home.

It would prove a grueling thirty-six hours for the volunteer boaters, bus drivers, food and drink handlers... then all would reverse, everyone filling boats to go back to their town-side lives, as it had to, leaving Squires Island to grieve in peace. Captain Dan was busily seating the ladies and the older ones first, and warned if there was no more room, the overflow would have to wait until noon. Toby had already decided it would be his lot, and was about to leave the dock when he saw Jaime trudging toward the boat, with Will chatting purposefully beside him. Jaime waved him away, and then he turned abruptly and impulsively to him, shoving an outstretched hand for him to take. They shook, wagging their heads in some mutual amusement, and continued to the ferry. Will smiled broadly at first sight of his friend, and then his face was as if a shade was pulled down over it.

Toby started to tell him he would be on the next boat, since this one was filling up with reservations, as Jaime boarded and began to take signatures, but shushed himself to hear Will say in a half-whisper... "I need some time alone with Carrie, Toby... you don't know what's been going on with us, and frankly neither do I, but it's not of this world, and she says she will explain it this morning. I even bought her this purple plant in her friend's memory, hoping she will trust that I really care about what she's been through. All I can tell you right now, so you'll let me get on that boat, is that it concerns the girl we found, and it has to do with her a lot!" Toby was already guiding him with his hand on his back, to the boarding steps. Will turned and grinned, relieved that his friend understood. "I swear I'll be there when you get off the boat at one. Then, if she says okay, we can all sit down together and try to get everything sorted out."

What could Toby say? He mumbled to Dan that he would be back to take the twelve boat, pointed a confirming finger at Will, and walked away. The boat left without Toby even looking back at it, because he was already thinking what he could do with this spare time, to prepare his case for Miss Carrie. He went to the newspaper office with an idea. The desk person offered that there was a local culture museum and gallery just out of town, opening at ten. Cool! Something was going right for a change. He drove to the place, feeling pay dirt coming. After about a thirty minute drive north, he found an old house that had been converted into a charming local art gallery and craft shop. The scope and variety of indigenous material was huge, and he was elated to come upon a small room full of related reference material. Having less than two hours to spend, he intended to ask his questions first, and purchase something to help him cram for he wasn't sure what. After a quick walk back to the lady behind the counter, he felt strong vibes he had come to the right place.

He passed through a lot of bright whimsy and primitive art. There were displays of intricate jewelry, and collages one could linger over, all vivid in color and texture. The hanging art was emotionally charged, and beautiful. Toby was making a silent promise to return with room in the Jeep for a haul, when he spied what he wanted. On a hand painted table near the desk was a book... an impressive old volume, very thick and use-worn, and when hc looked inside, there were numerous writings and symbols on the front and back inside covers, obviously put there by more than one hand. The clincher was an old etching, under tissue-thin vellum. It was an illustration of what he had been suspecting Will and Carrie were into, and now had to face full-on. He took the book to the lady at the desk, almost trying to conceal its' title for a murky reason. When the woman saw him coming toward her, she began a steely stare that nearly seared his skin. Her large head covering of red, orange and turquoise nearly fell off, as she inclined her head to stare even harder.

"You want THAT, child? How come you to want THAT book? It ain't for sale... Oh no! No, Son, I can't let you have that one!" She was back against the wall, her demeanor increasing Toby's resolve to have the book. "I'll give you whatever you ask for it, ma'am... this book is needed by some friends of mine on Squires Island, and I have to take it to them today" She recoiled even more. "You talkin' 'bout Aaron an' Carrie? They don't need this, they got the way to fix eva'ting, all up inside 'em... tell me, why you want my book?" Toby was scratching for the right words... and they came. "Carrie does have a need, one that tells her she has to use combinations of her own power, as well as those in this book. There is a person coming in over top of Clothilde's departed soul, and he needs help too. She doesn't need it for keeps, but if you let me sign my name, and leave my credit card for you now with my promise I will bring this book back no later than one week from today, just like it is now. Is that all right?"

She was still looking queerly at this brash white man, but not without trust, praise be. Toby had said words he would never have put together without intervention... "Is that you, Will?" He asked the air itself. The exquisite woman came around the counter to stand close to him, to look up into his face with even more intensity. She put her hands on either side of his face and spoke. "You got the aura... you know that? The light around you is there, strong and bright! I guess that makes it okay for you to take the book, if you promise to bring it back here yo'self. You can sign this paper... like you said, but it don't matter about no credit card, 'cause this here book could never bring enough money to replace it, no matter how much credit you got! Just you sign all two of yo' names, and I'll be easy, knowin' you're good as your word. And you tell Carrie Treacle I'm watchin' her, and she's gonna' be all right... And that boy, Clothilde Braswell's child, Aaron, will come to his high place when he does right by his mama!"

Toby almost asked her some whirling questions, but decided to wait for Carrie's answers... he thanked her graciously, and sped back to the marina. With a good hour left before noon he settled on the porch, and beginning with the first page, started to read. Not to be... strange as it seemed, at that moment he was compelled to call Linda Sue.

# Two People Very Much Connected, and Apart

Linda had not allowed herself think about Will and his friend Toby, at least for one day... No, not him... especially not Toby. All he left when he slipped out of town after turning her heart wrongside-out, was a business card and a cap, a faded, rusty-hued one, with a tarpon jumping over the bill. Nothing to invest her hopes and dreams in, or to make her be glad he had come into her life. It was as if he appeared to give her a tiny taste of her son, then he was gone, and she would have to wait for perhaps years, for another taste. Not fair! It was worse than knowing nothing at all. She had practiced ignorant oblivion, a scrubbed, empty heart and mind, ever since she saw Willie to the safety of her daddy's swamp place.

Since she had Mondays off from the gift shop, there was nothing pressing until time for her shift at the lounge. It never left her that all this work wasn't for making a living. Linda was financially secure owing to the untimely bequest, before Willie was born. She liquidated the tangible assets, and it was all invested for the time when the boy could use it. No, she worked for the work itself, a kind of atonement... no more being her own boss, she didn't want to be that rooted. If her life magically took a turn, she wanted to be able to bolt, with no ties, or the loose ends ties always leave behind. Linda was satisfied she had handled at least her fiscal life well. It was a good day to do bills, clean out the refrigerator, and soak up some sun on the deck out back if it wasn't too humid. A tall iced coffee, her worn accordion file, and out to the porch with bookkeeping chores. Just as she put down her glass, the phone rang. She went inside to answer it, fussing at the intrusion.

"Hello? You! Why did you leave without a word to me? You have no right to intrude on our lives... mine and Will's, then disappear like that! I can't forgive it of you, Toby! What?" She had begun to cry, trying to choke the sound back, so he wouldn't know. It was such pleasure to hear her sweet voice again, Toby forgot the purpose for ringing her, then he remembered... It was to give her the good news.

"I found him, Linda, and he's fine... I don't know, we haven't had a minute to talk, and I can explain that too, but not now. He's great, matured a lot, even in this short time, mostly because he's dealing with some grownup issues, and I think he's going to come out okay very soon." He let that sink in, and when she said nothing, he continued. "Linda Sue, I'm sorry for the coward's way out. I hated it when we parted so angrily. You're right, Honey, we can fix any damage done by getting together soon... the three of us. Don't let the idea scare you, it's meant to be. You haven't been through all this for nothing... to just forget you have a son. He's worth every day you've suffered, trust me. As soon as I can get him alone, you will be the first subject. When he knows you and I are connected like we are... no, I don't mean like that! It seems like I keep upsetting you!"

In a pinched effort to make the best of the call, choosing his words had fallen flat. Toby prayed a plea for the right way to say it, and went on. "I mean that we are together for HIS sake, and to help HIM! He'll come to know us as his best chance. I have to go... he's waiting for me over on Squires Island. I'm in Frenchport, waiting for the... Linda? Linda Sue?"

She had hung up. Toby dialed her back as fast as he could, but he guessed she had elected not to answer. Combining the few pages of the book he had just digested with that fractured phone conversation, Toby felt a stomach churning turmoil coming on. No matter, he had to buck up, and get to the boat. The book was tucked into his backpack, along with a few snapshots he had taken in Waycross, a couple of Linda's house, and even one of her going up the steps, when she wasn't aware... (That one was NOT for Will.) If they were to speak of his mom while they were on the island, Toby had the proof she was really out there, and he had SEEN her. Never before, except when Katie was sick, had Toby felt so alone... so vulnerable.

Back then, as his wife's condition worsened, he had often wished for his own mother's gentle strength, humble wisdom, and solid faith to keep him in the road, while realizing that she, who he adored, was surely dying. Now he had Linda's face and voice whirling before him... within him, providing a new kind of value, but he could not make out the words... the perfect, most concise few words to bring Linda back around.

Toby was even having trouble bringing her face into focus, to distinguish her features. He questioned his motives again as well. Was he doing this for Will and the mother he had lost, or had he become desperate to bring Linda Sue Parrish along for himself? Did the fact of his feelings for her justify any and all action, even using the boy... her prodigal son, as bait? He galloped down the steps... spending the trip to the boat in deep thought... the first objective evaluation of his feelings for Linda since meeting and leaving her. It was vital to be wrapped tight, with full insight, when he told Will about her. That ominous box was in his bag to taunt him further, with the picture of the bearded man secreted in his address book. What a day this could turn out to be. As he greeted the crew, his motivation was clear, and it was right and good.

# CHAPTER EIGHTEEN

Aaron was waiting in the Land Rover for Will, only because Carrie had asked that he go to fetch him while she set both houses to order. His heart was full of sadness for his mama, increasing the task of shaking off the now physical need for the drugs he had depended on every day, so valiantly flushed away after speaking with Aunt Carrie last night. He prayed to God, and his mama, to help him, said a fervent "Amen", and got out of the car to greet Carrie's guest. Will had already thrown his backpack in the rear door by the time Aaron reached him. The two boys, so near in age yet so different, stood awkwardly, each waiting for the other to make the first move. It was Will who offered his hand, saying, "I'm Will Parrish, and you're Aaron Braswell, aren't you?"

If Aaron hadn't been raised to respect guests, he might have rejected Will's overzealous greeting, on this sad day. He took the hand and shook tentatively. "Yes, I'm Aaron. It's a pleasure to meet you, Will." He was astounded at how his own voice sounded at that moment... almost Caribbean inflected, pitch and diction new and alien to him. They got in the car and drove to the big house with no more than a polite comment or two about the weather from Aaron, and Will's words of sympathy for his mother's passing. The driveway, crowned by twin rows of ancient live oak trees dripping with moss, were cushioned below by huge Hydrangea in early, baby blue and pale green bloom, and interspersed giant Gardenia bushes, their snowy blossoms' fragrance lifting the two of them from their seats as they idled around the curve to the house.

Will was gawking as they reached the porch steps and stopped. It was too much to take in all at once. Carrie was throwing out some scraps for the chickens and guineas scratching in the bushes, and came toward them with her arms out. "Lord Jesus, I'm glad you came. You can be a big old help to me and Aaron at this bad time! Aaron, did you greet this boy to suit? He's the one who saved Mister Massey's life when he fell so sick, and we got a lot to talk about, we three. Come on inside and have some iced tea and a snack, 'cause I know how you boys can eat!" They went in to the kitchen and sat down at the big round table, falling silent. Aaron was still guarded, a bit shy around a white boy he didn't know. Carrie served their tea and a bowl of cheese straws, seating herself across from them. "Babies, we got trouble, and I don't know yet how to meet it. Aaron, your mama would know, and she was near to tellin' me when she died. I think you have things to tell me, as does this child here, so if we can be true to ourselves and to each other, and most of all, to The Good Lord, we can do right." She poured some more sweet tea for them both, and folded her hands on the table.

"Will, you know what you were told on the dock this mornin', and you will be fine. I have something to give you as an amulet to keep close by you through this strife. It will tell you what you must know to find your way." She took the bracelet that was Franciene's from her apron, and put it in Will's breast pocket, closing and buttoning the flap with a pat. "You will know when to go to it for the help, this I promise you." Now you and Aaron get busy for me. I need the chairs and tables set up in the church-yard for tonight, and Aaron, you take Will right now, to see your mama's face. He wants to pay his respects before you go to work."

They did as told, and in minutes Will was let in the kitchen door of 'Tilde's little house. There was about a dozen in attendance, some in the kitchen picking for their plates from the loaded table, and the rest sitting around the walls in the parlor.

The smells of lamp oil and flowers mixed into a heady incense, and Will became a little dizzy. Some off-key humming and rocking to the tempo was giving the room life, while death presided beneath a riot of roses. Will and Aaron walked to the coffin and stood for a moment. Then a place was made for Will to sit beside Pansy. She was in another place, her eyes closed in prayer, looking very much like a Mayan priestess, her silvery braids circling her head. She patted Will's hand to settle his nerves, and continued her incantation. In a few minutes, Aaron tiptoed to Will and motioned him to come out with him. They went silently to the truck and drove off toward the church, as Carrie watched from the porch, nodding approval.

## IT IS TIME FOR LINDA TO GO TO THE ISLAND

Linda was on the road five minutes after she hung up on Toby. She had called and cleared three days off with both her bosses, citing a family crisis... which it truly was. Will was in danger, she was certain. He had innocently put himself in a situation that called for a mother's attention. Toby couldn't be trusted to handle it, because she believed he regarded Will as all grown up... not the sheltered child she knew he must be. She had last seen her baby when he was not yet four years old, when she took him to her father. Time had stopped for him then, and as his mother, for her as well. The trip would take about three hours, and she was praying she could simply appear in Frenchport, without revealing herself. It sounded, from the last words spoken by Toby, that they would be on Squires by then, and no one else in port would know her. What if someone did know who she was? She mentally spat the thought out, and as she drove toward, God knows WHAT, her mind played the unbelievable story for the thousandth time.

# Quite a Saga, the Memoirs of Linda Sue Parrish.

More than pretty, but terribly thin, the 1960 Waycross teen knew nothing of boy-girl love, other than what she conjured while day-dreaming about the film idols of the time. The emotions they evoked in her had the disturbing consequence of even more loneliness and frustration, and she shunned the boy-silliness she saw with her friends. Instead, she sought safe comfort in other interests... horses, painting, music, and culinary arts. The latter prevailed into her choice of careers, as she dreamed of becoming a world-class chef. It was crushing as Linda watched while girls her mother swore couldn't hold a candle to her, took up with first this cute boyfriend, then that beauty title, then another sorority or social club membership, while Linda wondered when it would be her turn.

Boys were marginally aware of her, and she had a few dates during her high school years, but more often than not, Linda Sue found herself alone most weekends, since the head of a sixteen year old boy seemed destined to turn toward the sassy girls, toting their luscious delights around in sexy, revealing attire. She tried to fill herself out with high calorie food and silly chest-building exercises, but when all efforts failed she resorted to wearing thick walking shorts under her skirts and slacks, and padding her bra, desperately trying to create the hips and breasts the others took for granted.

It wasn't long before catty girls she thought were her friends whispered to the guys that Linda Sue was not all she appeared to be. A dare cooked up by the football fraternity resulted in her blackest day, when a staged date with the star quarterback sought to prove what had been rumored. Linda should have been aware of the strangeness of the whole thing, since no one, certainly the star of the team would be calling such as her. It wasn't long at all after he picked her up, that she found herself parked in the local cemetery, his stilted comment being the moon was really pretty from there. He spent a few minutes in foolish conversation, and then, as if on cue, rudely groped up her skirt, and down her neckline, later crowing his discoveries to a cruel bunch of gossips who were waiting for the scoop. They went on with their cruel game by spreading the dirt around the small town. It would seem silly years later, that she even gave a damn, but that was the worst time of her young life, knowing she had to face everyone they had told.

Sobbing into her pillow night after night, Linda wondered if she had been born in the wrong time. Years later, during the skinny seventies, she was in vogue without denying herself a morsel. But the damage had been done, and she vowed no longer to regard vanity and its compulsions as her focus. Linda Sue Parrish would not be humiliated about her body ever again. After graduation she enrolled in a two year course in Charleston at a fine culinary school. The student body's male-female ratio was so heavy with men, Linda tried being one of the boys, for simple survival. It helped to have a coltish body with small breasts and long legs, and a derriere that wasn't much more than the terminus of those legs. She comically thought herself about as sexy as an ostrich.

She also had the personality that allowed her to be a good friend in the dorm. Her new best friend, Diane, was quite busy, since her face and body were glaring invitations. Linda didn't envy her one bit. Instead, she enjoyed the show as she moved forward in her studies and labs unencumbered by silly distractions. They had fun, took care of each other, emerging arm in arm with diplomas and lofty dreams. Linda was chock- full of talent and creativity, and Diane was her perfect counterpart, having a razor sharp business head and fine attention to detail. They spent a little down-time in Charleston, inevitably discussing the prospects of a joint venture, agreeing to give gotham-like Atlanta a shot. It wasn't long before the starry-eyed young women realized they were in alien territory, where everything is wrapped tightly in sticky red tape, and that it is WHO one knows, more than WHAT, and that being small fish in a big pond wasn't for them.

The two bruised ingénues finally settled on inventing a catering and party planning enterprise in the quaint, booming coastal town of Brunswick, Georgia. Being so close to Waycross should have been a plus for Linda, but she felt no strong ties there any longer, with her mother passed on, free at last from her miserable life with a traveling man. Years back, after one final fight, Linda's father packed his duds and his sportsman's toys off to a little piece of land he had kept on the edge of the nearby swamp for hunting and fishing and for sporting the town tramps. Linda went to talk to him on her mother's behalf, to tell him his wife was slowly killing herself with grief and loneliness.

What she found was a quite cozy, rather charming little cabin in a breathtaking spot, with vistas of the small bayou that led into the great Okeefenokee Swamp Park. Her father looked great, had put on some healthy bulk after quitting cigarettes, laughed jovially, and often. What could she do but go back and tell her mother to chin up... that he wasn't coming home. She stayed one night, trying to get him to go and talk to her mother, if only for a kind goodbye, but he was adamant not to see her again, perhaps because he feared he would weaken and stay. Finally, Bill Parrish would not be moved, and in a queer way, Linda couldn't blame him. He was fifty-eight years old, still virile, and his wife clearly wanted a "Sunday dinner after church, prayer meeting on Wednesday night, and no more nights out at the Dew Drop Inn with your redneck cronies", kind of man, like many of her lady friends had. Nope! Bill was sticking right where he was, by God!

Harriet Parrish was dead in eight months, taking what was left of her girlhood perceptions of love and marriage with her, and Linda prayed for the reincarnation theory to be true, for her mother's sake. She made the sad trip to see her daddy in April, after her mama's death, and discovered that he had dug up and transplanted twenty three pink and white wild dogwood trees, Harriet's favorites, and the number of years they were married, all around his place in her memory. They were in full bloom, and poignantly beautiful, like the gesture, and her parents' long lost love.

Linda and Diane's partnership was a go, and on May first, nineteen sixty-three, two excited twenty-year-old women opened their shop. Regionally correct to the Golden Isles, where they anticipated their client base, they named it, "Golden Styles Catering Company." Their instincts were right on target, and they were an instant success.

The lovely, historic oceanfront area was becoming home and second home, to many well moneyed, elegant people from around the world. A steady market from St. Simons, Jekyll, and posh Sea Island, kept the phone ringing to set up cocktail parties, family celebrations, and society weddings. Diane began to specialize in baking and creating exquisite desserts, quickly touted in three counties, and Linda saw expansion on the horizon.

Their lives were perfect... or almost perfect. Linda had no interest or time for the pursuit of dating and romance. Diane remained true to form, causing quite a stir in the coastal community and dating up a storm, with her range spanning bronzed island lifeguards, a few sailors, two interns, and a couple of stunning Georgia State Troopers she met when they changed a flat tire for her on Highway Seventeen one day. She fell hard within two months of the shop opening, after a whirlwind turn with a charter boat captain, a strapping, jovial, "calendar hunk", named Pete Bridger, exhibiting a ready wink for the girls, and the best dance floor seduction scam for miles. Diane hated to do it, but she left Linda with the business to move with her new husband to the little harbor town of Darien. It was sad to lose the steady presence such good friends shared, but they were not far apart, and when the separation pinched, they would call each other up, managing lunch occasionally when Diane was able to come to Brunswick.

Business went seasonably sour in winter, so Linda and Diane decided to spend some long overdue time together. Pete had promptly impregnated his bride within weeks of their marriage in late June, then announced she wouldn't be able to go to the Bahamas with him for the winter fishing season because of her condition. The plan had been for them to cruise together in the Caribbean that first year, but intuitively Diane suspected Pete didn't want her along, because he hastily arranged for a group of his buddies to go with him. She was disappointed to miss out on the tropical wonders he had regaled her with during their courtship, but happy to have her friend with her for the coming of her baby, due in March.

By the time Linda and Diane got together, Pete had moved her to an even more distant coastal town than Darien. He wanted the proximity to the offshore fishing St. Marys provided, and it was very near the Florida line. He over-explained to Diane that the primary reason he liked the move was that he knew people there who could book his fleet and help him with important maintenance. He had four boats, each specializing in a marketable fishing mode, and the charter docks in the new place were better than adequate. Diane didn't question. It was Pete's business decision to make.

Linda closed her shop the day after New Years, and put her lonesome butt on the road to St. Marys. She found her friend in a mobile home down a dirt road near the docks, and she was as depressed as a deserted, first time expectant mother could be. Sensing her gloomy mood, Linda hugged her tight and told her she was still as beautiful as ever. They were like children... a jumping and squealing reunion. After they calmed down, Linda made their lunch from the goody basket she'd brought, and they walked around the little town, their hands in each others' pockets, huddling against the penetrating sea fog.

That night, after avoiding heavy conversation all afternoon, they dressed and went to a seafood restaurant popular in the area. It was like the holidays had just begun for the two friends, and Diane, the teetotaler, even sipped a small glass of white wine in honor of the occasion. After their oyster buckets and crab leg remnants were dispatched, and they were sharing a piece of bread pudding, Diane suddenly lowered her head, crying softly.

"I was waiting for you to open up to me, sweetie, what is really going on here?" Linda was braced for the words telling her that Diane's marriage was already foundering. They spilled out in a rush. "Oh, he's not so bad, Linda, I guess I didn't look carefully enough at the whole picture... all the good things I'd wished for, crowded out any bad ones I counted in the middle of the night. Pete just steam-rolled me when we met, and the thought of being a sportsman's wife was so romantic and different from anything I'd ever done, or dreamed of doing. You know, he told me there were women in other harbors, waiting for him to settle on one, when he met me! Kind of like the old car salesman... "If you don't buy it today, it'll be gone tomorrow!""

She was so hungry, so needy for someone she could just talk to, Linda was heartbroken and silently berated herself for not coming sooner. When they got back to the trailer, Linda settled Diane on the couch in her robe and big woolly socks, and made them some kettle tea, a soothing warm milk drink, with honey and nutmeg. It was just about time to get to the heart of their talk, so she braced herself and asked the big question.

"Honey, how do you feel about Pete? I mean, do you think you only believed you were in love with him, or has he damaged your commitment beyond repair with so many disappointments?" It was a basic, easy question to answer, and Linda was surprised and proud of herself for thinking of it. Diane was quite ready to address it, as if she had been waiting for it. "You have asked the question I have to answer before I can go on, Linda. I believe this baby was conceived so Pete could control me, and assure my faithfulness and dependence on him while he went off to play for the winter. He refused to wear protection one night, knowing it was a risky week for me, when he had always agreed before. Linda, I found a letter from the Bahamas he got out of the ship's store mailbox. Hopetown, I think it was. I'm ashamed to say I read it, but I was so insecure about him. Do you understand?"

"Poor Diane", Linda thought. "She is really in a spot." She could almost recite what was coming next... it appeared the big truck had just run over Diane's world! She went on with the rest. "The woman wrote to tell him she would be on Eleuthera Island in mid-January, and the next thing she wrote was the crusher. It was an obscene, unrepeatable description of what she was going to do to him when she got him alone, if you know what I mean. The postmark date was December twelfth, and he took the boat out of here on the eighteenth, first to go tuna fishing off North Carolina's coast, then after two weeks, he was to pick up some friends who were chartering the boat for the rest of the winter in the Bahamas, and then the Caribbean, if they decided to stay longer. He couldn't even be here for our first Christmas together... me, with the baby inside me, to be left here like I was nobody!" She started to cry again, more pitifully than before. Linda was worried that it was too much strain on her, getting so upset, but she knew Diane had to get it said. She continued.

"It was so hard to watch him steam out of the harbor, knowing what he had planned. I haven't been sane since, Linda, and I won't bring up my child in this kind of marriage! I am convinced that Pete is not going to change the way he lives, and he expects me to attach myself and this baby to his ways, and not complain or question. What would you do if you had this choice to make?" With no hesitation, Linda answered her with another question. "How would you like to get back into business with me? I mean, here, or near here? This area is all about expansion, and we could be first out of the gate with our kind of service." Diane was snuffling back her sobs now, and looking intently into her friend's eyes. Linda was encouraged, and went on. "Let's get off the negatives and start a positive plan. You and me, and baby makes three, will haul ourselves up and take the world on together! Let's talk about this for exactly fifteen more minutes, and take the rest of the night to dream our very possible dreams... what about it?" They hugged, went right to bed, and to sleep.

The two rose early, still bubbling from their talk the night before. They went through the newspaper over tea and toast, and within a few minutes were in Linda's suburban with real estate catalogues on their laps. They were only an hour into their search when they found it... right across the road from the harbor in St. Marys. It was an old storefront-style building... likely for hardware or general merchandise... time-roughened wood, crude window glass, and a rotting but fixable porch, but inside, just what they needed. Both of them suggested in unison that a large showroom-plus-cafe was possible out front. There were glass-front cabinets with drawers, twelve foot ceilings, and peeling bead board all over... even a rolling ladder, perfect for storing and retrieving from the tall shelves. Behind the front room was another, nearly as big... with a bathroom, two closets, and a tiny corner room, ideal for an office. Linda was already plotting out the commercial kitchen, chattering away about where the stove, sinks, and work areas could fit.

Diane, overcome with grateful tears, went outside to compose herself and found a staircase on the back side of the building. She went quickly to fetch Linda. What they found was the clincher. At the top of the stairs was the answer to Diane's prayers. It was another peeling, moldy, dirty mess to be true, but all the same, a charming apartment, with a parlor, bedroom, bathroom, and a tiny but adequate kitchen. The two friends walked around speechless, wondering how they could be so lucky, then not wondering at all. Silently, both whispered thankful prayers for such a discovery.

On a creative roll, Diane suggested the little pantry room between the kitchen and bedroom could become the baby's nursery. They only needed to switch the door to the opposite wall, opening into Diane's bedroom, so she could be near at night... and there was even a little window... perfect! The breathless friends signed the five year lease with an option to buy, and went to the courthouse for papers to process for licensing and permitting. After the morning's triumph, Linda sped off to Brunswick to pack her car for several weeks away, and called her best helpers to warn them they would be in charge of the business for a while. Reassurances forthcoming, she went back to her friend with a clear mind and a full heart. It was tough, making a rustic but rough building into a home and business, but they did it, and with minimal contracting... largely alone. Linda had withdrawn a good-sized chunk from her bank account, labeled it expansion capital, and secured a small business loan to handle the large purchases.

It was February before they knew it, but they were so happy and hopeful, all had gone along like silk. Diane was in good health, as was the baby in her belly. It was confirmed to be a March delivery, so it appeared everything was going to happen within the same few days. They were opening for minimal service for Valentine's week only. Diane's talents as a baker would send their message to the area that quality food service had arrived. It was a sellout! At week's end there wasn't so much as one cookie left, the partners had prepared and sold every available morsel, and they were exhausted. They dined out and fell into their beds before eight o'clock, feeling like wonder women. When the shop formally opened, having been dubbed "Golden Styles II", Linda took over all of the physically challenging chores and set Diane up as public relations, marketing, and office manager... anything she could do while sitting down, with the now huge baby she was toting. She had heard nothing from Pete, and mercifully she no longer cared. The shop in Brunswick only needed two pump-up visits from Linda, and soon was successfully on its own, creating a groundswell of support for their new shop down the road.

Sure enough, both grand openings, the business's and Diane's, came within a week of each other. First, Diane was delivered of a roly-poly little baby boy on March third, and next, the shop welcomed its first full-service clientele the same weekend. Linda found and hired the nicest local folks, planning to train them from scratch. Personalities were first and foremost to woo the people in, so then they could deliver their product in style. Diane was well, regaining strength and her figure daily. The little one... named Darius, gained ten ounces in the first three days, and soon was spending more and more time downstairs with his ebullient mom. They girded themselves for Pete's return, with Diane firm in her resolve to continue without him, and Linda vowed to stand beside her, no matter what would come... No matter what would come... No matter what would come.

Diane was a new woman. It seemed years of maturity had been added to her character and resolve. "I have grown in so many ways since you came after New Year's Day, Linda. You gave me back something I missed so much and never realized it... you gave me back myself, and my dignity. I won't ever be able to thank you, or repay you for that." Touched but not forsaking her sense of humor, Linda replied, "I can think of a good way to do it... you can get your butt busy and make us rich!" They embraced warmly, and as they held each other in the middle of the showroom floor, there was an arrival in St. Marys port.

It was the fighting-lady yellow, sassy-handsome, Buddy Davis sport fishing boat named "Georgia Gal," with equally handsome Captain Pete Bridger at the helm in the tower. He was chock full of himself, and totally drunk, waving and whooping at those he recognized on the dock. It was March fourteenth, nineteen sixty-four

# CHAPTER NINETEEN

"Some house," Franciene whispered as she stepped through the foyer and into the great room of the Hoyt's pavilion-style mansion. There was a salt-and-pepper pair of sparkling servants in black and white, waiting to do their bidding when the trio stepped from the car. As their bags were removed to the house, the Hoyts ushered their guest through masonry portals, then into a fan shaped room that looked out over the pool, set so the water at its far edge seemed to blend with the horizon and the Atlantic. The gardens at each end were exquisitely landscaped with coconut palms and tropical trees in full bloom, giving the illusion of a desert oasis. Franciene had grown up in beautiful surroundings... exposed all her life to grace and plenty, but this pretentious splendor eclipsed anything she had known. The couple excused themselves after refreshments were offered, and Mrs. Hoyt pointed out her daughter's suite, where Francie could shower and change into her choices from the closet.

Figuring this was to be a fancy brunch, she went straight for the wall of closets. While she was flipping through as if in a boutique, she was startled by, "What are you looking for in my closet, or is it still MY closet?" When Franciene turned, she was facing a girl very much like herself, across the room by a wall of glass. Both girls were startled silent by their similar appearance. The girl was dressed in a safari guide-style romper, cinched at the waist with a military belt. For footgear, she was wearing high topped turquoise sneakers and white anklets. Her skin was copper, and her mane of hair, sun streaked in shades from rich gold to silvery platinum. Franciene found her voice and started to speak, but she was signaled silent. "Never mind, I know what you're doing here. My parents are handy at bringing home strays that remind them of me. You're a pretty good match. When did you get here? It must have been just now, because when I circled around behind the property, there was no car in the drive. I'm only here for a minute, so don't let me bother you. Just knock yourself out with my things... I'm ages over them!"

The disarmed Franciene wasn't accustomed to being treated in such a flip way, and began to explain. "I didn't want to come here, whatever your name is. My name's Franciene, and I asked your parents to drop me at Lauderdale Airport, but they insisted that I come here first. I was abandoned on the highway, but that's a long story I don't choose to retell. If you want to kick me out of here, you'll probably be doing me a favor." She was angrily twisting her hips from side to side, her fists buried in her tiny waist. The girl began to laugh. "You'll do, Missy. I like your sass. My name's Mandy Hoyt, and I'm right pleased to meet you!" When she put out her hand, Francie, not used to pressing the flesh with a girl, simply touched fingers, and sat down on the love seat at the foot of the bed.

"Listen, I'm sorry I'm in your way. I'm supposed to be cleaning up for brunch... what should I do now...leave the way you came in?" She was getting more nervous, and rose to pace around the room. "Chill, cutie, my reasons for being here are about a half-dozen, high limit, or no limit credit cards, usually stored in the foyer chest to the left of the front door. They're in an eel skin card case in the middle drawer. If you get it for me, I'll be gone like a cool breeze, and you can have the whole place, including my folks, for all I care." Mandy matched the strange girl's stance... now TWO pairs of little fists were firmly planted.

"What's going on with you anyway? Where're you from? What are you runnin' from... and to? I can't see you as my parents' brand new little darling. No, sirree! They'd be trading the devil for the witch, from where I stand. Come on, you know MY last name, and you've even met my parents!" This made Francie giggle, so she relaxed and answered, "My name's Franciene Thornedike, and all

I wanted was a lift to the coast, when your folks stopped. The whole story isn't important... I just want to get back on the road, and away from here." Whatever the truth was, somewhere in between her story and Mandy's interpretation of it, the older girl liked the thorny kid, and figured her a new sidekick, right then and there.

"How about if you help me, and then I'll help you, Francie?" Francie bristled." How did you know what people call me? I said my name is Franciene!" Mandy strutted across the room toward her. "Chill out, little sis," she teased, "Francie suits you better. Anyway, why can't we relax, and try to make some fun out of this?" Francie was of the same mind, but had no intention of giving control to this grainy bitch. All the same, SHE was the stranger here, and needed to gather some boundaries first. She cocked her head and feigned a tiny bit of submission. Mandy picked up on it, winked slyly, and they were on.

"Now! What you need to do is tiptoe out into the foyer, look first to be sure you're alone, and slip the card case out of the top middle drawer of the table in the alcove. Bring it back here to me, and Bingo! We're in the chips! Then I'll give you a lift anywhere you want to go. Maybe we'll stay together for some fun before you split, what do you think... sound good?" It was so good Francie suspected the girl was reading her thoughts. "I like it, Mandy, but we better get going now, 'cause they're gonna' wonder where I am for so long. You watch through the other door, and signal if there's anyone coming this way." Mandy clicked her heels, Gestapo style, and gave a military salute. "Good! I just knew you and I would match up," she whispered, taking her place at the bathroom door.

From where she was she could just barely see her mother and a part of her father in the library, probably checking phone messages and mail. As long as she could see this much of them, it would be safe. Francie stepped lightly into the foyer, looked either way, and then focused on the tromp de le'oile bombe chest by the entrance. In seconds she had the card case and was back in the room. Mandy mock-clapped her hands and mouthed, "Cool! That was' awesome!" She flipped the cards to see if everything was there, expertly accordion-ed them back into place, and whooped under her breath.

"They're all here, and there won't be a limit on them like before, since I'm eighteen now. My folks don't care what I spend as long as it looks legal to them. They are such woosies, they believe if they try to control the money I will start hooking or something! We better get the hell out of here. I'm shakin' this taco stand for good. You can't imagine what a jail this has been."

"Yes I can!" Franciene said to herself. "Oh, yes I can.

The sweaty little runaway would have liked a shower and some fresh clothes. Her shorts and crop top were beginning to look seedy after hours in the heat, so before they left the room she grabbed a few things from Mandy's bureau. She held them up with a questioning look, and got an enthusiastic nod. When they had collected their strewn belongings, they stole out the sliding door to the hedge by the house. One, two, three, and over they went, running headlong toward the yacht basin where Mandy said her car was parked. Franciene let her new friend lead her along... for now.

"We need to be careful for a few minutes more. My parents have the rent-a-cops always looking for a car like mine, and if they see one they are to detain it until they can come check it out. It's like having one of those APB's the cops put out on criminals. You see... last October I ran off with a couple of yachties on a sailboat. We cast off from the yacht basin here, did a bit of island-hopping, then after a month or so came back... but the security force had the guys' names and descriptions, and since the boat wasn't exactly theirs, they lit out." She was laughing so hard she could barely tell her story, but Francie was running along beside her, egging her on, "What happened then?" Mandy, delighted to be onstage, panted out the rest.

"I wasn't suspected of taking the boat or anything, but the cops figured I would likely hear from the boys, and there were some nice things missing off the boat. Hell, they sold everything that wasn't built in, for party money." They had gotten to the myrtle grove where she had hidden the car, so she waited until they got in to wrap up her tale. "Anyway, because there was larceny involved, my dear parents figured they had help finding me, and after I left in early November, they gave the order to the cops to call them as soon as they got a report that matched my car. There shouldn't be any problem for a while, 'cause I had a friend mail a letter I sent to them, from Rhode Island, so they would think I'm way up north and not likely to be dropping by. We just need to get out of the gate before we're noticed. I didn't recognize anybody on duty when I came in, so we may be in luck."

They took a route that would put them at the rear gate to exit where scrutiny would be minimal. Mandy had a silver Saab convertible, a mighty flashy car, but they could scrunch down with hats on, and drive right out. Within minutes the girls were headed North on A1A, the fine-tuned engine whining perfectly. "Well, where to, chickie?" Mandy asked, a wry smile tugging her face toward Francie. "We've got the world ahead of us for the taking. By the time our bills catch up to us, we'll be someplace else!"

The comely co-conspirators high-fived each other, and roared toward adventure. They bought a couple of newspapers, one from each of their origins, to check out any possible mention. They checked the papers while sitting at stop lights, but found nothing about either of them, a bit of a letdown for Francie... now she wondered if anybody had even missed her back home. She thought briefly of 'Tilde, and if Aaron knew about his mom yet. No sense spoiling the day with negatives, she reasoned, and the music was turned to ear splitting decibels while they sped toward route twenty-seven, and Lake Okeechobee. The trip northward was uneventful, with a couple of fuel and pee stops... and their own refueling at a White Castle. Francie predictably griped about fast food, since she had preferred a splashy seafood restaurant they passed a few miles back.

"You won't impress people just because you eat in the fancy joints, honey!" Mandy advised. "Save your bucks for more important things, like your appearance. Believe it, Francie, money does run out!" Francie wasn't even slightly interested in Mandy's advice. She had her own ideas. "How about Tybee Island?" she offered up. "It's a great place to get lost and found at the same time, if you know what I mean. I was there only once when I was about thirteen. Benjie, Aaron and I sailed to Tybee while they were taking care of some real rich Savannah guy's cat-boat. It was so cool! They came over and took me and Aaron's mother to the Back River, and we got a dinghy ride to the pier. Girl, there were clubs and restaurants and music, and the greatest lookin' boys I ever saw. Of course I didn't get to move an arm's length in their direction 'cause Aunt 'Tilde was watching me like a hawk as usual, but I always promised myself I'd go back there someday when I could." The girls found a motel room on the beach about dark.

Tybee is the funky-quaint island retreat twelve miles east of Savannah. Francie was right. It was a cool place. Everywhere there was a unique blending of old and new. The blending covered architecture, politics, amenities... and most important, the people. As in a good stew, a random sprinkling of vintage hippies and young professionals raising children to introduce to Tybee's magic, flavor the year-round population. Tourists, the ever-present scourge-slash-savior, attend every month, even in the dead of winter, coming to see and do what a place like Tybee can be famous for... dropping in, dropping out, and kicking back! It was so easy to become "Tybeefied", after a day or so, with its "Don't Worry-Be Happy", tempo, always beating. Mandy was instantly intrigued.

The two girls were bumping into each other as they showered and changed, anxious to go out among the carousing hoard they had seen as they arrived. "I'm gonna' get a big platter of crab legs, and a draft beer... how 'bout you?" Francie crooned in big shot fashion. "Good God! Are you always hungry?" Her pal teased. "I was thinking more about a beach walk to check out the night life the desk clerk told us about. There's supposed to be a pier, and a bunch of clubs down a half a mile or so. Let's do that first and we might get our dinner bought for us! Get the picture?"

Francie didn't want to appear unworldly, so she perked up at the idea, and the two, in Mandy's bright and clingy slip dresses and espadrilles, walked arm in arm across the pool deck and down to the beach. It was low tide, and there were numerous groups and couples walking either way, enjoying the twilight, and the sweet-salty, soft, northerly breeze blowing up the beach. The lights ahead were seductive... full of brilliant color and movement... and promise.

Francie and Mandy sashayed casually toward the show, but were eying everyone they passed, seeking possibilities among the strangers. Francie was absorbed in the buzz of activity so long denied her, along with the familiar comfort of sand and sea.

She had a fantasy working. It was mixed up... disjointed, but clear purpose waited on the edge. The delusional girl was sure if she had the chance to get away for good, she could top Mandy's act and have the life she knew was waiting for her. This was just a taste and she wanted much more. Freedom and the money to keep it, had always been Franciene's hidden obsession. The credit card would let daddy catch up with her once she began to use it. He would be sure to cancel it... reasoning she would call or come home when her pockets were wrong side out.

After years of butting heads with her bull-headed father, Franciene knew what his game would be as soon as he became more angry than afraid for her. The Hartsells would have called him worrying after Clifford by now. God! What would he be conjuring up? Statutory rape, kidnapping, crossing state lines with a minor, since she was four months from eighteen. He would be like a raging black bear, like the ones in the movies, or the monster she had seen in Godzilla! She couldn't help but giggle at the mental picture of the monster with her daddy's face, beating his chest... a big cigar in its teeth. Clifford! What if the gators didn't eat him, and he was found with his car? She couldn't worry about the prospect. The car was covered with that green swamp slime and a good-sized deposit of mud by now, it being so heavy. She had to believe her tracks were covered. No, it was worry for nothing, and she broke the thoughts off, back to here and now.

The two most striking females on the beach had walked into a clutch of people of all ages and stages of dress, the last of twilight's glow replaced by neon and mercury vapor. Closing in on a stretch of sand by the pier, they were surprised to find it was jumping for a Sunday evening. There was a good reason for the party. Graduation time had harkened the southern tradition of the "house party" and this island was a prime spot for land-locked young people... those new arrivals, from urban jungles like Atlanta... hot for a spring-break scene.

Since Tybee was easier to access and more wallet-friendly than Daytona and Lauderdale, it worked perfectly, as youth, booze, and banality came together. The place that ultimately beckoned the girls was a colorful, conch-house-style restaurant and bar. It was perfect! The little dive was pumping reggae... literally bouncing off the sand to the syncopation of the dancers on the deck. The two girls were thrilled! They clasped hands and trudged through the deep, dry sand, from the beach to the deck. "This is what I've been seeing in my dreams, Mandy," Francie breathed. They were lifted up and swept into the club by the sweet, spicy aroma of conch fritters frying, and pungent etoufee, making their tummies gurgle.

The place was rocking, and the girls held tight to each other as a small empty table popped up in the room. They sat down, pretending a bored serenity, and ordered banana daiquiris, a choice dredged up from some tacky movie. Looking around as their eyes allowed, they congratulated themselves with wrinkled noses and wriggling shoulders... girl talk for, "Ain't we something NOW?" Their drinks en route, the waitress was intercepted and relieved of them by two sun burnished studs who sat them... and themselves, down at the table. "We couldn't believe our eyes when you two walked in here!" The tall one shouted, as they presented the frozen cocktails with flourishes and flashing smiles.

"I'm Alex Renfro, and this is my buddy, Troy Bender. Just say the word, and we'll split. But c'mon," and he gestured with widespread arms, "What's not to like... right? You two didn't come out tonight lookin' that good for each other, 'least I hope not!" The girls affected startled poses, but jabbed each other with their elbows, at the attention they'd scored. Mandy motioned to the restroom, as they nodded their need to get out of the crowded seats. The two lads, well versed in feminine customs, graciously made way. They knew these two probably didn't need to pee... they just wanted to pow-wow.

As soon as the door closed behind them, Mandy wheeled on the younger girl. "Too hot! They're just too damn hot, Francie! Those guys are predatory! Something isn't right here, and you should know it! Why don't they have girls locked on their arms already, if they are as good as they look? They could be married with children, or axe

murderers, or something! I don't trust this whole thing!" Francie
had to convince her to the contrary.

"Look at us, Mandy," she argued. "We don't have dates, and
they could think the same about us! Let's have some fun tonight... I
don't know about you, but I'm way overdue for a good time." Mandy
relented, and admitted that their suitors were mighty cute. They
turned to the mirror, patted away imaginary problems, and rejoined
the table. A marathon round of bar-hopping and beach trotting
ensued!

Alex and Troy were staying in a motel behind "Sandy Paris"...
the club where they met, on the site where the Tybrisa Hotel presided during the Art Deco twenties and thirties. Grand events...
internationally regarded figures in residence for weddings and holiday parties ruled the years in her prime, but that changed forever,
when "progress" razed the edifice decades ago. The gothic structure
had to make way for practical and more storm-proof accommodations building codes dictated, with hurricanes a sure thing to come,
given the odds on the coast. It might be said, so much grace and
charm of seaside experience was gone, but not forgotten, with the
old town fathers and mothers holding fast to many stories and mem-
orabilia they cherished, making the grand old lady forever real to
them. Now, young revelers party on, never knowing they are merely
pretenders to the classy scene of old.

Many flashy cocktails and no dinner later, the darkened dunes
beckoned for a time, as inevitably the boys and girls paired off
for the real reason the young men were there. When Franciene
yelled her objections to being pressured to strip for a dip, with, "I
don't know you, boy... I don't know if I want to know you better, if
that's what you're about! You aren't seein' me nekkid without even
knowin' me!" Somewhere, her daddy was proud. She felt it cross
her mind for a second, and continued slapping the groping hands
from her person. Mandy and Alex, on their sea oats couch, were
convulsed with giggles listening to the sass dealt by a very drunk,
but in charge Miss Franciene. "She's a sketch, she is!" Alex whispered. "I'm glad you're more agreeable, Honey," he murmured in
her ear, a deft right hand at work under her skirt. Mandy was sort

of enjoying what he was doing, and returned his statement with a kiss, and a sexy squeeze in return, but it was not to go any further.

"This isn't going anywhere tonight, I'm afraid, Alex. It's too fast, and I'll bet you don't have protection, do you?" Her wish was his command, damn him. "As a matter of fact I do." Alex whispered triumphantly, hugging her closer. Now What?! She took a more logical tack. "We need to go somewhere else then... I don''t rightly care for sand in my britches. Let's wait 'til tomorrow night to take this to the top. We can make plans tomorrow, when we're better able to. I want to be with you a little longer, and in the daylight... you know, sane and sober... okay?" Alex had seen this coming.

This chick was having some teasing sport with him! No sex was about to happen, and she was in charge! He silently admitted she was good at the game, considering he was, by now, reduced to half-staff in defeat. He wearily got to his knees. "No problem, my sweet... we'll just see this done tomorrow night." He did not mean it, any more than she did, and was already dismissing her as a conquest. His whirling head was railing at his confused crotch. "What do these bitches think is going on anyway? They get all done up, smelling like the Garden of Eden, allow themselves to be led along, diddled with and primed up, then they drop the garage door on the hood of the car... Kerplunk!

Mandy adjusted her clothes, slapped away most of the sticky sand and grass, and started walking back to the motel alone... figuring not to disturb the other two, who had settled down after Francie's outburst and were making out peacefully. "Mandy! Wait!" It was Franciene, standing now, waving to her through the blowing grasses. She waited for the girl to run to her, breathing in little gulps. "Don't go! You stay with us. We'll quit this stuff if you stay. I had an idea, and I want you to listen to Troy. He's going to help!" The wind had clocked around and was getting up out of the south, sending sand down the beach in silvery sprays as they walked together. "What is it? What could he help US with?" she asked. Francie led her to the dune, and beckoned Troy.

"There's a Hobie-cat tied down in the dune, and it looks like it's been there a while. I looked around and saw no houses near to it, and nobody can see it from the motels, but," she continued quickly, "It's fully rigged, and ready to sail away. This wind will take us to South Carolina in a snap. We could be on Squires Island and back by daylight if we cast off within the hour." Mandy looked at her watch and blinked. "It's one-thirty, Sweet pea, why in holy hell would you want to sail to South Carolina in the dark?" Francie and Troy locked arms, and when Mandy finished her question, it was Troy's turn.

"I'm a documented world-class sailor, Mandy-girl, and I know what a kick this would be. The tide is flooding, so we'll have plenty of water over the bar out there, and Francie says she needs to get something important from her house without her daddy knowing about it. I know that boat, it's just like one we used to have on Longboat Key when I was a kid. Come on, and let's forget my friend, he's too chicken anyway... we'll take a trip by the moon's light, what do you think?" He had been into something... probably cocaine, Mandy deduced, and had shared with Francie, or they wouldn't be so wacky-impulsive. "I think you're both crazy, that's what I think. Francie, can I speak to you over there?" She led the bouncy girl to a spot out of earshot. "What's going on here? What do you need to get from Squires Island we can't get any way other than a pitch dark crossing of that black water? I can barely see the lights over there, it looks so far. Why is he so anxious to take us out on that boat...for what?"

"I'll tell you, but don't get mad. I told him I have a box hidden in my room with an ounce of pot, and a quarter ounce of hashish an old friend asked me to hold for him. We couldn't get to the Island without everybody knowing, since we have to leave from Frenchport, and I'd be busted so bad! That stash is enough reason for Troy to drag that boat into the water right this minute, but I have a secret reason for getting over there." She moved close to Mandy's ear in case she could be heard over the wind. "The safe in my daddy's study holds probably twenty thousand dollars in cash, and some stocks in my name that are worth a couple of hundred thousand dollars or more. He doesn't know that I memorized the combination from watching over his shoulder, and since I was the only other person ever in the room with him when he opened the safe, he would figure a professional thief opened it."

"My daddy would never suspect me, since I won't be seen in Frenchport before the theft, get it? After this trip, later, I show up, like, in a few days... go over to see my daddy, and ask for forgiveness for going off like I did this week. And, if he's discovered the robbery, he will have replaced the cash, as well as called to replace the stock certificates, just like it never happened." Mandy's head was spinning with Francie's flip details, but she listened. The little conniver was in her glory as she went on. "It gets better and better. See, since the theft happens before anyone hears from me, when I go home I can switch the old certificates we snatch tonight for the new ones daddy puts in their place, then we can go on our way, with no one the wiser. Just think, Mandy, the cash alone is reason to do it….we can travel anywhere with no credit card record….REAL Freedom!"

She was licking her lips as if there was hot fudge all over them as she went on and on. "All he will believe is that the certificates are the good ones he put back, and he won't think about them again, until after I cash them out! It is so cool, don't you see? He won't know about my selling the stock, since I can't do it until I turn eighteen. We'll put them in a safety deposit box somewhere, and when we want to fly to Australia or someplace, leaving here for good, it'll be too late for my dear daddy to do anything." Her eyes sparkled in the lights with manic anticipation. "His copies will be worthless, don't you get it? And he'll never know what happened until we're long gone." Mandy was gape-faced when Francie finished. She had truly underestimated this one. Her wild plan could work! She must have spent her life listening to every word her daddy had to say about his finances, with such as this coming forth in such a torrent.

# CHAPTER TWENTY

One hour from Frenchport, and Linda had barely noticed the miles as they flew, along with Georgia's rural landscape. Since it was years since she had rerun those life-changing times, she was challenged to remember the details she used to think would never leave her. Perhaps now that her little Willie was back in the forefront, she was viewing her life with new eyes, possibly her son's, and the twists and hitches would need to be made fresh and simple to follow if she was asked to tell the story. She pulled off to fuel up and get a soft drink, and as she passed the telephone booth outside the ladies' room, she was drawn to it, with a furtive wish someone was out there she could call and talk to. It was sad to acknowledge that there was no one... anywhere. Her times of pain and passion were hers alone. She got back on the road with the memories continuing.

## MARCH OF 1964... LINDA'S MEMORIES CONTINUE

St. Marys Harbor burst into action with the arrival of Georgia Gal, and in minutes everyone who had an interest in the boat's arrival was buzzing about. Linda was upstairs with Darrie after Diane had asked her to keep the baby away from the docks, while she went to the pub to wait for Pete. Linda gave him his scheduled bottle, delighting in the way he devoured it like a piglet, his pudgy little fists rotating under his chin with rapt satisfaction. She put him down only a moment before there was a sharp knock on the door glass. A toast-brown, handsome face filled the doorway when she opened it. She suspected he was a Georgia Gal mate right off.

"Hello Miss, I hate to disturb you, but we just rolled in, and from the look of things down there, Pete and his missus are going to need some privacy. Truth be known, they better get out of that pub pretty quick, before they get thrown out! I'm afraid one of 'em's gonna' take a beer bottle to the other's noggin' if we don't pull 'em apart." He was glancing around the room as he talked, remarking, "Look's like old Pete's got a nice surprise waitin' up here for him, less'un that's yours!" He clumsily tiptoed to the bassinet, cocking his head left and right to the cadence of Darrie's cooing. Linda instinctively moved herself between him and the baby, and blurted, "I'm Linda Parrish, Diane's friend and partner. Who are you, and what did you mean about her and Pete? Did you say they're arguing already?"

He looked down with incredible shyness taking over, managed to raise his eyes to hers and say, "I'm Dan Fuller, ma'am." He ambled toward her, the salt and sweat Linda could see, blending with days old fish smells and alcohol, causing a pungent wave to roll through the tidy room. She ushered him into the kitchen away from the baby, and bade him sit. He exhaled and went on. "We been out there for a month or more, and I beg your pardon if I'm skanked up for now, but I swear, we got to do somethin' about those two, an' quick!" Linda gathered the baby's poncho and diaper bag, and her jacket in a frenzy of fear, while Dan was step for step behind her, explaining.

"See? When we got here, Pete shot straight for the pub...said somethin' about that bein' where he'd left her, and that she knew damn well to be there when he come back. I wanted to get cleaned up right off, but he said a scant few words to his wife, then he shot back to me at the bar and told me to come up here and fetch his boy down to him. I think it would be better if you and the baby got out of here and let them come up to settle what's got 'em so riled up, before you and that little one get in the mix."

Linda had herself and Darrie dressed for outdoors by then, and nodded to Dan, "Oh God...Yes! But first I have to see if Diane needs me! Are they still in the bar? Let's go" They caught up with Pete and Diane halfway down the dock toward the boat, and Linda's sense of foreboding caused a sudden chill when she saw Pete Bridger's face. He was a thunderhead of temper and volcanic rage, as he turned and rushed toward a cowering Linda and her tightly clutched bundle. Diane was screaming at Linda to run, but the big man was on her in a moment, snatching the child from her before she could turn away.

"Diane!" He yelled to his now hysterical wife, "You come on with me, up to your little playhouse! I intend to find out what, and more important, WHO is starting up this shit with us! You ain't taking my son away from me! No Sir!" He headed up the stairs, as Diane passed by Linda, following the enraged ape, who was mashing her baby's tiny face up against his sweaty chest. "Diane, don't go up there!" Linda begged, "He's a maniac, and you can't get Darrie from him, any way you try! He'll hurt you, honey, not Darrie, I swear! Dan! Tell her not to go!"

Dan was half-running with them to the stairs, warning breathlessly, "I better go with him, Diane, not you. I won't let him hurt that baby, I swear, and I might get him to settle down some. He's always been a mean drunk, long as I've known him, but I never seen him hurt anyone, man or beast, and sure 'nuff, not a child! You stay down here 'til I call you to come."

He took the steps two at the time, and disappeared into the apartment. There was a loud crash, then another, and Dan leaned out to motion Diane and Linda upstairs. "I laid him out good, and while I regret he smashed the coffee table and a chair, he's calm now, and he had put the baby down before he hit the floor. Y'all come on up!" They dashed inside, and Diane scooped her little one up close in her arms. Linda led her out to the porch so Dan could deal with a now reviving Pete. The two women kept their backs to the room, afraid to look at him, until he and Dan stood calmly together at the door.

Pete started to whimper and beg. "I'm sorry, baby, I was crazy drunk and jealous when you told me you want a divorce, right off the bat." He was crying pitifully, and holding his arms out for them. "Please let me hold him just for a minute... I haven't even looked in his little eyes yet. I'll give him right back, and then I'll leave until I sober up and can talk better. Is that too much to ask? I swear you don't have to be afraid of me. Dan here just popped the liquor and the meanness right out of me, an' that's a fact!"

Linda didn't want her to do it, but Diane felt easier seeing Pete so penitent and weak. So, the kind girl she was, she walked to him and let him take Darrie in his arms. He turned to go inside, and Dan and Diane changed places, so she could stay close to them. Dan joined Linda, awkwardly patting her shoulder, as the sad little family huddled in the scattered living room. Linda was not handling it well, and with her foreboding raging inside, she whispered, "He's going to hurt them, I just know it! Why is he so furious? Did he say anything to you?" Dan turned Linda to face the water, and he was watching inside over her shoulder, ready to spring to action.

"He thinks she has another man, Linda. It's the only thing a red-neck boy like Pete Bridger can believe, to justify losin' his woman's favor. He said when he tried to kiss her, she turned her head and shook him off, and that was all it took, him bein' such a stud like he is, to have a woman deny him. He figures it this way, in his rock-hard head... he was out there tryin' to make a livin', and she was back here trottin' around with some man. There ain't any such, is there?" He was squinting in the window, as he watched them move to the sofa, seeing Pete sit her down with her baby, as he rattled on non-stop, pleading his case to her, while Linda vehemently replied.

"NO! Of COURSE NOT! That girl just gave birth on the third of this month, for God's sake! What kind of affair could she have been having? She found out about HIS woman in the Bahamas, and put it together then, that Pete will never change. You know that it's true, too... don't you? She and I set about making it possible for her to be on her own, running our business and living quietly here, she and Darrie, and that's all there is to tell. She's simply OVER him, and I would be too!" Dan listened, nodded, and continued anxiously watching Pete as his unruly body language began to tell Dan to act. He let go of Linda's shoulder and was taking his first step to the door when everything fell apart.

One shot! Then a shriek, and a scream, then the second shot, barely two seconds behind the first. The shriek was Diane's, the scream was Linda's, reacting to the first shot, and Dan nearly ripped the door off the hinges in time to see Pete pull the trigger of the pistol he was near to swallowing, the third shot sending his blood and brains to the walls and floor as he fell over his dying wife, and their blankly staring infant son.

It could not be real! Linda stood stupidly in the door... her jaw dropped, her mouth gaping. She was spasmodically reaching toward the mess, gesturing for help, or for it to go away... Please, God, make it GO AWAY! Dan turned her back out to the porch, breathing in gasps himself, hoping to spare her the visage he could not himself take in. "Oh, My Dear God Almighty"... he kept saying softly, tears coursing his ruddy cheeks. "This just didn't happen... it ain't true, honey, honest to God it didn't happen!"

At that, Linda jerked to life, and broke from him, back toward the room. "We've got to get help," she yelled, over and over, "Call 911! Call 911! The hospital is only five minutes from here by chopper! DAN! She clutched at him, crying, "Please, Dan, call them!" The poor rough-edged man had to tell her as gently and convincingly as he could, without letting her see why he knew, that they had all died the second the shots were fired into them, all three. The poor little family, with the tick of seconds, ceased to exist... lost to insane stupidity! He knew Pete's expertise with firearms after watching him painlessly dispatch many fish that would have died slowly otherwise, and had to reconcile facing this horror as so.

He sat her in a rocking chair, telling her softly, "Now! You just stay here, and be real still, while ole' Dan goes and covers 'em up and calls the police. I won't leave you alone... I'll never do that, I promise. You're too sweet and innocent to have to bear this much bad without ole Dan holdin' you up." He went inside and lowered the shades before he did his chores, to be sure she wouldn't look again, and see what he knew he would see in his dreams for the rest of his life. She had seen enough, and would be haunted the same forever.

Linda still saw it, even now, as she drove toward Frenchport, but it was a part of who she was, and now she could finally live with it. Dan had been her rock and all she could have hoped for, during the

darkest time she would know. It was enough remembering for now…
it was all she could bear.

Back to NOW, and she had arrived… Frenchport was just ahead.
She parked near the marina restaurant and locked her bag in the
car, knowing nothing of what she would find. It was just past three
o'clock. She saw the tables and the bar a little further along the walk,
so she gratefully headed toward a seat. A young girl, probably nineteen or so, came to her with a glass of ice water and a menu.

"Hi there' ma'am! We haven't seen you around here before, have
we? My name's Cissy, and I'm lookin' after the place while Ruby
runs some errands. You look like you could do with a beer, or somethin'. What'll it be?" Linda wanted nothing more than to sit, while
thinking of and doing nothing. There was so much ahead of her she
could not predict, and while her intention to be available for her
son's protection from his father, as she had always vowed, was of
primary importance, she was strangely pulled away from that venue
by another reason, one she couldn't touch on. Linda answered Cissy
by ordering an iced tea, and after she was gone, the weary woman's
head dropped to her forearms so she could be alone with herself,
hoping God would tell her what to do, and how it would come out.

## TYBEE ISLAND'S BEACH - VERY LATE AT NIGHT…

Troy called out from behind the boat, reminding the girls that time
and tide were important, and he began checking the boat's lines and
sails, still bagged up from last winter's storage. Mandy and Francie
went to their room for sailing clothes, purchased a six pack of beer
and drinking water, and went to stash the car in a safe place. While
they were gone, Troy horsed the boat to water's edge, ready to go.
The girls were quickly back, so Troy helped them up to the trampo-
line, and shoved out into deeper water. He had brought a spotlight
for checking overhead into the sails and shrouds when they were
underway. Once beyond the breakers, Troy unfurled the ginny and
hoisted the main, expertly tacking to wind. The eager little boat

soon snapped to, and they were off toward Franciene's Island home. Mandy popped them each a beer, and they began to sing, first in a whisper, then as loud as they could, to the silvery, starlit trail the moon was laying for them.

## FRENCHPORT HOSPITAL HAS AN IMPATIENT PATIENT

Massey's dinner tray was brought to his room on Sunday evening, and the nurse found him sitting up. He lifted the cover over the plate to check the evening's fare, but soon sent the whole apparatus screeching to the foot of the bed with a well-placed foot. "DAMN it! I want to go home!" he boomed. The nurse returned immediately after hearing the clatter. "Mr. Thornedike, what in the world is it?" She took the tray away, straightened his bed from all the thrashing, and stood near the foot, with her hands clasped in front of her. "I know, you're beginning to feel better, with all the medication and rest you've been getting, and the hospital is closing in on your big self, am I near to the truth?" She wasn't just near, she was dead on the money. Massey was still quite agitated, and he meant to be regarded.

"I'm not talkin' to anybody who ain't about to send me home, you hear? I got a daughter missin'... MISSING! Do you know what it's like to have your own precious little girl somewhere out there, bein' bothered with by who the hell knows? Add to that misery, one of my dearest old friends, more like a member of my family on Squires, just died, and the service is tomorrow! The sweet old thing is being laid to rest without me to stand over her. I just ain't havin' it! If I can lay my ass in this bed and raise hell, I should be well enough to sit this same ass in a pew, while people say nice things about Aunt 'Tilde." The nurse listened on, as patiently as she could. "Add another little thing to chew on here! I probably paid for a whole floor in this dog and cat clinic! If I get real mad 'cause you won't let me go, and at the same time something bad comes to my little daughter because I'm stuck here, there's going to be hell to pay! Just let me go home until the service is over, and my girl's found... that's all I ask, and I'll come back and let the doctors blow me up with their balloons all they want. That's my speech. Now... what 'you got to say?"

It was fortunate that Nurse Bell was on duty, when Massey blew his top. The truth was, ever since he had been admitted she had taken a unique interest in him, and had swapped shifts to be able to tend him most of every day. She sternly shushed him up as one would a noisy child, and excused herself to get him a sedative, since even though he had been upgraded to satisfactory condition, the level of stress he was conjuring could reverse him. She added the medication to his I.V., and pulled a chair up to Massey's more approachable side. "You know, you're right! I think you should be able to do all the things you want to do, and you give a strong argument for your side. The other side, sir, is that you need to get yourself well before you can be any good to anyone. You are still in danger of a serious attack."

She had to be careful not to turn him off. It would not serve to use the word, "NO", to men like Massey Thornedike...they needed to retain control of their lives, and those they are responsible for. The kind of power he was losing as he lay in bed was as important to him as food and water, and sleep at night. He felt castrated by the sterile, restrictive, passive conditions he was forced by his own body to endure, and was unable to look at her as they talked... he just stared at the ceiling, his eyes bright with fought back tears.

Mattie's untapped power, the spiritual sight she was using to deal with the frustrated man, was beginning to frustrate HER in a strange way. She was hopeful she could get him to agree with her, but it wasn't enough... he needed a compromise. "I have a thought, Massey," It was the first time she had used his given name, and it affected him positively. "What if I was to go to your home after my shift? I have a friend who will take me to Squires Island in his boat, and I can go to your house, call you from there, and the duty nurse here can give you the phone, so you can speak with anyone you want to speak to. "The lady named Carrie works for you, doesn't she?" He nodded sullenly. "She'll help with your concerns about the funeral, and I'll do what I can to find out about the search for your little girl."

She was bolstered by the fact that he had not yet stopped her, and went on. "You know, young people can be rebellious, no matter how much love and care parents give them throughout their lives. I'll bet she's just taking a break, your daughter. Didn't you say she is graduating this week? Lord! That age, they do all kinds of things. Why, I'll bet you can remember, not so long ago, when you were less than sensible about how you conducted yourself, and you turned out fine. I'd be willing to bet she's got your good heart, no matter what she does, doesn't she?" Massey nodded and wiped fresh, large tears at the thought of his baby girl's little heart beating someplace where he couldn't get to her.

Fearing he would think she was trying too hard, Mattie wrapped up their talk with one last heavy point. "And there's this... if you were able to ask her, I am sure your departed friend would box your ears for threatening your condition with the irrational request to leave this safe place of healing, to go over to her funeral. Don't answer that the way you want to... think about what you will say, and you'll tell me I'm right." She was sitting close to him with such truth in her lovely eyes, he took the hand she offered. His big shoulders relaxed a little, and as they looked deep into a shared place called trust, stubborn old Massey Thornedike was quiet, and he slowly nodded his tousled head. "Get me a pencil and paper, and I'll write the name and phone number of the man who can take you to my house when you get off the boat," he finally said, his eyes pleading for her help.

## TOBY'S ARRIVAL ON SQUIRES ISLAND

Toby craned his neck to see if Will was waiting as soon as the dock came into view. Finally he saw him, running toward the ramp as they coasted to a stop at the floating dock. Toby helped a few folks off, while a glowing Will transferred their bags, waiting for a proper greeting, until they hugged like brothers and headed toward the Rover.

"Wait 'till you see the house, Toby," he exclaimed proudly, "It's like an old plantation house, only it's done over... you know, all the conveniences like air conditioning and indoor plumbing and such. OH! I left that purple plant in the car on purpose instead of giving it to Carrie, so she'll think it's from you. Is that okay? I figured it would be a good ice breaker for you two. She was kind of funny when I told her I had a friend coming over today. I guess she's got so much on her now, what with the funeral, and that Aaron guy coming back early this morning. It was his mother who died. They've all been here since they were born, and it's kind of a private time, you know what I mean."

Having brought all of that forth seemingly without taking a breath, the boy became serious, and somewhat incredulous, as he continued. "But... Toby, she loves me almost like she's known me all MY life too! We haven't gotten deep into all the spiritual stuff yet, because she's had no time... even to sit down. Now that you're here, I bet she'll want you to know what it's all about too. I swear to God, man, when you hear what's happening, and what it feels like... I don't know how to begin." After another sobering pause, Will offered, "Aaron, the son, came off kind'a hostile when he came to the dock for me, but I pretended not to notice, and we got along after that." Toby listened and nodded as Will jabbered on, but he wasn't buying the Voodoo part, and he made a mental note to watch Aaron's attitude at work.

The Rover pulled into a circular oyster shell drive lined with enormous azaleas and hydrangeas, obviously decades old. They idled passed a trail leading to a couple of little rough wood cottages, one with three or four old vehicles in various stages of rust and ruin parked around it. When the big house came into view, Toby allowed to Will he was right, it was impressive. It truly was quite a house... built around the turn of the century from oak and rich heart pine, and looked as if it had never been painted, glowing with the silvery patina of driftwood. The shutters on the tall plantation windows were painted a rich black green, and the tin roof dripped a patina of rusty-red and silver-gray down its' pitch, like black cherries and cream. Porches wrapped around both floors, from front to back, and there was a gingerbread-frosted cupola large enough for a penthouse suite, sitting on top of the whole thing.

Toby was turning in circles, taking in the impressive lawn vistas and gardens, when Will called from the back porch. Toby thought to himself that Will seemed at ease here... in place, somehow, as he approached the porch, feeling strangely here, more like the younger one. In the kitchen the boy was pouring tea into two ice filled glasses. "I figured you might be thirsty. This is the drink of the day over here in Gullah Land." Will was loving it... comfortably consumed by the place where they stood. So, so strange it all was. Carrie hadn't appeared, so the pair of friends took their tea and hunted a place to talk. As they sat down in the study, both felt a force between and around them, but neither let on. After sharing a laugh at good ol' Neville Shirley's expense, Will stiffened when Toby mentioned his mother's hometown.

Back up! Detour! Toby put it off a moment, adding instead a few more highway tales, again lightening their mood. Will was genuinely amused with his stories of the road, and Toby sighed, aware they were at the place where he needed only to say, "I met your Mom, Will, and she's great!" But he stopped when he caught Will fidgeting nervously. "Let's take a closer look at the books and art in this fine old room, how about it?" Toby offered, deftly breaking the tension. Will stood stiffly and went to the library shelves, pretending to peruse book titles. A voice as strange as he had ever heard came at Toby like a laser.

"You've seen my Mother, haven't you?"

Before the startled man could reply, Will turned to face him. Toby hardly recognized the once fresh faced, now darkening person standing before him. The boy was decidedly younger, like he was standing on the knoll two years ago when they first met. His demeanor was the hook... a quaking, caved-in figure had replaced the stalwart, almost cocky young man on the dock in Frenchport a few hours earlier. Poor Toby wanted to cross the room and shake him back to himself. Instead, he could only stammer. "Will! Will, son... are you HERE? What is happening to you? What are you seeing?" The boy stood motionless, all but his eyes, which were darting around, trying to focus on what he was being shown in the room behind. Toby stiffened, wanting to help him, but unable.

Will's hollow eyes began to glow, and he spoke again, but this time it was different, as if he was speaking from another place. Hearing the voice terrified Toby, syllables came at him like darts. It was too familiar.

"He isn't going to have you, my darling, I won't let him take you, no matter what I have to do. You will not be brought up by him, to learn that you have control over someone just because they love you and would do anything for you. He has no other kind of power, only what he has here, in this place. We will go... now, and never return. He made a big mistake bringing you here, Will. He tricked us and stole you from me. I know now I will never take anything from him, no matter how much I will always feel. You are a Parrish, Will, don't ever forget that!" While the voice continued, Will unconsciously unbuttoned the flap on his shirt pocket. The bracelet found his fingers and he pulled it out and looked it over, back and front. A light floral chasing was on the top side, but underneath, two sets of initials. In script, LSP, and with an infinity symbol centered, and then in beaded block... WILLIE T!

His voice! It was HER voice! Toby shook his head to better hear it. He couldn't deny the truth. He was too afraid to speak, too enchanted to move. It was Will who made the first effort. He went to stand beneath a large painting of Massey Thornedike behind the desk, switched on the brass lamp over the frame, details popping out in the light. The subject of the portrait was posed in full shooting sportsman's garb, with a majestic golden retriever looking up at his face. An ornately chased, custom made over and under lay across his knee, the day's kill of summer duck at his feet. Then, at the bottom of the painting, in his dangling, big right hand, was a large, yellowed ivory handled buck knife, its' blade exposed and ready for dressing the birds. He was so wonderfully presented, it was hard to look elsewhere on the canvas, for all there was to admire. Toby reluctantly looked back up at that face, those eyes, and even with the fedora covering his forehead, it was indisputably the man in the photograph he had wanted Will to identify.

It was no longer a mystery. Toby went over to the boy and stood looking at him. All of it came together...the knife, and the photo in

Will's box, and now, up on the wall in this room, was the reason for everything.

"Massey Thornedike is Will's father!" Toby whispered. "That is why we are here!"

Renewed Gumption for what may Come…

At Ruby's table in Frenchport, Linda wasn't sure whether she had been asleep or in a haze of deep thought when she raised her head from her crossed arms. There was a tall glass of tea and a note in front of her, so she took a long drink and began to read. "I had to leave, but I fixed your tea first. Ruby will be back in a minute or two, so you wait here and she can help with whatever you need. You take care now." It was signed simply, "Cissy". Her eyes filled to brimming at the sweet concern of a stranger. She heartened a little, thinking her mission might come to good, if others were as kind. Whatever, the moment helped her to relax… but only for a moment. Ruby returned, and Linda's interrogation got underway for real.

"Howdy! My name's Ruby!" She announced herself with the same pride and relish Linda had regarded while watching Minnie Pearl on the Grand Old Opry with her parents way back when. Ruby went on without taking much of a breath… "I was just now told by Cissy that there was a real pretty lady needin' my help. What's your name, honey, and what can ol' Ruby do for you?" This lady has a curiosity bordering on nosiness, Linda decided. Hoping for the same compassion she had gotten from Cissy, she spoke her piece.

"I'm Linda Sue Parrish, from Waycross, Georgia. I need to be taken to Squires Island this afternoon if possible, and want to arrange for a ride to a home when I get there. Can you help me? Is that enough information to get it done?" It was enough for what she wanted to do… not enough to satisfy Ruby! She was drooling to ask more, but Linda's reserve stopped her, sending "Leave me be," in signals as plain as tom-toms in the jungle, so she relented. "I can take care of those little things for you right now! The captain is due back here in a few minutes so he can take you over there at four. There's a nice old man who lives near to the dock who can meet you, and for five bucks he'll take you most anywhere, except where you're not welcome, then he'll pick you up and meet the next boat for another five dollars. That includes carrying your things, an umbrella if it's raining, and a free tour of the island thrown in. There's an important funeral service happenin' tomorrow, so it might be a little touchy, but business is business I suppose. I'll call him right off. Where did you say you're goin' to?"

Linda was on her guard... there was no reason to tip anyone off, so she simply ignored the question. Ruby, being Ruby, repeated it, so Linda had to shut her down with, "I'd rather not say, if you don't mind." The woman minded, but let it pass. Linda was glad to change the subject by asking,

"Do you have a ladies' room I could use? I'd like to wash my face." Ruby, rebounding from her nose being knocked out of joint, enthusiastically directed her. Linda went in and laughed out loud. It could have been Lucy and Ricky Ricardo's lavatory. Sassy pink and maroon ceramic tile, pink dotted Swiss, crisscross window treatments, and a shower curtain with grazing flamingos on parade. The tacky humor was a welcome change, and she dispatched her cosmetic duties, feeling renewed and ready for whatever was to be. Outside she was quickly met by Ruby, with good news. "The captain knows all about you, and I have your ride meetin' you at five o'clock, Miss... Parrish was it? I swear, my short-term memory is just plain old gone! Did you fail to tell me whose house Jasper is takin' you to, or did I forget that too?" Lord, love this woman for trying... Linda said to herself.

If it would help her even one whit, to be told what she so rabidly sought, after all she had done to help, Linda would have considered telling her. But no, nothing would be gained by the news that it was Massey's house that was her quest. She also felt no obligation to tell her that this was her second visit to the island, the first being when Willie was a toddler, and... No! Not now, not when she was starting to feel stronger. Her recollections couldn't turn sour now, when so much depended on fortitude. She gathered up her resolve and let the old memories form in her mind.

# CHAPTER TWENTY-ONE

*Renewed Memories Return from 1964*

There was a miracle, and great joy following the black hole of shock and grief that consumed Linda's life on March fourteenth, Nineteen-sixty-four. It was six o'clock in the evening, by the time she was finally able to breathe regularly and not cry, after Dan had taken charge of all the necessary arrangements and steered police and reporters away from a heavily sedated Linda Sue. She was taken by one of the women on the dock into the pub, and led back into the manager's office. Dan had faced the whole tragedy from the porch, and since Linda was turned away when the shots were fired, and NOT a witness, he was able to get the press and the posse off her back for a while. The three bodies were removed to the funeral home after the coroner and deputies had their notebooks full, while Linda fought through murky, drug laden dreams.

An hour or so later, when the door opened, she roused and found herself looking up at the prettiest man she had ever seen. "How are you doin', darlin'?" The big man spoke so softly she thought she had died and was being addressed by The Angel Gabriel. "I don't know yet," Linda moaned. "I know it's true, but it just won't get into my head, you know what I mean?" He was nodding sympathetically. "I sure do, I truly do. In fact, you said it just right, how it is when the worst things happen."

Music seemed to be playing behind him, like in old movies. She let herself float along to the soothing tempo. "Can I get you anything? I was on the boat with Pete and Dan when it tied up today. Pete, along with most of those boys, are old friends from Citadel with me. Dan, the man with you who saw it happen, joined us in Bimini for the last of the good fishing and the crossing to Florida. Pete... Oh! I'm so sorry! Massey Thornedike's my name, from Squires Island, South Carolina. What's yours?"

What WAS her name? Linda was feeling something near to a spiritual awakening, later to be identified as love at first sight, even in her grief, and she said weakly, "I'm Linda Sue Parrish, from Waycross, Georgia. I'm pleased to meet you." She lifted her limp arm for his hand to take hers. He seized the chance to ply his charm. "I just KNEW you were a Georgia girl, honey. Nobody, not even Carolina girls can make words come out like church music that'a 'way!" God Almighty! This wasn't happening! How was it that she had gone from shell-shocked and desolate, to southern bell, madly in love? She feared the onset of the vapors any minute. Massey went out and returned with, of all things, a glass of chocolate milk.

"Drink this, Linda Sue Parrish, to ease those cramps." She was wide-eyed with wonder. "How did you know? My tummy and my throat are knotted up like they're bound with bungee cords. You think this will help?" He chuckled, intimately patting her thigh, "It's sort'a like comfort food. You know... chicken and dumplin's, mashed potatoes and peas, macaroni and cheese, a hot rum toddy. Now, you can't have a toddy, sugar, 'cause you been dosed with something for your 'nervous prostration', as my granny used to call it, and it doesn't do to mix the two. But just as soon as you get over this terrible thing, we're goin' out in a boat until we can't see land anymore, you're going to tell me every minute's worth of your life, and we're going to toast the God that made you, and your mama and daddy, too. How does that sound, Linda Sue Parrish?" How did he THINK it sounded? She was nodding her head like a little child, obediently, anxiously... lovingly.

The morning newspaper's account of the tragedy was so repugnant to her, Linda couldn't even touch the paper, much less read the words. After Massey took his leave, Dan had come to the pub in early evening with a detective seeking her statement, while she cringed on the office couch. The man was rabid to get "All of the story," for the record, and Dan made him promise if the interview came off, that police and reporters would stay away from Linda all the next day. She took a motel room in town to avoid the murder scene, and slept a drugged sleep only Valium can render.

Feeling better next morning, Linda was drinking coffee in the little café by the office, only eying the bowl of grits and cheese she had half-heartedly ordered, when Massey, a slicked up version of the salty character she had met yesterday, strode to her booth. "How's the prettiest girl I ever did see this mornin'?" He looked luminous standing there. Yesterday he had been an eyeful, as disheveled as he was, and as half-conscious as she was, but this! Clean as a pin, trimmed up, and smelling of Hawaiian Surf cologne, he was a vision...pleated olive, brushed denim slacks, a photo journalist's shirt full of trendy little pockets and tortoise-shell buttons, and from under it peeked out a soft-collared knit of stylishly faded flamingo pink. His web belt was held with a brass buckle and his boat shoes were the best money could buy, properly tied with monkey fists at the tips of the rawhide laces. She couldn't help it, she noticed the two-toned Rolex Submariner weighing down his blonde thatched wrist. A masterpiece of "male nauticality", carefully constructed to steal her heart. She found her voice and breathed.

"I'm a good bit better, thank you... and I thank you for your gallantry yesterday as well. You took me from the darkest place I've ever been, into a place where hope and life can still abide. I am sure I'm still in shock, and will be for a good while, but it's easier to bear knowing people like you are around. Have you seen Dan this morning? He brought me here last night, and I was supposed to meet him for breakfast." A hint of a scowl crossed Massey's brow, and he replied, "We had a couple of minor repairs to do on the diesels... nothing needing a technician, and since Dan's quite versed in those hummers, he got on them early, assessed the problems, and went to Savannah to get the parts. Pete had run the shit...Oh, I'm so sorry,

Linda, I've been on the boat with those jack legs too long. My apologies, please ma'am"

Linda was charmed by his chivalry, and she was glad she hadn't told him she had been quite numb to offensive language since childhood. At the moment, it was lovely to be regarded as a tender-eared lady. "Anyhow, he's gone 'til later tonight, so you've got me to deal with. What do you want to do with this fine day? It's already seventy degrees out there, and there's a workable breeze. I've had my eye on a sweet little day-sailer tied up at the marina with a for sale sign on her. She needs to be sea-trialed before we can buy her, don't you agree?" He always seemed to be near laughter, and invariably shook his head from side to side as if in awe of life itself... such a beautiful trait... such a beautiful man.

"You mean, you're going to just up and buy a boat today? Do you NEED a boat? I've always heard sailboats and tidal waters don't mix well," she offered. He spread his big hands with, "And you heard right, my beauty, but it's the best challenge for a sailor I can figure. Think on it a minute. Anybody can find a to-wind situation that complies with the destination, on a lake or in the ocean where there's no challenge. It takes a real moxie cruiser-man to manipulate the wind and water to compliment each other. No matter! Let's not complicate by dissecting it anymore. Go get some jeans and a sweater on, and I'll pick you up some boat shoes in the ship's store. Let's see... you wear a seven B, right? A small foot on such a treetop-tall gal... real nice! I'll see you at the marina in, say... thirty minutes? We are gonna' fill that gorgeous head of yours with so much fun you will come back full of life and hope!" Okay?"

Thirty seconds would have been okay! He was a true Angel from Heaven on a mission to save her, and to make it even more impossible to believe, Linda was madly, crashingly, adolescently in love with this man already. She knew... although she had never felt this way, not even close... that this was it! It couldn't be happening at a more wretched time, but this was LOVE, in the purest sense, as if she had created the emotion. She ran out the back door, looking back and laughing out loud, as she saw Massey slide her untouched grits bowl to his chest, picking up fork and salt shaker at the same time.

They sailed all day, talked the world out, consumed grilled grouper sandwiches he had made, drank dark beer, then red wine. And when it was so perfect they were nearly drowning in sensuality, Massey let the boom loose, lifted the rudder, and laid her down on the bow, while devouring her with kisses.

The delighted and humbled man took her virgin's body, mind, and heart to the skies, for the flight of her life. When a shared explosion came, it scattered their fragmented realities in kaleidoscope patterns like strong fireworks... like lacy snowflakes, all around the bobbing boat. And, as they felt the fragments flooding back inside them, he whispered in her ear, "If I tell you I love you, right now... will you understand and believe I never loved anybody so sure, and so quick. Never! Do you know it is true, Linda?" God! She believed it all! All of the unworldly components that were, since he had made love to this innocent girl, suddenly all there was.

A nearly delirious lover let his thoughts help him through the fog.

Frances had been the proper wife for a Thornedike, it was certain he'd done right by the family. Even the undeniable disappointment of losing her before a male heir could be brought forth, hadn't dimmed his devotion to her memory, and Franciene, their child, was his heart's need to beat. It was as if there was a compelling reason why he was here... why Carrie and 'Tilde had almost pushed him onto Pete's boat in January. He had found passion and wonder today, God help him, that he'd never had with anyone, not even Frances, as sweet and lovely as she was.

Linda surrendered her fiercely preserved purity to him so sweetly... so hungrily. He had risen on the white cloud of her chastity. She was a virgin! This was reverent, and precious...the loveliest time ever to happen to Massey... ever! They both ignored the little stain, and set about getting underway after a few moments, to begin breathing again. When the sail filled on a following sea, the perky little boat dipped her bow like a porpoise, almost as if she knew she needed to swab her decks, and the traces became part of the sparkling foam.

The boat was back in port just at twilight. It was nearly five, and the sky was streaked with color, as Massey tacked to the fishing docks.

He told Linda to jump off there, since the marina where the sloop was berthed was a bit of a walk, and she was visibly unsteady. She was nearly to the bluff, when she heard someone calling her name.

It was Dan. She turned to see where he was, and he had popped up out of the engine compartment of the Davis, grease-covered and quite drunk. "Where you been? 'You and Massey been together all day? Well I'll be a sumbitch!" He was on the dock, weaving toward her, wiping his hands with a red rag. An unprepared Linda was an even redder rag than he was holding, and he was too quick, too aware of her by now to miss the obvious. "Yep, I could tell soon as I saw you just now. Massey's been at you, ain't he? He is the lowest...! Why, he left me a list of parts to get in Savannah, so we could get Pete's boat fixed. Now I know he only wanted me out of the way"

She skipped noting the conflicting stories, and hastened, "Wait, Dan! No, he's not the lowest anything! I didn't mean for this to happen, but I think I am falling in love, for the first time in my life. Please, don't spoil this for me. I barely know you either, but it must be fate that I met you both, and needed you both so much, after what has happened. Just let it go for now, can you? I want to go to my room and lie down for a little while... alone, in case you're wondering."

Dan had crumbled in front of her, a defeated suitor. It was always this way with Massey Thornedike, he silently anguished. He always got the best of everything. Now it was a girl Dan had gone crazy about first, and was hoping to court. He was still standing there alone, when Massey came onto the dock, folding a piece of paper to fit his pocket. "WHY, Massey?" Dan moaned, "Why HER? Didn't you suspect for even a minute I might like her, and want to get closer to her? Don't you get enough pussy in and around Frenchport whenever you want it? I see you all the time on your secret little Jasper's boat trips, when the jism backup gets too strong for you to handle yourself! I ain't felt this good about a woman since Patty ran off, an' now you got this one too!"

He began a swing toward Massey's jaw, but it proved a dud when he spun himself too fast, and tripped over his own feet. He was in the water in seconds, treading furiously while shouting curses up at a chuckling Massey, who managed to call out, "Dan, I can't get you out without going in myself, so you'll have to manage alone. As for Linda, I won't discuss her with you, since she has come to mean everything, and I love her, old friend, I really and truly do. "Yeah, I'll bet!" The haggard figure, by now slopping up through the marsh growled, his teeth chattering, "Yeah, right! I've heard it before with you, more than once. Save all that bullshit for somebody who don't know you good as me!" Massey wasn't listening to him anymore. He had jumped into Pete's jeep, heading for Linda's motel and more brand new love.

The weeks were filled with warm spring days and magic nights. Massey up and bought the boat that first day, and since it was a cozy thirty-eight foot live-aboard, they set up housekeeping just fine. Linda sold her business in Brunswick and was able to move right into the new shop, since her name had been on the lease with Diane's. She never wanted to go up those back stairs again, and rented the apartment to a couple who worked for her, a chef and her handyman husband. It was all so easy, so many cosmically fitting pieces. Dan stayed a week longer, wished them well, even gave Massey a hug, and apologized. They had a beer together before Dan shoved off, to mend lifelong fences. Dan was a good friend... too good to lose. His parting words set the hook.

"I watched you with her, Massey, and I guess you really do love her like you say. I guess it shows I love her too, but it's different, know what I mean? Just take care of her, or I'll kick your ass all over Carolina! What about home, man? You forget about Little Francie?... your business stuff... all that? I can't see you just stayin' here, lovin' your days away!" Massey didn't need to be told he was being a selfish, lovesick fool. He was calling himself that and more every time he looked at Franciene's little face in the pictures in his wallet. Linda was as happy as Cinderella at the ball... her business was booming with the spring season, and waterway traffic increasing daily. Massey filled his days fishing, and tending the fleet of boats left by the tragedy. The judge had ruled the deaths a tragic murder-suicide misadventure. They learned the will that was left was a progressive one, since Diane had named Linda her heir, and custodian of her son. It was ruled she was the only apparent heir either of the two had, so she found herself the dubiously proud owner of a fishing fleet, a sassy Jeep, and the contents of both the apartment and the new shop.

The fleet...four fishing boats, was appraised at three quarters of a million dollars if maintained in present condition. Massey knew very well how quickly boats could depreciate, and suggested to Linda she sell two and keep two, investing the proceeds to care for the remaining two she would keep in charter. It was a welcome piece of advice, and Linda put the entire issue into Massey's experienced hands. He chose to keep the Buddy Davis, the pride of Pete's fleet and the most enduring asset, and a sturdy, steel-hulled vessel that would create interest in several markets, since it was large... near to seventy foot, and it was fitted as a head boat, easily converted to work-crew transport, or for ferrying. They celebrated the sale of the other two, a small scale shrimp trawler, and a fast and sassy twin powered Biddison, by taking a week' s sail to Bimini and surrounding Cays.

Linda had never been exposed to the crystal brilliance of Bahamian waters, with all the colors from purple, to navy blue, to turquoise, to coke bottle, to aquamarine, splashing onto soft white sand everywhere you looked. She didn't need anything but her man, but with such a backdrop it was better than Heaven. An ocean voyage together, even a short one like the Bimini trip, was perfect for new lovers. Their love was consuming... a force of nature no words could tell. If their first time had been so good, then the lazy, warm, sun splashed days in the Bahamas allowed for boundless passion.

Massey took his new boat and his new lady to places even he had forgotten about. She was a "Sweet surprise", this handy sloop, and as he liked to call her so, he whispered the same compliment in Linda's ear, every time she became the insatiable one, pulling his swimsuit from his hips at the oddest of times for her passion.

There were moments when Massey came close to telling her about his other life, but fear that she would up and disappear at the mention of Franciene, kept him silent. They finished their last day on Bimini with a lobster boil on the beach side...away from the busy harbor. Island music from the docks' bars brought to their party by the direction of the soft tropic breeze, was all the humanity they wanted. Linda wanted to talk about their future, but with Massey, it was always about today, never any other time. It was now mid-April, and while professing his deep love for her, he never offered up what was in his mind for them, and never anything about home.

She knew he had to have left a life back in some place called Squires Island, but he avoided any effort she made to draw him out. It was increasingly threatening to her that the reason for the silence was likely a wife or a girlfriend. Massey was only twenty-eight, still a very young, and she was here to shout, wonderfully virile man. Sure, that had to be it... he was spoken for by some perfect someone who was on that Island!

The lobsters were caught, cooked, and devoured, washed down with icy cold Fume Blanc, and they were stretched out on a blanket, looking through a three dimensional galaxy of clear starlight, just about to attack each other, when Linda asked simply, "Massey, what's next for us? Have you thought about it? It has been on my mind a lot lately. I don't want to press, I just feel the need to know. Don't you think it's natural, I mean, for a girl to want to have a peek into the future?" He got up and took his wallet from his shorts. When he sat down and opened the wallet to the photo section, Linda covered his hand with hers.

"I can't possibly look at another woman's picture, Honey, don't ask me to. I'm sure she's spectacular... just like you, and she probably has the right name and pedigree, and fills your life with joy, and all that." She was crying into her hands now, and it was the saddest sound Massey had heard since Frances died, when his infant daughter mewed hungrily from her bassinet, only a year and a half ago. "You are uncanny, my sweet. How can you guess my past so well? I'm pretty spooked about these powers you have, Linda. We're so damn fine together, and it's as it should be between us... has been since I first saw you. I had wanted to save this talk for when we get back home day after tomorrow, but if you are even a little bit upset not knowing, that settles it. First, come here."

She crawled over to be close to him, and he snuggled her up to his side while he went back to his wallet. When he had pulled the pictures he wanted her to see from their slots, he put them face down on the blanket, and reached for his spotlight. He turned her to face him, and began. "Everything you just suggested is right on the money, as I just now said. Darlin', I do have someone back home, and she is all the world to me. She's little, blonde, has everything she should have, and she loves me like a god." Linda was ready to scream at his callous handling of her breaking heart. "Stop it! Just shut up!"

The plea was so anguished and desperate, he was despising his own tongue for continuing. It had been carefully scripted by him to create such relief when he was finished, that she couldn't leave him...as long as it wasn't a wife or girlfriend. He took up the pictures and turned to her. The first photo was of an infant, no more than a few weeks old, held proudly in her daddy's arms. She was perfect, and dressed in a christening gown, that reached to Massey's knees. She wore a crocheted cap, and her mouth was drawn into a priceless yawn, like an elongated, tiny "O". Linda was transfixed for a moment, then put the picture down on the blanket, got up and walked to the water's edge. Massey was confused. Was she mad about Franciene? He trotted to her, and took her shoulders with a question in his eyes. Linda answered his eyes with a question of her own.

"How is THAT supposed to make me feel? Should I be happy because there's a child at home as well? Okay, I would never do anything to upset a little baby's world. There! Now you and the woman who fills your life with joy, have my blessing to forget I was ever anything but an easy piece for a few weeks! Now! How can I get off this godforsaken rock?" She was pacing and sobbing pitifully. "No! No, Linda, you've rushed to judgment on this one." He had risen from his knees, trying to get her to stop pacing and crying. "Honey, you're confused... you've jumped to conclusions I didn't give you." He finally stopped the pacing, and she was letting him hold her arms, gently guiding her back to the blanket. "Look at the rest of the snapshots. Please, Baby, just look!"

She reluctantly picked up the half dozen pictures, and laid them out under the light, one by one. There were six more shots of the child in various stages of babyhood, some of them with two different black women, one with a baby rabbit, and two more with Massey, one in a brightly colored wading pool, and the last one with him on a big bay horse... none with her mother! None with a beautiful woman who would be Massey's wife!

She looked for a few more moments, then, wide-eyed, at his face. He was crying in the spotlight's glow, tears already to his chin. "Linda, this little one is the girl in my life, and until you came to me, this was the only girl in my life, since the night her mother died giving her life." She drew in her breath and reached to touch his tears. He continued, "It was the worst thing, and I didn't think I would get through the guilt, knowing I had given her what took her life. I haven't done anything but live for my baby daughter ever since." He was sobbing softly, and he reached for the pictures, looking slowly at each one lovingly, so tenderly, that it made Linda cry even harder with him.

"Don't you start up again," he begged. "I'll never stop if you keep crying! I'm sorry I didn't tell you right away so this didn't have to happen. If you had known from the get-go about Franciene.... that's her name, Francie, my sweet little baby girl. If you had known all along, we could have handled it without all this. I'm so sorry." She reacted desperately. "NO! No, my sweetheart, I did this! I made you talk about something you weren't ready to share!" He stopped her this time. "I was always ready to share it, but I was so scared you'd run off. Some women don't want another woman's children, even if there IS no other woman. I was all about loving you so good, and it felt like enough, just like it was. I know I need to go back, but I can't stand to leave you... I just can't bear it!" He broke down for real at this, and she was holding him, and rocking him back and to, crooning comforting sounds to make him better. "We'll get through this, Massey darling. My promise to you is that we will be together, and we will fix what isn't right.

What was not right would surface soon. It had been a busy and happy April, food and fishing businesses both going great. Massey was providing Linda's kitchen with more than enough fresh catch to service all her clients, and they were able to sell the rest to the markets and restaurants in town. He was also stocking fresh-frozen seafood in the marina's bait freezer to take home with him, something he decided not to mention to Linda. She had not pressed him again since Bimini. It was such a traumatic night, and it took the rest of the trip for him to become his old self. He did tell her about the fine child caregivers he had in Carrie and 'Tilde, and the two of them were seeing to his daughter so well, that the little one was probably unaware he had been gone so long. He also told her that he wasn't expected until later in the month, so no one would be concerned yet. "After all, men go out of town all the time, and military fathers might be away for months, so my daughter is fine. Right now, I get to capture a little of myself, and I choose to spend it with you... is that wrong?" Linda held him and assured him it was not, but she feared he was trying to convince himself, not her. She was worried after his strange state, and tried valiantly to help him.

"No, darling, it's not wrong. The only things that are wrong are things that are intentionally wrought to do harm to others who don't deserve it. We have no such intent inside us. Life has given us a gift, and I am grateful to God that you showed me what a divine state mutually shared love can be. We will be happy while we can, and if you want more for us, I'll be with you." It was done. She had given him a perfect way out if he wanted it. The only loser would be herself. She feared she did not mean a word of it, but was convinced he would be able to relax with this revelation, and perhaps even commit to her more readily.

# CHAPTER TWENTY-TWO

*The Recollections Become Intense*

A day trip to Brunswick was two-fold in purpose. Linda needed to see her lawyer about finalizing ownership of the business, and she wanted to get a checkup. Massey was offshore fishing with a half dozen politicians from Atlanta, to return by dark. She was at the medical center at one o'clock on the button. The examination and mammogram were uneventful, and Linda was let into her doctor's office, to wrap up the visit as she had done regularly for the two years she'd been living in Brunswick. When she was seated, the doctor took a deep breath, and began.

"Linda, you're as healthy as ever, there are no deviations from your other checkups, except for one thing, and it's a big thing." She shifted in the stiff chair, and let him continue. "Are you involved in a serious relationship, my dear? I hope so, and I hope it will lead to marriage. I'm an old-fashioned southern sawbones, and I like two-parent families raising the future of our country." She gasped at the inference. He removed his glasses and stared at her blank face. "You look surprised, Linda. Have you been using birth control? I had treated you as a virgin until this visit, and had hopes you'd stay so until your marriage. My prize pupil, I think teachers call it. From what I can tell, you've been pregnant for about eight or nine weeks now, and I repeat, you seem in great shape to deliver a perfectly healthy little one sometime in late December."

This could not BE! She was pregnant! It had stupidly, and innocently slipped her consciousness to consider the possibility. Theirs had been such a hazy dream of impulsive happiness, combined with her lack of experience. Her mind was whizzing through many thoughts. How was it going to play with Massey? What would he say when she told him? Maybe he would ask her to marry him and take her home with him. Wouldn't it be perfect? She could become mistress of the Thornedike family. It was a good fairy tale, and she was consumed, as she drove back home, with just how she should tell him. Deciding on a romantic evening, Linda bathed and dressed in the marina changing rooms, since their tiny head shower was not very relaxing. She wondered if Massey had a hot tub at his house, would he buy her a horse so they could go riding together?... would the little girl be happy with her? Her woman's dreams were so joyful and perfect... so very perfect.

When Massey finally got back it was nine o'clock, and there were seven big cobia to clean, filet, and bag up. The bigwigs planned to take their catch to the seafood restaurant in nearby Eulonia, so the chef could prepare dinner for them. He got to the sailboat at ten, and found Linda all gussied up in gown and peignoir, with candles and wine. "What's this? What are we celebrating at this late hour?" He seemed a bit crabby, she observed, and since he was so tired, she offered to wash his back and rub his aching shoulders and legs. Massey was too tired to be bothered at all. He kissed her eyes, her nose, and her lips and said, "Darlin', I only wants a sip of this wine, and since we already had pizza on the boat, after my shower let's just cuddle up and sleep. Those big fish wore me out this day, but I'll banish the nasty bear overnight, I promise."

If she had left it alone right then, where it lay, it might have been different. But, the telling is about men and women, and they can make fateful errors where love is concerned. She was insistent that he let her minister to him, so he relented. There was some nice jazz softly playing, and she wiped his weary, burnt body down with a cool towel as they sat in bed and drank the wine with the candles glowing. He looked at her quizzically. "What's up Linda Sue? You look all floaty and glowing tonight. What's got you goin'?"

She giggled softly, and curled around him like a snake. "My darlin' and I are about to have a new toy to play with." He didn't catch on. "Why would we have a new toy, when we hardly have enough time to play with each other?" He laughed wryly. "What is it? Come on, Linda." She was instantly on guard, and very nearly made up something else, but instead, blurted out, "Massey, I'm pregnant, over two months now!" He jumped off the bed as if it was made of hot coals. "What did you say?" She started to cry. "I said"...she began. He was livid. "I got it the first time, but I couldn't believe I heard you right! Jesus! What were you thinking? I told you about Frances, and what happened, and how it nearly killed me when I killed her! You couldn't have been more than a tiny bit pregnant at that time! We could have fixed it! Why didn't you keep track? Haven't you ever heard of the pill? SHIT!"

To her horror, he was pulling on his shorts, and reaching for his things from the bureau. "You can't expect me to be happy about something that killed the last woman I knocked up, can you? My God Almighty, Linda, don't you have any feelings for me at all? How did you expect me to take this?" Never in a million years had she imagined he would react in such a way. It was a facet of his subconscious she hadn't figured on. He was obviously slightly insane from this part of his past. It was the guilt from impregnating a woman who died as a result, and he was carrying it around daily. She clung to him piteously, as he bounced from bulkhead to bunk in the little stateroom.

"Please listen to me Massey, I want to have this baby for us, honey, so much, and it's going to be my responsibility to take care of it myself, to be sure we're okay! I promise you won't be sorry." She was pressing against the side of the bunk with her body so hard, he had to lift her off the floor to move her out of his exit. As he sat her on the bed, he impulsively raised his arm as if to strike her, but stopped, and spun up the steps to the cockpit, and off the boat. Linda was dizzy with panic. She went up top in time to see the jeep careening out of the parking lot, but she was too shocked and sick to do anything. He had once been her cure, now he was her curse. She stumbled, helpless, down the steps to the stateroom, blew out the candles and went to bed as if in a living nightmare.

Massey drove without knowing where to, or why he was even going away. He knew he had not ever before reacted in such a way, to something that should be positive, so it had to be a powerful internal force. The girl, this woman he loved so hard ever since he first laid eyes on her, even before they met, had just witnessed what could very well be the end of their love, and it was impossible to believe. He recalled watching her that day back in March, as she was going up the stairs behind the shop when they were pulling into port. She was a head-turner, all right... but more, especially to him. She had a light inside her, strong enough to warm a cold night just by sitting next to her, and her smile let you fly straight to her heart.

The bad thing was, and he hit hard on this one...he hadn't reckoned on a thunder and lightning storm like her, when for a long time he had not cared whether it rained or not. With all he had on his plate, Massey had lost a young man's day to day need for sex, a pursuit men like him always admitted to. As with his fish stories, Dan was exaggerating about his friend's conquests. He saw Massey with a woman just one time since Frances's death, and the reason for it that night was that he had accepted a bold invitation to dinner by an acquaintance of his who had recently lost her husband, one of Massey's good friends. When he failed to raise Dan on the radio for a pick up, he asked Jasper if he could use his little bateau...big deal! Dan had used that ONE time, to create and gossip about the illusion of Massey the Playboy!

The more he thought on it, the more he began to doubt his own sense of reason. His child, growing inside a woman he was crazy in love with, and he could think of no one who would care if he brought her home for keeps. Well, maybe 'Tilde and Carrie would kick up a fuss about another woman in the house, but they'd get over it, and it would mean a positive for Francie to have a sweet woman living with them. As if in a trance, Massey was nearly to Jacksonville, tired to the bone and beginning to feel genuine shame. He kept going, believing he wouldn't have the guts to face her after how he behaved on the boat.

He would call her in the morning and beg forgiveness, finishing with a proposal! The situation could not be forced. He had almost struck the best and finest woman he could hope to find, bar none, and if he didn't win her back, Dan would be around in no time, soon as he heard about their fight, and take everything away from him. Massey needed one thing right then, even more than another chance. He had to get off the road and get some sleep, and then he would head back to his woman and their child the very next morning.

Linda wanted nothing more than to sleep either, and not dream of Massey and his obsessions. The first thing she was going to do tomorrow was get away from St. Marys. She would lease the business and the apartment to someone she could trust to keep the quality going up, and the overhead down. Next, she would put the two remaining boats' listings with a broker, let the catering shop use the jeep, and high-tail it right back to Waycross. This waterfront life was too much for her country girl roots. What a ride it had been, since she and Diane had first decided to expand. Somehow she had more gumption than ever before, maybe because she was living for a little life inside her...and now had to stand up to, behind, and maybe even staunchly in front of whatever would face her from now on.

\* \* \*

Back to the present, it was a few minutes before four o'clock, and Linda was feeling better. She decided a walk on the pier was in order, since from there she could see the ferryboat arrive. Ruby informed her in no uncertain terms that the boat was always prompt, and she was glad for that. She still found points to ponder popping up in her head, and she was better off alone and outdoors for this. Negatives took their turn next. She knew that if she was taken to Massey's house and encountered a wife, or hostility from her unheralded appearance, it would be what she deserved. If Toby and Willie were there, and her son was NOT glad to see her, nothing could stop her from turning and leaving, to spare everyone a very hard moment.

If Toby and Massey were side by side for her to test her conflicted emotions, she would have just cause for the trepidation engulfing her. It was a huge ball of worry, even without the negatives. Either way, there was life-changing reality waiting for her on Squires Island. There was a clean dock box beside the slip where the ferry would tie up, so she hoisted herself up to sit out the last five minutes with her chin in her fists, and her eyes closed to continue going down the list of possibilities.

Without a sound, there were two huge, rough hands on her wrists from behind, and they slid over her now wide opened eyes. A rattled whisper asked, "And who do you think THIS is?" She was right ready to send an elbow into his groin, when she suddenly realized, and turned to be enveloped in a bear hug by Captain Dan himself. "OH!" Was all she got out as the breath was squeezed out of her, before he released her to look, after more than eighteen years, into the still bright, baby blue eyes of her old friend. "I know I shouldn't 'a snuck up on you like that, but when I saw Ruby out on the fuel dock, and she told me what my lone passenger's name was, I don't think my feet hit the dock but a couple of times, and when I saw you lookin' even prettier than when I left you in Georgia, well, I just had to play with you a mite! How is my darlin', anyway? Where you livin' now? God! You are so purty, honey! I know I ain't done as good myself, but you make up for it. After all, I don't gotta' look at me, 'cept when I shave, and that ain't everyday!"

He couldn't stop babbling away, so happy was he to see her. She was laughing and nodding to his words, shyly acknowledging his praise, and realized they had walked back to Ruby's. "Where is the boat?" she asked, spinning prettily around, feeling strangely sassy. "I thought I was waiting by your slip!" He had kept hold to her hand as they walked, taking it to his lips several times to kiss. "I needed to take on fuel between trips, and I'm mighty glad I did, else we couldn't have a chance for a beer together. RUBY! Pop open two Heinekens for us. This here is one of my sweetest little gal friends, come to ride ole Dan's ferryboat!" Ruby grumbled something about not drinking on the job site, but knew better not to belabor it, and set up two greenies on the bar.

Linda was guarded as she asked about Dan's life since St. Marys, and he told her he had been married, and had a son who was his boat mate, and that his wife had taken off seven years back with a couple of boat gypsies bound for the Spice Islands, and had never looked back, either for him or for Jaime. "Shucks, honey, this here life ain't so bad, why, I get to be on the water I love, with my boy beside me, and the tourists are pretty okay, even tip decent some days, most times all they give me is somethin' to chuckle over my beer about. Back in March, the place was crawlin' with spring snowbirds, all of 'em not knowin' Shit from Shinola, and full of questions. I had one little lady come up to me at the helm one day, and, as pure as she could ask it, I swear to God, said, "Captain, is this REAL Salt Water?" He slapped his leg and laughed at the old story as if he had just experienced it, and Linda laughed heartily along with him. How good it was for a moment.

She knew what was unspoken by them both, and she regarded him as he wound on, taking stock of what life had done with and to him. He was still attractive, though much heavier. His once sun bleached, tightly curled ponytail was now in a shorter cut, streaked with gray, and receding a little over his eyebrows. There were unruly silver hairs in his bushy brows, but those eternally bright eyes stood for the man's spirit. He was attired in the usual captain's garb of khaki shorts and white polyester shirt, frayed shoulder boards and rundown topsiders. Overall, an okay sight to her, and she silently thanked him for being there when she was so alone, and for not questioning her about why she was going to the island today, after all this time.

Dan, on the other hand, was busting a gut to ask her, and while he could have stopped the whole show by telling her that Massey was in the hospital only a few blocks away, he feared for many reasons what the mention of his buddy's name would invoke. They took their beers in cups and walked to the fuel dock, chattering away about nothing and everything, to avoid the advent of the something they knew would arise once they were underway. It arose just as the bow was pointed to Squires Island's river approach across the sound. Linda was standing beside Dan at the helm, silently sipping her beer until he evened the pitch of the big diesels, enabling them to hear each other's voices.

"Now, Missy, you need to tell me what you're doin' here, and why you're headin' over to Squires today. I figured you'd long ago left that mess behind you, had married a doctor or a lawyer someplace, and started bouncin' babies right off. Don't tell me you been in touch with him all along. He ain't said a word about you, not since the day he came back here. Fact is, I never asked him about why he came home alone, since he was so sure it was the real thing and all. Did he ever tell you about Franciene? Do you know how come his wife to die? I don't think he's been right in the head since the awful night she passed." Linda listened as Dan got more and more caught up in his memory of the day Frances was delivered of her baby and died. Her heart lurched as he told her about their rum-soaked day and night at Ruby's, and how Massey grieved for weeks and weeks, that Frances had died in agony and fear without him there to hold her hand. Linda was silent until he was done.

"I have a lot to tell you, Dan, and you have a right to hear the rest of the story. The reason I'm going to Massey's house today, is because I've been told that our son, who I haven't seen since he was three and a half years old, is there." She paused for the truth to be absorbed by a slack-jawed, sputtering captain. He found his voice, and fired so many four word questions at her she had to grab his shoulders and shake him silent. "I will tell you all of it, in the time we have, then I want you to promise me to drop it! Forget that you know, because I need this time before everyone will know, and at last it won't matter anymore."

Dan was dumbstruck. He agreed to every condition, so she would get on to the story. Linda filled him in from when he left St. Marys in March of sixty-four, to the night Massey left her, pregnant and bewildered, on their sailboat. He listened for thirty minutes, his teeth clenched and grinding angrily, his eyes begging to let the heavy teardrops loose, but he would not allow it, throwing his head back repeatedly, to send them away. "I haven't finished, Dan," she said as she finished her beer and discarded the cup. "What I will tell you now is the hardest part to share." Dan's head snapped around to look in her eyes.

"You can't mean there's more, and worse than you already told me, 'cause if he was even worse to you than what I heard just now, I'll tear his leg off and beat him to death with the bloody stump! What happened next, Linda Sue? Did you have the baby all right? Poor Darlin', I just can't stand this! I would a' loved and cherished you forever if you'd a' chose me! I hate what he did... and I hate him!" He threw his head back once more, as new tears formed, squared his shoulders, and nodded her on. Linda chose the words carefully, knowing she was about to reveal a side of Massey that even Dan had not seen. She labored over how much she should say out loud, and how much she should keep to herself, but trusted her instincts and related the story that time, so long ago and ever since, had held entrapped.

## THE AFTERMATH OF LINDA'S HEARTBREAK IS RETOLD

Linda went first to Brunswick to wrap up her interests there, on her way home to Waycross to await her baby's birth. Her childhood home was pitiful to behold, but it was hers, and she was grateful to be able to afford to put it right. In a few weeks she stood on the sidewalk looking at a sparkling restored circa 1920's bungalow. The project was costly, since she had sprung for quick as well as quality work, but worth it, from its new tile roof to the brick walkway winding to the street between instantly vivid flower gardens.

The best part was that she resurrected her mother's overgrown rose vines on the South end of the porch. With Master Gardener-style advice, she pruned, cultivated, and retrained the old bushes to former glory in one growing season, and spent many summer nights swinging beneath the fragrantly abundant blossoms. December came, and with it, motherhood. Linda was delivered of a perfect, foursquare little son, with no problems. She grieved to herself that

Massey needn't have worried. Just like she promised him last May, when she said she would do it right.

Now he had a baby son, but he didn't know. It did little or no good to cry over spilt milk as Mama used to warn her, so she got strong of mind and body, and plotted hers and Little William Darius's life together. While the bequest from Diane was ample enough to let her be a stay-at-home mom, Linda wisely went to her family bank and put most of the half-million in the president's capable and caring hands, to be invested in trust until Willie needed it, and found a fine nurse to stay home with him while she went to work. It never left her that because of Diane, her child would never worry about his future, and she wanted to do right by him in grateful memory. The reason she chose to name her son after his grandfather and her dear friend's star-crossed little baby boy, permanently honored the two.

A position as catering and banquet manager in the town's best hotel barely compensated where so much fullness once lived, but Willie more than filled the cracks in her heart... most of the time. She would swear every morning that she would begin to heal, but like an alcoholic after a binge, she would slip back to her bottle of memories, and fall off the love wagon again. Massey would not leave her heart, no matter how tarnished his image had become. Little Willie was his daddy in miniature, and Linda had only to look into his huge blue eyes to drown anew. She became obsessed with everything there was to learn about his home, and after researching Squires Island at the library she daydreamed often about the pristine retreat it must be.

Going further with her quest, she would scissor out magazine pictures of pretty little girls who would be about Franciene's age, believing she nearly was her daughter. The status-quo remained, and she learned to live with it, even finding abstract pleasure in dreams that would wake her after a soul rattling orgasm from Massey's dream-borne visits. Linda didn't need a lover... she had one nearly every night. They were quite a pair in town, pretty mom and roly-poly baby son. The aging neighborhood welcomed the younger ones warmly. She was seldom without a bowl of yard eggs, fresh baked cookies, toys for the baby, and far too many offers to babysit for her nonexistent social life.

When Will was two and a half, she was pleased to hear from her old friends who had bought the shop in St. Marys, asking her to take over the business for a couple of days in mid-June, while they attended a family wedding in Florida. She agreed, and made plans to be away from Waycross for four days. St. Marys was going to be a challenge for her unresolved memories, but she was so happy to take her golden, husky little boy to such a pretty place on the coast, it was no contest. The boy had begun to shake his little head when he was happy, just like Massey had, and when he ran naked from his bath, his little torso, so like his daddy's, broke her heart. They settled in the rooms above the pub, and Linda went to work. Will charmed those who remembered Linda, and transients alike, and since a sparkling swimming pool had been added to the marina with a wading pool for children, their leisure time was spent splashing happy hours away together.

Linda soon had Willie dog paddling while she supported him, lustily cheering her pre-Olympic swimmer on to glory. It was so idyllic she decided to extend another day, encouraged by Tad, the ship's store clerk, and her old friends. The sailboat, Sweet Surprise", that had housed hers and Massey's love, was still there, causing a cloud over the visit. Tad told her that Massey titled it to her the same month Will was born, and that he still sent monthly checks for dockage and precise perpetual maintenance, so when she saw it, she almost expected to see Massey pop up from below, waving a greeting to her. Her thoughts went toward selling it, to remove the painful reminder forever. She never boarded the little sloop while there.

Their last day arrived, bright and warm. Willie tugged his mama to the pool, and there they stayed. Linda's skin had become nut brown, and her woman's body in the sleek black tank suit caused stares and whistles from the docks, but she was oblivious to the attention, as she and Will began their pool games. It was a perfect day, but not for long. Inside the store, a big man watched from behind a cast net display, his knuckles pressed painfully to his teeth. Massey turned to Tad, wrecked by what he was seeing. "Here's a hundred,

Tad, thanks for calling me yesterday. I had a feeling she would come back sometime, and since I couldn't go to her home and risk being sent away, I had to come here. I can't believe that beautiful little man is my son, you know?" He was crying openly.

"Ain't he the cutest thing you ever did see?" He was pitiful, and Tad was feeling deep compassion for him as he took the bill, his eyes questioning. Massey patted his shoulder and said, "Don't you worry, boy, I don't mean them any harm. I only want to see him and hold him for just a minute. You can help me, by taking the call that's about to come for Linda Sue, and going out there to fetch her while you hold the boy. I'll slip out back and around to the other side of the building, and while she's on the phone, you can let me hold my baby for just a minute, and then I swear I'll go. It's real simple, don't you think? It's my only chance to touch him, and whisper in his little ear that I love him." There was no choice for Tad. He nodded silently and pocketed the money he could really use. Sure enough, the telephone rang at eleven-ten, the call for Linda Sue Parrish.

Massey motioned Tad to the door and darted out back. Linda looked up to see Tad shouting between his cupped hands that there was a call for her. She wrapped a towel around Will, and Tad reached out for him as she went inside the chilly store. It was a lobster vendor from Jacksonville, so he told her, wanting the shop's business, and as she explained that she no longer decided those issues, she turned to see Massey, easily recognized as he dashed away from the pool deck.

She dropped the phone and ran out just in time to see him running toward a helicopter across the road, and a scream closed her throat when she saw Will's blonde curls bobbing in Massey's arms as he climbed in. The pilot shot up and away in a banked turn that took it instantly out of reach. Linda's arms stretched helplessly skyward, and she and Massey locked eyes for a second before he snapped his head away and the chopper was gone. The poor mother sank to the gravel and screamed like an animal to God for her baby.

A horrified Tad and others who saw it, rushed to her. The boy was inconsolable. "Linda! Oh, Christ! He said he just wanted to touch him for a minute, and then he would leave! I NEVER noticed that chopper across the road. They come and go all the time with anglers and boat owners here. I'm so sorry, Linda! What can we do? He's kidnapped Willie!" Linda was on her feet, replacing shock with rage. She sent Tad to call the state patrol and the Coast Guard on the radio, and went upstairs to pack their things. Massey was not going to have her child! She vowed silently to kill the man if she had to, to get little Will back.

# CHAPTER
# TWENTY-THREE

Memories of the minutes after the telephone call on that day, were causing nausea and chills while she made as palatable as the parts of the story she believed Dan could stomach, while they motored across the sound to Squires, leaving out the cruel, heartless facts of the kidnapping, and telling a softer version to Massey's best friend. All Dan needed to know was that Massey had posed a threat back when Will was a tot, but she would keep the vile truth of his selfish deed for a while longer. The rest of the story consisted of Linda's vow to shield her son from his father's control by placing him with her own daddy in South Georgia, and that she had learned of Will's arrival on the Island just that morning. She told a by now, stupefied Dan, that she wanted to be present at their meeting to give support and protection for her son, if he wanted it from her, while of course, she longed to hold him in her arms.

Dan hadn't moved a muscle, listening intently to her story. His heart was cracking at the thought of what this sweet woman had endured at Massey's greedy hands. He decided not to tell her about his heart attack and hospitalization, fearing she would want to go right back to see him. Massey didn't deserve her concern or her love... No Sir! He hoped she would forgive the omission when she learned of it. He had read between her words how deeply Linda still loved Massey, even after all the hurt he had caused. They disembarked without speaking after Linda was done with the story. Dan walked her to the head of the dock where Jasper was waiting, just like Ruby had promised. He put her bag in the back of Jasper's truck and helped her in.

When she looked at Jasper's dear old face and saw recognition rising, Linda put her hand palm down to quell his greeting. She smiled cordially, and said, "How are you? I'm Linda Sue Parrish. Thank you for taking me to the Thornedike house. I believe you are Jasper Griffin, is that right?" He was a quick-minded and clever man, following her lead without a hitch. "Yes Ma'am, I'm Jasper, and I'm pleased to meet you. Thank you Cap, we appreciate all you doin' for 'Tilde's services and all you still got to do. Folks like you sho' do help us Islanders out good."

Dan reached in and shook hands, adding, "Jasper, we are, and always will be, good friends. I'm here for you all, Buddy. Give my condolences to Aaron when you see him." He kissed Linda's cheek softly, and squeezed her shoulder. They backed away and turned down the dirt road to nowhere. Dan stood for a moment, and then he walked slowly down to his boat, shaking his head in confusion. Maybe he had done wrong. What if those two were supposed to be together after all? He was being selfish and manipulative, keeping this from Linda. He decided to put his mind hard to what was right, on the trip back across, while in the truck as they rode toward the past, the two unlikely comrades clasped hands warmly and spoke of their last meeting.

\* \* \*

At Thornedike's, it was a blessing to tend the mountain of chores Carrie faced before tonight's supper and tomorrow's service for 'Tilde. While friends and relations were bringing huge loads of food and drink for the meals, Carrie was bound to bake her traditional pies and cakes, and there were never too many biscuits and cornbread hoecakes for a gathering like this.

She left Aaron at his mama's side an hour ago, telling him not to prostrate himself too long, and to come help her like he used to as a child. He wasn't taking 'Tilde's passing at all well, still wanting answers about what made her die. In Carrie's basic, good heart, she wanted all questions left at the grave tomorrow, and thus let Clothilde's sweet soul rest. She hummed as she worked on, a hymn that would not leave her."Swing low, Sweet Chariot, Comin' for to Carry me Home...", and as she worked she thought about Will and his good friend, Toby Howell. He seemed nice enough, openly devoted to Will, and Will to him. If this boy was to be part of their work, it would be necessary to include Toby in their talks. Will wanted him there, and if Aaron agreed, then it would be so. The two friends drove to the beach in the Jeep an hour ago, and seeing the boy's strange demeanor when they came out of the study, she liked the plan. Toby had seemed to attentively guide a staring Will to the door, she was relieved to observe. But Carrie was still concerned. It was a bother to her that so much work stood between them... still, she knew she could fix everything after tomorrow.

"I looked over Jordan and what did I see? Comin' for to carry me home, a band of Angels a'comin' after me, Comin' for to carry me home." The piecrusts were perfect as usual.

* * *

Such wild beauty, this deserted beach, Toby was struck dumb by the vista... a two mile stretch of smooth white sand, lapped at by perfectly formed, mini-waves, lazily leaving a foamy fringe of shells and freeform chert along the tide line. The strand curved up against a uniform dune, crested with undulating sea oats and carnival colored gallardia flowers. Behind the dune was a multi-hued meadow, waving in concordance with the ocean, and an occasional palmetto palm, aged cedar tree, and monster long leaf pine tree, providing shade and music in the breeze. To the right was Tybee Island, its lighthouse an exclamation point at Fort Screven. To the left was the upscale island of Hilton Head, and across from there, Cusabo Sound and tiny Frenchport. A mesmerized Will spread his arms to the ocean a second time since they first came to this place. Good old Padgett's Island seemed as far away as Fiji to him right then, and Toby prayed that this would soon pass.

227

His young friend was deep in something he could only watch, and incredibly he seemed to be enjoying every mystical minute. "Will!" He shouted to him, "Let's take a run to clear the cobwebs, how about it?" He snapped to, and began to sprint toward Toby. They fell in together, and after modifying his agile companion's pace to his own aging prowess, the boy looked in his eyes with his old Will's smile and wink. The older man ruffled his hair and said, "Welcome back, sport! I missed you so much! If you want to zip our lips and just run, just nod, and I'll abide by it. If you want to dig into things as we run, then, go for it!" He did neither for a full minute, then let it out.

"Toby, I'm scared shitless about what's happening to me! What does all this mean? Toby had a good idea, but would Will be okay with what he would hear from a more mature, but detached perspective? He decided to plunge ahead. "Yes, I have an opinion, but first I want to talk about that girl, just so we are clear. She is stuck somewhere between real and unreal, if I'm guessing right, and we are here to sort it out to save everyone concerned from something that could happen because of her. How am I doing?"

Toby himself was stunned by the wisdom and concise quality of what he had said. It was a funny feeling... like the words were given, and he simply whispered his thanks for the help to who, or what... he did not know. The boy was looking at him trustingly as he went on, hoping the right words would keep coming. "Will, tell me what YOU believe." The young man took a moment, and then began. "Toby, I think Carrie and Aaron are joined for a mission or missions involving people who soon will need help, fighting evil and danger to their bodies and their spirits." He was so sincere, so innocently driven, Toby believed every word he was saying.

"That girl, Franciene, is at the heart of it, and if we aren't triumphant the outcome could be fatal, even worse... Soul-Stealing, for those involved. Some of what is coming may be good... and some not so good. I don't know much more than that I am called here, and that Aaron is acting in his mother's stead. Carrie Treacle is in, or very near the center on the good side. Carrie said earlier that we will have time to talk after the service is over tomorrow. There is a twilight service for Clothilde, with a big supper on the riverbank by the church, and Carrie wants us to stay through tomorrow, thinking we might be of help, as well as be more enlightened." Toby was rapt, watching the boy he thought he knew inside and out, now exhibiting a depth and spirituality he had not known was there.

"See, I know I am chosen, and I want to answer the call... I simply don't have a clue about what I must do! Please be patient for another day, Toby, and this will come clear. I ask you as my best friend, and as the father I would have picked out from the whole world." It was a strong case, so Toby elected not to present his. The fact that he did not call Massey Thornedike his father was perplexing. He guessed that he had been entranced while they were in the study... possessed even, and the post-trance kept the facts away. He had thought to ask Will to back off from this for three days, go see his mother, and search his head for the clarity distance might permit, but somehow could not summon the words.

They were relaxing in the beauty around them, when Aaron came through the dune. He was a dozen feet from them when he put out his hand, lowered his head, and began to sob. Will went to him with an arm instantly around his shoulder. "What's happened, man? Is Carrie all right? Why are you so upset?" Aaron was obviously in a bad way, so the two flanked him and began to walk up the beach. He looked at first one, then the other, and began.

"You don't know what I have to do today. I have to tell Aunt Carrie something I always meant to keep from her. My mama told me while I was beside her just now, to cleanse my conscience so I could carry on with her work, and I know what she means."

He had fear in his eyes that rivaled anything Toby had ever seen. "Can you tell us what it is, Aaron? Maybe if you talk it out it won't seem so bad. Let's go sit on that tree and talk. We want to help." The grieving, emerging young man expressed gratitude for the unconditional friendship and support from strangers, and he told the sad story of Carrie's son… his own best friend, and how he died. It was a terrible story to tell, but Aaron got through it with controlled sobs. Next, he revealed his subsequent drug addiction, and decision to cleanse himself after his mother's death. He appeared relieved to tell it, and they praised him warmly. Aaron had come to find them for this purpose, and Toby suspected without saying it that this wouldn't be happening without the work of higher powers. That book's first few pages told him that the history behind these powers allows to those involved, open doors to many rooms of wisdom.

The two young men, so different yet so much the same, walked off for a few minutes, and Toby considered it a good thing. Left standing on the beach alone, Toby became edgy for an unknown reason, thought it was his old-time cynicism, bred through decades of agnostics in school, pulling at this pure moment. He wanted to go back and call Linda again, but something told him she still would not answer the phone. What the hell, the whole thing was out of his hands anyway. That resolved, he walked in the opposite direction from the boys, daydreaming about... Her.

Aaron and Will set out down the beach in cadence, with Will the first to speak. "I want a chance to sit down with Carrie and you before we go back across, Aaron. I know you are busy with your mother's service, and all the people coming, but maybe we can steal a few minutes tonight or early in the morning before you get covered up with your duties. Do you know why I need the time?" He hoped Aaron was with him, and he was. He stopped and turned to Will with eyes that said it all.

It was so strange, but he stayed cool and detached. "What can you tell me about Franciene Thornedike, and what she has done? I have found something here on Squires Island that rocked my world, and it won't turn me loose or let me turn it loose. Man, that girl haunts me day and night." Aaron exhaled wearily. "Will, I was with Franciene yesterday in Florida, but with what the Gift wants from us, and what I believe you are trying to tell me, the truths are true to each of us, separate and apart." Will sucked in his breath at Aaron's admission. Franciene should be dead for nearly five days by now, if she died on the day they found her. That grisly bit of news he had overheard at the hospital about her arm being dumped on a shrimp boat deck was real. He felt his sanity slipping.

"How could you be with her? Where were you, and why did you leave her down there? Were you alone? What was the reason you were with her?" He had begun to yell his questions, frustrated beyond belief, and Aaron responded with calm, soft-spoken answers. He put his hand on Will's arm to settle him, and said. "It was for her graduation week, and she and Cliff Hartsell and I took off on a spur of the moment trip, to return in a few days. Francie was impossible to control, wilder than I thought she could ever be, even having known her all her life, and I opted to strike out alone before dark yesterday. I do not know where they are now, and until Carrie gives me the direction that will change my feelings, I don't really care where they are!" Will was totally confused. It was his turn to talk.

"I found her drowned body on the creek bank right here on Squires last Wednesday...what do you say about THAT? Why is this happening? Don't you think we're losing our frigging minds?" Aaron smiled slowly, with Will envying him his control. "No, although it is beyond strange, it has a reason and that will come clear, this I know. You are new here, and will soon know the trust I have had for a long time." Will envied Aaron's calm resolve, as he went on. "I think we should go back to the house now. Carrie needs me and so does my mama." That put Will in his place and the two new friends walked back to the Jeep.

* * *

Mattie Bell made it to the marina on time, having raced from her shift at the hospital to her apartment to grab a few things for overnight on Squires Island, and met her friend at his boat at five as planned. Help for Massey through his crisis, and exploring the strange sensations she was getting each time the Island was mentioned, both when she was in Massey's room, and most profound, when she encountered Will Parrish this morning, made the trip a must for her. It was more, much more than her charitable heart's directive to give aid...this was deeper. The chills began again as they cast off, heading toward the island. Dan was loading a fresh boat full of mourners across the harbor, hoping to be done in time to bring Linda back, solo. He had decided to tell her about Massey, and then do as she wished, regardless of his personal fears. If she wanted to go see the man, he would be her escort to the hospital. It was high time they put the past where it belonged, and see if good things could come to the present and future.

# THE TIME TO HONOR A
# GREAT LADY IS NEAR

So much good food was appearing at the big house, at 'Tilde's house, at the church, and even being dropped off on the dock by anonymous boats! Carrie was answering dozens of calls pleading, "Where we goin' to put all this?" She was truly touched by the kindness of folks. Pansy and Jasper were with 'Tilde, hosting the sittin' guests while she cleaned her pie- making mess away. The sun was splashing the yard and the porches with late afternoon gold... it was her favorite time of day. This was quittin' time... when work was done and everyone found their way to river and beach for ritual gatherings ending the day with the best the Island can offer. The women sit in buzzing circles punctuated with laughter and songs of praise, while dodgeball, hide and seek, jump rope and jacks busy the children, and the men fish from docks and surfside until darkness or gnats drive them in. Many a jump-up fish fry results from these twilight times, when their luck is good.

It was nearly six... an hour until dinner at the church as Carrie discarded her apron to leave, when the telephone pealed again. "All Right?" Carrie's colorful greeting was answered by Strahan Hartsell's tense voice. "Aunt Carrie? 'That you, Aunt Carrie? This is Strah...!" He didn't get to finish his first name when Carrie, tired and cranky, replied, "I know it's you, Mista' Hartsell, how you doin' today?" She braced herself for what was coming next, her eyes to the ceiling. "I think you know how I... how we are over here, Carrie, what with my son disappeared and Franciene missin', and the two of them probably gone off together! I took what's left of my near-to prostrate-family to the hospital, a hospital I damn near paid for, and they wouldn't let me see Massey, nor tell me when I can possibly see him! I'm rightly sorry, and you know I am, about his heart attack, but this is a crisis for us too, and we've got to deal with it NOW!"

The wise woman's eyes were now closed in an effort to be patient, and answered with, "MISTER Strahan, I can tell you that MISTER Massey would be just as worried up as you are if he could be allowed to worry, but right now he can't get upset, an' that's why he has not been told anything about this! I ain't been let see him myself, but they say he's better, and I' just got to trust the doctors." Strahan was sputtering as she spoke, and exploded when he got the chance.

"You know as well as I, Carrie, that this is exactly what Massey wants to happen... he's been dangling that little cookie in front of my boy's innocent nose since she got tits, beg your pardon, and I been watchin' and waitin' for something like this to happen. Why, at the Christmas party, when Cliffie was home, I watched her turnin' him just like a pancake that very night... first teasin', then ignorin' him, workin' him like a Jezebel."

Carrie's body was shaking with chuckles at the thought of Francie with a big spatula, flipping Cliff Hartsell in the air. While she was grievously worried about Franciene being gone, knowing her like she did, she was sure it was voluntary, and if she was with the Hartsell boy for fact, there was little chance of danger, although she would definitely be compromised when they returned! Strahan's outburst brought her back.

"Now I know, Carrie, you got a lot goin' on over there, what with Aunt 'Tilde's passin'. I'm so sorry 'bout that... and with Massey bein' away, but I need you to tell him when you can, that if that girl ends up in a family way, it ain't goin' to follow that she becomes Mrs. Clifford Hartsell! You tell Massey I' got ways to block such a thing, and he knows I can do it!" He hung up with force, and Carrie, shaking her head, chuckled some more as she resumed her humming and her chores.

While she readied to go to 'Tilde's, she thought on whether Strahan Hartsell could be right about Mister Massey's plot to get Franciene married off to the wealthiest boy in the state for selfish purposes. She wouldn't put it past her old friend and boss, but he must know who would suffer for it. If that boy took Francie off to dally with her, he could find himself drawing back a nub, in the most serious way! Franciene would allow his advances only if it suited her, and she would be in control of the situation. The Hartsells had reason to worry after Clifford, Carrie knew, but not from a shotgun wedding... A wedding would be the kindest thing that could happen to the boy.

* * *

It was a radiant Sunday evening on Alligator Alley, with colors most vibrant in the pre-twilight sun, and traffic near to nonexistent. If anyone had been traveling that stretch of the causeway, boredom would have been shattered by the clutch of activity at a canal-side rest area, where a trio of state patrol cars, whirling blue-splashed smokey bear hats, a growling wrecker at work near the water's edge, and the usual rubberneckers pulled to the shoulders for their thrill du jour, converged amid crackling radio transmissions. The object of the blob of blight on the landscape was something being hoisted from its' slimy berth. A trooper on his supper break had noticed, mid-bite, a glint of chrome in the duck weed on the water's surface. He finished his burrito before going closer to investigate.

What he saw was a vehicle's bumper, its curved edge all there was to see. Rather than soil his militarily perfect attire, he radioed for a tow truck and back up units. A wave of chills rolled over him as often occurred when a possible grisly discovery was imminent. It being a grindingly slow night for the road warriors, every patrol car in earshot rolled in. The officer first on the scene had stood by the spot, marking with a pylon the place on land that would locate the car if it slipped deeper underwater. The local sheriff arrived just as the little car was pulled free of the goo that was the tenuous bottom of the canal. He walked slowly to the rear of the wrecker, his arms folded and clasped at the elbows. Locking his knees with a rhythmic jerk, he remarked, "Damn! It's an Austin Healey roadster, and she was somebody's baby for sure!"

He was right... Clifford Hartsell's "Baby" was now dangling and oozing while everyone craned their necks to look for a sign of humanity. The truck moved up to high ground and surrendered its prize to the growing crowd. "Can you see the plate?" The sheriff silently begged for a New York origin as he hustled to the rear of the car. "It's a South Carolina plate, Doug," the trooper offered. "I can't make out the figures yet... wait! Now I see it! He wrote the plate number on his pad and tore the sheet off for the sheriff, not yelling it out. Sheriff Doug liked that. The long standing rivalry between state and county peace officers was legend, and each side was hard-pressed to be the bad guy. The onlookers were disbursed for a more secure crime scene as the poor wretched thing that had once been a treasure was rudely bumped to the ground. The police, to a man, donned gloves and slickers and were looking over their discovery. It was quickly determined that there was no sign of anyone, and no outward indication of foul play.

The incidence of doused cars out here was large... insurance companies knew the area well, and some thought Alligator Alley a fitting moniker. This case did not fit the pattern. No sane owner would want to destroy such a beauty for any amount of recovery, so the plot would surely be deepening. The trooper and the sheriff went to call in the plate information on their respective radios. When they met between the two units, the trooper, Corporal Charlie Wagner, was grim-faced.

"I know this family, Doug," he drawled, "They were in my territory when I was with the South Carolina Troopers, and it happens to be the uncrowned first family of the state. Mr. Strahan Hartsell pretty much turns the wheels up there. He's got a kick-ass plantation on the coast, and this was his son's car. Jesus! I hope he ain't in that canal, or ate up by gators!" The sheriff shuddered and they went back to the edge of the canal. "I suppose we need to drag for a body, don't you? I mean, if we've got a car like this one, there has to be somebody close by."

The trooper was older and wiser, but he knew to tread lightly on such an ego. "Not necessarily so, if the owner met with foul play somewhere else, being so well-heeled like this young man was, another toy was right around the corner, or maybe he was kidnapped...disposing of his flashy little sports car would be the first thing to do. No, I don't disagree with you about calling for a drag. It's going to be easy as pie to drag this canal, even a half-mile or so either way. I'll wager there's nobody down there, and that he was robbed and either killed or forced to relocate... before the car was brought here and sunk, get the picture?" He zipped his lip, vowing to quit popping off just because he felt like being heard. "You go on and order the dragging team, and I'll certify that this is the boy's car. Did you look in the glove box and the trunk, or boot, or whatever the hell those limey's call 'em? Maybe we'll get a clue or two yet."

He knew it was Strahan Hartsell's kid's car, knew it in his gut. The Healey was a signature of the good taste the family used. He wouldn't bother the Hartsells until after dragging was finished, to stretch out their oblivion. There was no sense causing agony just yet, with them waiting to find out if their son was in the canal. The john boat took its time, slowly crisscrossing the canal, big grappling hooks yielding everything else BUT a body. Each time the hooks were hauled up bearing weight, the trooper, who was called "Pieback," for some good old boy reason, sighed audibly. There was a moment of levity to break the pall, when just before dark, a gator as long as the wrecker truck followed the hooks out of the water landing halfway in the john boat. The two rednecks in the little vessel barely touched the water as they fled to the bank. The monster slid backward into the duck weed, disappearing with a hiss and a gurgle. Everyone on land, happy for the diversion, hooted and hollered as the two men waded, panting and cursing, to retrieve their boat from the reeds.

Dragging resumed immediately, to continue until they hit pay dirt, or were ordered to stop. More than one of the sour-faced officers was thinking the gator they just met, could have easily death-rolled a medium size young man and stuffed his body under a shelf of mud or an old log for later.

* * *

Back at Frenchport Dan was tired... to the bone. Add to the fatigue all that from Linda Sue, and the captain was ready for a rum drink. Ruby obliged and tousled his hair as she looked hard in his eyes. "What's all over you, boy? I know you been runnin' like a scalded dog since before daylight, but it's more ain't it? You can tell me to mind my own business, if you want to, but I'm stayin' right here!" She was propped on her sturdy elbows, waiting for his answer. "I'm okay, darlin'," Dan moaned, "It's been a bitch of a day, that's all. There's more, but it's real personal, and I can't tell it. It ain't I don't trust you, it's just what it is." He chugged his drink and pushed it to her for another. She was concocting a weaker one when the bar phone rang.

"Pick that up for me, Dan," she called out. He took the call and was astounded to hear Massey's shaky voice. "Dan, buddy, is that you? How'd you know to get the phone?" Dan summoned control and answered, "Ruby's gettin' my drink is all. How you doin', Massey? They lettin' you call out now? Must mean you're better. I ain't heard nothin' back about your girl, and I swear I been askin' around," he lied. There simply hadn't been time to keep his promise to poke about for Francie, and he was quickly red-faced with shame. "I know you have, and I'm worried sick about her." Massey replied weakly. "That's why I'm callin', Dan. I slipped the mobile phone while the nurse was way down the hall so I could call to ask you a great big favor."

A big favor to Massey was usually a mountain to climb for the poor sap he would ask, Dan knew this from experience, but he took the bait. "What you need, boy? I'll help if I can." The revelations from Linda faded when he heard Massey's voice... their long friendship ruled above all. "I need you to be here tonight at midnight, waitin' in your truck by the rear entrance to the kitchen. Keep the engine idlin', and the lights off. I'll be there no more than ten minutes later. I got to get the hell out of here, Daniel, there's too much to tend to out there, and layin' in here frettin' over it is gonna' kill me quicker!" The poor guy was near to tears.

"I' got a plan laid out, and all you got to do is be there. Will you do it?" What a crazy fool! Dan was about to laugh out loud, but stopped when he heard Massey sobbing. He had to do it, he knew, but spoke out anyway. "Man, this is nuts! You'll finish yourself off for sure! Don't you think the doctors know anything, Massey? How are you gonna' get out of that place? They' got security and orderlies crawlin' all over." He waited for Massey to argue his case, but all he heard was the same sniffing sound... until, "My baby's GONE, Dan! Out there, she could be gettin' gang raped, or even killed! There's pervert sum-bitches who would put a girl like her peddlin' on the street, for Christ's sake! I need to go home, see that Aunt 'Tilde's for sure laid away, and then go after my little girl, or I'll surely die tonight, right here! Please be there for me, Dan, I got no better friend than you to help me!" That did it! The best friend thing was the capper. Dan finally agreed, and sipped his second rum while Massey detailed his plan.

* * *

Jasper and Linda drove away from the dock engaged in friendly small talk... about Pansy, the island's politics, everything but what they knew must be brought up between them. Finally Linda spoke of it. "Would you mind if we went to the beach and sat together for a while? Do you have the time?" The man knew he should be back at the church where there was so much to do for tonight, but this was the best way he could think of to spend his time right now. He nodded, giving her a look that said he knew. She squeezed his rough hand, and went back once more in her mind, to their first meeting.

# CHAPTER TWENTY-FOUR

*Remembering June, 1967*

There was little else Linda could do when she got home alone, but wait until the police called her in Waycross with some word about Willie. If she went to Massey's Island home now, he would not be there, figuring that to be her first move. Perhaps the law would get that helicopter's flight plan, and track him that way. The house was so empty, so full of the scent and sweet essence of her baby. How could Massey tear her heart out so cruelly? There was nothing he could have done worse, nothing that would prove that he couldn't feel anything more for her, than tearing her baby from her arms. Finally, after two hours of nothing, she called for the Thornedike phone number on Squires Island. Trembling finger punches brought the first ring, the second... then an answer. "All Right?" A woman's voice answered. "May I please speak to Mister Thornedike?" She said timidly. "He ain't here at present, ma'am, could I tell him who's callin' when he comes? I expect him directly."

Wondering what she meant by "directly", Linda said, "No, but I would appreciate you telling me when he might return, whether today or tomorrow." Next, the woman shushed someone, and Linda heard a child's voice scream, "NO!" It wasn't little Will's voice, so it must be Franciene's. Such a poignant moment, for her to hear this child,

Massey's child, when hers was gone. Finally the answer came. "He went offsho' fishin' and he said he's comin' back tonight, about dark, or soon after." That would be five more hours, if he had been truthful. Linda tried to believe he would be on time with his daughter expecting him. Stupidly, she realized she was thinking of him as a human being, instead of the monster he truly was. She whispered, "Thank you"... and hung up. One more call to the number the police in St. Marys gave her, a recording being all there was for an answer, and she made the decision she knew must be made. In a half-hour, she was heading North on I-95, toward Carolina.

Clutching his little boy to his chest, Massey was flown to the shopping mall parking lot near Savannah where he had been picked up earlier. It had been meticulously coordinated by him ever since Tad called. He liked that boy, and hated to involve him in what was in law a kidnapping, but the past two-plus years of not knowing his child had been maddening. He had, over time, left six or seven messages on Linda's phone, and when no answer came back, he even sent a detective to check on them, receiving a grainy snapshot of mother and child in the front yard when Will was first walking, as his meager prize.

He didn't know what would happen as a result of the caper, but at the moment, it was worth it. Will was surely the sweetest baby he had ever seen! He had not cried even once since he was taken, and was content playing with the things Massey had brought from Franciene's outrageous toy chest. Finally, to complete his plan, he secured a safe-house he could count on to remain so, until he could figure out what was next. In fleeting moments of reality checks, he knew he would have to give his son back, but his impulsive nature ruled him, and he knew even more surely, that he would take his joy for as long as he could.

It was not lost on Massey that Dan was on a boat delivery and therefore ignorant of his stunt on that day. The crusty but chivalrous Dan Fuller would be tough to handle if he was made aware. He was certain Linda Sue hated him now, and while he regretted the pain she was in, his own pain at the loss of her love burned hot. But!... Massey reasoned as only he could, she had the luxury of being with the boy since his birth, and it was Daddy's turn now, while Willie was still a baby and so precious. Nobody keeps a man and his son apart... not THIS man!

Will was snuggled down in the front seat beside him when they drove out of the parking lot, as if he knew who he was with, causing Massey to weep grateful tears. Just as he was about to turn onto the highway, he spotted a nice jewelry store at the end of the mall. Scooping the child up, he trotted inside... back out in under a half-hour with a gift box. It was silly, considering his dirty deed, but he anticipated a special visitor, and wished to be prepared.

When she got to the unfamiliar harbor after her dizzying dash from home, Linda had no clue how to get a boat to the Island, so she walked out on the dock, intending to ask the first person she saw. No one was about, and the hour was nearly six. Cocktail hour, she mused. Finally she saw a man coming toward her. His skin was as black as ebony, and his build was slight, but strong. He wore black rubber boots up over his khaki-clad knees, a soft plaid shirt and suspenders. His hat was of wheat-brown straw, quite rakish... and his eyes flashed smartly from under the wide brim. "You need some help, Ma'am? I don't work here, but I know eva'ting there is to know 'bout the place... My name's Jasper Griffin."

He put out his hand, and she took it, answering, "I do need some help, thank you. My name is Linda Parrish, and I have to go to Squires Island this evening, to Mister Massey Thornedike's house. Do you know how I can do that?" He smiled slowly, his eyes even brighter. "Well, well! Massey's got him a caller comin'! I'm that glad to hear it! He's been alone long enough now. I live over there too, and I'm just about to cast off for home. How's 'bout you come with me. I'll take you right to his door." It might have been prudent to let the man know she was no friend to Massey Thornedike, but she bit her tongue and took his kind offer.

Neither of them had reason to talk... rather, each of them had reason not to. Jasper was a private man, always had been, and he respected others' privacy the same. He figured Massey would get around to telling him about his pretty lady if he wanted to. Linda on the other hand, had to keep her terrible story to herself while on Massey's turf. It would likely go against her if she confessed her fury. Linda's composure was borne of a fierce need to maintain and prevail for Willie's sake.

Jasper stopped at the walk, and announced, "Here you are, child, and I hope you have a nice visit. Did you meet little Franciene yet? She's quiet somethin', you'll see. Anyways, Carrie or 'Tilde ought to be right inside. Massey's not back yet, but I heard he had a boat set to bring him across at seven o'clock, so he's on his way. Shame you couldn't 'a met up to cross together, or is this here a surprise visit? Never you mind, that ain't no business of old Jasper's to know. I'll be 'round when you need to go back, an' Carrie'll call me for you... how's that?"

He was so sweet Linda wanted to fall on his shoulder and sob it all out, but she thanked him instead, got out of the old square-back, and went up the steps to Massey's door. She rang the wrought iron bell and Carrie was there in seconds. "I'm here to see Mister Thornedike, if you please. I know he isn't here yet, but I was told he would be shortly. May I come in and wait for him?" Carrie looked quizzically at the pretty young visitor, and opened the screen door wide for her to enter. "Sure you can, Miss! I'm Carrie, and it's good to have a visitor nice as you to come see us. What is your name, honey?" She was smiling and genuine, Linda observed, so she said, "My name is Linda Sue Parrish, and I'm pleased to meet you, Carrie."

They walked in and Linda was struck by the beauty of the house... its' center hall, a room in itself, sprawling from back door to front, a glistening creek moving slowly beyond the screen doors, the hall showcasing an antique piano, a ceiling high English break-front displaying fine old crystal and china, artifacts and sculpture, interspersed with dozens of family photographs in polished silver frames. There was a parade of museum quality, brass lamp-lit Early American art down each wall, and the runner on the floor was deep, jewel hued, and Turkish. Carrie showed her into the parlor, more of the same flavor, and she sat gingerly down on the raw silk, camel-back sofa. Constant manners in place, Carrie asked what she would like to drink, but Linda declined with thanks. Then she was alone... finally, free to amaze herself with this place.

She rose to walk about, and her heart stopped when she spied a watercolor rendering of a boat hanging over a kidney shaped writing desk. It was their sailboat, "Sweet Surprise", the name Massey gave to his two new "girls", while they were in that magic, long ago time. She turned when she heard voices, and faced Massey head on, but not for long... poor Linda fainted in a heap on the floor at his feet. Hazy figures and anxious mumbling brought Linda around to find herself a scant few inches from Massey's face. She was on the divan, with her upper body across his knees, while he rubbed her icy hands between his own. "Linda! Sweetheart! Come on back now! You're okay, little darlin'. I love you, Linda, love you so damn much! Look at me!"

She scanned the room and saw two black women, each holding the hand of a beautiful, though very frightened little girl, of about four years. Her roving gaze continued, until she once again, this time clearly, stared into the bluest eyes in the world, being those of her only love. Involuntarily she surged into his arms, but only for a split second, when dark realities wedged them apart again.

"NO! Let me go! You give me back my baby, Massey! I swear to God I will kill you if anything has happened to him!" She was on her knees, beating the big man's chest and face with futile fists.

He took her wrists effortlessly, while barking to the drop-jawed women, "Take Franciene to your house, 'Tilde, and you and Carrie wait there with her 'til I call. I need to handle this alone. Francie, baby, everything's okay, and Daddy'll explain all this later. Go along with Carrie and 'Tilde now!" They were gone with his last word, and he stood up, pulling Linda to her feet. "You' got to calm down now, Linda Sue. We can talk when you do, and not until you do!" The furious woman was choking on her rage, but composed herself enough to allow words to form. "Where is my little boy, DAMN YOU? Don't say anything else until you tell me!" He was cornered with that, and exhaled deeply as he began. "He is completely safe, I promise you, baby," She flailed at him anew, more infuriated by his use of the affectionate term.

"Don't you DARE call me that, you sonofabitch! I could strangle you right now, as outweighed as I am, and you're dripping honey like some fool! Give me back my son! WHERE IS HE?" He had moved away from her to the bar, and was pouring two snifters half full of brandy. She was aware of Spanish guitar music somewhere in the house, like it was coming from inside the walls. "He likes everything to be SO Perfect!" She spat to her own roaring brain. She knew she was not going to have the effect she needed to have, no matter what she said or did, so she stopped fighting him to hear his words.

"I am sorry for how this has hurt you, Linda, but the truth is, I have a son, my only son and heir, and nobody is going to keep me from claiming him and being near him... not even you, who I know I still love, and will always love. The reason I never came to you before, is just that, honey... this love that will not die. I know I can't make up for the past, and that you have every right to hate my guts, but my impulsive actions that awful night when you told me, just took me over, and I could not stop what happened... and I regret that night more than you will ever know."

He strode to her, where she had dropped to a straight chair by the doorway, and handed her the heavy snifter. "Drink this, so you can relax a little... it'll be like medicine, I swear." Linda didn't want to do anything he said at that moment, but when she sipped the brandy it seemed to soften her razor sharp nerves. Massey turned away a moment, then looked back over his shoulder, a thundercloud of warning on his face, thinly disguised by his crooked smile.

"Think before you answer what I'm going to suggest, Linda, then I'll listen to you. That boy's got me and my name in him... he's one-half part of me, there's no gettin' around that! I've got a little daughter here, who would kick like a steer if I brought a strange woman and another child into this house, but if you will agree, I can set you up nearby on the other side, in a place we choose together, with a nurse, and I can visit and be his daddy, send him to the best schools, and when Francie's older and I can make her understand, we can have a life together. I need to put my imprint on the boy, starting now, for him to be a true Thornedike, to grow up like me. Honey, it would only be good for him. He can stay where he is for now, until we draw up some kind of paper for my lawyers to approve, and then every-thing will be just fine. What do you think?" He went to the kitchen for a moment, while Linda gathered her rage into a salvo. When he returned, he took her snifter for a splash more. She followed him, resisting the urge to take up something heavy. Instead, she decided to answer him rationally, or at least to try.

"What do I think? I think you're insane to put this to me as even a remote possibility! I won't let you take control of our lives like this! You and I could have raised Willie together, as a real family! Instead, you abandoned me the moment you knew I was pregnant, and now you suggest uprooting and billeting us close by, while he grows up under your thumb... and me? I'm to wait until you and your daughter decide that I'm worthy of your acceptance? I say, BULL SHIT! Where IS he, Damn you?" She was sobbing pitifully, and gulping instead of sipping the brandy, until it was nearly gone. Massey began to notice the effects of the sedative he had put in her snifter while he was in the kitchen, and after a couple of minutes Linda's legs stopped working, and she began to slur her words.

A look of knowing crossed her slackening face as she helplessly allowed him to scoop her up in his arms, and take her, his lips in her hair, to the guest room on the second floor next to Franciene's. He gently undressed the by now unconscious woman, worshiping each lovely, familiar place he unwrapped, and put her under the covers with expert tenderness. Linda was snoring softly by then, and Massey had to smile when he remembered her good natured ribbing when he would snore, oh, so many millions of years ago. He sat beside her for a few minutes, rocking back and to, singing her into deeper sleep, then tiptoed downstairs and phoned 'Tilde's house to suggest Francie sleep there, offering no explanation. He knew the two women were a'twitter with curiosity, and Francie must be pelting them with questions about her daddy's unruly guest, but they couldn't have any answers... not until he did.

He went downstairs, poured yet another brandy, and made a call to check on Will. Satisfied with the report, he took the gift box he had picked up earlier in the day, went back up to Linda, and slipped the bracelet on her limp wrist. When the drug relaxed its grip on her a little, Linda's mind began to drum the message out that Willie was where she couldn't go, and she would be kept from him... couldn't see him, or hear him cry for her. Hell was a holiday when compared to what she was told in her dream. She woke slightly for a few seconds, and then went back to the misery of the nightmare. There were no words blacker than the ones spoken inside her head, with despicable cadence, like a cruel child's sing-song taunt.

"Massey has your son, Linda Sue... he has taken him away to where you can never find him. But no matter, you can survive, Dearie. There will be other children when you meet the right man. Just let it go, Linda... he will always win out... always. The child is a Thornedike. He is not yours to keep, Linda Sue, according to his birthright." Rolling tears dropped to the pillow from her chin, as she slept and dreamed on, with no respite.

A sudden storm promising gale force winds began lighting up the sky as Massey climbed the staircase to his rooms. Outside the windows the mammoth live oaks were being bent and twisted into impossible shapes, and he concluded conditions would prevail through the night. He was, by now, quite in his cups, the cognac decanter having been vested of its contents over the last hour. He slowed on the second floor landing, palpably aware of her... steps from him in the guest room. Lightning flashes and cracks punctuated the already surreal state in the shadowy hallway, as he gathered himself for the rest of the ascent to his bed- chamber.

After a brief, coma-like sleep, Massey sat up and checked his watch. It was one-twenty, and still blowing stink outside. He went down to check on Linda. She was on her back, arms and legs akimbo, breathing heavily in drugged sleep, and irresistible to Massey as he sat, weaving, on the edge of the big oak rice bed. She roused, to once again, impulsively move into his cloaking arms as he whispered hoarsely, "Linda, I love you so much, my darlin'. I never meant you to be hurt, and I'm so damn sorry." He laid her back down, repeating his devotion, just as Linda came into the moment.

"You are a vile monster and a criminal," she hissed, pushing him from her with little success. "Get off me... NOW!" He had been too long without a woman... in reality, since that night in 1964, when he left her crying on the boat... too long for a man like Massey. And here she was, the woman he loved, all the sweet and beautiful parts of her. He could no longer maintain his sanity. His need was all there was. Linda realized it too, and what love she still held deep inside was being choked by fear and anger, and by survival. She fought as hard as she could in her haze, but the difference between them was formidable... due as much to the scope of his desire as his size and strength, as her own foggy head and sapped strength from the sedative.

He pulled the bed clothes from around her body, pinned her arms and legs with his own, and was intent on orally consuming her from ears to knees, not letting her move until she was awash in his saliva. Then, without being allowed control even for a second, Linda was impaled with his, aching, needy member. Massey was sobbing regrets, as he raised his hips and thrust deeper into her again and again, his control totally gone. He was about the will of his hunger now, a man gone mad. Linda was spinning apart, no longer herself, but the pain and panic were very real.

This was Massey, and she had experienced his urgent, sometimes rough ardor before, while they were together in love, so now she instinctively met him as he took her. Getting hold of her sanity anew, she tried desperately to move from under him. He found her breasts with his lips, as he continued to slam into her, and sucked her nipples into his mouth, then deeper into his throat, causing her to cry out. Her cries of pain did not make him relent, and he pounded her steadily, still sobbing his love into her chest.

The hellish roller coaster stormed on for an unbelievable forty-five minutes... Massey spending and re-arousing twice, with no pause. Even then he wasn't ready to release her, but at one point Linda took advantage of his limp arms and legs, and managed to throw her body from under him. The quick move sent her off the side of the bed, and she landed with a thump onto the rug. She caught her breath a little when she heard him moan, knowing she had to get on her feet and get away from him. Linda realized dizzily that she was afraid for her life.

Since he was at the point of semi-consciousness, Massey hadn't noticed Linda's movements. He was oblivious of her leaving down the stairs after grabbing her dress and shoes. She took time to check the study desk for any sign of where he was hiding Will. Finding none, she dashed to the garage out back, praying the key to one of the cars was there. Deciding against starting up a noisy engine, and thanking God for horse-savvy, she ran to the barn where a big bay stallion pawed the ground and whinnied at her. She found a hacka-more for him and climbed aboard from the fence. They galloped out of the drive, and to the dock where she prayed for a miracle, to find a boat. No luck, so she turned the horse down a different road, end-ing at the beach. After dismounting, Linda crumpled to the dune while the spirited horse thundered away. Wracked with whole body trauma and fatigue, Linda Sue let herself breathe deeply, and fall unconscious in healing sleep.

# CHAPTER TWENTY-FIVE

However Massey felt about what had just happened in the guest room, it would soon become a lesser urgency, as he returned to reality. He lifted himself up from the ruined bed, shaking his shaggy head, worried that it might fall off of his neck and roll across the floor. "Too damn much brandy", he whispered raggedly. "What did you say, Daddy?" came forth from near the hearth, stabbing his heart. Massey stumbled into his shorts, as he waved his arms toward the voice. "What are you doin' here darlin'? Daddy sent you home with 'Tilde and Carrie, so you could spend the night! When did you come back here, and who brought you?"

Massey was too groggy to feel anger at the two nannies, but would have it out with them about this come daylight. He tried to pick her up in his arms, but she stiffened and moved away. "Franciene, have you been here long, honey? Why did you come in this room instead of your own... how come?" It was getting clearer by the moment that his innocent little girl might have witnessed his debauchery, and he became instantly nauseous. He dashed to the bathroom, and when he returned his daughter was gone. In a swift move he gathered the ravaged linen from the mattress, shoved it under the bed, and ran out into the dark, calling Franciene's name. He found her in the barn, in her pony's stall, crying and biting her knuckles as she cowered in a corner.

Her daddy crawled on his knees through the deep straw to her side. "What IS it, baby? He sang to her. "Tell Daddy what's got you so upset, and how he can help." Franciene was on her knees in a flash, and without a moment's hesitation, hauled back and slapped her daddy's face with stunning strength. "You hurt that lady on the bed! I saw what you did! She was a'cryin', and you wouldn't let her up! Daddy, is that why Mommie died? Is that what you did to Mommie, and then she died? Why did you do that to her? I don't wanna' be a lady if that's what happens! Does that always happen to ladies? Does it? You can't make me be one if that's what has to be! I just won't, that's all!"

Massey could have slit his own throat from the wrenching guilt at having exposed her to such unspeakable sights and sounds. He reached for her again, asking, "Why were you in there, baby?" She was flailing at him as she sobbed out, "I thought she maybe knew my mommie, so I sneaked out after Carrie was asleep, and I went in the room to look at her, and hid when you came in so I wouldn't get a whippin'. Then I saw you hurtin' the lady. Where is she now? I want to help her!" She got up and went to stand with her pony between them, screaming, "Now you go away... get outta' my pony's stall, I said! GET OUT!" The last words were more shrieked than spoken, so loud the pony whinnied and stomped in protest.

Massey feared the whole Island had heard her, so he threw his hands up and turned to go. He was the wrong one here, and she needed to calm down before she would listen to his side. Back at the house, he quickly started the process of laundering away his mess, sadly hearing Francie's pony's hoof beats retreating into the night.

Ocean sounds, and soft onshore breeze had calmed and comforted Linda, and she was grateful to the steed for bringing her to such a place of healing. She stood and slipped off her shoes, her dress falling away as she moved gingerly to the water's edge, wishing for the waves to soothe and cleanse the pain and shame she felt. Half-reclining in the lapping, moon splashed surf, she heard a horse running toward the beach on the road. "If that horse has come back for me, I know there's weird powers at work," she said aloud, but it wasn't the bay... it was a pony... with flying flaxen mane and a tail as long as its burnished body. As the dainty horse cleared the dune and romped out onto the beach, she could see a tiny girl in yellow pajamas, her hands tangled in the pony's mane, steering toward her. Linda waved, and Franciene nudged her mount into the rushing and receding waves.

"I'm here, Franciene! It's Linda Sue... over here!" She waved wildly to keep the girl coming to her, then remembered that she was nude... not good, especially when the child didn't know her with clothes ON yet. Still, considering what she had already seen of hysteria and outrage earlier in the study, it was a night of excesses and surreal events. She was sure the beach had welcomed skinny dippers many times, and that Franciene likely was accustomed to it. Linda took hold of the pony's halter, and patted the lovely child's leg."What are doing out alone this time of night, sweetie? Does anybody know you're gone?"

"I was riding to the beach and saw old Copper running back home, lickety split! Did you ride him here? Nobody rides that stallion but my daddy!... 'least we never saw anybody who could!" Bless her heart, Linda thought, she's everything they all said she was... besides being the epitome of beauty, she was quite the precocious little miss. No wonder Massey was so proud of her. No! She wouldn't allow a kind thought of him to pass through her mind. He was still the bastard who stole her baby, and he would pay! She answered with words she hoped would be bonding and warm. "Maybe since he didn't feel any fear from me, we started out even, what do you think? Horses are like that... they pick up on your feelings, and that's a fact!"

Francie had slid from the pony's back into the waist deep water, letting her trot up to the stands of sea oats for a late night raid. "You know a lot 'bout horses, Linda Sue? I want to learn everything I can, 'cause I love 'em more than anything in this whole world!" Her little brown arms extended from her sides to measure how big, "The whole wide world" was. "Don't you want me to go get your dress for you? You must be ready to get out of the water by now."

Linda was charmed, and near to tears as the girl dashed up to retrieve her dress. It was a break from the terror, and she was grateful. She put on the dress and they walked from the surf together, but Franciene bolted away and disappeared in the dunes. She returned with her arms full of twigs and driftwood. Linda watched, rapt, as the dainty child expertly fashioned a fire pit and lit the twigs, causing a burst of flame. The night breeze was chilly on wet clothes and skin, so Linda flopped down, close by, to warm herself.

"How did you light the fire so fast?" she asked. Franciene was brushing her hands on her pajamas, and replied proudly, "We have always kept matches and lighters in a Tupperware box behind that big fallen tree 'cause Aaron and Benjie used to come to the beach to smoke rabbit tobacco and cigarettes, if they could sneak 'em." Linda saw the silvery driftwood tree, once presiding over its place so majestically... now the children's secret hiding place. Her mind wandered, and wondered if there could be a better place to grow up.

"You have quite a good life here, don't you, Franciene? Would you ever want to live anywhere else if you could?" She watched the girl as she put her index finger to her temple and tapped, just as her daddy did, and after a minute, jumped to her feet, looked in Linda's eyes, and wisely said with a little frown of conviction, "There's no place like home"... and clicked her bare heels together three times, as if on her way back to Kansas with no need for ruby slippers. Linda laughed and hugged the little swimmer's body to her, her throat tightening from what might have been, had it not been for Massey's craziness.

Finally, they covered the fire with sand, and Francie whistled for Topsy. They began to walk to meet her, with Francie announcing maturely, "I'm going to take you to Miss Sandy's to spend the night. She's gone for the summer, since she's our school teacher. We know where the key is, in case Daddy wants to put company up there. I truly think she loves my daddy, but he says she's just his friend. He don't love anybody but me and Carrie and 'Tilde, I know that for true. He don't want you to come back to the big house, I'll bet, cause he feels bad about what he did to you. It was wrong he did that, and I told him so. My mommie died, 'cause he hurt her too... he said so to Carrie when I wasn't supposed to hear, back when I was little." Dear God, Linda realized this child witnessed what happened in that bed! What must her mind be fashioning about men, and what should be said to her right now as damage control?

At the most inquisitive time in her life she had been heaped with horrors she couldn't sort out. The questions that come naturally... where babies come from, what men and women do when alone, what parts of her body are for, must be a tangle after the nightmarish episode. She hated Massey even more, as she reached deep for the right words. "Honey, I need to help you with this." They were standing by Topsy, both stroking her silky neck as she stood, breathing heavily from her run. Linda found words, not altogether true, but for now, good enough for what this confused little girl needed to hear.

"I wasn't really hurt by your daddy, and he did NOT cause your mommie to die. He told me that her fragile body was too weak to get well when she got sick, so she went to Heaven. Now she's an angel who is assigned just to you, honey, and that's the truth. When I came to see him last evening, he remembered how much he misses your mommie, and he just tried too hard to show me, that's all. He needed to hug and kiss a lady like Mommie so much he forgot to be gentle."

God, this is so tedious, Linda thought as she forged ahead... in a strange way convincing herself, even as she tried to satisfy Francie. "See, when people grow up, they go out and find a partner to make them a pair, so they can work together, play together, make dreams come true, and most important, have children. Their games grow up too, and may not seem like fun to little ones like you, but they are fun, and they work when everyone is happy. Don't you worry, Franciene, it will all make sense when you are a young lady. All you need to do now is have fun and be good, and mind your daddy and the ladies who take care of you. How does it feel to you, after all's said and done? Do you believe me when I tell you that I'm okay? All Daddy did was drink too much alcohol, and get upset with something I said. I know he loves you so much, and would never hurt you... ever!"

Enough had been said. It was up to the child to take it in and rule on it now. A totally exhausted Linda agreed to go to Sandy-whoever's house for what was left of the night, so they climbed on Topsy and galloped the mile to her cottage, deep in the thickest part of the woods. It was a dear little lowcountry house, with screen porches, decks, and flower gardens creating the teacher's retreat. Linda and Franciene put Topsy in the fenced yard, knowing she would likely devour everything growing, and went inside. A strange emotion swept over Linda... one she couldn't define. Then she knew. She SMELLED her baby! Francie was turning on lights, when someone called out from the bedroom. "Who's there?"

Francie bolted to the back of the little house, and Linda heard her exclaim, "Sandy! I thought you were gone! What's happened?" Linda was racing around the house by then, calling Will's name. When she heard him cry, "Mama!" from the other bedroom, she stumbled in the door and there he was... standing in a crib with extra high sides. He seemed okay at first look, in fact he was dressed in a soft night dress, and smelled sweet from a bedtime bath. No matter, Linda thought as she lifted her baby from his cage... We're Gone!

Sandy Calhoun and Francie were in the hall by then, both wide-eyed with shock. "What is my son doing in your house?" Linda asked furiously, but in a low tone to keep from scaring the children. She knew the answer, of course. Franciene's hint about this woman's feelings for Massey had explained it. Sandy sat down on the sofa and began to cry.

"I had just gotten to Isle of Palms, to my brother's home for the summer, when Massey called me, to ask me to come back and take care of a friend's little boy. He said he would pay me twice what I make a month teaching, and that we could have supper together a couple of nights a week, so he could visit with the child, since they were buddies. As soon as I saw him today, I knew he was Massey's boy. There was no denying it. I told him so, and he finally admitted he had taken him from his mother so he could get to know him, and that our deal could remain the same, because he was going to work it out with the mother in a way she wouldn't object to. I should have known it was a sham, but he was so pitiful and desperate, it got to me, I guess. I assure you I have taken good care of him, I am a registered nurse as well as a teacher. He is a precious little boy, and we were getting on great. Whatever you do now, as his mother you have a right to do." She covered her face with her hands and went to her room.

"That is my daddy's little boy?" The girl had backed to the door, and was fumbling with the knob. Her face had contorted into something awful. "He can't be my daddy's baby! I'M MY DADDY'S BABY! HIS ONLY BABY! He promised me!" She flew out the door and was gone before Linda could reach her. She let her go, feeling helpless for the poor, confused little girl. Willie was settled in her arms and was turning a toy car over and over in his chubby fingers. Linda put him on the rug and went to Sandy. She asked for Jasper's telephone number, sure the woman could give it. Without a thought for the hour she called the number.

Jasper answered, and his voice was so kind Linda broke down. Sandy had stepped close behind, awkwardly trying to comfort her. Jasper was in his car in minutes, and soon was knocking on Sandy's door. It was nearly five in the morning and the earliest shafts of morning light were giving a ghostly glow to the moss laden trees over the cottage. He rapped sharply on the door, and Sandy opened it for him, her face reddened with shame. "What's happenin' here, Miss Sandy? This lady just called me all upset... somethin' 'bout a baby boy. You know what she means?" He then got a look at the sturdy blonde cherub in Linda's arms, and held his hands up in wonder. "I swear if Massey Thornedike didn' spit that child out his-self! Come here to ol' Jasper, you sweetest t'ing!" He held his arms wide and little Willie fell forward, anxious to be taken by the smiling, licorice colored man.

Linda smiled proudly at her son as he wrapped his arms around Jasper's neck and laid his sleepy little head on his shoulder. Jasper patted and rubbed his back lovingly, but was frowning at the two women who appeared so upset.

"Take this baby and put him down, and come back to me with the story. I don't want his tender ears to hear a word. I saw Franciene on that little yellow pony when she ran past me on the road. What does she know of this? You ought not let little ears hear what messes grownups get themselves into, don't you know that?"

He was so right the two women could only hang their heads. It was Sandy who spoke first.

"Jasper, you don't think I would ever hurt Francie, do you? She was here when it all came apart. I was taking care of the child because Massey asked me to, and I should have asked more questions. This young woman has been treated horribly, and I want to help her. It won't sit well with Massey, but right is right. He snatched this baby away from his mother, it's as simple as that. Now I want to fix what I foolishly took part in. If you can help them get off the Island before Massey stops them, it will be best. Can you please take them across now?"

Jasper was way ahead of her. He had told Pansy to get his can of outboard fuel from the shed and put it in the boat, and warm up the engine while he went to Sandy's to fetch Linda. He also told her to keep everything to herself, especially from the Thornedike house. Linda remembered she had left her purse and overnight bag, and when she told Jasper the hitch in their quick departure, he called Pansy back and had her slip over there again, quietly get the things out and take them to the dock. Linda monitored Jasper's efforts with wonder and deep thanks. Because of these two Godly people, she and her baby would escape. Sandy packed the things Massey had brought, and helped Linda into Jasper's car, still asking forgiveness. It would be longtime coming from Linda... forgiveness for any of it.

She nodded robotically, just to make her stop begging, but asked her one favor. She asked that Sandy refrain from calling Massey until at least eight o'clock, to give her time to be close to home. Sandy promised, agreeing that Massey would most likely follow her if he thought he could overtake her nearer to Frenchport. Willie was wrapped up tight in one of Sandy's blankets, so he was asleep for the trip to the dock. They were trooping down the pier, Jasper, Pansy, Linda and son, when Massey appeared at the top of the ramp, resting a shotgun across his loins. "I just left Sandy's, Jasper. It was pretty clear somethin' was goin' on when I heard that old busted muffler of yours grumblin' down the road. You get up early old friend, but not early enough. When my daughter came back home, I was waitin' up for her. She lit into me like a banshee, all about me havin' another baby to take her place. Just you tell me, all of you, how could you do that to her?"

He was beside himself with rage, and Linda could not help herself from speaking up. "Not another accusatory word to these good people, Massey Thornedike! "You will NOT berate them for helping me take my son away from here, and away from you, after they heard what you did! I won't have you misplacing any blame you yourself deserve. Now get away from there and let us pass." She started toward him, but Jasper stopped her. "No honey, don't provoke him right now. I know him like my own. He ain't bad, he's just stubborn like the worst mule I ever saw. He won't mean to hurt a one of us, but this is when bad accidents happen. Let's just go to my house right now, and I'll let you and the little one stay with Pansy while I reason with him. Then I'll take you to town when it's light. He half turned toward the river, and looked into a furious face.

"Massey, you might as well go on home to Franciene, now, since I'm takin' these chillun' home with me and Pansy, and you can't do a thing about it for now. You run along, son, and go take hold of your girl." It was perhaps the bravest thing Linda had ever seen. Jasper was confident that Massey wouldn't harm them, any of them, but she knew he had lost face in her presence, and wouldn't rest until he was restored.

At any rate, he stood speechless as they turned and went to the square back, got in and rumbled to the house down the road. He followed, stupidly turning in behind them, and sitting in the Rover... watching as they went inside. It was daylight, they were all frazzled from the lack of sleep and the stress brought on by Massey's confrontation. Linda was saddened by the rift that had developed between Massey and the Griffins on her account, and said as much, but Pansy and Jasper wouldn't hear of it.

He patted her shoulder and said, "That boy has a lot to learn 'bout how to be a man, Honey. He can't run things to suit himself like he thinks, and his child is learning' some bad lessons from him. I'm goin' to speak to Carrie and 'Tilde today about these here shenanigans, and they'll jerk a knot in his tail for sure. Pansy's makin some breakfast for us, and after that, you and the baby can try to take a little nap 'fore we go across. Massey won't be back this mornin', you can be sure. He knows ol' Jasper won't have anymore of that bully-boy bidness."

He chucked Will under the chin and went to help his wife. Linda was grateful to tears again, sitting in the big rocking chair on the porch, rocking the sleeping child it had all been about, as he slept the innocent sleep of an angel. She suddenly noticed the silver bangle bracelet on her wrist. Slipping it off and turning it over, she saw that there was an engraved inscription inside. When she read it, her fury caught fire again, and she flung the bracelet across the porch.

# CHAPTER TWENTY-SIX

There would be no consoling Franciene. Massey returned home, full of self-loathing and dread about facing his daughter. He was still stinging from Sandy's tirade about his subterfuge, when he went to her house for Will after Jasper had taken them away. After last night's histrionics, he figured he might as well tell Carrie and 'Tilde, prepared for their disdain. He went to the barn where Franciene was holed up, to try and repair the damage, but she exercised the option of stony silence, and turned her back to him as she groomed Topsy.

"What a spoiled, selfish child I have raised", thought Massey, as he left the barn. If she wouldn't listen to him and understand what he was enduring, then she could do without that new pony cart he had coming next week. He went in to cancel the order, sputtering like the spoiled child he was himself. As for Francie, she was doing what most children in crisis do… she was pushing all the conflicts and confused issues she had just faced, deep down inside her, rather than deal with them. She was just too young for such. The facts now flooding her naive mind…a woman her daddy seemed to like, or even love, that she never knew existed, the things her daddy did to that woman last night, the fact that she truly liked Linda Sue… liked her so much, and yet she had to reject her because of HIM!… because of that baby boy of hers.

He just couldn't belong to Daddy! Where could he have gotten him, and why did he need any other child when SHE was here? If he couldn't make all this go away, then he could go away too, and that was all there was to it! She heard Carrie whooping for her from the porch, but it was probably just to come for breakfast, so she swung up on Topsy and took the shortcut to the road leading to Jasper and Pansy's. Everything was in the boat except the people, and Linda was still trying to think of a way to thank the two earthbound angels who rescued her and her son. They decided to walk from the house to the dock, to delay their goodbyes. Jasper and Pansy were walking together, each holding one of Will's fat little hands, and Linda followed, smiling and hugging herself at the sight.

They all turned to look when they heard the pony coming. Francie sailed from the horse before she slowed the canter, and fell into step beside Linda. She looked up at her, squinting one eye in the sun, as she blurted, "It ain't that I don't like you, Linda Sue... I love you. It's just that HE can't be here with my daddy! You got to take HIM away for keeps! Maybe you can come back sometime when he's not with you, and we can ride all over the island together. Would you like that?"

The child had such a look of desperation and panic on her face, Linda was filled with pity at what had become an obsessed daddy's girl. She lifted the child in her arms and hugged her close, saying soothingly, "I will be back, Francie, I promise, and we can go riding as much as you want. Now, as for Will, you try to understand and accept what is the truth, here... that you will always be number one in your daddy's life, and nothing can change that, but there will be others he cares for, coming and going as you grow. I hope you will be a big girl and let this pass for now. See? I'm just fine this morning... there's no harm been done. Do you believe that?"

What a joke! She couldn't expect Francie to believe it if she didn't believe it herself. But Francie nodded solemnly, and Linda put her down, because they had arrived at the dock. Everyone waved as the boat moved away...with Pansy holding Francie's hand while they called out farewells. When they had walked back to the house, and started shelling peas on the porch, Pansy asked her young guest to tell her what she thought about Linda's little boy, Will.

"I don't want to think about him at all, Aunt Pansy. He don't mean nuthin' to me, OR to my daddy! Linda Sue promised me he wouldn't NEVER come here again, and I know she'll keep her promise!"

Pansy sighed in defeat, sad that this little one would never know her only brother because of selfishness, and went inside with the bowls. Alone on the porch, Francie began her usual snooping expedition, a habit since she had crawled about as a baby, picking up wrapped candies and tiny toys Jasper would purposely leave about for her. The silver bracelet tossed away earlier, beckoned in a sunbeam, and she slyly plucked it and put it in her shorts pocket. Triumphant in her stealth, she tiptoed to the doorway, and called out, "Gotta' go, Pansy!'" She tripped down the steps, and was away in a cloud of dust.

When Linda was finally able to unlock the front door of their home and collapse on the sofa, she was able to let go. After all she had been through... truly, after all they had both been through, she was still convinced it wasn't over, and that she could expect to hear from Will's angry father very soon. The baby was fed, bathed and put to bed while his mama pondered every option that could protect them. She had an idea, and spent the rest of the evening before allowing herself to fall into bed, packing a few days' worth of things for them. The next morning, well before the sun, Linda rose, and taking her precious baby, got in her car once again, to seek peace. Her daddy would know what to do, and Massey knew nothing about the remote place where Bill Parrish lived. It would help her immeasurably, to feel her father's comforting arms again, and Willie would be thrilled to be in the magical swamp.

An hour after they were gone, Massey paced the floor of his study as he counted the rings... four, five, six, seven, Eight! He slammed the phone down for the third time that morning. She had run away with his son, he was sure of it! In moments he was calling to re-engage the investigators to stake out Linda's house, and to call him immediately if they returned. Massey's arms ached to hold his boy, and while it was a consuming need, he had come to realize that the need beyond, and more consuming, was his desire to have Linda back. The way he had treated her, he was certain, would keep them even more impossibly apart than before, and he was loathe to beg her to consider seeing him. At the heart of the truth, even though he had lost the love of the woman, he could not fathom conceding the loss of his child forever.

Carrie and 'Tilde had no idea what to do for their little girl. Since the day she was born, there was no sign of strife between father and daughter. Now after one visit, and over one night, everything was different. The girl would not come in the house, choosing to stay with her horse in the barn, and could be seen galloping away at times without a word of notice. Mister Massey was closed in the study, not answering their knocks and calls in, to please open the door. There were other reasons to go to the Griffins, but when Carrie arrived, and the trio was seated on the porch with iced tea, Jasper's first words were of Franciene and her daddy.

"Carrie, you notice anythin' not so good 'tween Massey an' his child? I s'pose you'd know if somethin' wasn't quite right... ain't that so?" He was adept at calling folks to the hard line of the truth, for a strict accounting of what they could contribute to it. Carrie, on the other hand, would reveal only as much as she deemed proper, about her "family", near to the same constraints an attorney uses with his clients. She took a sip of tea, rubbed the moisture from her glass with her hanky, and put it down on the arm of the swing. "I ain't right sure how you mean, "Not so good", Jasper," she said slowly, "We all know there's a powerful lot of mulishness in those two, an' all them Thornedikes."

They chuckled in agreement, then fell silent to wait for more. She continued carefully, "I guess you wonderin' 'bout the lady that was here last night, is that what we doin' here? Well, you just mind your 'batata 'til your gravy cools, Jasper Griffin, 'cause I don't know nuthin' 'bout that young woman, an' you don't either, do you?" It was more a command from headquarters than the question she feigned. Carrie was as wise as Jasper, making these kinds of tête-à-tête's mostly end in a draw. Pansy came to Jasper's aid this time, and the mystery began to take on colorful proportions.

"You know", Pansy said slowly, "I saw somethin' in Francie I never noticed before, and I love that child good as anybody. She's a jealous and selfish girl, for why I don't know, but it ain't pretty on her, that's for true. She ain't 'bout to share nuthin' with nobody, never mind how close they is. Why, I'll bet she won't ever have any friends, the way she's bein'. Like my mama always tol' us girls... "Pretty is as Pretty Does!" It was enough for Carrie. She stood, went to the kitchen to leave her glass, and without a word, left by the back door... leaving Jasper and his wife looking at each other, shrugging their shoulders wordlessly. When Carrie got home and looked for Massey and Francie, she found neither one. Clothilde reported to her that, mercifully, father and daughter had taken a gallop to the beach together, after Franciene learned that her longed-for pony cart hung in the balance. They returned in time for supper, Francie bobbing along from the barn atop her daddy's shoulders. "Hallelujah!" whooped Carrie and 'Tilde, and they sparked their dinner efforts with blackberry dumplings and fresh churned ice cream for dessert. After Franciene had been read to sleep, and Massey said good night, and thanks to the two ladies at the door, he lit a big Cuban cigar and took his brandy to the front porch, just like always.

* * *

Her daddy's porch was comfortable enough for sleeping, but Linda was wakeful most of the night, while Will slept soundly with his "Bunky Bear" beside him in his new best friend, "Gampah's" bed. The hardest decision she could ever have to make had filled the night. With daylight breaking over the misty swamp, she paddled one of the old canoes to the ranger station's dock and drove home with the feel of her baby's hair still on her trembling lips. Her daddy would read the note, and accept their plan as they had discussed it, delighted to be of service, and have the company of his little grandson.

* * *

Linda's recollections from years back, and the fill-ins from Jasper as they sat at the beach, left her drained. She had vowed to treat the experience they secretly shared as something buried, or at least left to die of its own weight, partly to protect the elderly couple. Jasper had become most timorous, when she told him why she was on Squires. He didn't tell her about Massey's illness, since he was no danger to her where he was, and if Will was here, that meant they could finally be together again.

His sweet old heart had nearly broken when he learned that she had sacrificed the early years most precious with her son, just so he would be safe from the domination of his father. When it sank in, Jasper was as proud as if she were his own daughter, for her brave and selfless act. He told her of his pride, and then suggested he could drop her at the Thornedike's, or she could catch her breath with Pansy and him for a while, but she convinced him she wanted to stay at the beach for now, and watch the sky change colors.

She recalled the way to Massey's from there, even though it had been fifteen years, and nothing seemed to have changed. She promised to call them if she needed anything, and Jasper rolled away up the road. Now it was time for "Coming to Jesus", as her mama used to call it. What could she say to her son that could explain why she left him sleeping, never to contact him, or try to find him all this time. She prayed for the words and the strength to face Massey, yet again. It was possible he and his son had acknowledged each other, and she was girding against the wrath she could endure from them as a unit. Adding Toby's presence would either save or destroy whatever strength she was mustering... feeling what she now knew was true devotion for him. It was no wonder she simply sat on the beach, not wanting to move, while God's palette was smeared across the sky for her solitary gaze.

Everything was ready for Clothilde's family and friends to gather at the old church for the twilight supper and testimonials. Will and Aaron as greeters were engulfed by the boatloads of guests. There were probably more than three hundred in number already, with more to come throughout the next twenty-four hours. Two wallowing paddle wheel boats had brought the bulk of them from Savannah and Beaufort, and were anchored off the bank beside the church property to wait for day's end.

Carrie was still at the big house, and Toby remained with her in the kitchen. It was already seven o'clock, in fact a few minutes past, but Carrie was running behind with all the interruptions. She had her helper spinning in circles, somehow managing to get an apron tied on him. The perplexed "volunteer" was almost done packing serving utensils in a box, when she frantically waved at him, "You get that ham out the oven, Toby, while I wrap these last four pies!" He wasn't sure how this happened, and why he was left on kitchen detail while Will and Aaron did men's work, but he suspected Will volunteered him, so Carrie and he could get better acquainted. It hadn't happened yet... no time, but Toby staunchly intended to ask a couple of questions before they got out to the supper. He went out to back the Land Rover up to the steps, and observed an old Volkswagen creaking into the yard. A lovely young woman alit, soft luggage in hand.

She thanked the driver and came toward him. She put her hand out confidently, stating, "I'm Massey Thornedike's nurse, Mattie Bell... and you are?" He told her who he thought he was at that weird point, and took her bag as they went in the house. "Carrie, this is Miss Bell, from the hospital", he offered. "She just got dropped off. Where should I put this?" He held up the bag with a questioning eyebrow. To his surprise, she rushed to the young woman, wiping her hands and exclaiming. "Oh, I'm so glad to see you! How is my baby'? I done been so worried!"

Mattie shook hands and sat down at the table. Toby, figuring he could load the car alone, retreated to the cacophony of both voices in unison. "Your 'Baby' is much better, Carrie, and I am here to keep him that way. He was about to fly to pieces over his friend's death with him not here to see her laid to rest, along with his biggest worry, being his little girl's disappearance. Have you heard anything about her? We're supposed to call him with any news, and I know you want to speak with him."

Carrie was beside herself with relief. "I sho' 'nuff DO! No, child, I don't think anybody's heard a thing from that bad girl. She just up and left! I need to tell Mista' Massey that he needn't worry, though. She's a smart little one, and I know she's jus' gone off to play, that's all. Let me go see if that boy's got away from here with all that food, and then we need to call my Mista Massey, is that alright?"

Mattie saw tears welling in Carrie's eyes. She took her hands between her own and said calmly, "I know there is a purpose for me being here, and you do too... a purpose so much greater than the one I just gave. Carrie, you have it too, don't you?" Their eyes were locked, and as their spirits blended, Carrie's tears became lit with the brightest colored lights imaginable. Shafts of color transferred between them, as Carrie said, "You know! Matilda Miranda Bell. You came to help us... Aaron, William, and me, to put dear souls at rest in our Clothilde's sweet name. I charge you with the task of pulling Will and Aaron into our circle, so we will have the best and strongest arms. We will only speak through our eyes from this moment, and you must not betray us to anyone... do you under... ?" "Yes, I do," Mattie sent back silently, and Carrie smiled.

They went to call Massey then, a call of comfort between two old friends. After the emotional call was done, Massey was even more certain that he must leave the hospital as planned, though he didn't reveal any part of the scheme to Carrie, sure she would blow his cover to stop him. He was mentally rehearsing for the caper scheduled for five hours later. At the same time, Dan pulled his jeep behind the hospital, advance testing Masse's instructions. He had his john boat tied behind Aaron's cabin on Turtletail Cove, a clever twist Massey would find brilliant, he bragged to himself.

* * *

Back on Squires, the supper was in full swing. Will hadn't known of a time when he had seen so much food in one place. The tables, fashioned from saw horses and sheets of heavy gauge plywood, were fast filling up with course after course, from a table of salads and breads, to another with meat and seafood... platters of fried and smoked fish and shrimp, and crabs, deviled, barbecued, and steamed... haunches of venison, beef, whole roasted pigs, and barbecued hams, ribs, and butts. Turkeys, fried, smoked, and stuffed and roasted, and chickens, fried, roasted, stewed with dumplings, and barbecued, a mountain of smoked sausages, pickled pig's feet, and the ever popular oxtail stew.

After the meats marched the sides... macaroni and cheese, mashed potatoes, red rice, white rice and gravies, candied sweet potatoes, and all the garden vegetables in bowls to their brims... collards and turnip greens, butter beans, squash, pole beans and pigeon peas, and traditional First Night fare on New Years Eve, Hoppin' John, with hog jowl, and blackeyed peas and rice. And finally, the queen of Island vegetables... Okra!... gumbo, fried, boiled with fatback, every way known, trailed on the table by jars and crocks of every possible pickle, a dozen relishes, chutneys, vinegars, and a dozen kinds of hot sauces to tease the tongue.

If that weren't enough, Will stopped beside a dessert table out of dreams. Tall cakes... chocolate, red velvet, coconut, applesauce, upside-down, carrot, pound and nectar, on and on, and pies of every variety, followed by candies and cookies, a big washtub filled with ice and fresh churned tubs of ice cream, fruit... melons, peaches, berries, and bowls of honey, sorghum molasses, and preserves, and the biggest tub of butter in the world. All that glorious food was to be washed down with rivers of iced tea, lemonade, and some contraband beer and homemade wine, hidden in the usual place. Everyone was rarin' to go at the tables, but Aaron held them back until Carrie could arrive, so the reverend could say the blessing, and the tribute to his mama. There was scapula singing everywhere, Will noticed, giving a lilt to the scene. Will also noticed the Rover come up to the tables and Toby unloading from the back, but before they could meet up across the big field, Toby had driven off. Will guessed rightly that he was going back for Carrie, so he returned to Aaron's side.

"Hey, Will," Aaron said warily, "I ain't used to this, man. To tell the truth, I was always kind of bashful in crowds. Funny, it ain't so bad right now. Maybe it's my mama helpin' me." Will patted his back as an affirmative, and suggested they take a walk down to the river to cut the tension. Nothing was said until they found a spot away from the others.

It was a radiant evening, and the sunset promised to suit the occasion. The voices humming and singing behind them gave background to what Aaron suddenly said. "I got to tell Aunt Carrie about Benjie tonight, before the funeral tomorrow, Will. My mama, she tol' me NOT to lay her away 'til it was all said. If you think what I told you sounds okay, then that's the way I will do it. Mama won't give her powers up to me until she's sure I can work them right. Carrie needs to deal with me about this, and she might never forgive me, but she is so damn goodhearted, I'm hopin' and prayin' she'll understand what a foolish boy I was back then, and not now, and how much my brother Benjie was to me."

He was looking at the ground, pushing an oyster shell around with the toe of his shoe. Will knew what to say. He put his arm around Aaron's shoulder as he said, "If anyone has a forgiving heart, it's Carrie, Aaron. You can say just what you said to me on the beach, and it will do just fine. How about we go find that lady and Toby, and get your mama's love supper going?" Aaron laughed shyly, thanking God and mama for this new friend. They walked into the gathering together, Carrie and Toby, with him feeling like escort to the queen. The crowds parted, everyone murmuring affectionate greetings and "Don't she look jus' beautiful this evenin'," to each other. Lines were long at the tables, and, God bless her, Carrie simply had to check the presentation before blessings were said, and the signal given to dig in. Will and Aaron came to stand with them while the reverend blessed the food and drink and spoke glowingly of the new angel heading up to Heaven right now. Then it was, "Now everybody Eat!" with a cheer of approval rising up.

Carrie was swept into the crowd and passed from group to group like the matriarch she was, with Aaron at her elbow. He accepted the hugs, back slaps, and condolences good naturedly. Toby watched as Will watched them with deep love. He was obviously moved, turning away when tears came. "Did you see her, Toby? Mrs. Braswell, I mean? She was the tiniest woman I ever saw. Aaron let me see her face when we were alone in the house. He has a hard time leaving her coffin open, because he thinks she is looking bad after this long. I agree with him, but not out loud. I swear, these folks sure know how to send somebody off, don't they? That lady has been gone for days, and they have been honoring her, non-stop!"

Toby told him he had not viewed Clothilde in repose, and would not, since he had not known the lady in life, and it just didn't seem proper somehow. It came to him again and again how very young the boy is, and how many things he was coming upon for the first time. They headed for the Rover, poured a couple of beers into cups, and sat on the tailgate. Will turned to look at Toby, and without blinking, asked, "Who's here?" Toby did not know what he meant, and when he asked him, the boy got up without another word, and walked slowly down the road toward the Thornedike house. It wouldn't have suited to follow him, somehow, so Toby joined Aaron and Carrie's entourage.

After the talk and the call to Massey, Mattie politely declined Carrie's invitation to the supper, saying she needed to be alone. She was content to stroll around in the house at first, but when she went out on the porch and discovered the gardens at their peak, she knew where she would spend most of her time. A small pier about ten feet long led her to the narrow creek that washed in and out of the marsh on the side of the property. It was a vista of incredible wild beauty. This was how all people should be able to live if they were pure and good, Mattie decided.

She had been sitting there about ten minutes when a hand fell onto her shoulder. It was Will Parrish, with a look on his face that could only be called delight. "Mattie Bell? What are... ? She stopped him with, "I'm here on Massey's business, and I hoped you would be glad to see me too." Their smiles matched in radiance as she continued. "I was invited to the dinner by Miss Carrie, but felt a bit out of place. Are you going back there?" Will didn't answer because his throat had closed with emotion. All he could do was nod.

She stood with his help, and he regarded her for the first time as a person other than a nurse. Dressed in pale blue linen... walking shorts and a sleeveless shell, with a tiny gold cross at her throat, she was a vision. Her skin was golden brown, her eyes now a brilliant hazel, (instead of the strange fluorescence he had been caught by when he looked into them at the hospital), and her chestnut hair reflected the sun's flashing demise... yes, she was lovely.

"How is Massey?" Will managed as they moved toward the swing. He had been anxious for news of him, and was sure Carrie would be easier if she could hear. "He is a little better, and will be a whole lot better, if he gets enough of a chance. I came today to relay news back to him, as well as ease everyone's anxiety. Carrie and I even spoke to him a little while ago. He can not relax and stabilize, while so much of his energy is here. The lady who died was like a mother to him all his life, he told me, and he wants to be here so badly." Will watched her face as she spoke, admiration for what she was doing so very strong.

"Add in the fact of his daughter running off like she did, and the problem grows. Have you any word of her to send to him?" He sat her on the swing, and gallantly began to push it from behind her, focusing on the nape of her graceful neck, wishing his lips could be there. What he knew about Franciene would shock her to her toes, so he lied and said, "No, I'm afraid I know nothing at all of her. She's been a mystery to Toby and me." Mattie put her sandaled feet out to stop swinging, spun around, and cast eyes of green fire into Will's. "Why do you lie to me, William?" He felt as if lightning had struck him.

"Did you not know that we are joined? You cannot lie and continue this work. We know when an untruth is told, and you must know that your value depends on complete openness. We are dedicated to the truth and what it can do to save some important people, and you were brought in for reasons you will soon know... you and your friend, so we could avert danger and destruction of life and spirit." Was this the same, sweet nurse-lady he met yesterday? What a different energy she was presenting now... Will was so intrigued, but remained silent. She had barely taken a breath, and continued.

"I hoped our meeting at the hospital had fixed you in place, but you are so new, I must be more patient. I know about what you found here on the edge of the creek, William, and I am sorry for your bad time, but you need to compartmentalize that event, somehow, and delete it from your mind while we adjust and adapt and try to succeed. What you found is real, but it is stuck in a place not unlike limbo... while this confusing time is seen through. As strange as you may find it, that discovery has no validity, at least not yet. Let's wipe out the fib, dear Will, and continue."

It was as if a tape had been rewound and edited, and Will was telling Mattie the story of finding Franciene's body. He hated calling up the images he loathed, but Mattie was gently keeping him focused, so he could air the awful thing, in order to purge himself. He finished, wiping tears from his eyes, realizing it was the first time he had related it aloud. "See?" Mattie said lovingly, looking up under his bowed head at his face, with misty eyes and the sweetest smile. "Doesn't that feel better? You had been choking to death on that terrible thing, and now it is out of your throat, and we can share it, causing us to be squared in our power over ITS' power over you!"

She's perfect! Thought Will, as Mattie jumped up and declared, "Now! Let's go to that supper! I'm suddenly starving, and I bet there's plenty for two skinny white folks like us." She hugged him with genuine ardor, allowing Will to seek her lips with his. There was a second's hesitation, then Mattie answered his kiss with purpose. What was happening between them must have been puzzling, with what they were already dealing with, but it felt so damn good neither was about to protest. They set out on the road, hands clasped and swinging between them... just two fresh young lovers about to bloom.

# CHAPTER
# TWENTY-SEVEN

The food tables were still three deep with hungry folks, over an hour since the blessing was said. Toby watched... his refilled plate in his lap. It was tough to keep his eyes focused, so stuffed was his gut, as he strained to keep up with her... Carrie working the groups clustered around the church yard. She had the most distinctive aura... as if she was an incarnate angel, so personally connected to each one she spoke to. Aaron sat down on the bench beside Toby just then, following his stare.

"Ain't she sum'thin'? My mama was that way too, but she was so damn little she would'a disappeared in this crowd." He laughed as he said it, and Toby returned. "No, buddy, they would have parted wide for her just like they are doing for Carrie, you can be sure." Aaron nodded gratefully, and Toby saw the moisture well up again in his eyes. "I got to know why, and how she died, Toby," he said sadly. "There's got to be a way to know. It's buggin' me so bad, you know? She was just fine! I had no word that she was sick, and somebody would a got word to me. How can I find out what happened?"

He had put a big question to this new friend, and Toby knew the only thing he could do for his peace of mind, was to stop this beautiful ceremony, and take her straight over for an autopsy and tests. He hesitated, but said as much, and Aaron nodded at what he had known all along. Toby could feel his tortured indecision, poised to jump up and cry "Foul", but not letting himself, keeping the promise he had made to his mama to abide by her after-death wishes. It was as if he was hesitating for other reasons, but Toby couldn't open that up for discussion. He was a stranger, and had no place to offer an opinion. Carrie might know... she probably did know, but was of the same mind with Aaron, and had taken the high road as well. "Wonder what happened to Will?" Aaron said after a few minutes. A tall boy like him needs to keep pilin' in the food, and we sure got plenty!"

Toby had not brought up Will's strange and untimely walk just a bit ago, but wondered silently about the boy as well. He was about to take the same walk when they appeared, hand in hand, Will, and he was with a captivating pixie of a girl. The two sprang to their feet, as Will introduced them. "Mattie Bell, this is my best friend, Toby Howell, and my newest friend, Aaron Braswell. It was Aaron's mother who passed away." He said the last part of his intro in a whisper, and Mattie put out both hands to the son, causing a shower of phosphorescent sparks when their fingers touched.

"I appreciate you comin', but how did you get here?" Aaron asked, knowing the boats had only allowed card-carrying mourners aboard, to insure privacy. Will jumped in before she could speak, offering, "Oh! I forgot to tell you! Mattie is Massey's nurse, and she came at his request, to be his eyes, and report back to him how all his folks are getting along. He wants to get out of there so bad, and he needs to stay, so Mattie's here to keep the peace. You probably know well how stubborn he can be." Aaron shouted his, "Oh Yeah!"... lending a bit of humor to the moment.

It was not lost on Toby, that two young hands were still tightly clasped, and that two flanking shoulders touched every few seconds, remembering when he Katie and were similarly rapt with newfound love. It looked the same for Will and Mattie, and he approved, considering his first impressions of this girl. There was a feeling of parental sadness within, that Toby had only heard about, when children become men and women before your eyes. He shoved them affectionately toward the serving tables, as the last second and third helping group grazed the remnants of the feast. As soon as all were finished eating and there was an expectant hush over the crowd, Carrie raised her arms high over her head on the porch of the church, and all gathered in front of her without a sound. She clasped her hands in front of her batik-swathed body, continued her Heaven-bound gaze, and began to sing.

"Swing Low, Sweet Chariot", while everyone swayed and hummed along. Aaron went to her side, and only then did she lower her gaze to lean her head to his shoulder. He knew she had held up in the loss of her sister as long as she could, to get the work done, and he held her in his arms while she sobbed her old hymn out, in harmony with her people.

* * *

It was nearly ten o'clock, and Massey was getting antsy. He could not get to the phone again without drawing suspicion, and since the charge nurse had broken rules to let him speak to his home earlier, he had no good reason to cajole its use again. All he could do was lie there until the time he and Dan had agreed on. The nurse brought his oral medication at eight, and he had gestured as if to swallow, but let the pills fall into his cupped hand. The pills were for sleep promotion and to calm him, and Massey figured he would need them later more than sooner. His things were stowed in the locker behind the door, easy to get to.

The tricky part would be disconnecting from the monitors and I.V. needles without alarms causing the troops to descend. Years ago, he and Strahan sat together on the same board that saw to the renovation and construction of upgrades to the hospital, and he had intimate knowledge of every nook and cranny, as the architectural review committee passed on each expenditure. He mentally mapped the shortest route to the kitchen wing, and by using staff access and egress routes, would be unnoticed at the midnight hour. He said a prayer... asking not to black out, please God... at least until he was in Dan's Jeep and away from the medical campus. Ultimately there was nothing to do but count those god-dammed ceiling dots again, since he got a different total every time, and wait for zero hour.

\* \* \*

Confirmation of ownership came at eight-thirty, and the news was grim. The 1963 Austin Healey 3000, was, in fact, registered to one Clifford Augustus Hartsell, address given as Palmland Plantation, Beaufort County, South Carolina. The trooper stared at the printout for a full minute before he shared it with the sheriff, already preparing himself for the worst. The dragging would resume at first light, but the lawmen knew what had happened to the boy's body, if in fact it was ever in the car. They kept their own counsel, each man, the ugly pictures of past discoveries flashing like a peep show in their minds, and neither said the possibility out loud.

\* \* \*

The boats were loaded, and they stood on the bank, waving, as the scene took on Mississippi riverboat departures from the old plantation wharfs Will had seen in history books and movies, and he chided himself for the stereotypical thought. It was late... nearly eleven, and they were all tired, but Carrie was incandescent, and behaved as though she had just arisen from twelve hours of sleep. The remnants of the crowd, besides islanders, numbered about forty, and Carrie set about herding them toward the bonfire, still sending flames and showers of sparks as high as fifty feet in the night sky, competing with the stars for control of the blue-blackness. The near-to-being-High Priestess spread her arms wide to catch those of Aaron and Will, saying with conviction,

"We should circle the fire and join hands in a prayer of thanks for our sister Clothilde now, and ask that she be received with the full complement of tributes she has earned here on earth. Tomorrow, her pitiful remains will be laid under the Island soil she loved so dear, and we will sing the last hymns of praise to her, and to God Almighty."

There was much concurrence in the group, through the signifying sounds of "Oh Yes, Lord", and the simple, "AMEN!" that said it all. Carrie went on, more quietly and more intimately than before. "Her work here will continue, never fear. There are those already in place to carry on. So, we will sleep well, because the lady we honor would not trade places with a one, no, not a one of us tonight, because she is in Paradise right now."

She bowed her head, squeezed each of the hands she held, and said tremulously, "Oh God, and Dear Jesus the Son, receive our sister to be in Your Company this night, and let us, as a sign from You, have our eyes cast on the star that is now Clothilde Poinsett Braswell." She, and everyone in the crowd, raised their heads and were drawn together, to look at a particularly bright and twinkling star overhead. Not a sound was made for a minute or more, and then Carrie lowered her head and breathed, "AMEN". It was done. The group silently left the churchyard, some riding, some walking, all humming their favorite soul satisfying hymn. Carrie was ahead of the little procession going to 'Tilde's for the last night of sittin' up. There was a trio of young women the newcomers didn't know, Jasper and Pansy, Mattie, Will and Toby.

It was decided that Jasper and Pansy would take the first two hours, and the three women the next, so Carrie and Aaron could sleep the first part of the evening, then be with 'Tilde when the sun came up on her buryin' day. Everyone parted, leaving the rest wondering what to do next. Will had an idea that seemed untoward, but tough to dismiss. He rubbed his hands together, and said, "I don't know about you two, but a beer would be mighty tasty right now, and there's a little bar, I hear, down the river road about a mile. It might be just the break we need in this. What about a vote?" Toby looked quickly at Mattie, she being not just the only lady, but considering the solemnity of the evening, he wondered if she would be offended by a funky bar scene. Personally, he was up for it. "I'll bet you two think I'll decline. Listen, I'm as ready for a beer as you are, and a fun break in this two day event would be welcome! Let's go!"

Toby took one arm, Will the other, and they went off down the moonlit sandy road, singing "Lions and Tigers and Bears, Oh my!"

skipping the traditional steps. For the first time since he arrived on the Island, Toby had a sense that everything would end up all right. He just hoped tomorrow would bear him out.

When Aaron and Carrie got inside Carrie's house, she slumped in a slip-covered chair as if the air had been released from her floating body. I'll get you some hot tea, Aunt Carrie", Aaron said hurriedly, dashing to the kitchen to put on the kettle. "No, Aaron, the tea would keep me awake all night, and we need rest. I believe I'd sooner have a taste of my prickly pear wine, if you'll look down in the cupboard by the sink and fetch it for me. There's two little glasses beside it. Bring one for yourself," she said weakly. Aaron was delighted that she was going to have a "taste" with him, like his mama and she used to do together after a long day... things that are handed down from generation to generation... so good.

In case there is any doubt, ladies on Squires like to tipple as much as the men, given the opportunity, but will always ask for, "Jes' a tas'e", to avoid gossip. No one would be fooled by the request, but faces are saved just the same. The wine Carrie asked for was barely fit to be called "WINE", except for its potency, tasting much like sugary fingernail polish remover, but a lifetime of acquired taste seemed to make it palatable, if not downright pleasant, when occasion demanded. The abundance of wild or cultivated fruits and berries, as well as the fruit of the prickly pear cactus, allowed every house a satisfactory larder of spirits. The boy sat the glasses on the table beside her chair, and with a flourish, poured two drams, then sat on the floor by her knee and raised his in a toast.

"Here's to my Mama, and to you, Aunt Carrie. I love you. YOU' my mama now." She clinked and nodded with teary eyes, and they drank healthy sips together.

It was time. Aaron knew there could be no better time than now, with the love swirling around and between them, to tell her what he knew he must. He hoped he could do it right, and that she wouldn't be too upset, or worse, angry with him. He poured their glasses nearly full, to Carrie's wide eyed pleasure, and took her hand. "I got to tell you somethin', Dear Carrie, I never wanted to, but I been tol' I must, by a mighty powerful voice. You got to promise not to take on, or hit me in the face, or say you hate me, or nuthin' like that, and I promise to take anything else you got to send." Carrie's face had twisted into a fearful mask, and she started to rise from the chair. "No, please don't stop me now... I just got to do it!" She sat back down and said, "I don't want you to go on about what you did after Benjie died, honey lamb, it don't matter no more. Your mama was spared the pain, and that's all that matters."

She knew. She knew that wasn't it at all. She knew it was about Benjie's death... had known someday he would come to her with what really happened in that boat. It was just that she was so weary of death right now, that bringing it back would knock her down, as fragile as she was.

"So, what if it does?" She was told in her mind. "What is more important, my dear sister? The pain of an old loss, long ago dealt with, or this boy's redemption... Perhaps it is his soul's very salvation? Let him speak. I demanded it of him, and I demand it of you because I love you both so dear. Let him tell you now." Carrie's eyes were closed, and she nodded her head as she opened them, swimming in tears, and clasped Aaron's hand in accordance. She wanted nothing more than to do 'Tilde's bidding. It took him an hour to stumble through his story. There were parts of it he could manage, but the worst parts took a few tastes extra for both of them, and when it was time for the "Aaron is to blame" part, Carrie nearly told him what happened instead of the other way around. She sat back at last, and took a few moments before she spoke.

"Benjamin was all I had for my own," she began, causing Aaron to bury his face in his hands, preparing for her wrath. "He made me so proud, you know? I just knew he would'a been somethin' out there one day... and not just a football player, runnin' around all dressed up like a fool, and spendin' money on false people, or for false doo-dads. No, I saw him makin' a fine leader of people. His own people first off, but then he would 'a showed even the finest white folks how we should treat one another. Yes, he would'a made this little place so proud." She wiped her eyes, and looked at Aaron with a steely stare. "But he's gone now, gone to God, and there ain't nothin' to do but wait 'til the Rapture when we'll be together again forever! In the meantime, I can work my days along, and keep dreamin' of what he might have been, and it fills me up, almost as good as if it was true." Aaron had no idea what would come next.

"Aaron, it was bad what happened, child, but it was more bad for YOU than anybody else. You got to remember how it truly was all your days, and for that I'm so sorry. You was a baby then... you' a man now, and I am thankful to Jesus you rose from the death of your past life and come back to me."

"I forgive you, and I take you as my son, from this night, in place of the one I gave up to the Lord. Now! You come here and give your mama a big hug around the neck and a kiss on the cheek!" He did just that, and stood up from her arms a man reborn, and free... He tossed his head back and shouted, "Thank you, Mama! And thank you God!"

They went to bed within minutes after Aaron's epiphany, each aglow with wine and the spirit. Carrie set her clock's alarm for five AM, and was asleep before she could say her ritual, nightly prayers. Aaron was a bit wakeful, still victimized by his addiction, stimulated by the alcohol he had consumed. He was more at peace than he had been since the accident so long ago, but his mother's mysterious death was as yet unresolved. It might never be explained, he figured, but it would take him a long time to accept that she just up and died like they said. He managed a plea to the ceiling of Carrie's extra bedroom, asking his mama to help him with his doubts about her death if she could, Amen.

It was quite a place, this bar called, appropriately, "The Hole". Built as a store of doomed-to-fail description, it had been added to and renovated several times, giving it a rambling, pieced-together look. The outside was many colors of old paint, attesting to ever-changing proprietors with as many tastes, all of them peeling in tandem, allowing a pleasing mosaic effect. Inside was a shrine to the eclectic, dominated by the expected nautical motif, cast nets with papier-mâché crustaceans trapped in them, bottle floats and faux scrimshaw, a bar constructed of large wooden casks topped with the traditional cedar top, polyurethane finished to a fare-you-well. A twenty year old Seeburg pumped out twenty year old tunes in a corner behind two exhausted billiard tables, obviously the primary activity.

They entered through a side door, and it was a relief to find a table by one of the camp-house style screened walls. Will and Mattie were speechless, soaking up the color without comment or critique. Toby, having been in hundreds of these colorful scenes was having a ball, watching them regarding the clientele, from one end of the social spectrum to the other.

Being a waterway establishment on the list in multiple cruising guides, one was likely to see mega-yacht crew, world class sailors, government contractors off of barges and push boats, mixing it up with the locals, both black and white, young and old, and the occasional "Fice dog" waiting for T-bone steak remains to be tossed rheir way. It was up to Toby to get their beer from the bar, and he wasted no time doing it. When he returned to the table, no one was there, but a quick spin found them swaying slowly to "In the Still of the Night", by the jukebox.

Brushing away a pang of envy, he sat down to enjoy the sight. It was the old man's turn next, Will allowed, and he agreed, choosing to circle the small dance floor with Mattie in a smooth, up-country shag, to "Rainy Day Bells", one of Katie's favorite dance tunes. It didn't hurt so much, and he was glad for the chance to relive a nice moment. They were walking back to the table when Mattie slowed a bit. Toby slowed with her as she said, "I like you Toby, you're really good for Will. He will need you so much in the next forty-eight hours. He still hasn't reacted to the reality that Massey is his father, has he?" Toby stopped in his tracks and looked at Will, now readying a shot at the far billiard table, and not looking their way. "How did you know? He didn't?..." She was expecting his measure of surprise. "No! Of course not! The truth will surface when he's able to deal with it. I know, because I am given what I need, to do the work."

My God, she's in this too! Toby extracted. She read that one, and nodded solemnly. Toby kept an eye on Will while asking another question. "What is the work you all keep talking about? Is it dangerous? 'Cause if it is, I'm taking that boy off the island this very night!

He is not going to get involved in some hokey Hoo-Doo, that may cause him harm. I got a book from a gallery that scares the shit out of me, and it's for damn sure you know what I mean."

She was still nodding firmly as she walked away, and Toby realized she had no intention of telling him anything! If anyone ever felt helpless in a situation, he could sympathize heartily at that moment. He knew he was the least important part of the mix... a place he wasn't accustomed to, and was not comfy with, and the secrecy was thick and ominous. Maybe it was the beer and the tequila shots they had hoisted a few minutes ago, but paranoia had covered him over like a second skin.

He figured it was time to leave them alone, so he went to Will and told him he would be walking on back to the house. He was about to object, when he realized he and Mattie could finish the evening as a couple, and pushed his friend's shoulder with his fist in gratitude. Toby wanted to go back to find his designated nest on the sleeping porch, and do more research in the book. If he was going to be excluded from their circle, he could at least get some background on this so-called power.

He hoped he was wrong... that they weren't about to spin Will into a world he couldn't come back from. Selfishly, he wanted him to stay where he was safe and happy, where they had been until last Wednesday. God! It seemed like a year ago! A lovely night to walk in such secluded beauty, Toby was walking along in the moonlight, pounding his fist into his palm, fuming. Linda Sue should be here, damn it! She needs to be his mother, and help him choose the way he should go. He doesn't even know what's happening to him... he has a father he isn't able to acknowledge because they are keeping it from his conscious mind for their own purposes.

He went inside the house and dared to pour himself a healthy splash of the fifty year old cognac from the bar, then went to the kitchen to see what was in the refrigerator for a snack. He had eaten as much as the others, but it had been of little benefit, due to all the worry. There was a note on the table to them from Carrie. She said there were pillows and light blankets on the porch, and they could choose, or fight over where they wanted to sleep. He looked outside and sure enough, the screened portion on the corner was a mini-dormitory of day beds, a sleeping swing, and even a comfortable hammock he was sure Will would grab. Carrie had put a reading lamp and a radio on the table between the beds, and a bowl of fruit. Toby continually marveled at the woman's savvy attention to detail, given her marathon duty of the last few days. The crickets and frogs were singing a song bound to knock anybody out cold, but Toby enjoyed a banana and some delicious grapes, closed one eye, and read a few enlightening pages, soon followed by oblivion.

## Linda is Back on the Finest Beach

Finding the same tree where Franciene had the matches stored was easier than Linda expected... It was about a hundred feet from the road's end. She still remembered how the girl had scurried around for weeds and wood for a fire, and in minutes had a happy little blaze going for them to warm beside. She had always thought a crackling fire, or an aquarium full of colorful fish, to be the best catalyst for meditation. It was past dark when Jasper had reluctantly agreed to leave here, and had driven away. Now, after several more wood safaris, she checked her watch, and was startled to see it was nearly midnight. God, she was hungry! Maybe she should have gone to Jasper's to plan her next move, but she didn't want to intrude by complicating their already busy evening at the church.

No, she would be fine for a little while longer, then when she was sure everyone was asleep, she would go to the house and wait until morning to make her presence known. When everyone in the house realized she was there, she knew the gamut of reactions, from elation, to shocked disbelief, to hostile dissent, would be visited on her, and it was going to take some preparation time. The house was large enough for her to find a place to curl up in, and she might, if there was a God in Heaven, be able to see and speak with Toby first, before the others, and he could help her. No one would be able to intercede with Massey, she was sure, except perhaps Franciene.

It had been a long time since they had parted when Will was so small, and she feared Franciene's resentment might have grown with the years. There was so much to ponder, and so much unpredictable time ahead for her. There was a freshening breeze on the beach... she huddled closer to the warmth. Her bag made a dandy pillow, and in minutes an exhausted Linda was deep in sleep. Her dreams were a kaleidoscope of faces... some dear, some frightening, but all of them would be touching Squires Island soil that night.

# CHAPTER
# TWENTY-EIGHT

The effort and raw nerve needed to get out of his "jail", had Massey doubting his sanity. Yet, here he was, checking his watch every few minutes, mentally timing each part of his escape, and praying that Dan wouldn't let him down. He didn't expect a purposeful no-show, but who could know what might happen... he could have a flat tire, be hijacked, or that decrepit old jeep of his could throw a rod... he decided it was stupid to worry that the mule would go blind before the field was plowed, and looked at his watch again. He was glad his watch had been given back to him today when he asked for it. He told that Nurse Bell he would behave if she went to the Island to see to his affairs, and he damn well wanted his Rolex in the room with him! She went to the safe and signed it out before she left for the day, never suspecting his need for it. Eleven fifty. It was time. He had seen the two nurses go in separate directions less than five minutes ago to complete their rounds by midnight, giving him the next ten minutes of guaranteed moving time.

He was surprised how strong he felt at that moment, and gave his imminent freedom full credit for the lift of spirits. In less than two minutes, he had stripped himself of the needle and the connectors that monitored his vital signs, causing a beeping alarm to be set off. It would be no time at all before his jailers would be rushing to the emergency, so he scooped his clothes and shoes up in his arms and dashed to the stairs. They had approved the building for no more than four stories for aesthetic as well as safety reasons, and he arrived in the ground level, back corridor, next to the kitchen doors with dizzying speed. It was eleven fifty-five.

He was early! What if Dan wasn't there to speed away with him? What if he was going to be found standing on the loading platform, and dragged back upstairs after all his efforts? Couldn't be helped... he went through the kitchen and out the back doors, nearly stove in from anxiety.

THERE HE WAS! Good old Dan! He was sitting there with the engine rattling softly, and when he saw his old friend, he jumped out to hold the door wide for him. Massey dropped a shoe in his haste down the ramp, and as he stooped to retrieve it, Dan got a headlight-illuminated view of the open back of his hospital gown, displaying lavishly, Massey's furry ass-crack, and causing whoops of laughter. "Shut up, you Ass-Hole!" Was the reaction, the curse's reference to what had caused the outburst, giving way to even more guffaws. Galloping toward the jeep, Massey was waving Dan to his place under the wheel as he dove into the seat and grabbed the door.

They tore out of the driveway just as two security guards appeared at the ramp, helplessly watching them careen away. Dan told his passenger of his plan to use Turtletail Creek, as Massey pulled the polo shirt over his head. He stopped dressing, thought for a moment, and chuckled, "You old fart! You love this kind of shit, don't you? Well, it IS a great idea, I must admit. Right now, what I want you to do for me, is stop this sonofabitch, so I can get my fuckin' pants on! This tore up old seat is eatin' my ass a new one!" Dan really let it rip then, and as Massey zipped his fly by the side of the road, their laughter could be heard for a quarter-mile.

The nurses had sprinted to Massey's cubicle to find it empty. The alarm summoned the doctor on call, and security as well, but Mr. Thornedike's escape had been perfect, they deduced, and the charge nurse went to the phone to inform the deputy sheriff and Dr. Benjamin's service. "We will have the doctor return your call as soon as possible", was all she got, and they could do nothing more than go about the rest of their duties and hope he wasn't dead in a ditch somewhere. He wasn't. What he was, was motoring out of the little creek, the john boat's flat bottom easily negotiating its grassy path through the flooding channel, its square bow pointed toward home.

The man amidships was now feeling the stress and exertion of the last few hours, and was weaving slightly. He had put his hoard of medicine into the pocket of his khakis as he ran out, and slipped one into his mouth as soon as he could. When he turned to look at Dan, it was as if to say, "We made it!" But Dan saw in his eyes another question... "Where is my little girl?" He put his big hand in that of his best friend's outstretched one, and shook his head sadly. They were far enough from the creek mouth, and in the shadow of the tall grass, so Dan killed the motor for a moment.

"Massey, I know how bad this all is, buddy, and I already promised to help you find your girl, but if you're dead, you sure as hell won't get to see her come home, ain't that right?" He nodded solemnly, and Dan continued. "Let's get you home to your own bed first-off, an' then we'll start first thing tomorrow, even before Aunt 'Tilde's service. You're safe now. They can't make you go back there, but if you die, it'll all be for nothin'! I ain't gonna' be moved off'a this, my friend. You got to lie down for a time now. Tomorrow's gonna' be full as a tick of Shit AND Shinola, and you got to be rested for it."

While knowing Dan was right, Massey still had a feeling he was being patronized. Dan had started the motor and was powering up, to get to the pier on Thornedike land in the shortest time possible. When they idled up and Dan tied the line, Massey stood to step to the end of the pier, but became dizzy and had to sit back down before he fell into the water. He knew his endurance was spent at that point, and allowed Dan to support him while he stepped from the tippy little skiff. They walked in the shadows past 'Tilde's cabin with the lamplight glowing from the parlor. Massey stopped and began to sob into his hand, imagining the scene inside, but Dan kept a firm hold on him, and they went up the steps to the study door, Massey's private access to the house, and went inside.

God! It was good, even as bad as he felt, to be back home again. The familiar smells and his things around him gave him cause to moan, "Oh, Francie, baby, where are you?" They increased their pace to the stairs, with Dan still pressing his case. "I ain't shittin you, Massey, I didn't go through all this bullshit, jus' so you can get in here and show your ass and have another attack, or even DIE! You got to get in that hot-shit mighty bed of yours and REST, and I don't mean findin' a reason to choke your chicken or somethin', you hear me?"

Massey managed a whispered, "Blow me!", but squeezed his friend's shoulder weakly with gratitude, as Dan half-carried him up the two flights to his rooms. The lovingly tended suite was perfect, as if Carrie knew he was coming. Fresh hand pressed linen, the counterpane turned down, a pitcher of water and a glass and straw for ease of drinking while abed, and a vase of fragrant roses and lilies close enough to see and smell. Dan shook his head at the thoughtfulness, realizing she would have been doing the same thing every day, until the man came home... what a lucky old sum-bitch Massey was to have such devotion.

Dan undressed him, laid his robe on the foot of the bed, and when Massey waved his clucking away, tiptoed backward, not closing the door until he heard the soft snoring signal that he was asleep. He was asleep all right, but it was a sleep laden with images fraught with extremes and hallucinations, endured while he was awake. They would have been explained by the medical community as drug-induced, but these dreams were Massey's true life experience and fallout, playing away in his desperate mind.

Water... lots of churning, blackness, and a little teacup with children in Dr. Dentons, hanging on for dear life inside it. He saw that his daughter's little angel face was one of them, just as a huge sea serpent raised its snake-like head, spitting a red forked tongue and green bile, and devoured them, cup and all. His big mane shook the dream away, only to be replaced by another, and another, until he, too worn out even to dream anymore, fell off the last precipice into unconsciousness... where there was nothing but rest.

# SAILING TO SQUIRES BY THE MOON

The perky sailing contraption bobbed and rocked over the water in the moonlight like a rubber duck in a tub full of babies. No one was outwardly worried, but Mandy would have been the best bet to have a faster heart rate. She was not accustomed to boating like the others, and had not been dipping into the marching powder for false courage like them either. Troy was a happy captain... he had not had a sailing adventure in far too long, and this one would sustain him for months. He guessed right... the winds were fair and steady, with nothing to complain about from the boat or its crew so far. It was a half hour since they hoisted the sail, and they were better than halfway across the sound between the two islands already.

The young man was relaxing now, with mental perusal of sea shanties of yore, while the girls sipped beer and sang alternately chosen tunes. He took stock of the two new women in his life, and allowed that Franciene would be one to cultivate. She intrigued him, perhaps because she appeared not to care whether she was his,"Femme du Jour," or not. Rather, the way she had regarded him earlier was similar to how one treats luggage, or the vacuum cleaner... purely as objects to supply comfort, or expedite a problem. He was surprised that it turned him on, instead of the opposite. Yep! This was a tantalizing little package he looked forward to unwrapping at some future date.

On impulse, he got on his knees and called out between cupped hands, "Francie! It doesn't look like there's a lot of water between here and that point off starboard! What do you know about this stretch?" She held a hand to her ear, so he motioned her to join him, glad for the excuse to be closer to her. Mandy smirked, and poked her with a warning finger as she giggled and crawled on her hands and knees to sit beside him. "I think for the next few minutes you need to help me navigate. There must be a negotiable channel between the point and the other bank at the mouth of that creek we're entering, and we sure as hell don't want to miss it. Getting this thing off a bar is doable, but not any fun in the dark!"

Since she had spent most of her young life finding fun on her Island, Francie had a life's worth of familiarity with the way the tides and bars worked around the point, from a dozen summers of daylight to dark beaching, but it was strange territory in the dark water. Toby called to her ear, over the sounds of the sea and wind. He was trying valiantly to tend to business. "I've forgotten when you said high tide is, but if you can tell me pretty close, I'll know if we're safe to scoot straight across the bar, or go around it to port."

She was puffed-up proud of the astuteness of her theory, and knew Troy was enjoying her. "We should be ebbing high at about three-thirty, Sugar, and it's just past two now. Do you feel good about going for it or not?" She shot a tan little arm straight out from her side to point ahead to go for it, and Troy whooped and sheeted in for speed. The young girl's perfect eyesight scoped out her Island looming in the gray haze, fringed with a glowing necklace of sand, but they still had to get safely over the treacherous bar that had foundered many a handy craft. Unfamiliar to the area, hundreds of boaters had spent hours waiting on the tide to float them free from its clutches, to the glee of Islanders watching from shore.

It was a cruel game, but taking bets whether this or that boat would get lucky and find the slot, or bury their keels and lower units in the sand, whiled away more than a few hours at the beach. The fear and the game subsided for many with increasing use of technology, as boats were told by electronics to veer away from skinny water. The Hobie was a skimmer, but her fully engaged centerboard was not, needing three to four feet of freeboard at all times. With no auxiliary power for the option of putt-putting through unsure or becalmed moments, the trip was a test of Troy's mettle.

They slowed a little, and Troy was busy watching Francie's spectacular butt as she scanned the water from port side approaching the marsh, indicating the mouth of the creek that passed alongside Thornedike land, to the point to starboard, and its relation to the size of the channel. She snapped to action gesturing to port, and said, "It's over that way! The channel's there, maybe a hundred feet from us. I know, because we bar-walk from that dead tree on the point out to the channel at low tide, and it's right there!" She was so excited to be navigating, and wriggled her glee, causing Troy to clasp her knee in appreciation. "So if I tack to port about forty-five degrees, I'll be in the deepest water, right? Then all we have to do is head straight into the creek and we're there."

Francie was nodding happily, and put her hand over his on her knee, wanting it to stay. After the mauling she had endured from Clifford, it was fine to choose being touched. Her mind forced itself to go back to that shower scene, in spite of the upbeat mood she was in, and she frowned and cursed silently, recalling when she had needed to slap him away from her, because he had actually bitten her inner thigh! It proved a plus later, since she had snapped the rude bruise with her camera, intending its use to fluff up her story to her daddy. She still held to her conviction that if that was making love, she could do fine without it. It didn't hurt the boy one bit! Just the girl, and she wasn't into pain... at least not her own. Textbook sailing took them steaming straight across the bar and around the shallow point, then neatly into the creek. Mandy joined them aft for a celebration brew, and they hugged all around, growling, "AARRRRGGGHH, MATEY!--THEM THAT DIED WAS LUCKY!" at regular intervals until they were well inside the mouth of Muddy Cow Creek, tacking toward the pier by Francie's house.

They had come this far, with very little more to go, by three-thirty. Even at that late hour there were still stacked showers of bright stars frosting the night sky, and the air was so clear even a freshly waning moon couldn't dim their twinkling. The youngsters tied up as per Francie's instruction, with her suggesting the two of them wait in the boat for her. The last thing she needed now was a disoriented dummy howling from the pluff-mud on three sides of them. Alone, Francie could toddle off to the house if she were blindfolded, and she needed to get inside, do her business, and get out clean.

The girl ran like a fawn through the trees, noticing Aunt 'Tilde's cabin still lit up. What could be going on? Dismissing the thought quickly, and like a dog that won't look at his reflection in a mirror, she turned away and padded up the porch steps, not seeing the three strangers sleeping in the dark corner. Once inside, the as-ever smell of the old house made her dizzy. She steadied herself and looked up the finely carved oak staircase, toward her daddy's tower. What she was about to do would cut his heart out, not because of the money, but because she was in the house... this near, and didn't even want to see him.

"I'll give him that much", she thought to herself, and began to climb, as so many times before, when she would tiptoe in and tickle his face with a peacock feather, or put a kitten in his bed, or sail onto his chest with a report of how high Topsy jumped in the field, much too early on Saturday mornings. This was strange, sneaking up to see him, hoping this time he won't wake up. She pushed open the big door, and instantly caught the presence of him. He was breathing steadily... not snoring, to her surprise. The gnarly oak limb by the window blew away long enough for her to see his face clearly, and she was shocked at how old and pale he looked. She put her hand to her mouth... suddenly afraid for him, but no guilt accompanied her fear, and the selfish girl recovered instantly with the rationalization that he would be better off if he didn't know she was there. Blowing a kiss and whispering her love, she retreated to the hall and down the stairs, stopping in her room to grab the little powder box full of designer drugs, and downstairs for the real purpose of her visit.

Out on the porch, Will roused a bit, blaming his disturbed dreams on a full bladder. He slipped out of the cocoon that was his hammock bed, and tiptoed off of the porch to discreetly drain his own lily in the fragrant Easter lilies bordering the garden. As he returned to the steps he thought he heard someone inside, but knew he hadn't, since Carrie and Aaron were likely sitting up at 'Tilde's. He leaned over Mattie, snuggled up on one of the day beds, a cotton blanket pulled up to her neck in the night dampness. She had chosen to sleep in her clothes due to the accommodations and the company, but he was still aroused just listening to the soft sleep noises she was making. As he tucked the blanket closer around her shoulders Will brushed her forehead with his lips and thought he saw the corners of her mouth turn up in an answering smile by the moon's light. Emboldened, he repeated the kiss. Toby was opposite, and Will thought at that moment he couldn't be in better company. He crawled back in the hammock and laid there swinging gently, strangely aware of impending doom, but not able to define it.

Franciene was at her daddy's desk, feeling around in the middle drawer for the compartment that held the safe's code she needed to be sure of. She nearly whooped out loud when she found it, and using her daddy's penlight, she went to the floor safe under the round Turkish rug in the room's center. She studied the numbers, realizing that the combination was her mother's birth date! Unfazed after a moment, she quickly did what she had seen him do over and over, then put her hand on the stacks of cash right away, and stuffed the entire twenty thousand in the big pockets of the parachute-cloth jacket Troy had put around her shoulders. Feeling further, looking for the stock certificates, she discovered there was nothing there but a few lousy government bonds and some legal papers!

Francie was fuming! They have always been here... right here in this safe! Those stocks were worth hundreds of thousands of dollars last time they discussed them, and considering their blue-chip quality, were sure to triple in value over time. She was about to freak out and run, when she remembered a wall safe Daddy had put in a few years ago behind his portrait. The frame was heavy and cumbersome, but Francie was empowered, like a small woman lifting an automobile off of her child. Once the painting was on the floor, she tried the same combination, but it wouldn't open. Time was wasting... she had been too long in the house. Suddenly, she had a flash. HER birth date! The three number combinations might work. She tried... once, twice, and on the third try, the safe was open. Without a second's hesitation, Francie scooped the worn parchment envelopes up and tucked them in her jacket. After the safe was closed and the portrait replaced, she fled the room and the house, barely touching the floor as she ran.

Will was still awake, and started when he saw a flash of long shimmering hair and longer legs jump from the porch to the ground and disappear into the trees. Franciene's diaphanous form harkened a fairy to mind. It wasn't... it couldn't be! He shook off what must have been a half-awake delusion, and settled back in to try for more sleep. No more tequila for him, his foggy head vowed.

In the tower Massey dreamed on, but now his dream was embellished with a factor not there before. Arguably, his brain was being marched on by the medication, but this was no hallucination. He was detecting a sweet, flower-like scent, a cloud of soft, citrusy musk essence he knew very well. His mind processed the memories the fragrance evoked. Was it Linda? Was it? Yes! It was a scent Frances had worn, but it was more recent than any memory of Frances. It had to be Linda Sue. He smiled and snuggled down, hoping the dream would return, but... it wasn't Linda Sue either!

Then it was no longer a sweet dream. He knew it was a perfume Franciene just began using... the bottle they had given her last week from her mother's dresser. The dream was now a full-blown nightmare, and he was dashing from room to room in a filthy, web laden, abandoned house, calling her name over and over, louder and more anguished. He found her in Linda's arms... they were naked, and they were sitting up high in a blooming dogwood tree that had grown out from the floor. Both were shades of putrid green and gray, their faces falling from their skulls, the rotting flesh played upon by scores of grubs and maggots, and their once beautiful hair was tangled with coils of dirt-covered worms. They were rocking side to side, humming something that sounded like one of Carrie and 'Tilde's favored hymns, and staring through him toward some kind of Hell beyond.

Through the dream's frenzy, Massey feared he didn't have the strength to fight his way out, and that he would die from the jolting horror, but just then, as deep as he was into the place, he was suddenly out again, and wiping beads of sweat from his face, he reached for the pills on the table by his pillow. It was four-thirty... too early to be awake, but the essence of his daughter was strong in his nostrils, and would remain there to taunt him.

In the little cabin down the lane, the alarm rang rudely. Carrie complaining to the clock that she was positive she had just closed her eyes, because when they flew open they felt full of sand. A quick splash of cool water solving the problem, she then tiptoed to Aaron's bedside, affectionately shaking his shoulder. "Wake up, baby, we got to go be with your mama in a few minutes. I got the coffee perkin' already, and the biscuits are in the oven. Get on up now... we need to let those two ladies go on home, 'cause they got to be tired by now.

Aaron didn't want to get up, and he didn't want to spend any more time at the scene in the parlor. His mama needed burying real bad, and this day hadn't come any too soon for him. He was still in the bed when Carrie came to the door and announced she was going on ahead as she pulled off her apron, prodding him to be quick about coming behind her. She was right of course... he shouldn't be so damned no-count! He padded to the kitchen for coffee, ate a biscuit wrapped around some of last night's salty ham, and freshened up at the sink, before walking the hundred yards to his mama's cabin.

It was nearly five when he reached the corner where Thornedike acreage began, and he turned sharply left to use the path along the creek bank he had always taken as a shortcut. He would pass the barn and the workshop, and bear right toward the back porch. His thoughts were filled with frustration about why his mama was dead. The prayer he whispered before sleep came, still rang in his head. "Mama, please, if you can, send me a sign so I can put this doubt away from my thoughts." Hoping it would get through, he said it again, aloud to the indigo sky.

The sleepy boy had just passed the barn when it happened. At first, he thought his shirt tail had caught on a bush growing by the path. He waved behind to free himself, but incredibly, his hand was held tight by another one he could not see, although the moon was casting its light brightly around him. The hand was tiny, like a child's, but rough and withered, and disproportionately strong. He tried shaking free, but could not, and was being pulled backward, toward the buildings he had just passed.

All at once a peaceful, agreeable emotion filled him up, and he began walking freely along, the invisible hand nestled in his with great love. He was drawn up at the door of the old workshop beside the barn as the hand left his, and the door of the shop swung open, bidding him inside. The smell in the shed was a combination of damp, mildewed soil, paint and turpentine, and garden chemicals, long ago discarded in favor of fresh ones. Aaron was hard put to breathe the foul air, but disregarded his own comfort for the sake of the hand that now pulled him toward a shelf unit in the corner.

When it released him he stood frozen to the spot while a rusty can was raised to his eyes, then it was lowered for him to take. There was just enough light coming in from the doorway for him to make out the fading and rusty skull and crossbones. Quick as the hand had come, it was gone, and Aaron began to tremble and cry. The truth he had just been given caused him to cast his eyes toward the sky... to acknowledge his mama's gift of truth, terrible though it was. As soon as he could function, he sprinted off toward the little house, eager to tell Carrie about the sign. He heard a sound near the pier across the sloping lawn. There were voices... two, he figured... a couple talking and giggling. He stopped to try and hear what they were saying, when a third person appeared, running through the trees.

"Oh, DEAR LORD JESUS! It's Franciene!" Aaron breathed, as he stared at the girl jumping from the dock to a boat below. He was shocked into paralyzed silence, only able to watch as the sail was hoisted, allowing their departure. What was she doing here? Was it another vision? Aaron could see himself slipping into insanity if he didn't get to Carrie quick, and make her tell him what was transpiring. Carrie would know... She could make sense of it. The can was still in his frozen grip as he jumped to the porch in seconds, Carrie opened the door for him, and she said, "You found what you were asking to find, didn't you, child? You know what happened to your mama now, and by whose hand."

Aaron had not gotten that far. What did she mean? He sat down at the table, and put his head on his arms, totally vexed. Carrie sat beside him, and while rubbing his shoulders, she explained. "You must help this to be resolved and reconciled, Aaron. The girl is in torment, and she doesn't know why. What she is doing to others, she is doing to herself as well. We cannot bring back the ones who are now gone, but others may be spared with our help. I do not know who is next, because she doesn't know herself. When she is about to take another, they may be too far away for us to act in time." He could not catch his breath as she went on. "It is so hard to believe we are speaking of her this way. She has the demons of all creation inside her, Aaron, and her poor daddy is sure to suffer with her.

He is about to be given knowledge he will find hellish and unbearable, and I want us to help him too, but first we must tend to your mama's needs."

"What you mean, Carrie? Mama's long past our help, and knowin' how she died ain't gonna' bring her back. You think she gave me that poison can so I would know what killed her, but you can't make me believe that Franciene done it! I don't guess I'll ever know for sure who gave her the poison, but if Mama wants me to know who it was, she'll find the way to tell me!" He was getting panicky, wanting to keep talking so she would never say what he feared was true... what simply could not be! "Aunt Carrie, she would rise up from her pillow and strike me down dead, if I was to put this at Francie's feet. Oh, she's a bad one, but she loved my mama, and you too! How come you to say there's two gone? Two WHAT? You ain't gonna' sit there and say Francie's done killed my mama and somebody else! Who else?"

He stood and drew Carrie to her feet to look him in his eyes, and asked again, this time in a bellow of shock and disbelief. "WHO ELSE, Aunt Carrie? Don't say it if you don't know it for true! Oh Lordy, I can't stand this if it's so!" He sank to his knees, after taking from the woman's eyes all the truth he had feared. Franciene had, in fact, poisoned his mama, and Clifford Hartsell was likely dead by her hand as well! He felt as if he wouldn't be able to use his knees for support again, and pitched forward on the floor, sobbing and shaking his head furiously, trying to make it stop.

"I need to know what this is for, Carrie! If that girl is murdering folks, right and left, you got to tell me how we can stop her! Do the Hartsells know? What did she do to Clifford? Oh, Jesus, why did I leave them?" Guilt and fear were heavy on him, and he struggled to make sense of it. "I knew she was goin' real bad down in Florida, an' I just wanted to get away for myself, instead of tryin' to help her. It's my fault, ain't it? He's dead 'cause'a me!" It was one of the worst moments since Benjie's passing, and Aaron believed in his gut that he was not worth drawing breath, and wanted to die right then.

The woman knelt beside the boy, and took his face in her hands. "It don't serve, this blamin' yourself, boy. Francie has been ripenin' for this all her life... she's a bad seedlin' through nobody else's doin', and needs fixin', or we will all feel the blame. Will has a place with us, you know that now. He's Thornedike blood, same as Franciene, and is our family too. If Mister Massey was to die, he would be head of this family, Aaron. We need to give to him what he needs." All at once, Aaron could read her words before she spoke. It was like an echo, and maddening to endure, as the words came.

"That poor arm found in the shrimp net the other day is somethin' we need to get from the hospital, somehow, 'cause it will give rise to trouble out of place, that needs to be covered over for the time bein'. I want you to go and get it... you and Mattie. She's allowed in the place where it is, and you can go with her at first light." He was nodding as if a child to his parent, and Carrie trusted him to follow her directions.

"Aaron, put that thing in an ice cooler and get back here 'fore anybody else is stirrin'. I think those men folks on the porch won't even hear you when you fetch Mattie to the kitchen at about six. They went to the bar last night, and Mattie didn't take drink as much as they did. You can be home in plenty time for the service, an' we can leave that cooler in the big freezer in the shed, where nobody will find it. I don't rightly know why, but I been told to fetch it here to keep it from somebody who could hurt us. It's gonna' be all right, honey, it's almost over, I think... don't you? Can't you feel it?" No, Aaron couldn't feel it, or anything, but fury and the need for revenge. If Carrie knew the way Francie was going bad, why didn't she try to stop it? He asked, with gentle words, why Carrie thought this had happened, this need for Francie to destroy the lives of people who meant her no harm... who even loved her.

"She hates control, honey, no matter what kind, or who was doin' it... her daddy didn't mean to cause her to turn this way, but he had a lot to do with it. His, "Do what I say, not what I do", rule was what was the hardest for the child to bear. Mister Massey sat on her too hard, while she saw, plain like, that nobody ever sat on him." Aaron knew this all to be so. He listened on. "I was hard on her myself, and in the last hours of your mama's life, I was a lot of the reason why the girl took on so, and got so bad. If anybody was to blame, it might well be me, instead of you. I was the one told her daddy she ought not to go to Palmland without a chaperone, and he took my advice. That's why your mama died... she was goin' across with the girl, and the girl wa'ant havin' it, 'cause you know what she was plannin'! Now we got a chance to stop her, and those two men asleep out there can help us."

"We got to stop the police from findin' out what she did, Aaron. I want to get everything that can connect her... Francie can't be accused of causin' death... even your mama's. Her daddy, my poor Mister Massey, will surely die hisself, if he hears, and if he finds out about the arm from the sound, you know it would stop his heart before we could explain." Poor Carrie, thought Aaron, she is never to be at peace if this doesn't go by. "I don't want the police, or some reporter, to get to him about it, 'cause it's goin' to say nothin' but that his daughter's out in that deep water... dead and gone! We'll be havin' another funeral right here on Squires Island, if that happens." She was holding tight to his hands as they sat on the floor together, as if the world was falling from beneath them.

# CHAPTER
# TWENTY-NINE

Since it was only an hour before first light, Troy separated himself from the two reveling girls, to maximize the benefit of a freshening breeze. He sheeted in and began to tack expertly over what was now ample water. They would cross in about half the time it took going, and he was sure they could replace the boat, and be inside before being noticed. Even if there were any all-nighters still by the pool, the trio could lock arms and pretend to stagger along until they were safely in the room. It wouldn't take much to get the two chicks to sound incoherent... they had done a good job polishing off the rest of the beer, and combined with a bump of the cocaine Francie had salvaged, they were flying. Troy had seen this so many times he was used to it... women were a fluffy, albeit indispensable lot, with no outward care who was in charge, as long as the booze and favors held out. He was to regret that shallow observation.

The first signs of daylight had yet to appear, but Massey was wide awake. He actually felt better, and attributed it to being home in his own bed. All at once, the reality of his little girl's disappearance and 'Tilde's funeral day came crashing back. He couldn't get the fragrance out of his nostrils even now, the scent that was purely Franciene. He believed she was reaching to him for help, and he raised himself up in the thick, pewter darkness, making ready to rise and do something about her. He gulped a pill first, and then gingerly slid his feet toward the bathroom to pee. The stream was as limp as its source... causing vexation for a moment, but it couldn't matter now. Vowing to check his equipment later, he chose cargo shorts and a white, Sea Island cotton shirt from the chiffonier, and slipped his feet into the boat shoes always under the bed, before easing down the stairs, ears cocked for sounds of anyone who might be awake. No one but Carrie would be there, he figured, but due to the funeral she might have invited overnight guests, knowing her Mister Massey would oblige.

The perfume was wafting through the stairwell... and in the foyer below. He went into his study, now that he knew he was alone, and after inhaling an even more intense hint of his daughter, went out the side door toward the garage and barn. He needed some beach, and right now, for clearing his head of the cloying vapors in his house. It would be good to wash off the hospital goop in the surf, while the blues and grays of the predawn sky gave over to mauve and then peach with the sun. He would never, ever take such luxury for granted.

There were no keys in any of the vehicles, damn it! Carrie at work, of course, with so many unfamiliar people around these two days, she would have thought of securing the cars. A snort from the barn gave Massey a start, and his face was slashed with a grin as he turned to Copper's stall. "Good old boy! Good old pretty man!" He crooned, as he took saddle and bridle from the wall and began to dress the stallion, whose huge head began bobbing with delight at the chance for a morning gallop with Daddy. "You'll be ready for your oats when we get back, won't you boy?"

Massey led the big horse out to the lane, and noticed 'Tilde's windows aglow. No matter, he thought, believing they couldn't hear him from the end of the drive, and swung gingerly into the saddle. Without allowing himself to think about negative effects, he nudged a canter, and delighted when Copper, many weeks since ridden, gave a gleeful buck and increased his own pace to a rolling rack, trained into his gaits long ago for comfort on Island rides. "How did you know, son?" Massey laughed, slapping the arching neck several times in gratitude as they headed for the beach. As he rode along it came to him that Carrie might find his unmade bed on her ritual house patrol. Perhaps not, he hoped, since she was sure to be overtaxed with duties today. He wanted to come in to the kitchen this morning feeling well and surprise her, so they could share this very important time together. Franciene was still filling his head too, and the fears from what could be happening to her even now, were too daunting to dwell on until he had the time at the beach.

Copper had to be reined in and around the dune mounded up in front of them, and Massey was careful to take the path they had made between two sand hills, to protect the integrity of the fragile dune barrier. Feeling a slight tightness in his chest, he slowed his pace. There was nothing to disturb a perfect early morning on the beach, all things considered, so he felt lucky to be alive. He remembered Mattie's advice, and began to breathe regularly without gasping, to settle his heart down to the pace.

When he rounded the point and headed back, thrilling to the colors appearing in the sky, Massey went to the water and waded up to his knees in the soft, warm surf... his mind covering a lot of ground in tandem with the waves. He was safe, since all he had to do was whistle for Copper, but his condition took a backseat... as Franciene flooded his head again. "Dear God! Where is my little girl?" It was inescapable to face the truth that she was practically grown, and coming to the time when he had no say in her choices.

He felt as if a black tarp was drawing over him, and he even tried to shake it off, physically waving his arms to help, but truth is fixed and large, and the truth was that she was no longer a baby girl, saying "Yes, Daddy", and behaving in a way he chose for her. Now he had to accept the NEW Francie, the one who was her own person. How could it have come so soon? She was still his little one, and the thought of a dirty fingered full-grown man touching her in forbidden places made his blood rise. He had to stop that way of thinking... he wasn't strong enough. The depth of thought had dredged up another facet to his meandering. Maybe his own reckless and shallow early years with women had caused the panic he felt about his daughter. Those dozens of bimbos and bar pickups, long before he settled on Squires, and his casual treatment of them, was to blame for his refusal to let Francie grow up, all those ugly scenes... the rejection after exploitation... the laughter in groups of his buddies about what was visited on the girl of choice, all of it unthinkable when his fears put it to his little princess. He thought of Frances, his sainted wife. If she hadn't died things would have been so different. Francie would have learned dignity and self-respect from her mama, not the ugly, male-oriented rules and regulations her daddy laid down. Then there had been Linda Sue, his true love, the one he had always hoped to find. She had shown him the sunshine after so long in the dark. He was deep in love with her, from the first moment, and she had returned his with hers so purely.

She would have been his forever... anywhere, anyhow. And she had borne him a son! The missing jewel in his family crown, and how had he repaid her? By deserting her, then snatching her child away like one would a nursing foal, too much to shoulder, until it was weaned away from its mama. Massey realized, right there on the beach, how simple it could have been. She wouldn't have had to lose Willie, just like he hadn't needed to lose HER. It had really been about Franciene! IT HAD BEEN ABOUT FRANCIENE!

IT WAS ALWAYS ABOUT FRANCIENE! It was always about...Oh! My! God!   always about Franciene. He had forsaken those lives, denied all of them a fair shot at happiness, because it was always all about Franciene! He couldn't listen to that mantra again, so he turned and walked deeper into the surf, letting it cover him over for a moment, but only a moment, when he broke free of the spell and splashed out of the water, gasping and blowing his nose free of the stinging salty water and foam. He was hardly aware of moving back up toward the dunes, and wiping his eyes clear. As soon as he could see, he found a supporting place on a tree, silvered by the sun, and reclined to catch his breath, very near to bitter, frightened tears.

* * *

Down the beach she was awake now, amazed that she had slept until sun-up. Linda knew it was the unavoidable day of reckoning for her, with everyone she cared about. She checked the time against the position of the orange-red ball making its way out of the ocean's grasp, and saw that it was 5:35. There was time for a walk, she decided, and started toward the point, walking just at the water's edge. When she reached the place where the beach curved she picked up a driftwood walking stick and trudged up the dune to get a better view of all there was to see. It was truly a magic place, all hers alone for now, and she felt the power coming to her from being one with all this. The warm wind was fluttering around her, brushing her with the sea oats she had walked into. She felt like a growing, changing thing herself, in harmony and context with all of nature, finding the time as perfect as it could be to go and face her life.

When he had begun to relax, Massey made his way to the point, intending to summon Copper for the ride home. Then he saw her... the girl on the dune. She was standing there with the wind blowing her, looking like a stand of sea oats herself, springing from the crest of the dune. Was it? Could it really be? He whistled for Copper, hoping not to dispel the visage he couldn't take his eyes from. Unable to wait for his horse, Massey began to walk toward her, his arms out, calling, "Linda! Linda Sue!"... as loud as his cracking, hindered voice could manage. He didn't realize he was running until he felt the elephant's ass on his chest, settling down for a spell.

The weight, the pressure, the pain was so consuming, as hard as he tried to keep moving toward her, while she was unable to hear his cries, he sank to the sand. When the roar both inside and outside his head continued to intensify, he lay, stretched full length on his side, his arms reaching toward her, and prayed to God to help him live. Copper's gray velvet nose was brushing his corresponding gray cheek, nickering encouragement, when Linda found them. She fell over his body, calling to him to wake up, and please not to die. When he opened his pain-filled eyes for a moment, her face was there, causing an incredible smile to emerge from a grimace. "I love you, Linda Sue," was all he could manage before he slipped back away from her. She took Copper's mane and climbed aboard, and with no need for reins to guide him, the horse wheeled and galloped away, intent on his mission.

* * *

When Aaron went to the porch to wake Mattie, he stood in the open doorway for a moment, wanting to hold onto the loveliness of the dawn, for his mama's memory's sake, and for the amazing times they all had come into, lest they somehow forget how truly good life is, in spite of dire issues they faced. Carrie was right as usual, the trio was still deep in sleep. He could probably capture Mattie without disturbing the other two, since she was most likely used to being roused early and easily in her profession, so he didn't mind shaking her until her eyes opened.

"Oh! What?" She said in a breathless but canny whisper. Aaron put his finger to his lips, and whispered, "Aunt Carrie wants you and me to go to Frenchport this mornin', to see after Mista' Massey and fetch somethin' from the hospital. Can you come in the kitchen pretty quick?" She was on her feet in an instant, fully dressed, he noted, heading for the bathroom under the stairs. "How did she know that was there?" Aaron wondered aloud, but didn't waste time on it, given the scores of recent weird happenings. He went to the kitchen to tell Carrie that Mattie was up, but she wasn't there. He poured another cup of coffee, thinking she must be at his mama's, but he was wrong. Carrie had come in and gone up to Massey's tower rooms with strange resolve. She was right in her foreboding... he had been here! His bed was slept in, and like it always was in normal times, with the big down pillows all lined up in the center, and the little one folded in half for his head. She supposed he slept with that army of pillows out of loneliness, missing a woman next to him. She tossed the counterpane back, stupidly looking further for him, ran to the bathroom, and spied the hospital gown on the floor. She picked it up and crushed it to her breast, looking to Heaven and letting tears fall down her cheeks. "Oh, my poor lamb, my poor child."

Outside, the dawn was bringing them around. "Where am I? Oh, I'm on the porch of Will's father's house, a father he can't acknowledge, for so many reasons. Damn! What is today going to bring? This is the funeral day for Aaron's mother, Massey Thornedike is in the hospital very ill, Linda Sue is who knows where, angry as hell at me, and afraid for her son." Suffice to say, Toby had quite an eye-opening moment. The days are all so screwed up since they found that body, Toby had trouble keeping up. Carrie, and Aaron, and Will, and even little nurse Mattie, seem to be miles ahead of him in awareness of what it means... all he ever wanted was to find Will, go to the fucking beach, get a little sun, and do some writing!"

The thought pattern was so oppressive, it was as if he had said it out loud, and he looked around to see if anyone had heard. Will was still snoring in the hammock, a sure-fire hangover cooking in his head, but Mattie's bed was empty. A full bladder commanded, and he tiptoed down the steps to the side garden, so no one would come upon him in mid-stream. Not to be. He was still sighing in relief when he heard a giggle behind him in the haze. "Sorry, I was just taking a stroll." It was Mattie, fresh as a daisy and grinning with a flushed face at Toby's predicament. He was quick to recover, and waded from the flower bed, grinning foolishly. Hey! She's a nurse, right? He rallied and hoped he wasn't too red in the face. "SO... How did you sleep?", changed the subject nicely. "Oh, like a baby, Toby. I hope you did too." She was truly lovely... as well-bred as anyone he ever saw. It oozed from her, confidence and easy grace all in one.

"I suppose Will is still out. He tried to match you, shot for shot last night, and we both know how unseasoned he is when it comes to drinking. Don't you think it unwise to encourage the sporting life in him so early? He is young yet." Oops! An obvious scolding from the young lady... she's also strong and forthright. He was stuffed with admiration for her, and not even slightly offended by what she said. "You know, I HAVE had misgivings about that. It's easy, given his mature cunning, and I've added years to his few for my comfort... I've been wrong. I'll tell you what, my dear Miss Bell, you have my word on it. No more! From this moment, all we will share is an occasional beer, and I will begin counseling him, so he won't seek out other hoisting buddies in my stead... How's that?

With that, he bowed lavishly, more serious than he appeared to be. She, herself, was so serious on Will's behalf, she didn't heed his playful attitude, and nodded happily. "Thank you, Toby, I thought to like you right off, and now I know I was right." They were walking toward the pier on the creek, when she stopped short and whirled around. "What am I doing? I have to go." She looked at her watch, as did he, his own watch reading six-fifteen. "Hey!.. where to? How could you have plans so early? Aren't you going to stay for the service? I know Carrie and Aaron would want you to. You've made some fast friends here, you know."

Mattie was walking faster, leaving dark green prints behind her in the silvery dew. She tossed back some anxious words as she sprinted to the house, and Toby had to run to hear. "I can't tell you... I just have to go, that's all. Tell Will I'll be back by nine-thirty or ten, I promise." What in hell? Toby was completely curious, as he followed her in the back door. Carrie was standing stiffly at the sink, staring out the window. When she heard the screen door bang, she said without turning, "Aaron's at 'Tilde's to see to his mama for a minute, then you all can go down to the dock."

When she turned around and saw Toby, she seemed to melt a little, losing a couple of inches of her nearly six foot height. "Oh, Toby, I didn't know you were there. Mattie, go on now, you got no time to spare. I'll explain to Will." Toby went to her side and helped her to sit down, relieved Mattie hadn't regarded Carrie's state, not knowing why. "What is it, Carrie? You're almost pale." He smiled a little, hoping she would appreciate the attempt at humor, but she was unaware of anything but her shock.

"He's here, Toby! My poor Massey was in this house last night. He slept in his bed!" Oh, Lord, she has simply snapped her twig, he decided, holding her hands tightly in his own. "What do you mean? How could that be? Did you dream about Massey last night? That's what happened! I wouldn't doubt it, with all you've had on you these last few days." She was shaking her head furiously, unable to speak. All she did was point up overhead, indicating the upper rooms. He left her and trotted up the back stairs, taking them two at a time. The upper hallway, a mezzanine overlook down to the foyer, terminated at the smaller back stairs. He crossed to the main staircase and continued climbing. The next landing accessed three doorways. First was a sitting room with a connecting door. When he opened it, Toby knew Carrie had not dreamed it. Someone had slept there. He picked up the hospital gown wadded up at the foot of the bed, and returned to the kitchen. "Carrie, was this up there this morning?" He laid the garment in her lap. Her hands clutched it, and she nodded, putting it to her face. "If he was here, where is he now?"

He had barely gotten the words out when the screen door banged again. Linda Sue was standing there, covered with sand, her face streaked with tears. "Massey is on the beach. I think he has died." She collapsed in Toby's outstretched arms, while Carrie fell to her knees, her own arms raised in pitiful, begging incantation. He took Linda out to the porch and laid her on the day bed he had slept in. Will woke up, grumbling incoherently. "Will! Be quiet! Do you see who this is? Boy, it's your MOM! She's been on the beach all night, and she just told us Massey is out there, and he's had another attack! We don't have time to waste, son, we have to get to the beach, right-damn-Now!"

The boy shook off his fog, bent to eye-level with his mother, speechless with crashing emotions. Linda was still out, her poor mind shut down for respite. Will looked from her face to Toby's, whispering, "God! Toby, she's beautiful!" His buddy nodded silently, but wasted no time taking his arm and jerking him to the steps. They dashed for the truck. Shit! No key! Will ran back inside to get it, just as Jasper pulled in the drive. He jumped out and ran up the steps, calling frantically for Carrie. Toby got out of the truck and followed him inside, hearing him say, "Massey's in the back of my car, and he's bad off! I was worried after Linda Sue this mornin' cause she made me leave her to the beach last night, and... Oh God! I drove down the beach, followin' horse tracks, and... let's us go to the dock right now! He ain't gonna' last if we don't get him across quick! Call and get an ambulance to meet us." He asked for help putting the big man in the boat, and they were already in the front seat. Carrie was dialing up 911, when she put her hand to her mouth... her eyes rolling skyward.

"I sent Aaron and Mattie to town in your boat just a few minutes back, Jasper. I didn't want to wake you when the need came. I'm so sorry. What can we do? I prob'ly done killed my sweet lamb!" Jasper shook his head, and actually smiled! "No worry, girl... I took the sparkplugs out of that old motor last night to keep the grandbabies that's over here from goin' joy ridin' in the dark. I know my own grands...they ain't above such, but they sho' wa'ant goin' nowhere in THAT boat. Aaron's probably lookin' inside it to see what's wrong right now. Let's us get goin'!" Carrie saw the men out, and went to see after Linda, still out cold. She slipped the limp woman over on the bed, shook the blanket over her, and patted her clammy cheek, wishing she could get some of the sand off. Poor Carrie, it was time to get back to 'Tilde's... she had been untended too long. She went to the phone and called Pansy to come sit with her. It was after seven, and there was a whole difficult day ahead. "Please, Dear Lord, give me strength," she said to Heaven.

## TYBEE MORNING

The tide was flooding near to high when the Hobie-Cat was deposited on the beach by a fair-sized breaker. The young trio used three successive waves to slide the craft so near to the dune it was easy to horse it to its resting place. Troy had marked the spot by counting the lights on the dune walks... perfect work! In less than thirty minutes from their landing, and no one would know the catamaran had been anywhere. When they trudged up to the pool deck at their motel, Troy was first to suggest what was next. "I'm shuckin' off and diving into this pool, right now! Who wants to join me?" he asked, hoping Franciene would take his dare. Mandy spoke before her friend could.

"We can't right now, Troy! You go ahead. We've gotta take the stuff and lock it in the trunk. Be back in a flash, and then we'll see." They walked out of the lights toward the car. When the spoils of their adventure were safely stashed, Franciene suggested Mandy go across the street to the all night market for food, and she would go to their room for a quick rinse. Mandy toddled off, suddenly starving, leaving Francie to her devices. Troy was swimming laps... his athletic, tanned body gliding like a porpoise through the water. When he reached the shallow end on his last lap, he stood down, wiped his eyes and beheld, posing in Esther Williams-fashion, a stark naked, gorgeous vision that was Franciene, standing on the diving board. She jack-knifed expertly into the water, coming up inches from the boy, letting her breasts and tummy glide up against him. He was hopelessly lost to her in the early dawn.

Their Aquarian coupling was brief... Troy found himself hastily dispatched by her intense underwater pleasures. He hardly had time to enjoy what was, exactly the way the she wanted it...no more, no less. The mocking, amused girl then gave him a dismissive hug and left him standing there, wondering what the hell! She pulled her clothes on with a flourish, waved prettily, and told him to meet them by the pool at ten, so they could decide what to do next. She was in the room toweling off when Mandy returned with donuts and chocolate milk. They fell quickly asleep in their bed full of crumbs.

# CHAPTER THIRTY

The fields on either side of the oak lined drive were fluorescent with the morning sun's light, as the patrol car approached Palmland mansion at seven-thirty on Monday. Trooper Wagner had requested the duty of calling on the Hartsells personally, since they had been acquainted. Out of respect for the family, South Carolina Patrol sent an escort car along to wait outside while the grim news was delivered. While the canal had not yielded a body, the discovery of a shoe... a very nice hand sewn loafer, and a sterling money clip, monogrammed "CPH", the "P", for Andrea's family name of Palmer, tangled in the net on one of their last drags, providing sufficient cause to inform the parents.

Wagner stepped out of the unit, the plastic bag of personal effects stashed behind his back, as he mounted the steps... thinking how ironic it was that after all the abject envy he had heaped on this man, he was happy not to be Strahan Hartsell on this radiant morning, about to lose his only son. He learned from the local constabulary that Hartsell had been all but up their asses the last two days since the boy was missing, dishing such scathing criticism to the officers that they were happy to have outside help. The corporal was curious to see what would be Strahan's next move after his visit. He could go either way... deep depression, denial, or worse... rage and revenge.

He told the trooper in the waiting car to stay put until he was back outside, so they could get the hell out together. This particular trooper, though youthful in appearance, had been with the patrol for five years, having done more than one off-duty stint as security at lavish Hartsell soirees, so he knew what might be coming. Wagner rang the door chime, and Strahan himself opened the door, saying in a whisper, and with overt disdain, "Well, corporal, what brings you way out here to my door this hour of the mornin'?" His demeanor was deliberate. If he acknowledged the officer cordially, it might make him comfortable enough to say it right out, and he didn't want that. What Strahan wanted was for him to simply disappear. But it was not to be. The corporal was good at his job, and the agony was in motion.

"Mister Strahan Hartsell, Sir?" He waited for confirmation..."Yes, I am he." It came back with a wooden nod. Behind him, in a ball gown of a wisteria-flavored peignoir, Andrea Hartsell appeared, making things even more impossible for the hapless officer, leaning her head on her husband's arm, her mouth agape. "Sir, there may be no cause to fear the worst, but we have discovered a nineteen-sixty-two, red Austin Healey 3000 roadster, registered to one Clifford Palmer Hartsell, in a canal off of Alligator Alley, in South-Central Florida, last evening." Strahan and Andrea clutched at each other, like two sightless people who had turned onto a raucous avenue.

"Let me continue," the trooper said quickly. "Before you say anything, can we go inside? Wouldn't this be easier sitting down?" They turned like robots, walked into the parlor, a large but welcoming room, and Strahan indicated the sofa across from where he seated his wife. He remained standing, and the officer continued. "There was no sign of foul play in the vehicle, no indication that anyone was in it when it went in the water, and no one has reported knowledge of any disturbance, and that's a good sign. Perhaps your son wasn't even in possession of the car at the time, and is perfectly safe elsewhere, but we did find these items when we dragged the canal." He offered the bag to the ghostly pale man, who took it without looking down. Wagner went on. "If he was robbed and abandoned elsewhere, it makes sense the perp or perps wouldn't have wanted to be found with such a unique automobile, don't you agree? I need to know what you know or think you know, about your son's actions since he left here Saturday. Who he was with, and where he was going. Can you help us to help you?" The woman sat straight and still, as her husband walked slowly to the wall filling bay window, staring out across the lawn. His sagging shoulders began slowly to square, and he flexed and locked his knees before speaking.

"Corporal," he began without turning around, "We became concerned after our son on Saturday morning, when he failed to appear for one of his sister's graduation festivities, but were not worried until that evenin'. You know, it is about youthful impulsiveness and all it entails." He still had not turned around, and seemed to be imparting to the hedges and trees, his voice gaining volume with each word. "I wanted to formally report my son missing," an edge now to his voice, "But!" He turned on the word, and Wagner shrunk into the sofa's down pillows as the man walked over to face him, by now screaming, "I was told I could not, because he hadn't been GONE long enough! DAMN YOU ALL TO HELL!"... Andrea Hartsell had robotically slid the bagged evidence to the edge of the marble table, opened it, and was now stroking the ruined loafer at her breast, staring blankly, dry-eyed and elegant.

Strahan continued his tirade, aimed at the domed ceiling. "Doesn't even the stupidest, most brain-dead SHIT-ASS know that if someone who is missing meets with foul play, it is most likely to be within the first twenty-four hours, or at precisely the time his folks report him gone?" He had finally reached crescendo at that point, and was shrieking, shrill and ear-splitting incoherent words to the chandelier, tinkling nervously in useless retort.

Andrea was up, on some obscure cue, whispering entreaties for him to compose himself, but by then Strahan was positive he had just been told that his boy, his only son and heir, was most surely dead in some unholy fucking, sucking swamp, somewhere in South Bumfuck, Florida! He covered his face with his hands, and let his wife lead him toward the library and the brandy decanter, while the trooper mumbled something about them coming to the patrol station as soon as they were able to manage it, as he let himself out.

In the library, Strahan flopped on the leather couch, while Andrea poured a snifter half full for each of them. She summoned Amos to come minister to Mister Strahan, now drooling in shock, while she, her elegance and grace under fire, went to her rooms and allowed herself to faint, falling hard to the antique Aubusson garden floor beneath her. Downstairs Amos, who had "inherited", the Hartsell family from his father, and his father the same before him, set about gently bringing the traumatized man to his senses with cool cloths soaked in witch hazel, and a recipe of smelling salts the household had used for generations. When he finally came back, Strahan looked deep into the fine old man's black eyes and fell into his arms, sobbing his broken heart out. Within a minute he rallied, and stormed up to his suite with Amos right behind, to dress for a trip to town and the sheriff's office. It hadn't occurred to him, in self-centered fashion, to go to his wife before he left the house, and she lay unheeded where she had fallen, to awaken and re-live her blackest moment... alone.

## MISSIONS OF CHAOS CONTINUED

They were stymied...Aaron and Mattie, attempting Carrie's mission to the hospital, now standing in the marsh beside the disabled bateau. The first thing checked was the fuel tank... half full, and more than enough for the crossing. Aaron was versed in ancient outboard engines, so he deftly removed the cowling and began to wiggle things around until he saw the plug wires hanging loose with nothing to do. "Damn! Who the hell? Mattie, somebody's taken the sparkplugs out! We are stuck until I can find some more." Mattie slogged up on high ground, and got busy rubbing the black mud from her shoes on the grass.

"And where will you find such? At the parts store?... I don't think so!" She sat down hard on a piling in defeat. "Now, don't you despair, girl," Aaron wiped his hands on a rag from the boat, walking toward her. "I bet Jasper has a spare set in his shed. You sit tight, and I'll go look." He trotted off to Jasper's house, visible from the boat. It was seven-thirty, and time was at a premium if they were going to be back before the funeral. Neither of them had spoken about the purpose of their trip. Each knew what to do. Mattie's perceptions were growing by the minute, since she was receiving directly from Carrie now. Females had traditionally been better psychics, while males were best used in the execution phase of the missions. Mattie began to hum a favorite tune, when she heard the rattling roar of a car with a busted muffler. It was speeding toward her, sending damp dust in a spray behind it. She stood to face the VW, knowing already that it was bearing Toby, Will, and Jasper, to save Massey's life. Mattie ran to meet the trio, now out of the car and taking the prostrate man from the back. Aaron had heard the car's approach and ran to help. It would take all of them to lift and carry the big, dead-weight of a man.

"He was here last night!" Will was breathless, but panted out the words. Mattie laid her ear to his chest, while taking his slack wrist. "He's not breathing! I get no pulse!" They put him in the boat, a cushion under his neck, at Mattie's direction. Jasper was already replacing the cover on the power head, and Aaron had the motor going in seconds. Will got into the boat and Mattie started CPR immediately, with Will ready to share the procedure if necessary. They sped off on the glassy water, as Jasper and Toby stood praying together. They watched until the boat disappeared around the bend of the river. It seemed like a year since Toby first looked at that same view last Wednesday. They went to the square back, and drove toward Linda Sue.

What was going to happen next? How could five days become any more bizarre? He could bet on one sure thing... somehow they would. The family that never was, was now touching in a most intimate, and vital way. There would be permanent consequences to this morning's events, and Toby believed he was to be no part of them. If Massey lived, who could deny him his son, and the woman who was meant to be his... especially if his daughter was gone? Toby felt superfluous at these thoughts... an interloper. When he got out of the car at the house, Carrie met him in the yard. "She's still out, but now she's just sleepin'. I can tell the difference. Poor thing's wore out. Toby, that's Will's Mama, and my Massey's his daddy, I know it's so. I' been a'knowin' that sweet girl was meant to be here. I recall when she came a long time ago, and Mister Massey was just beside himself! He wouldn't tell us nothin', 'Tilde, Francie, and me. It was like he had a secret life, just now come to us all." Her eyes were full, but she remained calm and spoke with purpose.

"Francie was upset for a long time, 'cause of the little boy they were fussin' about. She didn't want NO other child 'round her daddy... No Sir! We never spoke of it, he and I, because that's the way he wanted it, but it never let him rest again. I gave Will a bracelet that I found in the girl's room, 'cause I was told by the inner voice it should be his. When I asked Francie where it came from awhile back, she told me to mind my own bid'ness! Just like that! She'd never talked to me like that before, so I let it go. Toby, that girl's turned bad, and she has done things God and man won't allow. I'm tryin' to save her little soul, for her AND her daddy. I'm already seein' it work. You'll know what I mean when it's all over. Trust me, trust Will and Mattie. Be a good friend to Linda, 'cause she'll need you in the next few days. We will round out the week to Wednesday, and then it will be done. I know you went and got that book from my friend, Sara Gaines at the gallery. It is not necessary that you read any more of it. In fact, you could vex us if you know more than you should." Was she warning him? Toby listened carefully to her words and the way she was saying them, so not to miss anything.

"You and Will are going to be involved enough when tomorrow comes, so be prepared to defend yourselves, and keep everything you have discovered, for the tools you will need. I will say no more. Let Linda sleep, let her breathe. Don't pressure her about anything, you hear? She will make her own way back to us." With that and no more, Toby was politely dismissed. Not convinced the book would be no help to him, he mentally reserved the right to continue digging.

* * *

"You bastards better get on this thing YESTERDAY, you hear me?" Strahan was nearly foaming at the mouth, as he crouched over the sheriff's desk, inches from his startled face. "Do you know what my wife and I have just endured? A shittin' peon from Florida comes to my home announcin' to me that my son is, by now gator feces! I have tried to be mindful of your bullshit policy about waiting seventy-two hours, watchin' my wife and daughter gettin' more and more hysterical, now it's likely too fuckin' late!" He stopped for breath, wiped his eyes and nose with his handkerchief, and went back to it, pacing the room.

"Now, I want you to hear me. Somebody's snowy white ASS better be on the road in minutes, got it? I'm goin' down there today for some answers, but I want an officer from here, to keep things official, and goin' like I want 'em to! I'll be leavin' from the house at ten. My attorney, Jay-Jay Coleman's takin' up the other seat, and I'd better see you or yours down there by four this afternoon. I didn't put my full support into this constabulary, to be treated like some friggin', worthless, boat gypsy!" God, he was hot! The sheriff stood, finally, walked around the desk, trying to put his hand on the raging man's shoulder. No way! Strahan wasn't having any phony patronizing. He was about the business of his son's life, demanding plans and actions! The portly sheriff folded his arms across his chest, and nodded his acceptance of the orders as spouted. He spoke softly, and with sincere empathy.

"I'll choose a good, smart officer to go, Strahan, and you can count on him being there on time. I will keep contact with him, and we'll do all we can to help from this office. I do need one favor, if you please. Before you take off this morning, would you ask your wife and daughter to speak with me quickly, so I can prepare the papers and get some background information about the hours before Clifford was missing on Saturday? It would help if you jot down your memories as well. I'm so sorry this is happening to your family. You don't deserve it, none of you, and I will pray he is returned to you safely."

It was enough. Strahan raised his hand in a gesture of truce... turned, and left the office. The sheriff picked up the phone and asked his dispatcher to come it with the duty roster. "I swear to God," he drawled to the younger man, "Between the dope pushers, hippies, and drunks on the one side, and the rich folks, lawyers, and politicians on the other, it's a wonder I don't weigh a hundred pounds, and stand three foot tall, with a constsntly sore asshole!"

\* \* \*

Tybee dawn… it wasn't nine yet, but Franciene was wide awake, and fidgety. She slipped silently out of bed, dressed in shorts and a crop top, leaving Mandy sleeping. She had seen a pay phone by the pool bar, and she had a pouch full of coins in her bag. Dialing her number, the trembling girl added coins, and waited. One, two, three rings. "All right? Thornedike residence," came Carrie's familiar voice over the line. The girl tried to speak, but nothing came out. She tried again, "Aunt Carrie? It's Francie…are you still there? I'm scared, Aunt Carrie. Help me. Tell me what to do."

Carrie was saying the child's name over and over, choking on the tears that were flowing into her throat. "Honey child, where are you, darlin? Tell Carrie where…" She had hung up, just like that. Francie returned to her bad self before the Franciene that made the call could answer. She blithely trotted across the street to the market and bought a sack full of MaryJanes and Circus Peanuts, some Juicy Fruit gum, a big bag of Cheetos, a Dr. Pepper, and a teen magazine.

Shopping done, she set up camp in a lounge chair by the pool. It was quite a morning, she observed… a good day for a fresh start. Since she was keeper of the cash, she intended to devise the plan alone. An overnight stop in Savannah, or maybe they'd go up to Charleston. It would take Daddy a few days to have the stock certificates duped, the old ones voided, and the new copies stowed in the safe again, so she didn't want to return prematurely. In the meantime, she could figure what to do about the other two. Troy, she decided, might be her first conquest. He was cute, she was affected by him, and she knew he liked her! This morning, when her bad self was in the pool and did that to him, she had been told there was another Franciene to do the things she didn't know how to do.

## Another Crossing… another Crisis

Their emergency trip was cut measurably, due to slick calm conditions and no other boats about. Mattie kept the resuscitation tempo going smoothly, and her work was rewarded with a weak heartbeat and a pulse. All Aaron and Will could do was watch helplessly from the stern, praying to see him live. They were greeted by paramedics as they pulled into the harbor, equipped with everything they needed to see him to CICU. As the gurney was being rolled to the ambulance, Dan arrived for his first run. "What the hell has happened! MASSEY! Oh no, what have I done?" Will heard, and took Dan's arm, jerking him to a stop. "What do you mean?" Dan knew who this boy was by now, and shrunk from telling him about last night, but there was no way around it.

"I took my best friend home like he asked me to, boy, and I'm the one's gonna' have to live with it if he dies. He all but forced me to help him... told me he would die in that hospital if I didn't get him out. I swear I took good care of him, son, I did everything I could." He started to sniffle, and Will could not stand to see the crusty man break down. "Okay, okay, I guess I'd have done it too." He put his arm around Dan's shoulder and they walked up behind the gurney. Mattie asked Aaron to ride with her in the back of the ambulance, and as they sped off, Will asked Dan, "Hey, why don't you and me go to the hospital?" It was good, the two of them. Will was on the edge of awareness, and Uncle Dan would be there when it happened.

Over on Squires, Carrie heard the phone ring and went to answer it while Toby sat beside Linda, watching her sleep. He wanted her to wake up so he could tell her everything she did not yet know, but he let her sleep on as long as she would. Carrie returned to the porch, silently beckoning him inside. When he joined her in the kitchen, she told him. "It was Franciene, Toby, she called just now. I rang the operator back, but she couldn't tell me where she was." He sat down with her, stunned and disbelieving. "How can that be, Carrie? You know why I'm asking don't you? Please tell me what we are facing. Is Will... are Linda and Will in any danger from her? What do you think she'll do next? I don't understand a bit of this. Can it be, that Franciene and the people I care so much about will meet up in this mess, with her endangering their lives? If the girl is doomed to being a wayward soul, she can be a threat to her brother, and the woman her father still loves." She felt his anguish as he spoke his heart.

"Carrie, I think you know I have come to love Linda too, but I am ready to give up, freely and gladly, if she wants to stay here with Massey. If the girl is coming after them, you just watch me! I'll sweep both of them out of here like you sweep this kitchen floor!" He couldn't believe his own voice, so full of powerful purpose. Carrie surprised Toby as she took him in her arms. "Lord knows, I understand you, Toby," she said, "Fact is, she has me vexed, and good. I feel her nearby, but just where is hard to figure. I could smell her essence in her daddy's rooms this mornin', she's so close. As for danger to Will and his mama, it's possible. She's got a vengeance brewin', since long ago, if not for Linda, then Will, sho' nuff! He's the one she fears the most. As to how to find her, I venture Will's the best chance, since he's blood kin. I wish he was here now so we could get started. It's in me that she's comin' back soon, the reason she called here. There's a little piece of her wants to be helped, Toby, so she's still got good in her. You go on outside and see about that sweet woman now, and pray for Massey."

So, Toby went out and sat in the rocker, next to Linda. When he could look at her, Linda was staring at him like a doe in the dark with a light trained on her. "Toby, you're here! I'm glad you're here. Is my... " He put his finger to her lips, saying softly, "Now, don't you stress yourself, darlin'. Yes, he's here, or at least he was. They took Massey across to the hospital, and he went with them. I don't think he has brought the fact that he's his dad up to the surface yet, but it won't be long. He's already talked about it while in a sort of dream state." He held back the part about spirits at work, since she needed to get stronger, and it would only confuse her. "He saw you briefly before they left for town, so you won't be a complete surprise. By the way, he thinks you're a knockout!"

She was trying to rise up on her elbow, but he made her lie back down. "You wait a little, before you jump back into your perky self. I'm sure there's something here you can change into. You're a mighty sandy little gal right now, and I prescribe soaking in a tub of bubbles before we go on into this any further. I bet you could eat something too. While you bathe, I'll do my fancy omelet specialty for you. Stay put, and I'll find you some duds." She called out as soon as he turned away.

"Wait, Toby. My bag is in the barn. I can't imagine when or how, but I put it on my back before riding off the beach. How did Massey...?" He answered the one last question before leaving her, before she finished asking. "He was brought here from the beach by a land angel whose name is Jasper Griffin. The sweet man that he is went to fetch you, probably missed you by minutes. Did you come back by a different way?" She shook her head to clear her memory, then she said, in a whisper. "It was the horse, Toby, I just hung on, and he made a bee-line over land, through sweet grass and scrub palmetto, jumping ditches and scaling berms, to get here quicker. He knew, I swear he knew his master's life was his to save." The tears in her eyes caused his own tears to form. He smoothed back her hair, and wordlessly went to get her backpack from the barn.

When he got to the aisle between the box stalls, a pony whinnied at him as if to say, "He's over there." He went into the open stall across the way, to find the marvelous stallion on his side... and still, his heroic heart at rest. Linda's backpack was by his noble head, and as Toby took it, he closed the huge, staring, now expressionless eye with his fingers. The last thing he could do for him was cover him with the coolout sheet he found hanging on a hook, allowing him some dignity in death. On the way back to the porch, he decided Linda didn't need to know about t

\* \* \*

It was getting late...Aaron would be hard pressed to get home in time, unless he could break Mattie free, long enough to do "the thing", for Carrie. He paced back and forth outside the double doors, while Will sat with his face in his hands, enduring too much for his years. Mattie came out at last, went to Will and whispered, "No news," then motioned Aaron to follow her. They were around a corner before Will could notice, and down the stairs to the basement. Mattie was several yards ahead of him, and Aaron was surprised to find himself jogging to keep up. When they got to the morgue, she waved him back and went inside. Aaron couldn't help it... he peeked. The small window in the door gave a view of the office that admitted authorized persons further inside. Mattie was one of those. In a few minutes, she reappeared, toting a cooler with, "PERISHIBLE!" stickers on its sides. She came out and they hustled down the hall to an outside door.

Once on the sidewalk Mattie placed the cooler in Aaron's arms, warning him, "Get this damn thing to Carrie in record time, Aaron. She will hide it in the freezer, the one with the lock that no one goes into but her, and then we can all breathe easier. That box holds untold truths that can become dangerous to our mission... even deadly, if the wrong ones know them. I warn you as well, not to open the box! You don't want to see what it holds, and you won't be helped by seeing it. Believe me when I tell you, it is not yet validated truth, until it becomes confirmed of its existence. Do you understand me, and do you trust me?"

Aaron was clutching the little safe in his forearms, as he nodded, solemnly whispering, "Yes, Mattie Bell, I understand, and I trust you to be right. I will go now, as fast as I can, to Carrie and my mama. Thank you, Sister Mattie, for all of us." They said their goodbyes, with Mattie stating plans to stay with Massey until he was out of danger, and vowing to call with any news. She said she wouldn't let Will be alone too long... that she planned to slip out for lunch with him. As Aaron left, all Nurse Bell knew was that Massey wasn't dead, nothing more. When she returned to his side alone, she was able to lean down and tell him, "Come back to us, Massey Thornedike... your life begins fresh on this day. We will help you along, but you must put your foot on the first step now. Linda, and Will, and Franciene are waiting for you at home." She bit her lip on the lie about Franciene, but if it greased the wheels of his recovery, a lie was excusable. She stood up, thinking, that it wasn't the first time a lie had been used to save a life, and it wouldn't be the last.

"What? What did she say to me?" Massey heard the voice, but he couldn't believe what she said. "Linda! Will! ... and Francie! All waiting for me! God, let it be true, please let my family be there!

I want to go now, but it hurts so much in my chest, and I can't breathe right! They've got to help me go home! It really was Linda Sue on the beach! I DID see her face before I died. I DID die...I know it! I saw Frances there, and my Papa. I wonder where my mother was? [Probably checkin' the mirror one more time, she's so prissy]. God, please don't let this be as far as I come back! If it is, I'd rather be back there with Mother and Papa, and dear Frances. Don't leave me here in this purgatory!"

There was a buzz around him at that moment... a happy buzz. "He's breathing alone! His pulse is almost normal! It's spectacular!... unbelievable! Look at the EKG!...it's settling down to a stable pattern! He's gonna make it!" All the positives were being passed around the room, and Massey was hearing them. "Yes, yes, Lord, I hear...Thank You Dear Jesus, Thank You."

# CHAPTER THIRTY-ONE

If Carrie had found herself watching volcanic lava flowing toward the house, or a tornado bearing down on the Island, she couldn't have felt more pressure than she did waiting for Aaron to return. An old remedy, she diverted her anxiety by cooking...baking a big ham for the house, a massive bowl of potato salad, a sour cream pound cake, and her renown bread pudding, all in an hour's time. Lord knows they didn't need it, but it worked, and Carrie even found herself humming a little. Pansy had come to 'Tilde's to stand by, and Jasper was waiting at the dock for Aaron. The phone in the Thornedike kitchen had rung off with offers of help, but magically, all was ready for the service, beginning in less than two hours. Pansy was full of family stories, since a big brood, four generations-worth, was at her house.

They would load 'Tilde's coffin into the back of Jasper's quaint old ox cart, a tradition steadily waning. The regal bovine dubbed, "Sam," charged with pulling the cart for the last fifteen years for weddings and funerals the same, died in seventy-nine... so a replacement had to be gentled and made familiar with the task. The successor to the shafts was dubbed, "Trouble," hinting that he had stood up staunchly for himself during the process. Jasper vowed a smooth day, and the cart would arrive, decked with flowers, to get 'Tilde to the church with time to spare. The weather was perfect, respectfully still refusing to get warmer than the eighty-five degrees of the last several days. Carrie took a few minutes to freshen up and change into her traditional mourning costume, then went to join Pansy to greet the last few visitors to her friend's little house before they would follow the cart to the church. As she took the path, she heard Jasper's car. "Thank you, Jesus, for that noisy old car," she said aloud, slowing so Aaron could catch up to her.

He dashed to Carrie with the white box, concealing it as best he could, and she led him off to the tractor barn... her private freezer domain, holding all the frozen meats and ready-baked goodies. No one could even open the lid of the big chest but her, after Massey himself, craving a rib roast while Carrie was away last year, had failed to secure the lid, creating a great thaw! The resulting impromptu barbecue was little consolation to her loss, so she purchased a padlock and kept the only key tied inside her apron pocket. As soon as they were done, Carrie shooed Aaron to the big house where she had laid out his funeral clothes. Her good old heart finally slowed to normal, believing all would go well now. Aaron dressed, and at ten-fifteen, Clothilde Poinsett Braswell in her finery, was lifted to the cart, to make the final trip down the lane to her church, and the send-off she deserved.

\* \* \*

If it hadn't been for Linda, Toby would have gone with Carrie and Aaron, even though he had not known the lady of the day... He felt strangely aware of her now, sensing the deepening connection between her death and their arrival on the Island. He firmly believed his place was with Will's mother, to support her. As for Linda, Toby was starting to worry. She had been soaking for thirty minutes or more, and selfishly, he wanted to be with her, so he tapped on the bathroom door. "Come in, Toby," was the startling reply. "Are you decent?" he asked, hearing back, "I'm up to my neck in bubbles, so... yes! Please come in... I'm covered up." He was woozy with the prospect. God, be still my heart! All that, under those fizzling suds! He opened the door, and stood wordless, looking at his dream.

"Sit next to me." She patted the toilet seat. "I want to settle what's between us, while we have this bit of time alone. Is everybody really gone?" He nodded, still unable to speak. She began with a firm but affectionate tone. "Toby, I don't know what this is inside me, because it changes, minute by minute. Is that how you feel?" Once more, he said nothing, hoping she would say more. She did. "I know now, since this morning, that I am in some sort of love with you. What sort of love is unclear... but it is real, and you now know it hasn't happened to me but once before. I have long believed, since Massey, that he would be the only one, and it may still be true. But I realize, since we've spent time together, that you've got it all over him in some important ways. Do you know that?" He stayed silent, wishing this dream would never end. She had much more to say.

"In you I've seen brilliance, humility, compassion, equality, humor, and let's not leave out this huge physical attraction I have been trying to ignore since we met. Will's father is my only love, my only... only, well you know! Perhaps you have captured my curiosity because I've wished there could be, and please don't judge me, another lover for comparison, somehow. There! I've said it, and I can't take it back!" She was blushing beet red now, an irresistible aura in the white collar of bubbles beneath her chin, now beginning to dissolve from her shoulders. It was way past time to say something, so Toby got up and walked to the opposite wall before turning to say, bluntly.

"Linda, right now I want you so much I ache from it. You, there in that tub, saying things I've slept on for days, is driving me nuts! You deserve more than one lover in your life, sweetheart, and any man you would have would be enriched, just to touch you one time, in real, giving, worshipping love. If you want Massey Thornedike... if he lives, and wants you, I will put your hand in his with my blessing, but only after you can fairly decide between us." It was said, and he could not take it back, nor did he wish to. The words hung between their locked gaze, in the hollow silence only bathrooms hold. He was about to go out of the door, to lick his wounds alone, when she said, softly but even more firmly,

"Why do you think I'm still in this bathtub, Toby? When I saw you earlier, even after all that terror on the beach, well, I am embarrassed to admit this, but I wanted more from you too. I know it's brazen, and you must think me so, but I wanted you to come looking for me like you did, even to find me naked. What now? Do you walk out like it didn't happen, or do I simply stand up? I want you to tell me." Toby, as breathless and wordless as ever in his life, took a big towel from the shelf and held it out for her, wrapping it, and his famished arms, around her as she stood. There were elaborate minutes spent in the drying-off process, after which they went together to find a pretty room with a big bed. Linda was a glorious woman to behold... and Toby took his sweet time beholding her. He had waited far too long between Katie and this moment, so he savored her, inch by glorious inch.

Forty seconds became forty minutes... after which neither of them could speak for a while. What had happened? What it really meant, failed to come clear, except that they knew there had been glory between them. Linda fell asleep wrapped in his arms, like an angel. He carefully moved her from his shoulder and covered her newly adored body with the spread, before dressing and going outside for a head-clearing walk. It didn't take long for the truth to return... she was not his, not really. She was Thornedike's. Toby knew he had only tasted love with Linda... Massey would have the banquet for life. There were nearly twenty years between their first meeting and this one, and Toby suspected nothing had changed for her. He was fooling himself if he thought that much devotion, that, and a shared child, could be wiped away by an hour of gourmet sex, even though he knew that he loved her with more depth than mere bodies create.

It was close to noon, and he expected Will or Mattie to call, so he went back inside. To Toby's surprise, Linda was in the kitchen on the telephone, asking for information about Massey's condition. So... he was right. She had chosen. When she hung up and came to him, she had been crying. "They wouldn't tell me anything, Toby! I even asked for Will, but he was gone with Mattie...something about lunch. I want to know how HE is too! Don't you think they know something by now?" She had all the affectations of a woman with deep concern for the man she loved. He had to be a friend to her now, while maddeningly fresh from where they had just been. He longed to ask her about his place with her... whether it counted for anything, but he just couldn't set up for the pain of her answer. The phone ringing sent both of them to it. Toby got there first... for her sake.

Will's voice was saying, "He's stable, Toby, they've brought him back! Mattie and I went downstairs for a sandwich, and when she went back in, the miracle had happened. Is my mother by the phone? I think I want to tell her myself." No words were necessary... He handed the receiver to Linda and stood back. Her eyes were wide and fearful as she put it to her ear. "Hello? Willie? Oh, darling, yes, it's Mama! I love you, honey, I always have!" Her face was washed in tears, and Toby was quick with a handkerchief. "He IS? It's amazing! Willie, when I left him on the beach, he wasn't breathing at all, I swear! After so long with no CPR, what do they think it has done to him?"

It was a natural question, but Toby wanted to protect her once more, so he took the phone and asked the question again for her. Will heard, replying, "Hi Toby. No, I don't know the answer to Mom's question, because they won't know until they can test him, but the vital signs are indicating no abnormalities, and his breathing is shallow, but normal, for what he's been through. Thank God Mattie's here... She keeps bouncing in and out with smiles and thumbs up's." He was quiet for a moment, and then he said, with a strong measure of emotion,

"Toby, I want a favor... My mom should be here, and I need you to bring her... soon as you can. I can't leave my daddy, but I really want to see Mom, and you too! Dan had to go back to stand by on the dock, but he said he would come if we need him." He gave Toby the captain's number, and said goodbye. Raw sensations from the interlude with Linda were still strong, and Toby abhorred being asked to deliver her to a reunion that could close her off from him forever, but it was Will who was asking, not Massey.

If he could possibly manage it, he would reduce the scope of his feelings for her between the docks, to protect his own heart, and for the boy. Will's two words, "My Daddy," were all he needed to make firm his conviction to see Will and his mother reunite. Toby knew they had come so far together, he and Will. They owed each other as much as each needed from his friend in turn. The call was made, and Linda and Toby readied themselves to meet Dan's boat, avoiding each other's eyes. They fully intended to stop at the church to tell Carrie and Aaron the good news, but before they could leave, she came in the kitchen, breathless and worried.

"What is the news from town? How's my lamb?" Linda and Toby both began to tell her at the same time, but she managed to get the gist, and pealed out relieved laughter. "I jus' knew it! 'Tilde told me, as we laid her away! She said I should go be with the ones that need me, now that she's in the Arms of Jesus!" She was so elated she couldn't be still, putting on the teapot, wiping imaginary specks from the counter. Toby went to her and took her hands. "I have an idea, Carrie. Here you are, all gussied up, and you look so pretty, I bet Massey would get better still, if you were to go see him right now! We were about to go meet Captain Dan ourselves, so it's settled!" Tears came down her cheeks again, and she hugged them both. "Aaron's in good charge of the celebration at the church now. I saw him 'fore I came home. It is true that The Lord works in those mysterious ways I heard tell about. So, let's go! Dan's goin 'to be sputterin' if he has to wait!" Always in charge, Carrie led the way to the Rover, waving her arms in Thanksgiving. Toby cautiously took Linda's hand, and she squeezed his purposefully, saying all that needed saying.

## THE SHADY TRIO IS ON THE ROAD

The decision had been made to Franciene's liking. They would take lunch in Savannah, afterward, driving the hundred miles to Charleston's historic Battery District. Mandy was sullen. She had not wanted Troy to join them, since she suspected a pairing in the works. The electricity between her two companions was palpable, and to Mandy, tedious. Troy even suggested he and Francie sit in the backseat, but Mandy nixed that, ordering him back there alone. They dropped the top, and were lunching on blue crabs and shrimp in the little riverside village of Thunderbolt, before noon. Francie and Troy were courting all right, mock-pinching each other with the crab claws, each pushing food at the other's faces, and giving Mandy a Royal PAIN! Back at the car, she suggested Troy drive, and climbed in the backseat herself, for a snooze. Troy had been in full rut since his encounter with Franciene in the pool, so he relished taking the wheel, with her sitting prettily beside him. She was full of herself as she chattered away.

"When we get to Charleston, I can show you where to go. I stayed in a little hotel built into an old antebellum mansion, right on the park. They call it a "Bed and Breakfast Inn," because you get a little piece of cheesecake and a silver pot of coffee before you check out. Let's get adjoining rooms, what do you think? I want one with a rice bed in it." Troy, amused by Franciene's childlike exuberance, would have said yes to any idea, but, considering his own plans, the connecting room idea was her best yet. They left Mandy sleeping in the car while they registered as a brother and two sisters. Troy used his credit card so their names wouldn't appear, to Francie's relief. She was really warming to this boy, more than anyone before in her small social circle, but she had not the first clue what to do about it.

It was getting to be a bore, she realized, always having to consider the other ones. Francie wanted to do what she liked to do at home... spend time alone in her room, wrapped up in Francie. She begged off from a walk into the tourist district with Mandy and Troy, so she could do just that. It was a different, more complex Franciene Thornedike, but the former hadn't given thought to the latter, at least not until this morning, when she had called Carrie in confused anxiety.

It was a good thing she hung up before she really blew it, giving herself away. Carrie sounded so safe, so close. But if she had figured out where the call was coming from, her daddy would have found out, and walked across the water to get to her. She simply had to stay undercover until those stocks were replaced, then she could go back like she planned, make her peace, then pick another fight daddy couldn't possibly win, and take off, this time for good, and this time... alone!

She wondered if he had discovered the missing safe contents yet. It being Monday, his tradition was to spend the morning in his study, so it was likely. Oh, God! He would be a sight, fuming and cussing around. He truly wouldn't think she had anything to do with it, figuring her to be off somewhere, under the bad influence of her friends. No, he wouldn't tie her in. Not his baby. Besides, she was sure the Island was filled to overflowing with all the people there for the funeral. Surely Daddy would suspect one of them first. She pulled the wrinkled envelopes out from their hiding place between the mattress and springs of the fine old bed... slipped the certificates out, and... WHAT?

Franciene was on her feet in a second, gaping at the stocks... at the names on each one. They were HER stocks! Daddy showed them to her a bunch of times! She had believed him! Yet, her name was not there where it said, "Bearer." She shuffled through all of them, then back through again, but it was true. The name on them was, "William Parrish"! Who the hell was He? Francie threw the papers on the bed, raked through her hair, and turned back to look one more time. It was there! "William Parrish", not, "Franciene Thornedike"! And to make it worse, her daddy's initials were on each of them! He had taken them away from her without a word, and had given them to someone else! "WHY?"

The red-faced girl screamed to the ceiling, crumpling the sheets in her fists. Then, as if a light was turned on in her brain. William! Will! Willie T! What was the "T" about on that bracelet? Could it have been for Thornedike? She began to spin like an abused top. "I've got to go back home and find out about this!" She wasn't think-ing... only reacting to the infuriating stimulus she'd found. What to do? She couldn't let Troy and Mandy find her wigged out like this! No, she had to get control somehow.

She went in the bathroom and washed her face, looking in the mirror, and not recognizing the witchy creature staring back. "OOOOOOOHHHHHH," she covered the gargoyle face with her hands, silently thanking the mirror for shaking her back to her senses, and bee-lined for her bag. In ten minutes, a serene, doll-like vision strolled into the sunny courtyard, in place of the shrew she had been. Clear-headed, but coldly enraged, Francie felt trampled by unseen beings, as they tried to remove her from her rightful place. All these five days. More... all her life, she had been building a bridge... a bridge away from that Island, from him, without realizing the possibility that she would want to return some day in the unimagined future, and claim all that was hers.

Now, it was being said that she would be sharing, or even losing the prize that was the Thornedike legacy. Her daddy would forgive an adolescent prank like this runaway, and he would be so glad she was safe and even contrite, it would be forgotten by July Fourth. She could admit to a lapse of good judgment, while being coaxed by the excitement Clifford had promised.

CLIFFORD! What about the Hartsells? What about Aaron? No, she wouldn't freak out again, it would do no good now. Clifford could have gotten in trouble AFTER she left him to come back home. GREAT! Her conniving mind had begun to spin the perfect story... She would tell Daddy that Clifford wanted to go too far, not that he did... it would serve no purpose to use the rape angle. That stupid plan with the bed sheet was long gone, discarded in Florida when she realized it would not hold up as evidence if daddy wanted to formally charge Cliff. Heinz ketchup and Coppertone Lotion would do nothing in her favor, once tested.

She could use her innocence to get Daddy to drop any thought of going after the boy. Mister Hartsell would be easy. He was forever panting after her, acting like an old fool. She had worked him more than once, to get around compromising situations at Palmland with Sonja. He would roll over if she told Daddy to tell him he wouldn't pursue a kidnapping case, if no more was said. What a good plan! She was almost done, and actually anticipating going back home, when she thought of the last obstacles. First there was Aaron. He could blab about the drugs, but he wouldn't. No, she began to relax again. Aaron had more principles than that, she was sure. He could be a help, really. She could say they gave him a ride south, which is true, sort of, and he could agree to lie and say Clifford left BOTH of them, somewhere to be determined. Cool!

Franciene was mentally turning her attentions on them as two and three, when they appeared, obviously fresh from a conversation about her. Mandy wouldn't look in her eyes, and Troy was much too jovial to be for real. She walked to the gate to meet them, calling out, "Now I'M ready to hit the streets! What did you scout out for us?" The two sat down on a tabby bench and took glasses of minted ice tea from the table, before Troy offered, "We found some fun to be had, but I feel like a nap myself, and Mandy said she wants to take a swim in that pretty pool over there. Why don't you come in and sing me to sleep, Francie? I think a power nap in the rice bed would make me go all night." Francie was intrigued, and while Mandy went to change, she and Troy locked themselves in the pretty room. "Project Troy" was in action.

Stroke, stroke, Mandy was swimming furiously, working through her anger. Visuals kept flowing into her brain, fogged by chlorine fumes, and her own. How did she lose control of the little bitch? SHE was suddenly the bomb, not Mandy! It started when they sailed to Squires Island, she remembered, while Troy was flirting with her, and she was giving directions. Mandy re-ran the events... not without including her own high intimidation quotient, when she had to admit the boy was choosing Francie over her. Why? She knew she had a more exciting body... more womanly, bigger boobs, and she had been around enough to know how to make him howl at the moon if he would let her. Now she was sure of it. Mandy had feelings for Troy she had been pushing back until now. "Here I am, she thought, "paddling in this pool, while they do God knows what, in that room!"

"God knows what," turned out to be nothing more than a little making out, when Troy attempted some first base work he figured he'd been encouraged to do. Francie untangled herself, and ran giggling out the door. The boy was miserably let down and frustrated, 'and decided to take Francie up on her offer... the pill on the nightstand she said would relax him. He popped it, drank deeply from his tea glass, and conked out. What he had taken was an equine tranquilizer her daddy used, when he wanted to barge his horse to the vet. The big stallion, refusing to be trailered since a yearling, was always at risk of injuring himself while loading for the voyage to town. Francie had found the tin of pills while looking for that infamous poison in the shed, and had slipped three of them into her pocket, not knowing why.

There was no way Troy would wake up before morning. Franciene planned to rebuild her bond with Mandy now, sensing she would need her loyalty later. She found a swimsuit in the tangle of Mandy's bag and changed quickly, running and cannon-balling right on top of the surprised girl. They spent an hour in the pool, picking on each other, telling boy stories, and painting splashy verbal pictures of their future. It was good...they were like sisters again, like before Troy had happened. "I think we ought to go to Frenchport tomorrow," Francie offered up as they treaded in the twilight.

"Maybe it would be a mistake to wait before I go back home. The longer I'm away, the harder it will be to explain where I've been, and what I've been up to." She no longer cared about the stocks, since they weren't hers anymore. No, all she wanted was to get back there and find out what she could about the boy who was trying to steal her daddy and her inheritance. If she stayed away, his chances to poison everybody against her would be greater. There had to be a way to go back for another look in Daddy's study, unnoticed... for anything about the boy.

## THEY COME TO THE REUNION

Jasper happily zipped his three VIP passengers across in short order. When they got to the hospital, they found Will asleep on a bench, curled fetally to allow room for his long legs. The waiting room was empty except for the sleeping boy and Dan, reading an outdoor magazine. He jumped to his feet when he saw them. "Well, this IS nice!" he said as he bounded over. Toby noticed his eyes locking on Linda's without a second's pause. He led her to sit beside him and began nervously massaging her hand, talking about everything at once. Carrie and Toby went to the desk to ask for Mattie, and were told she would come out in a moment.

Toby was curious-to-nosey about Dan's attention to Linda, disregarding his silly jealousy as sophomoric and degrading. It was tough, dealing with infatuation, or love, or whatever it was. To distract himself, he mercilessly shook Will awake for company, while

Carrie chatted with the aide she obviously knew, at the desk. Plainly, Will was suffering from last night, so Toby was careful not to pick on him. Instead, he asked about Massey. He had risen to a sitting position, and shook his head before answering. "Mattie came with something, but it wasn't much. They still don't know if he's suffered any permanent brain impairment, or, if they should go in now to work on his heart. There are still blockages, we knew that, but if the centers in his brain can't protect him through the surgery and after, it might kill him, trying to save him. I'm so confused, Toby. Is he my real dad? Did my mother…?" He realized she was in the room without looking her way, just as she had risen to walk toward them at the same moment.

Will stood, turned and bent down, lifting her feet from the floor. He rocked her back and forth like a rag doll, saying, "Mother… My Mother," at her ear. They were sobbing together, and Toby went to stand with Dan and Carrie, to watch the beautiful moment, joining them in their own emotional reactions. "Praise God, this is a happy thing," Carrie whispered. Dan was batting tears, and nodding, "This has been too long comin'…those two needed each other all these years. I hate that they lost so much time, you know?" Toby agreed, but couldn't feel any cloud over this. His best buddy was in his own mother's arms, finally, and it was worth everything. Now they had to face Massey's crisis, but they were together, and they could do anything. Toby hesitated, but went to them and put his arms around them both, and from behind, Carrie and Dan joined in. They looked like they were playing one of those tangled games to people passing the door, but they did not care, this was their moment, and it was good.

Mattie came into the waiting room, saw everyone in the weepy huddle, and crossed to them with her arms waving to get their attention. "We're going into surgery in five minutes! I have permission to let you in to see him for a half-minute each, the four of you. Who's first?" They looked at each other, and put Dan in front. He composed himself and went with Mattie, while they stood and watched them disappear. It was Linda who spoke first. "Dan feels responsible for Massey's attack. I disagreed. It could have happened here just the same. He needs to see his old friend, to tell him he did it out of love. I'm sure Massey knows, but Dan wants to say it. Those men have been through a lot on my account, almost lost their friendship, and it has to end in there. Toby, Will, you'll know the story today, but not until we know that man... Will, your FATHER, is going to live." As they listened, Toby could tell Will was having a break-through. "I don't want him to die, just when I have him back! I want both of you... all three of you! After having no one to call my family, I think I deserve it!" He had lost his hard crust...now there was only a tender, vulnerable boy who had had enough of being strong.

# CHAPTER THIRTY-TWO

The last paddle boat to Savannah was nearly out of sight. Aaron had seen all the funeral guests to their embarkations himself, and thanked them all for coming, and he was worn out. After a few minutes with Jasper and Pansy, thanking them for their help and their love, he pointed the jeep toward home... now his home. No more Mama, except in his heart. It was five o'clock, and the most brilliant time of day. The sun did magic things as it gave up the stage. What had just been ordinary green, was now fluorescent chartreuse, even drab tans and browns were blindingly splashed with fiery orange, gold, and red. The trunks of pines and oaks were regimentally ignited in the sun's last hurrah.

Aaron was most awed by the palmetto palms grown tall, while weaving gracefully as they sought sunlight, now slashes of Indian red, crowned with plumes of incandescent fronds. The drive was fearsome, as his view of the road was obscured by splash after splash of blindingly bright light, strobing between the trees. It tends to make one believe in magic. Before going to his cottage, the bleary boy decided to raid the refrigerator in the big house. He had neglected his belly all day, and the smells from Carrie's baking this morning made him drool as he recalled them. A quick inventory brought forth the ham, potato salad, Carrie's bread pudding, and a pitcher of sweet tea. Aaron filled a plate, went to the front porch and ate his fill.

There were a few dishes in the sink, so he set about tidying up for Carrie. He took her apron from the hook, and while smoothing down the front, he felt something in the pocket. It was a key... a padlock key. He knew in a flash. The freezer! The cooler was in the freezer locked by this key's padlock... the one he had been warned away from. What had she said? "The contents won't be the truth until they are regarded." How could that be? It was the same question as, "If a tree falls in the woods with no one to hear it, does it make any sound?" Aaron had always believed pragmatically that it would, and he had his doubts about that cooler's mystery as well.

While he washed up the dishes, his mind kept wandering to the tractor barn. What could it hurt to look? He simply wouldn't tell anybody, and if Carrie got a sense of his disobedience, well, he would just admit to being overly curious. Mattie was too bossy anyway! He didn't have to take orders from some kewpie doll nurse he'd met only yesterday. In minutes he was standing before the freezer, key in hand, about to break the rules. A small noise from overhead caused Aaron to look up, and as he did, he dropped the key to the oyster shell floor. A Mourning Dove perched in the rafters, stretched and flapped its pearly wings as if to say, "It was me!" But it wasn't only the dove...It was a warning sent by all the Powers, to stop Aaron before he looked in the cooler and made it the truth.

## IT WAS TIME FOR GIVING COMFORT, NOT FOR RECEIVING IT.

"Hey Massey-Boy!" Dan was whispering close to the groggy man's ear. Half afraid to disturb him, what with all the paraphernalia he was hooked up to, he plunged into the speech he had been rehearsing. "I never meant to cause this, man. If I could'a figured you'd go South on me, well... you got to get better, 'cause there's folks out there waitin' for you. You got a fine boy, and Linda Sue's with him, and Aunt Carrie, and your girl... Massey! She's comin' home! She'll likely be at home when you get there, soon as you get well enough to go!" He was a good liar, and this was as good a time as any to use the gift, if it would give the man some hope. He knew his time was up, so he put his hand on Massey's bicep, and was startled to feel him shrug his shoulder ever so slightly. It was a weak sign that he'd heard him, Dan was sure of it. He patted him in response, and left the cubicle. Massey had to take it as the truth. If Francie was coming home, he would believe he could too.

## CHARLESTON REALITY

Troy woke up to a headache like he'd only heard about. When he looked out, he saw that it was still light outside. He had a quick power nap. Where were those two girls? He struggled into some shorts and a shirt, and went outside. Hey! There was dew on the grass, and the street by the garden was deserted. He looked at the time, and went to the main house, but no one was about. The sign said they would be open at seven. They wouldn't know anything, anyway. The little bitches had left him there, that's all! His head was still pounding, so he decided to go back to bed. Maybe they had just done an all-nighter, and were having blueberry pancakes somewhere.

They were having pancakes all right, but in Beaufort, not Charleston! Franciene had convinced Mandy that Troy was the problem between them, and she had readily agreed. When the check came, Francie said she would take care of it when she went to the restroom, and instead, rushed to a pay phone. She was connected to Troy's room, and breathlessly begged him to wait there for her. Fine, he growled, and began snoring again in seconds. "What's next? Where do we want to go now?" Mandy had allowed Francie to spirit her away before dawn, with nothing offered but a promise to allow more equality in their plans. Mandy had only wanted a light, fun-filled adventure, and it had gotten much too complicated... even to the extreme of night sailing to robbery. "This girl needs a keeper," she thought to herself, "But I'm not taking the job."

"Mandy, I want to get away from this part of the world bad as you do," Francie replied to an unanswered question hanging in the air. "I know you don't want anything from your parents anymore right now, but you might change your mind one day. I mean, what if you found out that one of their little wayward waif projects had managed to get herself in their will, and you were out in the cold?

Wouldn't that fry you, after all you put up with all your life? It would send you back home to get rid of her so fast you'd leave me standing here sucking my thumb!" Mandy was spell bounded! Just what was this all about? Mandy could hardly wait to hear the rest of the mess. Francie was about to tell her.

"I have something to see about at home you don't need to know, and if we could head that way for a day or so, I'll do anything you want after that. Can I go across today? I would only be gone for a few hours, and there are some cute shops, and a place to have lunch by the dock that I recommend highly." She had always hated the food at Miss Ruby's, but it didn't matter to her WHAT Mandy shoved in her face, she had to get home and see if that boy was there with her daddy. She would find Jaime, and sweet-talk him into taking her over without Captain Dan, so he couldn't call and warn anyone. She wanted to surprise everybody and catch them off guard, and if that Will-boy was truly in her house, well, he would be sorry.

Daddy would be so glad she was home, he would send him away, and she could leave when all was well again. Aunt 'Tilde dying had probably upset them a lot, and she could cheer them up like she always did. After that, she would figure it out as she went along. Mandy just HAD to say yes... it was her car... she wasn't about to spend a big chunk of her money on a car of her own, so she needed her for transportation, and Francie didn't want anybody else in this for now. They would go to Frenchport today, and that's that! Mandy would realize this was a mandate, and she did... she gave in... One more time! "Okay, but I plan to spend the time alone making our itinerary up for the next two weeks, at least! When do you think we'll be there?" They were already on the road by the time she agreed with Franciene, less than an hour from Frenchport. Poor Jaime, he was about to be vamped again, by that irresistible Thornedike girl!

## FRENCHPORT HOSPITAL

It was Carrie's turn to go in. Both excited and scared, she composed herself at the sight of her sweet Massey, tubed up and gray-faced in a green swathed bed. Mattie stopped her before she spoke, whispering, "Don't say anything about his daughter being missing. Pretend she's home if you have to, it may give him more purpose. Dan told him she'd been found when he came in. Also, it might be better if he doesn't recall 'Tilde's passing right now, if it hasn't yet come to him. Now, you go give him a kiss."

Massey was aware, though paralyzed in his crisis, and the restraints that held him still. "What's going on? It's not time yet, I know, 'cause I haven't seen that white light again... but why is everybody coming to my side now? I wish I could speak, I'd tell them I love them all, just in case. I can't die yet, because I've got to see my girl. Please let her come, God... I'll live for you every day I've got left. Who's that? Oh yeah, it's my Aunt Carrie." She was there all right, stroking his forehead, saying his name over and over. He tried hard to speak, but the medication had made him nearly catatonic. She hummed a tune from his childhood, one that settled him right down. "Eva'ting's goin' ta be jes' fine honey, you'll see. We' all out 'dere waitin' for you to come home wid' us."

She used her old way of speaking to soothe him like in the old times, and it worked. Mattie said it was time to go, and that his heart rate had slowed, and become more rhythmic, while she was with him. It was all Carrie wanted to hear, and she left his side, thanking God. Mattie went with Carrie to send the last ones in. This time she suggested Will and Linda go in together, to save time of course, but to have the most positive effect. Massey heard the voices speaking to him, but he couldn't absorb the truth he was hearing. What did come through was the way she smelled... her hair and her skin, when she brushed his cheek with her lips. It was Linda, like on the beach. Will put his big hand on his father's, and said one word, "Dad?"... to cause him to turn his hand, palm up in his boy's, and curl his fingers in a weak clasp. He knew... they could tell he knew. Linda said all she could choke out then, whispering, "We are here, Massey, come back to us."

\* \* \*

The girls were nearly to Frenchport when Francie had another idea. "You know, I think I'd like you to go with me to Squires! You don't have to go to see Daddy with me. You could wait for me at Sandy's house. We can go to the beach, and you can see the place where I live. What about it?" Francie's plan was taking shape. Mandy had doubts, asking, "Who's Sandy? I don't want to have to make nice with somebody strange, you hear? Why do I need to go to Sandy's house?" She didn't want to agree to anything, from a sense of being manipulated, but Francie was ready. "Silly! Sandy's the teacher, but she's gone for the summer. We always look after her house, and I know where the key is stashed." It satisfied the older girl for the moment, and she actually was looking forward to seeing the Island in daylight.

The call was made. Jaime would meet them by the boat in Aaron's backyard, to avoid nosey Miss Ruby and Cissy, and since the tide was springing extremely high that afternoon, it would be easy to put them right on Thornedike property. Francie's diabolical plot seemed to thicken by the minute. She could pull it off just right if they could get to the Jeep without being seen. She was almost positive everybody was at the church or visiting because of 'Tilde. If they had all gathered at her house, she and Mandy would just have to hike to Sandy's. So be it!

* * *

Toby was about ready to take his awkward ass out of that hospital, and leave them to whatever was to come. In fact, if Mattie hadn't said something to him at that moment, he might have never seen the two people he loved, ever again. Once in the hall, she lit into him with a vengeance. "I know what you're thinking, Toby, and you're so, so wrong! You are a crucial person here, and we all need you to stay. Forget YOURSELF for now, and keep digging! You must be armed to help Will, to keep him safe from what is coming. Why did you stop reading the book? That is where you will find the answer, I swear! Where IS it?"

Toby told her it was in his pack, on the Island. He wasn't ready to say that Carrie told him to stop reading it. Was there a conflict between these two strong women? Were they each protecting different people, on opposing sides? There was something that made him believe HER, and want to take HER side, if there was such a thing. Her eyes, while set in a youthful face, were wise and ageless. This mess had been a long time coming, from all Toby had seen, and that young girl, Will's half-sister, was the seed of it, whether she was aware or not. If there were evil spirits working inside her, causing things she wouldn't have been party to otherwise, Toby believed he could learn by going on with his research. It was the only way he could think of to help, and if Mattie believed it too, that was good enough. He went to Dan.

"Can you take me back over to the Island, Dan? I have to go now, if I'm going to help them." He must have seemed desperate, because Dan slapped his back, with, "Let's go!" They ran down the dock to find the boat gone. Both men scanned the horizon, but there was no sign. Dan asked a fisherman if he had seen the boat leave, and he said it was there at three-thirty, about an hour ago, but he hadn't seen it pull out. Dan borrowed his skiff, and they sped off in minutes. Halfway there, they saw Jaime coming toward them. He didn't stop, only waved and kept going. Toby heard Dan swear something raunchy, and as soon as he was on the dock, the angry dad horsed the little boat around and headed back, obviously after his son's hide.

Toby was glad to see the Rover still there, and planned to call back to the hospital to tell Mattie where he was. He had just settled on the porch with a beer and that eerie book, when Aaron walked up the driveway. He looked so strange, almost entranced, but he acknowledged Toby, and walked out to the pier. "Where are you? Show yourself!" Toby heard him scream out, the anguished sound echoing across the marsh, and it caused him to shake as if he had a chill, while it was a balmy eighty-four degrees.

\* \* \*

After a strange, silent trip, Jaime left the two girls to find no one home at Thornedike House. They could not have known Aaron was there, searching for the key to the freezer in the shell floor. They sprinted to the jeep, started it on the first try, and sped out of the drive. Aaron's frantic scratching around had drowned out the sounds they made, and when he gave up, he went to his mama's house and cried his heart out. After he composed himself, he went to the kitchen to find a pot simmering on the stove. In it, he found a perfect, just done, blackberry dumpling, like his mama made. He turned off the stove, thinking perhaps Pansy had left it for him. He lifted it to a plate and turned to the table, not hungry, but too touched not to have a bite of it. The table was set for two, and in the center, with the cream and sugar, was the can of poison from the shed! The plate crashed to the floor, as he knew that moment how she had done it. They had always enjoyed this ritual, just Francie and her Aunt 'Tilde, when the berries came ripe. At that moment he knew she was there, on the Island somewhere. He was certain. The Rover had come in the yard, and he ran to see if it was, in fact, that evil bitch, but it was not, it was Toby.

## TWO BEACHCOMBERS ARRIVE

"I'm really glad no one was home when we got the jeep. Let's go to the beach right now!" Franciene and Mandy put their backpacks down in Sandy's front hall, and were already in the refrigerator for whatever they could find. Mandy liked the whole feel of things on Squires. It was as if no one could ever find her, or guess she was there. She was enchanted, just like everyone else who found the place. Francie was digging out her bikini, shucked off and changed right there in the living room, nagging Mandy to do the same. They grabbed two of Sandy's beach towels and raced the quarter mile down the sandy path to the deserted strand. They were at last, as free as they wanted to be... for a while.

# ALLIGATOR ALLEY

It was nearly four o'clock, and still no Carolina cop! Strahan and his attorney had been crisscrossing by chopper the miles surrounding where the car had been found, hoping in vain to see something the ground crews had missed... anything! Maybe he had crawled off somewhere and was lying in the rushes, or by the road, or in a gully. They had raked the Florida officers over the coals as soon as they touched down. Hartsells do that...had always done that with impunity, whenever they, or theirs, were threatened or slighted. They were set up at the discovery site, having had a tent and supplies brought from the coast, complete with radio phones and scanners, surpassing the capabilities of the police equipment by miles. It was amazing to Strahan that his boy had only been missing for days... it seemed a month, but the police assured him, since they had a well formed plan of action, they would find him before long.

Yeah, right, Strahan thought. These wing-nuts are really top drawer, all right. If he hadn't shown up with his balls engaged, they would have dropped the case without a thought, and resumed whatever bullshit they usually do down here in the swamp. He had finally phoned Palmland to see after Andrea, being told she had packed and gone to their mountain house up-country, taking Sonja and the dogs, and asking not to be disturbed until Clifford could make the call himself. That was Andy, preferring not to be bored with trivia like the rudiments of the search. He asked Amos to call him if she returned or requested anything, and dismissed the feminine half of the family with a wave.

What next? What could he do now to make this nightmare end? That damn little chippy, she and her daddy, sick or well, would answer for this! He rang up the Thornedike home, but no one answered, then he remembered Aunt 'Tilde's funeral was today. His next call was to the hospital, to check on Massey, and was shocked to learn he was still in CICU. No use pursuing that outlet for his rage... Massey Thornedike was indisposed in such a way even a Hartsell couldn't usurp. Strahan's temper was ready to bubble over anew, when his friend, Jay-Jay came to him under the tent with an idea.

"Man, you need to relax! It's nigh on to cocktail time, and there ain't any place to get a decent martini within forty miles of here. That trooper from home finally got to headquarters in town, I heard it on the radio just now. What say we go chat him up, and find a good restaurant for some supper." Strahan knew Jay was wondering why he had taken on this debacle, and agreed to humor him into staying. The fact was, he needed a friend more than he needed a barrister. They asked one last trip of the chopper pilot before he signed off, and got themselves delivered to a car rental agency, then proceeded to get drunk.

While they were in Naples, the only town Strahan gave for dinner options, Trooper Stacy Mayes pondered the strange talk he had just had with the boy's father and his attorney. They had met in Golden Gate at the patrol station for only ten minutes, while Strahan pressed orders into his chest with a locked finger. "I want YOU to find my son, do you hear? These Rubes and Conkie Joes couldn't find pussy on Priscilla Presley, and it makes no difference how many platitudes they bleat at me, I know it's up to US! I believe he's alive, By God, and he's out there hurt and possibly dyin' by the minute!" In reality, Strahan didn't believe any such thing, but he had cleverly put the trooper in a place where he wanted to believe it too. He continued.

"Get yourself fifteen... twenty local yokels, tell 'em I'm offerin' ten thousand in cash, tonight, if they find my boy, and you work with them all night if you have to. You'll get twenty K yourself, if you find him alive, but don't tell the others. We' got to do this while the swamp cops aren't around, so get busy! You got two more hours of daylight, and after that you can use the torches from the tent. Leave one of the dumbest ones to guard base command, and call me on my radio phone... this number, if anything turns up. I'll have it with me at all times." With that, he and Jay-Jay drove off in the rented DeVille.

Well, that was strange, thought young Stacy. He had heard about the Hartsell manner of doing things, and knew he had just sampled a vintage slice. It worked too, because the stalwart trooper was immediately to the task, finding seventeen boys in one saloon on their second brew, and they had jumped at the chance to have a romp... and maybe get rich on the spot. Within thirty minutes they were crawling all over the area, while Stacy took the boat into the canal for another look, deciding that if he found the boy's body he would give half of his reward to those guys out there, to divide up. They would never see money come that easy again, he allowed. He could hear their voices, hooting and laughing at each other's antics, as he nodded his plan into a covenant

## TOBY IS IN IT NOW!

What was that about? Toby heard, but didn't understand. Aaron was still on the pier, looking slowly right and left, when he got to him. "Whoa, man! What's wrong? Is this about your mother? It's been too much for you, all this happening so fast. Let's go to the porch, and I'll pop you a cold beer. There's nobody else around for a change, and"... Aaron wheeled to face him, and spat out, "SHE"S HERE! man, she's on this Island right now! I don't know just where, but I feel her as sure as if she was this shirt I'm wearin'. Toby! Franciene has come back!" Toby didn't want to dispute him, or get into the webby mess of her body on the bank right off, so he led him to the porch, sat him in a rocker, and dashed for the beer, half afraid to leave him alone. "Why do you think that, Aaron? What gave you the feeling first?" Aaron inhaled and told Toby what had happened

"I was in the tractor barn, about to open the freezer, when the key flipped out of my fingers, and got lost in the shells on the floor! I couldn't find it nowhere, and it was while I was lookin' for it, I felt her nearby." They both rose and went around the house toward the barn. Aaron stopped at the garage, staring at the place where the jeep had been. "Toby, the jeep was here when I went into the barn! I noticed it from the kitchen window, 'cause somebody had left one of the doors open. I closed it on my way to the barn!" They got a closer look at the tracks... deep and serpentine, as if it had been driven away in a great hurry. Toby took his arms and asked, with all the earnest concern he could give.

"You didn't hear it leave? It seems hard to believe it went right past you and you didn't hear it," He said. They then went to the barn, and Aaron knelt down, running his hands back and forth, through and over the oyster shells, said nothing, but looked at Toby as if to say, "See?" He was right... the noise would have masked the moment of the jeep's departure, especially if one was kneeling close to the ground. Aaron rose to face him. "If I try to find her it'll backfire, since she's likely capable of sensing that we're coming for her. I have to do this my own way. I know, Toby, I know she killed my mama with poison she put on her dish of blackberry dumpling last Saturday morning. You might think you know something that would dispute that, but it's true. Mama gave me the answers... I'll show you."

They went to the cabin, and he showed him the table, and the dumpling on the stove, still warm. Toby picked up the rusty can, knowing Aaron didn't set this up, but not believing his mother's GHOST did either! Aaron faced Toby with the most lost look he had ever seen on a face. "Toby, that girl is here to do harm to people you love, and you got to join me to help them. Carrie is a good woman... she's my second mother, but she loves Francie with a fierceness that's next to blind." He was about to get deep into the heart of this mystery as he knew it, and so was his friend before him. "Aaron, Carrie wants to stop whatever the girl is doing... she told me! I don't think she's blind at all! I came back here this afternoon to get into the book that can help unravel some of the secrets of the power behind all this, my friend."

Suddenly struck by lightning, Toby exclaimed, "Wait a damn minute! Carrie told me to stop reading the book! She said I didn't need to know all that... that she had all we needed to stop Francie already inside her! It was Mattie who told me to get back to reading, only just today. It IS Carrie who wants me to stay dumb!" All he could do was nod soberly, and hang his head. They turned away from 'Tilde's display, resigned to the sad fact that they had Carrie to buck. They left the cabin, and while they walked back to the house, both trembling from uncertainty and fear, Aaron said,

"Man, you got to understand where Carrie has been. She loves Massey Thornedike and that girl of his, like they was her own.

She sees herself saving Franciene for Massey's sake! She knows the girl is evil, and that what WAS Franciene, the sweet little angel, is now a murderous bitch on the rampage. Even Carrie and her powers can't fix her. She knows if I get to her first, or if the law figures it out, she can't save her for her daddy. Jesus Knows, I wish it wasn't true too, we used to be like family, Toby, but she KILLED my mother! She probably killed Cliff Hartsell too, and she's here because Will is a threat to her, this I do know! Call and tell them not to come back here tonight, man, I swear it's not safe!"

Toby was starting to trust his version of this twisted mess. "I need to tell you what I know, right now, if you will listen. We have been here since last Wednesday, Will and I, and life has been like a bad B movie ever since. I'm glad the boy found his family, but before that, we found a pretty young girl's body on the creek bank that first morning, and our initial plan was to get away from the scene and forget it. But Will struck out alone through a sense of duty to tell her family, that turned into providence, when her daddy turned out to be his as well!"

"The weirdest of all those weird moments, was when we learned the girl wasn't dead... she had run away. That truth flip-flopped again, when a severed arm, still wearing the same jewelry the dead girl had on, was dumped on a shrimp boat deck over the weekend. Will told me he was at the hospital when reporters were buzzing about it. Reality seems to be flipping back and forth between before she died, and now... man, it's crazed! If the girl is alive, then whose arm is that in the hospital morgue?" It was a question to be answered only when all truths came to light. Aaron stood before him, blinking in silent awareness as the first of those truths sunk in.

# CHAPTER
# THIRTY-THREE

If anyone had seen the two girls on the beach, they would have watched them for a long while. They were nature's rapture... running, dancing, body-surfing in the easygoing waves... simply being kids on a beach belonging to them alone. Mandy asked as they dried off, "Why did you ever leave here? It looks like you had the run of the place, and you were always safe and out of reach. It would be heavenly to me, after the pretentious old-fart trap I was snapped up inside of." She's as stupid as she looks, thought Francie. Her mind spoke to her from years of convoluted rationale. Why was it, that nobody was ever happy? Every damn body who had ever come to Squires said the same stuff Mandy had just said... "If I could choose anywhere in the world to end up, it would be on Squires Island!"

Hah! If that were so, you couldn't stir 'em with a stick over here by now. She was so tired of the phony words people blurted out before they thought about them. Wiping away the bitter moment, Francie turned and smiled at her companion. "Come on, Mandy, you know that old, "Grass is always greener", drill, don't you? I wasn't about to hang around for more of that. Daddy had my future so planned in advance I was sure to be fifty-five before I got to be twenty-one, with five or six kidlets, and a big old fat ass to sit around on, I will NOT sit still while the rest of my life goes into the toilet! Now you remember that you can NOT answer the phone unless it rings once then stops, then rings again. It is my signal wherever I am, so I am sure the wrong people do not get my calls. I am going to see Daddy now, so you just have fun here until I come back, okay?" Yes, it was okay, Mandy sighed, as she readied for the beach. Let the silly chick do her thing, and after that she would make her turn the planning over to a better head.

Of course, Franciene was on quite a different tack. She found Jaime waiting for her in the creek where they had left him, and was waving him to get going, and right NOW! "Just hold on, Missy, I need to be sure I don't get spotted by anybody Pop has lookin' for me! After you girls left the boat I saw him in Ruddy's skiff, pokin' around, much too close, lookin' to me to whip my ass! Francie did not care about his "POP" whipping his ass one bit, but she did not want to be spotted by her daddy's best friend. "JAIME! Are you sure he didn't see you? That would be bad for both of us, since I am going back with you, and you are messing up the ferry schedule to beat the band! What did you do when you saw him?"

She pretended pouting and very contrived concern for him, and he ate it up, especially since with it came the way she pressed into his side and rubbed his hip with her long fingers. "Oh Boy! This might be it!", Jaime whooped in his head, wondering if the vee-berth was halfway decent. He puffed up and answered her in as casual a tone as he could muster. "All I did was go up in Gnat Creek, and fished for awhile until he got tired of lookin' for me. He'll be pissed, but I figure it'll be worth it, if you're sweet to me on the way back. Where's your sexy friend? Man, she was somethin'! If I can't sweet talk you, I bet she'll listen!" She could tell he was having sport with her, and it was nauseating.

"He is ALWAYS trolling around", thought Francie with a shudder. If she was going to get him to swear secrecy, though, she had to feign interest. "Mandy is at Sandy's waiting for me to go visit my daddy. As you can plainly see, I'm not visiting Daddy at all. I'm going to Charleston, and coming back later. She doesn't need to know that I've left Squires, and if you help me, and keep it to yourself, I promise we'll make you glad you did." With that as a teaser, Francie leaned in his face and took his mouth in hers so lavishly,

Jaime almost lost control of the boat. He had yet to touch, let alone kiss her. It had been one of his favorite pleasuring fantasies... making out with Franciene Thornedike... getting closer and closer to conquest. He had not enjoyed the end of his dream, because he always exploded before the best part. It had been enough just to imagine touching her without clothes, to cause him to spasm in a lunch-whistle climax. Now she was tickling his tongue with her own, so sharp and slick, he could have eaten it like a piece of candy. As quickly as she devoured him, she was away, primping and giggling.

"Look what you did, girl! You got me all stirred up!" He turned so she could see his tented shorts. Francie laughed loudly, as she covered her face in demure farce. Jaime pleaded on, "Come on, honey, that was no innocent kiss between old friends! I think we need to stop somewhere and deal with this!" Francie was running out of patience with this fool, but she held off. It would be so easy to get rid of him, but she still needed his help, at least until he got the canoe for them. "Don't you DARE stop, Jaime! I' got no time for you now! It's mid-afternoon already, and I' got a long drive yet. You know I only have a learner's permit, so I've got to take it slow. If I speed, I'm busted. I'll take the wheel while you take on your problem, how's that? I promise not to look." Jaime couldn't believe his ears! This girl was something else! His arousal had waned by then, and he punched playfully at her tan midriff.

She jumped out behind Aaron's house where they had left the car, with words of warning, and an order. "Okay, boy, I'll be back sometime later, and I'll call you, but while I'm gone, and if you want me and Mandy to set you spinnin', you need to get me a canoe... a light one, but it has to be big enough for two. Two paddles, and two life jackets. Bring them here and hide them in the bushes. I'll need you to take me and the canoe back to the island. You got to promise to keep quiet about seein' me at all, you hear? If anybody finds out, I'll be comin' after you, and good! Do you promise, Jaime?" Jaime dutifully promised.

He was so intrigued... there was something different, a strange compulsion he hadn't seen in the girl he had watched with relish as she grew. It was a weird kind of fun... having her all to himself, sharing a conspiracy. They parted, and he hurried to round up what she had ordered. He knew of just such a canoe, and he could easily slip it away from its shed, since it was behind a seasonal house on the sound. A little larceny was small price to pay for the reward he anticipated. Franciene was away in the Saab before Jaime could get cranked up. "She's trouble...and I don't know, or care, how much." He watched the rag top out of sight, and as he motored out of the creek, a gusty, too chilly for the season, breeze slapped his face.

"I won't need that fool anymore after tomorrow", thought Franciene, on her way to fetch Troy. If he handled the canoe, and got her to Squires in the morning, that might be it for him. She began to chuckle aloud as she imagined what he expected to happen with her and Mandy as a reward. "Reward?" She sneered out the word, and gunned the car into cruising speed, always watching the speedometer to avoid getting stopped. Her daddy would be called in minutes after she was caught with a restricted license. "A few more months and I'll be eighteen... Freedom!" She stopped at a pay phone, called the code to Sandy's house, and told Mandy to sit tight, that her visit to her daddy was getting tedious, and she might stay the night, but would call later. Mandy was fine... who wouldn't be, with a house just off the beach, a stocked fridge, and no chance of being found.

\* \* \*

Whatever had sparked their talk, it was worth it. Aaron and Toby were, at last, on the same page. He was having trouble swallowing that Franciene was alive, but whatever psychic phenomena was at work had shown itself to him in that little kitchen, and he was not pooh-poohing any possibility. "Why don't we take a ride to the beach?" Aaron asked. "It will clear our heads, and I admit I want to ride the roads to see if anything gives me a clue about Franciene... Mama wouldn't have set that scene up for nothing." They took the pickup, and when they reached the beach road, Aaron skidded to a stop, nearly putting them in a ditch. The jeep! It was in a scrub palmetto thicket, almost hidden. They ran to it, expecting anything.

There was nothing to tell who had misplaced it, except for a peculiar scent... fresh and youthful, one Aaron assured Toby was HERS! Wordlessly, Toby got in the jeep, and followed the truck back. No beach... they had been given their clue, and their heads were all too clear. Back at Sandy's, Mandy was oblivious to anything except the video tape collection and the strawberry ice cream she had found, settling in to wait for her friend's call.

* * *

What a shitty deal! Troy wondered why and how he could have ended up waiting in a sissy room for a silly chick to show up like this. His head was still heavy from that pill, and he was hungry as a boar hog. All Francie had said when she called was that Mandy was on her Island, and they would pick her up later. The boy had decided to tell them it had been nice, but that he was done with two crazy girls offering up NO NOOKY for his trouble. The money and stocks they lifted weren't his, and he wanted no part of getting busted for the theft when her daddy reported her to the cops. Franciene was too stupid to figure that he would know right off who had opened the safes. First, she was AWOL, then, she had watched him go through the combinations many times past, and had always known what was there. It was all about the adventure that night, Troy knew it now. If only he had left with his buddy and never looked back, he wouldn't have the shaky, sick sense of foreboding that was growing inside him.

It was then that Franciene appeared, fetchingly attired and breathless. "Did you miss me?" She flopped on the bed by him, tickling his toes with hers. "I bet you're starving, 'cause I am, and boys are always hungry! Let's go have ourselves a snack before we take off." It seemed now, that everything she did irritated Troy, and he wondered how he could have been so dumb. Nevertheless, he got up to leave with her. They were headed south in less than an hour, nibbling the last of the onion rings Francie had taken away from the barbecue shack on Highway Seventeen.

She sensed he had changed toward her, and it was puzzling. Perhaps he was tired of waiting for her affection... she knew she had been toying with him unmercifully, but if that's what he was waiting for... tough! Soon as they got to Frenchport she would give him what he really deserved. He was surprised when she laid her hand on his thigh, and squeezed ever so gently. No fair, he thought... a gesture like that meant something was going to happen, from his point of view. He smiled at her with hope, but she was staring at the road, humming tonelessly.

By the time they got to Beaufort, her attention to him had shifted to positive again, and she was excited about going to a little waterfront bar. She led him into a dark, rustic hole in the wall, begging a flashy drink. Several umbrellas later, they decided to sit in a swing by the harbor to sober up for the last hour of their drive. Francie was suddenly all over him, kissing and stroking him to madness. Troy thought, what the Hell, as she took his hand and led him to a fishing boat on the charter dock, sneaking aboard. They found a stateroom and were naked in seconds, the girl pushing him down and straddling him as if she did it all the time. After so much fantasy, when Troy at last had the real thing, he believed he would just die from the pleasure of her body. This was perfection, pure and simple, and the way she used what she had was spectacular. She put his palms on her proud breasts, moving them around while moaning softly to the rhythm of his hips. He obeyed all her unspoken encouragements, and wasn't at all prepared when she slapped him hard across his face.

"You hurt me! I didn't intend for you to hurt me!" She kept moving up and down on him until he could no longer hold back, and he gave up the ghost, in a heart stopping climax. It was barely subsiding when Francie dismounted and ran to the head. He was dressed when she reappeared, composed and stoic. "I'm sorry I hurt you, but you didn't have to pop me like that. Shit, girl! You made me do what I did!" She tossed her head in a superior gesture and waved the subject closed, flipping a quick remark at him to punctuate her attitude.

"I knew you were mad because I hadn't let you do it to me, so now you did, and now it's over. Let's go!" She was off the boat and running up the dock in the moonlight. The boy shook off what was left of the ruined afterglow, and followed her to the car. Francie threw the keys to him and was asleep as soon as she told him to follow the signs to Frenchport. Her dreams were full of violence, and the face of her victim was alternately her father's, and a blonde boy she didn't recognize. Troy could hear her moaning and struggling as she slept, but he cared not... just wanted to get the hell away as soon as their trip ended.

Franciene directed Troy to Aaron's creek house when he woke her for directions. Since his was the only dwelling, nobody would be on that dead end road, and she could leave him there while she went to check with Jaime about the next morning. She needed time alone to plan everything so that they would all get their due.

## AARON AND TOBY AND THE THICKENING MYSTERY

If he had not been disturbed about Linda Sue, and frustrated about the vortex he and his young friend were in, Toby would have seen how dangerous it was becoming from all sides. The whispering in his head was constant now, that if Franciene WAS here, and as involved in evil pursuits as Aaron suggested, danger was their closest companion. Aaron had almost lost it when they found the Jeep and he declared the clinging fragrance was the girl's. It was less than a week since they first came to this place... tomorrow was Tuesday, and Wednesday would be the seventh day. How it could be only one week, considering the world of life-altering events they had endured? If Will and Toby emerged with nothing but their sanity, Toby knew he would be grateful. He phoned the hospital when they got back to the house, and waited while being connected to the CICU waiting room. Linda answered with a shaky voice, but rallied when she realized who it was.

"Toby, this is taking so long! How long has it been now? I can't keep my thoughts together." She sounded scared... that much he could sense through the phone. It kept the fear going that she would be choosing Massey should he live, and Toby had to forget what had happened earlier. RIGHT! The sweetest moments spent since Katie, and he should forget! He was not going to do it! He let her take a breath, and consoled her as best he could. "That's really a good sign, Sweetheart. If he's holding up after this long, they must be encouraged to keep working on him. Don't forget what a strong man he is. You should know more than anyone what he's made of. What about Will and Carrie? Did Dan come back?"

She said Will was walking around the grounds, too nervous to be still, and Carrie had spent the last two hours in the chapel... said Jesus and 'Tilde felt closer to her there, when Will went to see about her. Dan had called, said he was looking for his son... something about running amuck in the ferry boat. Toby chuckled to himself, remembering how pissed Dan had been when Jaime had passed them earlier. Linda was spared all of this bizarre Franciene stuff, Thank God, because no one had told her anything except that she had seen fit to go sashaying off with some friends on Saturday, not knowing about her daddy's attack. Linda was so preoccupied with everything she had been dealing with, it was explanation enough for the time being. Toby was on tender hooks, fearing the whole mystery would emerge, with no plan to deal with the fallout.

With nothing to do, Toby was tempted to the beach again, this time alone. Aaron had gone to Jasper's to visit and help clean up after the big day. Their family went home on the last boats, and Pansy had a mountain of pans, bowls, and trays covered with baked-on food to be dispatched. Toby was graciously refused his weak offer of help, and left to his own devices. This time he walked the two miles to the shore, drawn by its rhythmic pounding.

As he turned the last corner to the dunes, he saw a girl coming toward him. She was blonde, tall, and lovely, wearing only a swim-suit bottom, and a batik wrap tied around her hips. He waved to get her attention, but she seemed not to notice, and left the road to go into a little house set in a youpon thicket up a narrow lane from the beach. What to do...? Should he go and knock on the door, satisfy-ing his curiosity, or leave an obviously private young lady alone? She was Will's age, maybe a little older, so Toby wasn't interested in her "that way," but there was something about her....

Inside, Mandy had hidden behind the door, watching as the man walked by. Francie warned her to lay low, and if she was seen on the beach, not to let on that she was staying in the teacher's house. She was getting a bit antsy, wishing Francie would call again, or better still, come back before dark. It was getting on to twilight, and she would have to turn on more lights than the one left burning night and day, and she was worried someone would come snooping. She was hungry again, so she hurriedly nuked a frozen dinner and sat on the floor in front of the television, choosing "Bonnie and Clyde," from Sandy's video collection. The glow from the screen wasn't visible from the front windows, and Mandy relaxed a little as she became absorbed in the twenty five year old flick she had never bothered to watch before.

When the phone rang, she jumped, and ran to it while the code came through. She snatched it up when the second set of rings began, and shrieked, "You bitch! You didn't tell me it was so scary here! I'm freakin' out alone in this place! A man was on the road when I came off the beach earlier, and he knows I'm in here! What next, Miss Smart-ass? Are you coming back soon?" Franciene was at a pay phone, leaving Troy with the excuse of a trip to the marina for drinks and chips. She was careful to not be seen, pulling a big canvas hat she found in Aaron's house down over her face. She didn't count on Mandy being discovered, and when she was told about the man, and couldn't get there until morning, she played her next card, asking Mandy for a description before offering an explanation.

"That was probably the deputy, making rounds before he goes back to Frenchport at dark. I'll get Daddy to call and tell him we have a guest using the house, so quit freaking, okay?" She waited while Mandy digested the fix, then, knowing there was no patrolling deputy, wondered fleetingly just who it HAD been, before she went on. "I'll try to get away from here for a bit and come see you, but if I'm not there by nine, don't expect me. Daddy has a tight clamp on me since I got home and I've got to stay close. I called Troy and he's gettin' impatient. I don't think he's going to hang around waiting. Said something about calling Alex's folks to tell him where he is, and splitting the whole scene. I say good riddance! I've got to go, Mandy, now you stay low until I see you tomorrow morning, you hear?"

She hung up without waiting for an answer. Mandy cursed the handset before replacing it, and petulantly rewound the movie back to Clyde Barrow's first bank robbery. Franciene slipped into the convenience store, purchased some junk food to pad her excuse, and went back to the house on Turtletail Creek, determined to keep Troy's hands off her no matter what. He was walking around in the yard when she turned into the drive, his fists stuffed in his pockets, his shoulders hunched as if readying himself to butt a door with his head. Francie got out of the car and approached him with her patent patronizing attitude.

"What're you doin' out here? I wasn't gone so long. It's not even ten thirty yet! I got some chips and salsa and some Mountain Dews. You like that?" Troy didn't answer, only took the bag and went inside the shabby house. "Well, if he wants to be a turd, then let him!" Francie mumbled, as she followed him inside without a word he could hear. Troy had words aplenty for her. "What are we doing in this shit box? This SUCKS! I want to leave right now! I thought things were going to get better, now we're stuck again! Where is Mandy, really? Did you dump her too? And what's going down tomorrow? You said we were going to do this thing together. Answer me, Francie, NOW, or I'm walking out of here! She stared at him, and broke into laughter.

"Things ARE better, stupid! What about what just happened on that boat in Beaufort? Are you telling me you didn't like it? If that's so, you just go ahead and leave! We're going to the Island tomorrow, and Mandy is right there waiting for us, just like I told you. She wanted to stay on the beach instead of more riding in the car, so I told her we'd be there early tomorrow. I've got a friend who has a canoe, and we're going to get him to take us across early tomorrow so we can paddle all over the back side of Squires, and I can show you where to find cool Indian stuff. It'll give me a chance to set things up with Daddy to get those certificates. He'll tell me when they'll be here, without being suspicious. Come on, Troy, I want to have fun, not fight all the time. We're almost done here, then you get to say where to next, now doesn't that sound better?"

She was crouching submissively in front of him, her hands on her knees, looking up into his face with as sincere a look as she could muster. He had no argument. They turned on the tube and sat on the dingy braided rug to snack and watch some inane sitcom. She munched Cheetos and half-heartedly studied his rapt face while silently planning his last hours on earth.

* * *

Whatever the outcome, the vigil for Massey Thornedike had taken its toll on the vigilant, for a wide range of reasons. He had been in surgery three-plus hours, and there was no way to know, other than Mattie's assurances that the length of time meant that the patient was withstanding the rigors of the procedure sufficiently to continue. Will was so delighted to be with his mother, he had to keep reminding himself the circumstances were dire, with his new-found father's life hanging by a thread. Mattie was able to peek out with encouragement at spare intervals, but he felt good about Massey's chances for some inborn reason.

Linda was not as optimistic, wringing her hands and wiping tears that would sneak out and down her face without a word. Will knew she was thinking back over the years, and all they held for the three of them, as well as dealing with her anger at Massey's other self. Finally, after nearly four hours, Mattie joined them, all smiles and hugs. "That is one strong bull of a man! He faltered one time about halfway through, but seemed to have been given a cattle prod zap, because he actually jumped and stabilized at the same second. After that, the surgery was almost what you could call routine! His blockages are clear and he has a reworked valve system. If he can behave, and cut out those bad habits of his, get a good exercise regimen, and most important of all, cut the stress in his life to near ZERO, well, you have him back as long as you want him!" Will grabbed her in a grateful hug, and Carrie and Linda embraced and asked immediately when they could see him.

"He's in recovery for now, and then he goes into post-op intensive care where he will be constantly tended through the night. You won't see anything but a lot of technology and a worn out, pitiful and slack-jawed Massey, who may or may not be conscious. We are hoping he will sleep through this stage, to avoid any harm to what was done. I think we all need a break from this hospital, and I need some hair of the dog. What about Miss Ruby's, then we can all go back on Dan's boat for the night? I know the folks over there would like to know how it went." She always seemed to have the best ideas.

Carrie and Linda nodded in concert, with Carrie the first, agreeing to head for home. She was weary, and Aaron was in need of her... she could feel it... that, and more. There was something that needed tending on Squires, and tired as she was, she was itching to get to it. Will went to call Dan, and quickly rang Massey's number to see if Toby was there. He was sure his friend was just about to his patience limit and wanted to reassure him. It crossed his mind that until his half-sister was found, alive or dead, they weren't going to be able to go anywhere. There was no answer, so he wrapped his mom in his long arms, breathed, "I love you," in her grateful ear, and they left the hospital.

Massey was barely conscious, but he seemed to know to be very still and quiet. He had almost died back there! He felt it again, like before on the beach. It was the same, only this time the one to turn him back to life was Aunt Clothilde Herself! He was so glad to "See" her, he did not care how she came to him, as she told him to go and fix everything with those who needed him and loved him. When she appeared from the big light, she was covered with blooming vines... Blackberry vines! But they had not had any thorns. Their white blooms were huge... as big as Cherokee roses, exactly like the ones that bloom wild at the beach every spring.

He didn't question anything, somehow it all made sense, like so many dreams do, until you wake up. He let her turn him around by taking his shoulder and directing him back away from the welcoming light she was part of. The last thing he remembered was that she called out, mind to mind, that he would be all right now, and that she loved him dearly, and forever. Even in his dream state, he made a note to tell Aaron about his mama, soon as he could. Massey's third chance at life gave him peace, and he let sleep come.

\* \* \*

On Squires, Toby was intrigued, but suppressed thoughts of the strange young lady at the beach. Aaron wasn't back from the Griffins, so he went in the study to fix a gin and tonic, his summer drink of choice, with lemon and a dash of bitters. The room always felt creepy, likely from his misgivings relating to Will and his new family, but for the first time, he felt a chill while stirring his drink. Maybe it's the ice, maybe there's a breeze coming from the ocean, or a touch of sea fog. It was real enough to question, but he let the mystery be, and went to the porch, trying to relax and not think too much. Halfway through his highball, the phone inside rang. He got to it on the third ring to hear Will's excited voice saying his name. "Toby, are you there? TOBY!" He slowed him down and got control, to hear him say, "Massey's going to be okay! Mattie said he is strong enough to have withstood even longer surgery. Isn't that cool?" It was indeed cool, but he had to fight down a twinge of regret that Linda would now have a new chance with her first love. He told Will how glad he was, and he asked about the group's plans. He had been spending far too much time on the edge of all this, and it was not feeling okay anymore.

Will's excited voice came back. "We are at Miss Ruby's, sort of celebrating, but Dan is going to take us across as soon as he fuels the boat. Seems Jaime has been joy riding all afternoon, and he's in deep shit with his dad. Is there a car at the dock, or can you or Aaron meet us?" Remembering, but discarding Aaron's warning that no one should come back tonight, Toby told him Aaron was at Jaspers in the Rover, and he would have him wait there for them. He asked to speak to Linda, but Will said she was upstairs with Carrie, kind of freshening up, so he simply sent good wishes. Toby wanted to hear her voice after the good news, hoping to catch a hint of her feelings, but let it go. It really was not his party, although he had thought it so for a little moment.

They hung up, and Toby found Jasper's number on the list Carrie had on the refrigerator door, called Aaron with the news, and the plan for their arrival. God! What next? The moment called for a refill, so he obliged himself, and stood sipping a more potent mixture, staring at the face of triumph in the portrait behind the massive desk. "Oh well," he said aloud to the room, "I can walk away with no less than I arrived with, maybe a little more, if love's road rash counts as a lesson learned. Cheers!" His glass went aloft to the image that was looking through him... and out the door, for his baby girl, his precious son, and perhaps his lost love.

Linda Sue and Carrie unlocked the door to the guest room Ruby told them to use to freshen up, and they realized, now that they could relax and regard one another, that they were becoming closer, more family-like. Carrie had, through this terrible day, prepared herself to give her sweet Massey to Jesus in that little chapel, and had already planned to ask Linda and the boy to stay awhile, at least until Franciene was found. That would not change with the good news. They would need to close ranks even more now, to be of help and comfort for Massey in this most timorous time. If the girl was found alive, there would have to be reckoning for her deeds, and her daddy would suffer horribly, most likely more than if she was discovered dead, or never found at all.

Carrie knew that frozen forearm was still safely hidden, and made a silent note to check the lock on the freezer tonight before bed. The proof of Franciene's evil acts must not be exposed, unless she herself knew it was time. That poor thing was undeniable evidence that recent events in time had been played with, as were Will and Toby, and their discovery last Wednesday. She simply HAD to shuffle things to right before Massey came home, and his life depended on how much she could keep from him until he could handle the truth. The two women rearranged their rumpled clothes and splashed their faces to relieve a grueling hospital wait, saying nothing until Linda patted the bed, asking Carrie to sit close to her. Linda spoke haltingly.

"Carrie, with all the upsetness, we've not had a chance to talk about what happened when Will was little... you know, that terrible time when Massey took my baby from me and brought him to his Island. That time left me a changed, bitter person who has not trusted anyone since. Can you understand, even though you love Massey as your own son, how it ruined me to find that the man who had been the only love I ever knew, could tear the sun and the moon from me?" Carrie was having the reaction she hoped for, as she held both of Linda's hands firmly in her lap. She needed for this wise lady to affirm her responses to so much anguish, so she went on.

"I know why he did what he did, Carrie, it was in order to have control and input so he could influence my child away from me later, with promises I could never afford to match. I know he didn't tell anyone on Squires Island the truth, and his little girl was badly in need of an explanation, first and foremost, so I want to tell you now, if you will let me, how we came to the place where this could happen." Carrie was looking in Linda's eyes, seeming to listen, but she was in fact, only waiting for her to finish speaking. She knew what was to be said, as long ago, when she first saw the frantic young woman on the porch, demanding to see Massey Thornedike. She kept Linda's hands in hers as she replied. "You poor child, I know what you have suffered, and I know what my sweet Massey suffered too. All his life he wanted to live in peace with folks and do good work. He's still the same young man you loved, honey, and when he stole off with your Willie, he was a lost soul, in guilty mourning for the family he should have claimed and didn't."

Linda was aghast. She knew Massey had not told her all of these feelings... he wasn't put together that way. This woman has connectors and receptors way, way above the ordinary. She had watched Will and Mattie, and yes, Toby too, regarding Carrie in a special way, ever since she got to Massey's house today, and now she knew why. The unasked questions in her head would remain so, as she settled in to listen further, her hands resting on Carrie's, steadying herself.

"You shouldn't have been treated so badly that night, and he deserved the wrath of both you AND his girl, when he came to his senses. Do you know she wouldn't let her daddy come near her for days after that night, she was so mad. You were someBODY to Franciene, Linda Sue, the first woman she believed like her mother she had felt so strong for, 'cept for Miss Sandy, her teacher. I tried to help Mister Massey with her, but she took on so bad we let her be awhile." She seemed far away, as if captive of the memory. "The bracelet she threw away on Jasper's porch was meant for you. Massey had it engraved the day he took your child, thinking he could make amends somehow. Your boy has it now, and is using it as an amulet to help him with his heart's direction. I can't tell you what is going to come to us... I would if I could, but for now Francie is out of my reach."

The anguish was twisting Carrie's sweet features so alarmingly, Linda reached to her cheek to give her pause, but she brushed her hand away, and spoke on. "She is in her own kind of hell, and has more evil things to do before we can stop her. Tell me you remember the sweet child you knew her to be back then, and your good energy will flow to her, this I know. She needs our help. We got to find her before her daddy comes home, and if it is my last act on earth... if it kills me, I will see justice for those who should find it."

She suddenly stopped speaking... as if she were switched off. Linda feared after the words she spoke, that Carrie was in a semi-conscious state. She patted her hands and said her name twice, before Carrie turned to look at her. "I am grateful for your words, Carrie, and yes, the time with little Francie was magic, and I will never forget it. She became my caretaker, and my friend. I want to help find her... for myself and for Will, as well as for you and Massey. He knows nothing about all this?" Carrie shook her head sadly.

"Honey chile, even if he knew every word like I just told you, he wouldn't believe it of his perfect daughter. Franciene was the reason you couldn't be here, you know. Massey asked her to let him bring you and Willie to live in the house, and she took such a fit, he feared she would do herself harm. His love for that girl is deep as the deepest ocean, and he can't see around it most times. I'd say she's the most kept back child there could ever be, and it has hurt both of them terribly. 'Tilde and me knew what was happenin', long time ago, same as did Aaron, and even my poor Benjie, rest his soul, but you know how hard Massey's head is!" Oh, yes, she knew! She had first-hand knowledge, from the day they met in South Georgia, to the way he fought his diseased heart on this very day. She felt miserable about Franciene and her disappearance, but there was a need to press Carrie on other matters.

"Carrie, do you know why Toby and Will have become so entwined in this place? It is all so strange, since I met Toby only a few days ago, when he came to my house in Waycross looking for Will. There was a compulsion, an obsession about the way he showed up there, as if he had been sent to find me as well as my son. I was mystically drawn to him, and I think you know I still feel the attraction. Now we are at odds because of Massey and our past, and I'm torn between two strong forces. How can I be so confused about how I feel? Are you able to explain this?"

Carrie nodded wisely, and said, "You have a choice tedious to make... whether to follow a new path that waits for you, or retrace and continue on one lost before. Let the next days fall, and be guided by your wisdom and your heart. We all are going to be sorely tested soon as we return to Squires Island, mark my words." She reached for her and hugged her close, still speaking. For your own safety, stay close to me, Linda... and to Aaron, and Mattie. We can help, but I must admit I am torn like you, between doing what is right, and what will hurt my family the least. Child, there has been pain spread wide enough already, and it must stop. Trust me, trust all of us, and most of all, Honey, trust in the Lord. He is lighting our way with choices. Now we got to go. They wonderin' what in the world we're about up here. Splash some of this Lilac toilet water on, so's they think we been busy primpin'!"

"God, please be with this woman as she works for good, and help me to help her", prayed Linda silently as they went downstairs to join the others. She kept her feelings for Toby close inside her, not knowing what to do with them... not knowing what his were for her, since their lovemaking. It would have to wait, she decided, and took up the joy she was feeling for Will's reentry into her life as her banner. He was more than she had hoped for in a son... straight, and good, and she thanked God for the blessing while she was at it.

# CHAPTER THIRTY-FOUR

It was twilight, and beginning to breeze up in the harbor. Dan was holding court in the circle of stools at the bar, telling foul weather stories with aplomb, when the two women joined them. He stopped and spun Linda around in a joyful hug at the news about Massey. "That boy is bein' saved for somethin', and I think I know what! He wants to have you again, darlin'! It was a shame you lost each other, when I see what you could'a been. You saved his life today, you know, just like Will did on Saturday when he first took sick out there. It seems a lifetime ago, don't it, Will?"

The boy nodded, reliving the days for the umpteenth time. Dan, satisfied with Will's silent signal of agreement, rambled on cheerfully. "When ya'll wanna go across? The boat's filled and ready, and there's a cooler full'a Heinekens, and even a cold bottle of Jose Gold for brave hearts. I know, Aunt Carrie, you believe we ought to be drinkin' well water and cider, but Shit! It's a party, and nobody ever had a good party without spirits, right?" Everyone agreed again, and they set off down the dock.

As they were idling away, the phone rang at Ruby's elbow. It was Toby's frantic attempt, with the book under his arm, to stop them... too late. They were all coming to whatever tomorrow would bring. He reread the paragraph that had sent him flying to the phone, helplessly flopped into a kitchen chair, to be startled to his feet by the phone ringing. It was Aaron, checking in, and when he told him they were just leaving Frenchport, the young man's sigh was ragged and loud. "We got bad times comin', Toby, I jus' know it. It might be tonight, or tomorrow, but they comin', that's for sure!" Toby remembered old Copper still lying dead in his stall, and when he told Aaron, after he had stifled a sob, he said they could drag him out and bury him tonight after everyone was asleep. It was looking like sleep deprivation would be as formidable a foe as the forces they had yet to face.

Toby hung up carefully, already filled with dread and a heavy weight in his chest the gin could not dissolve. He decided to put aside those things he couldn't control, and opted for a shower, shave, and change, from what was now a diminishing selection of attire. It would be khaki shorts and a white oxford shirt, or khaki shorts and a yellow LaCoste, or faded jeans and a blue oxford. His meager wardrobe was becoming weary, but he had laundered everything while drinking this afternoon, and the wrinkles were at bay for awhile. Linda's regard was mighty crucial, for reasons the heart alone can tell. He went for the jeans and blue oxford, recalling a few times when his eyes were noted as being the same blue as the shirt... vanity eternal.

While toweling his hair, he stepped out on the porch, the sky now nearly purple. From where he stood, he could hear the pony in her paddock, galloping around and whinnying excitedly. It was the first time she had acted up, and Toby walked to her gate with a soothing word. That fragrance was back, or perhaps it had never left. He looked around for a flowering bush or tree that would lay the mystery to rest, but there was nothing close enough... only the pines and oaks in the woods next to the barn. What does it say, this essence, this heady hint that a girl-woman is here, or was here a moment ago? The pony recognized it... that explained her fractious mood. Relief washed over Toby to think he wasn't going crazy.

It was creepy in the increasing darkness, and he went back in for another tonic. Blessed juniper juice! The book was still open on the table, and he sat down with his cocktail and flipped to the page that came after the one that had disturbed him. He read what was to be the last words he would read before everyone arrived, and they were as chilling as the others... fulfilling Aaron's prophecy of imminent danger to his friends and to himself.

## BACK TO THE ALLEY

It was quite a night on the Alley. Strahan and Jay had spent the night in town, after far too much food and beverage. Over port and Romie and Julies in the best eatery they could find in Naples, the two weary aristocrats vowed to see this through to the end together, no matter how long and grisly it became. Jay knew things looked very bad for the boy... his sophisticated tutelage would have produced something by now if he had any control at all over his status.

It had been three days since Cliff was placed in Frenchport, on his way home from school. Strahan's version of what happened would be the best scenario for his son to come out safely. If he was with the Thornedike girl, well, who knows what sham they had set up to stay hidden, even to the extent of staging foul play. It made no sense why a boy with all Clifford Hartsell's advantages would go off so half-cocked like he did. Jesus, he could bed any round-heeled baby-doll in the state, just by dropping his name and address. He knew the boy's mama must be deep in the vapors by now, but Strahan had made no new move to contact her. All told, Jay felt it best to leave the man alone. He would not squat down at his knee for any meddling in his personal business, especially his marriage.

They had secured rooms above the restaurant... nice ones, with all the comforts, and no one had to rock either one to sleep. Sometime in the earliest part of dawn the radio phone sounded by Strahan's head. He struggled awake and mumbled, "Hullo, Hartsell here. What the hell is it?" The trooper was on the other end. "Yes, Mr. Hartsell, I have a bit of news. The civvies you placed out here have had themselves quite a night. They're all back at the tent asleep, except two. Appears they are following some sort of trail out there, and told us to let you know it's big enough to be human... no signs of a lesser animal. They have a radio phone... said they will call with news either way. When you comin' back here?"

Strahan jumped to his feet, turned on the light, and was readying to go. Just that moment, his inner voice piped up. "Wait! Go back a minute. What kind of trail? Are they telling you it could be my son flopping around out there? Well, have you got the choppers ready to go up? Answer me!" He was done in the bathroom, and was banging on the connecting door to rouse Jay-Jay. The officer who had bitten off too much, too early in the morning gathered his courage and spoke. "No sir, we wanted to wait until we know more. Those boys aren't the sharpest knives in the drawer, and it would be better not to jump the gun. I tried to call them back a bunch of times but they don't answer. I'm afraid their radio phone might be out of commission... you know, they could have dropped it or something... "

He knew exactly what was brewing on the other end. Even as he said the words he hated them. What bullshit it must have sounded like to Strahan Hartsell. What he didn't know was how hung over the man was at that moment, or he never would have called. "If you have nothing more than what you just told me, Shit for Brains, I am going to hang up now, that is if you don't mind." He had sprayed the words between his teeth, Kirk Douglas-like, and got his message across. Jay came in, towel around his neck and nothing else. It was not a pretty sight, but Strahan didn't notice. "Jay, I don't care how much trouble, hell, or expense it causes, I am bound to find Clifford TODAY, in however many pieces I can... are you with me?" Jay knew this man well enough to see he was all in. He was against the wall. He went to his friend, forgetting his nakedness, nodding his head solemnly. "Get away from me with that ugly thing hangin' out, you asshole! Go get dressed and we'll get some things movin'!, was all Strahan spat at him.

It was beginning to look like there might be some greens and blues in the world after all. Daylight... finally, blessed dawn was breaking. The two fumbling youths had just about run out of everything... phone juice, rum juice, and adrenalin juice, all had bottomed out, but the trail was REAL, and they knew what they were seeing. They tracked a path through the waving grasses, and something like footprints and wallowed out places for about a mile. The signs where the car was found and beyond for a good way had terminated, and now, at first light, they searched frantically, moving in the direction of the highway. They were having a rough time negotiating the muck, hoping to find something soon, something they could cash in for the grand prize.

# TOBY PREPARES HIMSELF FOR... WHAT?

Time spent with that book only ratcheted up Toby's angst. It told him that forces can gather over short periods, and when they do evil, destructive things, they are calculated as stepping stones seeking a crescendo of revenge and triumph over their perceived enemies. The most telling part was the paragraph dealing with inevitability if the force is unchallenged... and not diverted. If Carrie is putting up road-blocks to protect Massey and his daughter, and they are all in the way, they could all be destroyed! Toby gleaned that much pretty damn quick! It was hard to believe she could let bad things happen to inno-cents like Will and his mom, and little Mattie, to protect the other two.

What he preferred to think was that she was being single-minded, believing it would all work out just fine as long as her family was alright. The guess he had was she might even be thinking they could create and hold their own defense, since they have strong counter forces like Aaron and Mattie, leaving her free to save Massey by redeeming Francie. The pages did not yield any advice on tactics or rudiments, but there was one small part that became his mantra throughout the crisis. He read it aloud, every few minutes, to imbed it in his brain.

"The basic truth you take from this writing, is that no matter what else is true, it is so that all good works are known, noted, and weighed for their worth, and all evil deeds the same. What solves the equation of which side is to rule, is the one manning the scale." Their side could count on surviving, and even winning, if the fight was fairly wrought and refereed. Toby was about to call Jasper to see if they had arrived yet, when the house came to life with their voices talking all at once, doors slamming, and Will calling his name, obvi-ously in great spirits. Toby went to the study to find Will and Linda, flanked by Aaron and Dan, as they stared up at Massey's portrait, needing no words to punctuate the moment.

"He'll look like that again, with all of you loving him back to health." Toby was behind them now, his arms around their shoul-ders, and it seemed to him as though he was giving his blessing to their reunited family... maybe he was, maybe it was coming from some other place to the left of his control. Carrie and Mattie lingered with Jasper and Pansy, to be brought home after Carrie got current with the outcome of the day. It was a good thing, since Toby wasn't ready to confront her until he had a "Come to Jesus" talk with Aaron.

They were likely to be faced with a jagged corner of hell within hours, and if they came to stand against it, as well as Carrie's blocking and misguided purpose, they, as one, needed to make a plan. Toby did not want Linda and Will to know until they had to... Will's insight was joggled by his father's crisis and his mother's arrival... he seemed to have lost awareness of the mental exchanges with Carrie from before. When they moved to the kitchen, a unanimous move since it was long past supper time, Toby motioned for Aaron to come outside. He took a few seconds to indicate items in the refrigerator for a cold buffet, and stepped onto the porch.

"I know what this is about, Toby." He whispered sarcastically. "I told you it was a bad thing to let them come over here tonight... NOW what do we do? I swear! The vibes from that girl are on me like a cattle prod... Zap! Toby, I'm for everybody but you and me gettin' the fuck out of here... now! If they ain't here, we just might be able to eliminate the danger of harm to them." Taking mental inventory and a deep breath at the same time, Toby answered, "I get your point, and I agree in part, but we are going to need Mattie, and Carrie isn't about to go anywhere. This is her bailiwick! Man, she is here for the show! Fact is, she may well BE the show, but I sure as hell hope not. I want Dan too, for brute strength and his close ties to the family. How about we get Jasper to take Will and Linda back, and while he's over there, he can round Jaime up."

Aaron hated to admit it, but this white man was right on. The two boatmen might not be able to put their combined and imposing bulk to use, given the spirits' impervious powers, but they would be a comforting presence, no matter what might come. He was afraid, but in a different way than Toby. He had grown up with an edge of savvy about The Power, and as he grew, his mama hinted that he would inherit her place, and his Aunt Carrie did the same with her boy, Benjie.

BENJIE! Was it about Benjamin with Carrie? Was she so affected by what he had confessed to her, that she had shifted gears? Had her pure mission become tainted by grief and maybe even revenge? His mind raced back to see if he recalled any hint of bitterness that could have festered into this. It seemed she had been compassionate and forgiving, almost dismissive, to spare him, the night he told her. It was a normal reaction from someone as good as she is. Still, deep feelings can surface, so strong, that Carrie could be unable to control herself.

There was no time to do the digging now, he needed to get with Toby and act fast. Franciene was present or nearby, and coming... and she was pissed! When Toby finally got her alone, unexpected things came from Linda Sue. She clasped his forearm in both her hands... tugging him out to the porch and down the steps to the garden with deliberate speed. When they stopped behind a hedge of prolifically blooming hydrangea, she locked her arms around his neck, with the appearance of bestowing a kiss on his slack mouth. But she stopped, leaned away blinking, and said,

"Do you know your shirt, these blossoms, and your eyes are the same electric shade of blue?" Then, because he could not help himself, he gave HER the kiss! Oh, how Toby Howell would always remember that moment as one of the tenderest he would ever know. As before, when they reeled into this place, there seemed to be no words to fit. He spent a full minute deep within her eyes, finding answers there before the questions could come. She laughed the twinkling laugh he was, by now, addicted to, and they began to walk to the pier in perfect step.

Toby needed to speak, but could not. When they reached the end of the pier he helped her to sit down with their legs dangling into the waxing darkness, and turned to her saying, "You, darling, are so sweet and lovely I have trouble taking it all in. Aside from that... What does tonight...what does all this actually mean? I know how confused you were after we made love, and you have just faced and dealt with two huge events... your son's re-entry into your life, and his father's fight for his own. I expected to have no more time with you, and now this. What am I supposed to believe? Linda, Linda darlin', where is your heart?

The words he hoped would come were drowned out by a scream so shrill and agonized they grabbed and held onto each other as it began. One... two... the third shriek was cut off short, as if a hand was clamped over the mouth. They scrambled back to the house to join the rest on the porch, where all were looking wildly about for someone who could be in such terror. Aaron took Toby aside and whispered, "It ain't a person, Toby man, that's something unreal and full of badness, as if warnin' us how near it is to us. Listen here, Toby Howell... we are set up against that thing I ain't sayin' it's Franciene, but she's in it deep, and I'm feared she's not the worst of it. Where's that damn book, Toby?"

They slipped inside, hoping not to be followed, and took the book upstairs to the porch off of Massey's rooms. Toby sat on the floor under a table lamp with Aaron and opened the book to the place he had marked. It was BLANK! Nothing was on the two open pages but a sticky purple stain and Toby's bookmark. He frantically flipped through the entire book from front to back... not a word of print was to be found. They looked into each other's eyes and then to the door-way where Carrie stood, glowing from a light, weaving back and to behind her like some sort of familiar in attendance. In an instant she was beside and over them, but they both were struck that her bizarre movements did not cause fear... it was Carrie, for goodness' sake! They rose to their feet like two little boys, caught looking at the "Doctor Book"!

Carrie still did not speak, but moved between them to pick up the volume. She held it to her breast and then, almost in defiance, opened it to show them that all the pages were restored to full print. Then she spoke, not with her own voice, but with a sound like the wind. "I don't have time or patience for your meddling now. There is much to do and those who need me may not see another day, if you try to redirect or stop my work. You are wrong if you think I mean to harm you and the others. I love you... all of you, but I must help my children above anything. There will be less trouble if I can be left to my mission."

She turned away and went back out to the porch where everyone was still gathered. There was silence as she spoke. "You all must hear me. The time is here to take hold of the unraveled ends and bring them together. You have very little to do except stay close by each other, and aware of where you are at all times. Tomorrow will be soon enough to leave the Island, since all that is here tonight is her Hag, or more known to you, her familiar... her host. Franciene has no power of her own against you yet. Besides, I am feeling good things from her. She wants to be back home, safe and good again, I am sure of it! Those times out of proper order were done so to cover for her, but not by me. That scream was not by me, and not by Francie. It came from 'The One Most Powerful', like a wild animal announcing its approach, to make us prepare for what it can bring."

"'The One' is neither totally evil nor totally good... and we know nothing of its' reasons for being, except that The Lord Jesus told us there would be demons and their company in our midst through-out all time, and I and mine are charged with dealing with them, between them and you good people." She turned slowly, as if she feared she might crumble and fall to the floor, then she stopped, facing Mattie.

"Mattie Bell, I hope you can help Will back to where he was this time last week, when he and I were connecting. I can not, because I will betray him to Franciene, and she hates him because she fears him. Aaron, you and the girl have had much between you since you were babies, so you should focus on those times, to try and cleanse her soul with the innocence and purity you shared." She moved to the next ones, and as she had just done, gave a directive.

"Linda and Toby, I want you to stay as unattached as you can for your own sakes, but mostly because I don't want too many people to worry about. If I can use you, Toby, I will call for you, and you too, Linda, if the girl gives me any sign for you, it may come suddenly and without time for you to prepare. She is confused about who and what you are to her, so you have an advantage." She stepped back three steps to hold out her arms in a loving gesture.

"That is how I see all of you in our walk through this dark and forbidding forest. I must go and be alone to receive whatever comes to me, so I can know what is meant for me to do. Be sure, each of you... I am afraid, as afraid as you are, and when we finally know where we will be on the other side of all this, I pray to God we are all safe and all together. Go With God, children."

She turned, the book still in her arms, and seemed to fade away instead of walking out. Mattie spoke first. "That was magnificent. I wish it was recorded on tape for us to keep. She was warning us, is what she was doing." Aaron had walked a few steps following as if drawn by a magnet, and he shook himself and faced everyone again. "Y'all wait, mark my words, there's gonna' be a come-uppance in the mornin', sure's you born!" He slammed the screen door rudely as he went inside.

No one else spoke until Mattie offered up a suggestion that she call about Massey's condition, an idea all applauded. They needed something positive to ride on. She came back with the expected announcement. "He's resting comfortably, vital signs stable, and should sleep right through the night." It would serve them all, Toby suggested, if they try and get some rest while they could as well. Everyone agreed, and they went to the kitchen to raid the bread pudding one more time, then to their respective beds. Toby squeezed Linda's hand as she and Mattie took the stairs to the guest room... THAT guest room. He did not realize what it would mean. Not then.

What was spinning around in his head was the way he was feeling about Linda in the garden compared to the possible mortal danger she and her son might face tomorrow... perhaps tonight, if Carrie was off base about Franciene not being an imminent threat. The fear she would target the two most threatening people to her was growing, and if she was as resourceful as she was starting to exhibit, Toby feared he might be unable to protect them. Poor, over-whelmed Will had fallen asleep within moments on the bed next to Toby's, and was now breathing the peaceful rhythm of the inno-cents. He tiptoed down the steps and jogged to Aaron's little house for another dose of support. He could see he had been in bed, but it was now empty. Toby followed his instincts and walked down the road to Carrie's.

There were flickering lights in the parlor windows and shadows moving about behind them. He wasn't sure what to do, but his need to know pushed him to the screen door. They were walking in a circle, Aaron and Carrie, with the aura Carrie had shown before, acting as an axis... a hub in the center. Toby was so angry at what he saw as Aaron's defection, he burst in on them, shouting disruptively. "Well, isn't this colorful! What are you doing, you two, summoning the bitch and her goblins to tell them we're ripe for the kill? Aaron, I can't believe you'd go over to her side!"

They ceased their incantation, and were standing so still, and with so much serenity, it was surreal. The bluish "thing" had faded away as soon as Toby entered, but he still felt its' chilly presence. Aaron spoke first, as Carrie stood frozen in place, her eyes closed. "Wrong! You are wrong, Toby! I came to Carrie to try and contact Franciene, to pinpoint where she is and what she is planning. It was working too, man, until you broke it off. All I could get was her fragrance again, like in the jeep. I'm sure of it! She is THAT close! Ask Carrie!"

Toby was about to do just that, when she raised her hand to silence him. "She is very near, and she is even more dangerous to her enemies than ever, my sons. Others are falling by her hand to make way for the primary targets of her fury. Massey will be spared knowledge of the trouble we soon will have for a little while, at least until he gets well enough to ask questions we can no longer fend off. I am reaching deep... to find a way to help all of us, but she is stronger than ever, and I fear she has attached the power from another, or others, to her own."

Toby perceived she was only telling this to help him understand, and that she would rather not take this precious time. He felt a wave of great tenderness and some shame for his intrusion. She finished. "No one knows why what we are turns good or bad, but I have to believe that good is inherently stronger than evil. We can do nothing more tonight, it is broken for now, but I will go to my knees by my bed, as should you, to ask for the Greatest of All Possible Help from our Dear Lord." All Toby could do was raise his palm to her in a salute of agreement.

* * *

Whatever the outcome of their reunion, Franciene was sure there would be a big time on Squires when they arrived Tuesday morning. She and Troy were barely speaking as they staggered into daybreak. He had balked at sleeping on the moldy glider cushions out on Aaron's screened porch, but Francie had all but locked him out there last night. He wasn't about to try anything... he told her just that in so many words, to an offensive degree. She did not want him either, but her female ego was waving wildly, especially since he was the first boy she had ever seriously pursued. He had added insult to injury by chiding how cool it would be to see Mandy again, with a raised eyebrow she was meant to see. Yep, he was asking for what was coming, and Franciene was counting the hours.

Jaime showed up at seven, replete with coffee and donuts, a few supplies Francie had asked for, the canoe and its gear, and a detailed waterway chart they could use on their exploration. He was visibly upended by Troy's presence, figuring him to be a rival suitor. Francie took him aside pretending to check the supplies and told him Troy was leaving later in the day... joining a friend on his sailboat, en route to Savannah. Also, Francie was so hostile to Troy, Jaime soon relaxed, and they pushed off for Squires. Francie stuck to Jaime's side like glue all the way across, chatting and teasing him to a fair-thee-well, partly for his pleasure and partly to vex Troy even more. "We'll get off on the beach, so you can just dump everything there, how's that?... and we will stow the canoe under Sandy's porch so nobody will take it... okay, Jamie-Boy?"

He didn't quite get it, that he was being dismissed by her with nothing she had promised. She could NOT be shitting on him so bad, he couldn't imagine such a dirty double cross. He was waiting to be alone with her long enough to plan their rendezvous after Troy was gone, so he cheerfully did as he was told. The two passengers and their gear were soon deposited on the deserted beach, and Jaime sped away with a wave and a silent gesture with his waggling finger to Francie, who simply waved a lazy, limp-wristed goodbye.

"Come on, Troy, help me!" She began to organize the canoe, so he ambled over to help. "Take the cooler and that bag and we'll go up and get your little Honey!" Her tone was as caustic as lye soap, but Troy ignored her and wrestled the cooler up the path. Francie knew he was too occupied with his burden, and too pissed off, to look back at her, so she had no trouble winding up and swinging the anchor at the base of his brain. He went down without a murmur, convulsed once... dead when he hit the sand.

Francie, unabashed, was quickly about digging a fairly deep grave with the canoe paddle in the soft sand behind the dune. In fifteen minutes she had rolled him, (both his pockets and his body), and his pack into the hole, covered him, and expertly placed dead grasses and a driftwood log over her work. Barely breathing hard in the fresh morning breeze, she took up the supplies and pranced off to Sandy's to wake Mandy. "Come help me, girl! I got us a cool canoe, and we are going to have a time!" Mandy, too jumpy to sleep upstairs, was sitting up on the couch, yawning and scratching. "Where did you come from? I didn't hear the jeep. Don't tell me you canoed here from your house!" She went to pee while Franciene quickly conjured a good answer.

"I was going to get out of there early, before anybody could slow me down, and ran slap into good old Jaime in the creek. He tied the canoe behind his boat and towed me around to the beach. Said somethin' about comin' back to see us later, but we won't be here, will we? Look, I got some good stuff, and the canoe's on the beach waiting for us. Let's get going while it's still cool outside."

There were questions, but Mandy decided to wait until they were in the canoe so she could pin Francie down. She started to shower, but Francie stopped her. "No sense gettin' all primped up, we're going to sweat and strain today... it'll be good for us, and we can come back later and clean up to go out in Beaufort tonight. This time of year the rich boys are all over the place. Here! Try this on! I wore it only an hour last night, and you would not believe how cool and comfy it is!"

Franciene held out the sun suit she had been wearing when she went to get the snacks at the marina in Frenchport last night. But Mandy bucked! "I don't want to wear your cooties! I'll wear something of my own!", the grouchy girl pouted. Franciene was insistent, and Mandy finally gave in. "Anyway," Francie chirped, "I want to wear your leopard bikini, and you didn't bring anything else this easy to paddle in." No big deal, thought Mandy, at the same time observing the play suit was mighty cute. They were dressed, (or undressed), in moments, and had the canoe splashed in jig-time. The tide was high-outgoing, so they set to paddling resolutely with the current to the mouth of the creek, and away from all that pesky surf.

Francie had folded the waterproof chart to suit her before casting off, and she set about choosing a good route. The Island was honeycombed all around its banks with winding, undisturbed little inlets and sloughs barely negotiable except at the highest water levels. They had entered a particularly sweet creek, when Mandy began her interrogation. "Where is Troy, Francie, and why did he fall out of the plan? Why haven't you even mentioned your visit home, and what happened about that safe? We were all involved, or did you forget? This is WAY too shady for my taste. What are we really doing here, with you acting like nothing matters but a stupid canoe trip, Francie?" The hysterical girl hadn't stopped screeching questions since they got up in the creek, and Francie was over it... it was time to finish what she started. She rested her paddle on her knees, quickly removing her bracelet and ring... putting them in her backpack. She needed to know they were safe before she got busy.

\* \* \*

Dan couldn't help it... he just had to go to the hospital to sit up for Massey. Dammit! When it came down to the bottom line, the two of them were like brothers, and Massey was alone in there. Dan was sure if things were reversed, his old friend would be warming a bench for him. Jaime was already gone, volunteering to do the ferry runs so his Dad could be freed up if Massey had a bad turn. He wondered if anybody was coming from Squires early, but avoided calling for fear he would wake that worn out bunch over there. If they were coming back early, Jaime could bring them on his first return, about nine o'clock.

# CHAPTER THIRTY-FIVE

Dan went straight to the nurses' station to ask about Massey's condition, got the babble he expected, and sat down with coffee and their "Daily Mullet Wrapper", of a local newspaper. His eyes widened as he read that the Hartsell boy's car had been found in a South Florida canal, and that the father was involved in the search. Good God! Massey could not see this! If they were searching for Clifford Hartsell, they might find Franciene with him, in Lord knows what condition! He went to the nurse to warn her that Massey must not see a newspaper, was assured he would not, and took off for the marina. Ruby had just set out the muffins, and poured his coffee as he lumbered up to the bar.

"Ruby, I need to call my boy on your radio! Have you been monitoring at all? Is he bringin' anybody back from the Island that you know of?" She stirred the sugar into his cup as she shook her head. "No, darlin', I haven't heard, go on back and see yourself. What's got you so frazzled this early of a mornin'? Don't tell me it's bad news about Massey! Everybody was so happy last night about his good chances. It ain't about Massey is it?" She really loved her old friend, Dan knew how much, and he was quick to update her, since he had just checked on him, and then told her the news about the Hartsell boy.

"Do they think he's dead?" Here we go again, thought Dan wearily, this woman will cause me to order a beer far too early if she keeps it up. "All I know is what's in the paper, Ruby. Strahan's down there, probably runnin' the show like he's a'mind to do 'bout everything. I'm gonna' call out to Palmland and ask Jesse what they know this mornin'... maybe they've found them by now." Ruby really puffed up then. "What you mean, 'THEM? Dan Fuller, don't you go tellin' me you think Franciene Thornedike is with Clifford down there in the swamp! Lord God, if Massey was to hear that he'd light out of that bed with all the tubes and wires stringin' along behind, just like he did before! Do you think he'll get wind of it, Dan? He simply can't!"

One more explanation done, and he went back to the radio to call Jaime, got no reply, and banged the mike back onto the hook, swearing. "I have told that scamp to keep his ears on so many times I hear it in my sleep!" He went to call Palmland then, leaving Ruby nibbling one of her muffins and shaking her tawny head in dismay. Who said it was boring here?

Dan rang Palmland's main number, hoping Jesse would answer. If Andrea should pick up, he would simply hang up to avoid upsetting questions. Jesse did answer, sounding as though it were his own kin in trouble. "Oh, hello dere, Cap'n... yes I know 'bout de papah tuhday... ain' it so sad ta fin' out sum'pin' lak dat from a piece o' fish wrappin'? No Suh! Dere ain' no news yet dis mawnin' fum down dere, an' Miz Andree an' Miss Sonya, dey tuk de dawg an' gon' to de mountain house soon's dey heah de bad news. I sorry I ain' no betta' hep, Cap'n, you call back latah, 'n' I'll tell you whut come new. Bye, now." And he hung up. Dan had been brushed off as only Jesse could do it, without a mark on him.

* * *

The mountain house was tucked away on forty acres of virgin land bordering on Sumter National Forest, bisected by a crystal stream that performed wondrous cascading feats over rock faces and down steep slopes. It was a summer place of the first order, and host to many family gatherings over the last hundred years. Strahan and Andrea were the first of the line to change the original state of the house, with modern kitchen and bath additions, including a custom jacuzzi on the upper balcony, cleverly supported by a slab of limestone left as a natural bridge, from the deck to a trail that rose to the top of the mountain. If any place could embrace and comfort a weary and demoralized body, it was the Hartsell's prized Laureland Mountain Retreat.

\* \* \*

The two distraught women helped each other get settled, after which each went into her own personal misery. Sonja took the dog for two hour walks, leaving her mother on the porch in the big swing bed, staring out over the blue-gray peaks, not seeing a thing. Once, when Sonja tried to call her daddy, she was overheard by Andrea and stopped, giving her the short, toneless excuse, "Cliffie will call when he gets home, darling, put down the phone... I want to keep the line free."

The young girl had no one but her burly Clumber Spaniel, Cudgel, to give her solace, so she was never without him beside her. When the phone did ring, and it was Jesse asking if they were safely settled in, he was sternly reminded that no one should call the mountain house but young Mister Clifford..."When he gets home." Andrea would endure the respite of the damned, with her decanter of Green Chartreuse standing sentinel.

The Island wakes up.

The time was seven-thirty, and Toby had been awake since before sunrise. His thoughts and fears were all about the three people in the house with him. It was Tuesday, now a week since he and Will had been in this stranger than fiction world, and he believed it could be the day of all their fears come to be. Somehow the people he loved were going to be dispatched from the Island this morning, as soon as he could arrange it. He heard a motor sound from the barn and went to see. Aaron was there, preparing to use the pickup to pull poor Copper's carcass to a large, grand piano-size grave, about fifty feet into the back paddock. It was quite a feat, and he had obviously been at work on it since before dawn. Toby ran the last few steps to help.

"I wanted to get this done before the women might find him. I'm sure Massey would want him buried on the property. His horse was his best friend, even better than Captain Dan, and he saved his Daddy's life by giving his own. I made a sling from an old jib sheet I found in a boat box in the shed, so he should come right along behind the truck. The sail will make a good shroud, don't you think?" Toby was tearing up, it was such a sweet gesture... his next emotion was shame and self-loathing for doubting Aaron last night.

Toby signaled him to start pulling, motioning as close to the hole as the truck could get, then unhooked the rope and directed him to pull up behind the horse to gently nudge him over the side and into his final place of rest. It was done in minutes, and they both shoveled and shoved the dirt until it was mounded neatly into a dome. They stood back, swabbing their faces on their sleeves, when Aaron spoke.

"He was truly a prince among horses, that one. It was an honor to have looked after him through the years. You know, when he was a young and snappy stud he used to walk around the fence line with his best friend, Belinda the nanny goat ahead of him, and he would actually hold her tail in his mouth, just walkin' along like that! We used to just laugh and laugh, me an' Benjie, to see such a fool horse! Used to run this back paddock so fast and so tight, he'd fall right on his ass from his feet goin' too fast for his body." The vivid pictures Aaron could see in his head caused him to slap his knees in boisterous laughter.

He stopped then, a sob choking off the words of the next tale, and hung his head. "I'm gonna plant this mound all over with oats so he can have all he wants forever." The tears came then. Toby put his arms around his quaking shoulders and they hugged and mourned the passing of a hero. "I'm sorry about last night, I really am," Aaron's friend told him when they gathered themselves. They then went to the walkout where Topsy was pacing back and to, looking for her old friend. The dainty Rocky Mountain Pony laid her ears back viciously, warning before she lunged at Toby's hand on the fence. He pulled back just in time, and Aaron yelled and swatted at her in rebuke.

"Damn! She ain't NEVER acted mean like that! Silly and sassy, yeah, but never set out to bite before! What's up with you, little gal?"

Topsy only reared, swung away to the back of the pasture and stood pawing and bobbing her fine little head. "Toby, I think we might have found what's been giving off the essence of Franciene. I need to ask Carrie, but it could be she's taken up inside that pony of hers. It would explain a lot."

Please Jesus! Toby began to scream inside with frustration and too much hocus-pocus to process. He couldn't stay sane if this didn't let up! He stared first at Aaron, at the fractious pony, then back at Aaron's eyes full of truth and sincerity. "Now suppose you tell me what I'm to answer THAT with! How can I get in the same tub with all this shit afloat, and expect to come out clean?" Aaron was so sure of it he was already taking the latch off of the gate to get closer to Topsy. Toby tried to stop him.

"Wait a minute! Why go in there if that's what you believe? Come back here... she'll trample you if she can!" Toby wasn't able to control what came from his mouth... the warning came by way of some deep instinct. The young man slowed, but kept going toward the back fence, where the palomino doll baby stood waiting. If Aaron believed his flash theory, he didn't show any fear as he walked deliberately toward Topsy with his hand out as if there was a palm full of sweet feed for her. She studied him, her ears pricked... the tips almost touching, with intense regard.

Watching, Toby was rooted with shock and fear of doing the wrong thing. He had to trust Aaron with this, and in a crazy way he needed to trust Franciene, if she was in fact hosted in the pony's flesh. She pawed the ground furiously and Toby almost called out again, but Aaron waved behind his back for him to be still. He was within six feet of her nose, still holding his hand out to her, when she reared up on her haunches, screaming like she was stabbed with a hot poker. Her front hooves came down less than six inches from Aaron's head.

He jumped clear and ran to the gate with the enraged horse behind him, snaking her neck, trying to grab his butt with her bared teeth. No time to open the gate, Toby grabbed his upper body as he dove for the top fence rail and they both rolled on the ground, shaken, but safe. Topsy was no match for the tall fence, designed to contain big old Copper, so she galloped back and forth in frustration, whinnying and blowing her nose at them.

"See? See, Toby?" Aaron was brushing his khakis off and talking so fast Toby had to listen closely to separate the words. "I KNEW she's in that pony! They were so close, and she'd had her since she was four years old and the horse was a yearling. I swear, she never acted fool like that in her whole fourteen years!" I got to go tell Aunt Carrie what happened!"

Maybe it was okay to tell Carrie... maybe not. He was gone like a bullet, so the point was moot. Not knowing what else to do, he stood at the fence staring at the lovely critter, who might be their worst nightmare, and again, found himself in disbelief. Maybe Carrie was the only person who could tell them what might be coming next. She and Aaron were hustling toward him, lines of concern deepening into Carries already weathered face with each step. Toby waited without a word for them, taking Carrie's arm as she stopped beside him. She stared into the velvety brown orbs that were Topsy's eyes, her own narrowing in scrutiny. The horse's countenance softened at once, her ears relaxed to their normal forward pitch, and she even nickered affectionately at Carrie, nuzzling and tasting her fingers. Carrie patted and rubbed the pony's cheek, and turned to the two men, whispering, "I swear I can't say yet. This pony has always loved me, since I'm the one who gives her all those delicious fruit and vegetable trimmin's from the kitchen. Maybe if I could stay here alone a little while, I could get deeper with her. You all go on inside... I'll be along presently."

They had to obey, and Toby wasn't worried for her, since Francie would have no vengeance toward her Aunt Carrie. They went inside to finally have a first cup of coffee. Linda and Mattie were there, showered and dressed for the day, whatever it would bring. Toby hugged them both, coffeed up, and went out to see about Will. He was sitting on the side of the day bed, rubbing his face with his hands and looking weary. "Here, buddy, you look like this would do you fine right now," Toby handed the cup to him, got another for himself, and sat down. Will looked at Toby with such dismay, it was similar to the trance-like scenario in the study, until he spoke.

"Toby? Toby, I think I had a visit from her while I slept. She swam at me from a dark, swirling place as if she had just landed from another galaxy, soft of... I don't really know how to tell you so you can see it too, you know, like when a dream can't be described? Anyway, God! Let me say this right... she wasn't dead, not then, and so gorgeous she could have stopped hearts anywhere. She seemed to be lifted out of the water, which was more like ink... all bluish purple and kind of thick, like syrup... or oil. I was glad, Toby, glad to see her, I don't know why. Then she glided over to me, like she was on wheels almost, with her hair all streaming out, and she had on that pink sunsuit we found her body in, only it was made of printed material. It was bright pink leopard-like, instead of plain. She was smiling and waving to me, so I went toward her, but when I got close and took her hand, HER ARM CAME OFF! IT CAME LOOSE FROM HER SHOULDER!" He shuddered with the memory of the horror, swallowed hard, and went on.

"I can still feel the weight of it as it fell down, with me still holding her warm little fingers. Then her fingers turned ice cold, and the skin on the arm changed from the golden tan of before, to sick, putrid green, and I could, and still can, smell the rottenness coming from it. She got really mad then, and shrieked... it sounded like an animal's scream...full of torment... full of rage. She came toward me again, this time menacing me, spitting words of hate and revenge. She said something over and over... but it is still hard to recall. It was something like...'Time is mine to set...'" His eyes squinted with his struggle to remember. "...and death makes one forget." I think that was it."

He turned to Toby from the rail, so like the boy when they first met and he begged to follow along, the older man felt weak in his knees. Toby took his shoulders to steady him, and asked, "What else was there, Will? Don't you see? She WAS with you in your sleep, and you have been warned. The "Time" thing, was about the strange fluctuations attached to the way the week's cluttered string of events came to be... there was a thought that it was Carrie's doing." Toby could see Will brightening as he took his words in.

"Franciene used time to confuse everyone so they couldn't pin her down to a place, and blame things on her. This is all making sense!

You heard a scream alright, but it was the pony, with Franciene's energy inside her. We were out at the barn when it happened about three quarters of an hour ago! I think she's targeting you, and using everyone else to throw up a smoke screen. Carrie is out there with the pony now, checking whether there is a sign of Francie's presence. I'm going to go get Aaron, and I want you to go out there with us right now. Are you up for it?" He was.

Linda wanted to come too, but Mattie suggested she stay inside while she called about Massey. She even offered the possibility that Massey could speak with Linda for a moment, something she wanted very much. It wouldn't do for her to see the weird behavior Topsy was exhibiting, and what could happen as Will appeared. When the three men got to the paddock, Carrie wasn't there. Looking around, they saw her walking back from the mound that was Copper's grave. Her face was sad.

"She told me you buried Copper over there behind the barn. When did he pass? Why didn't anybody tell me? Franciene herself told me about it. And, she said she knows something is wrong with her daddy... demanded to know what. I don't know what to do... if she goes to Massey's side full of demons, well, it could kill him. She can find the way herself, using her power. She has a compulsion to be first with him... now more than ever." She looked drawn and years older than when she went outside, and waved away attempts to support her.

"When Linda came looking for her boy years ago, Franciene was so little all she saw was somebody soft and sweet... like the mama she had never known. It was clear later, that with Linda, there came a threat to the child's place in her daddy's house like she could never tolerate. We know how much trouble she's in now that there's 'Tilde, and Clifford Hartsell, and another I'm gettin' more word of every minute. No, Massey needs to be spared this reality. Let's leave that poor pony be for a while... it just ain't fair!" The seductive smell of bacon frying lifted them into the kitchen, and even though there was anxiety in the air, they pitched in to make breakfast before deciding what to do. Aaron explained to the women what happened to the old stallion, and tearful tributes were passed around the table from each who had been touched by him.

Mattie was pleased to report that Massey was being difficult with his care givers this morning... a good sign of great improvement. He had demanded to be allowed to call his home, but Mattie didn't want to speak to him, for fear of increasing his anxiety. It was a quandary to know which was worse... being kept in the dark about his family, or knowing all about the past week's turmoil. He was asking after each of them in turn... his daughter, his son, Linda, Aunt Carrie, and for sure, how the funeral went without him to help. His brain function was normal, that was obvious... and a blessing.

Toby asked Linda to walk outside with him, desperate to see her alone again. She was, once again, guarded and silent, and when he tried to hold her, she stiffened in his arms. "What is it, honey?" He let her go and she turned away with her head down. "Toby, I can't keep up with my confusion... my flipping thoughts. I need to spend more time alone with Will, not you. It's selfishly immature of me, and it must be bothering him, that we seem so intimate. I don't want him to know about us until we can all feel safe, and his father is able to speak to him again, as a man who will be in his life."

Toby had feared this the most. She was tipsy last night, and her dormant passion, now awakened, was giving her the guilts. He made no move to touch her, it was no longer right. This was an elevator he wanted to exit for now. He looked at her for a full minute, before winking... nodding that he got it, while turning back to the house. "I'm sorry, Toby, please understand!" She said in a half whisper Toby would have heard from Frenchport.

\* \* \*

An hour had flown since Dan called Jesse, and he was still sitting at Ruby's, not knowing what to do next. When he called Massey's house, Mattie had said Massey was awake and raring to go! He was afraid if he went back to the hospital, he would somehow have to face his friend with no way to avoid the facts surrounding the past week. He decided to walk down the dock to look around for sight of his boat, when he saw it idling up to the fuel dock. He jogged down the ramp, waving his arms and calling Jaime's name. "Where the fuck have you been, boy, and where are your passengers? I thought you would be picking up from the landing on Squires! Is your head COMPLETELY up your ass?"

Jaime had begun to fuel the boat with a sheepish grin on his face. He waved his hand in front of his dad's face, repeating, "Cool it, Pop! Cool down a minute! I came back for fuel and to find a mate for the trip. You don't want me to break the law, do you? Besides, if I scoot, I'll be there close to time. It's only eight-thirty, and I've got the wind and the tide with me. Why don't you go call Jasper at the store and tell him to keep a lookout for people coming for the boat, an' tell them to wait, then you and me can high-tail it!"

"God, spare me from a smart-ass kid!" Dan thought to himself, admitting the boy was dead-on right. He trundled back up the dock, puffing from his bulk on the hoof, and dialed the Island store. Jasper worked half days, until noon, and the postmaster came in when the mail arrived, to finish the schedule. It worked well, since Jasper enjoyed the work and the extra money the Island Association paid him. He told Dan he had seen no travelers yet, but would inform whoever appeared. "I might call over to de Thornedike's, an' see is any of them studyin' a ride 'cross, so dey ain' gonna miss you all." They were about to cast off when Cissy ran down to them, asking to ride.

Jaime and Cissy had not been speaking since the night Jaime kicked Will off the dock, and the poor contrite girl had spent several nights wrapped in deliciously devastating melancholy. That morning, she had waked up with firm resolve to make up with her guy, no matter what she had to endure. Jaime waited stoically for her to step aboard, before he asked sarcastically, "You got a date over there or somethin', Little Miss Round Heels?" Cissy winced and ducked as if she expected to be popped in the chops. "No, and you don't have to be so mean! Captain Dan, tell him to apologize. If I talked that way to him every time HE made a mistake, why, I'd never shut up. I just want to talk to you, is all. Where're ya'll goin, anyway?"

Jaime sneered and spat out another jab before his dad could shush him. "As if you didn't know! This boat always runs to Squires this time of mornin', girl, and you know it! No big deal, though... if you want to ride, you can ride... just you go sit aft and be quiet, okay?" He waved her away without letting on that he had noticed she was wearing his favorite outfit, namely cutoffs as ragged as they could get, and a rib knit crop top stretching reluctantly over her bra-less breasts. He would turn purple before he would let her see him lusting after her.

Besides, didn't he have the most amazing babe in the state in his debt? And wasn't he due to collect from her, and her bodacious friend, as soon as he could get back over to the Island alone? Who needed Cissy the redneck, when he could be the salami for THAT sandwich? He was getting so aroused between his fantasy, and Cissy's, by now, wind-hardened nipples under that tight top, he suc-cumbed to playing pocket pool when no one was looking. HE WAS HORNY! This wouldn't do, or he'd end up giving in to the bird in the hand he could have in the vee berth right now, while his daddy took the helm. NO! He was determined to give Cissy her comeup-pance, and save himself for better stuff, so he conjured up the time he got that shark hook buried in his calf, and his arousal returned to the at-ease position within seconds. The day it happened, he was sure he'd never get it up again, and the memory worked every time he called on it.

Dan had to choke his laughter watching Jaime with Cissy. He loved this part of having a hot shot son... so like his own coming of age, it was the purest macho entertainment. He shuddered at the thought, if Cissy was his daughter. As amused as he was in the pres-ent, his mind slipped back to Massey and the others. All those wild young days, the snipe hunt they put Strahan through one freezing January night in the swampy up-country bog at the base of the foot-hills. God! They scared the Bejesus out of him! Such awful bullying and ridicule directed at Strahan, Dan had come to realize long ago, was borne from resentment for his place in society, and the status they all knew they would never reach, as the good old boy jocks with looks and luck, but not a drop of blue blood.

Now, after all these years, and with his old boyhood feelings for her rekindled, Dan was anguishing about the terrible torture Andrea Hartsell must be enduring, it was difficult to imagine how self-centered and dismissive her husband was being, when she really needed him. Captain Dan wasn't much of a man to lapse into prayer, but sometimes... his head bowed, he closed his eyes, and placed his order for Clifford's safe return to his mama, while hope failed him. The ferry docked on Squires only twelve minutes behind schedule, with no one to meet it. Dan sent Jaime and his pouty girlfriend up to the store to check on riders, lit a cigar butt and waited. He thought he saw a canoe about a quarter-mile up the river, but it vaporized in the steamy haze between the grass and the horizon. "Hmmmm," he mused aloud, "Wonder who THAT might be?" On Squires Island, you always, "Wonder who THAT is?" It is part of the fun, living so quietly away from others.

# CHAPTER THIRTY-SIX

*Here they ARE!*

The girls had paddled well up into the small creek, with Mandy still pressuring a fuming Franciene for details of their time apart. Francie could feel her head whirling faster and crazier, allowing less and less room for reason. Mandy could not be spared, even if she wasn't being a total bitch! She thought of telling all before she did it, and derived some pleasure silently constructing her speech. Mandy only grew more furious with the girl's rejection and non-response to her badgering.

"Listen, Francie, I haven't had much fun since we met up in my parents' house, and I think it's time to split. You can have your Island and all its mystery... to my mind it's just rednecksville, and you're perfect for it! Now, let's get this thing pointed toward civilization, you tell me where my car is, and I'll see YOU sometime, NEVER!" She was right about that.

## FRENCHPORT HOSPITAL'S PRIME PATIENT

At least he was alive. Massey thanked God for that. Not much of yesterday was clear yet, but since he woke up an hour ago, he had managed to answer the staff's test questions as well as his own internal ones with certainty. They had calmed him after the first few minutes, when he demanded to know about his daughter. Now, since he realized he was recovering from near-death trauma and surgery, and that his stupidity had caused it all, he was mellowing somewhat. No, he was going to be a model patient this time, and give them the chance to minister to him, that Mister Thornedike was not master of his own destiny... not this time. From his bed, he begged of everyone who came in to his cubicle for his friend, Captain Dan Fuller, to come and see him for only a minute, so he could ask about Franciene. Dan promised him he would track her, and Massey believed him.

That second promise, the night he went home, was written in stone. The girl wouldn't have run off like that if she hadn't been coaxed away with the promises of some lying bastard, and he knew somebody had to see her with "him", before they disappeared on Saturday. He had been awake long enough to have some chicken broth and Jell-O, then the sedative in his I.V. cocktail took him out again, to the staff's great relief. What was waiting for him was enough to thrash the strongest heart. When he slipped between half and full sleep, the Hag, Franciene's disembodied spirit-lackey, presented herself at his bedside, at once poking and picking at him, disturbing his rest enough to keep him from drifting off.

Massey tried mental tricks to dismiss it, but Hags are persistent as well as mischievous. It did not speak, but left strong assurance that he had been visited by Franciene's alter-ego. The proof was on the hand that tickled him maniacally under his chin, just like his little girl used to do. It was wearing his dead wife's signet ring! The damned apparition wanted Massey to know who it was! What he figured from the visit, was that Francie wanted to reach her daddy to ask for his help. He was amazed that he had no fear of such an eerie thing, but if it was his baby, how could he shrink from it?

Instinctively, he wanted to call the nurse, but did not, when he admitted to himself she would put a medical label on what he would relate, and chart medication side-effects, giving him added sedation. He wanted... he needed to be sharp now, if he was to help her. All at once he had an idea. Carrie would help him! She and Aunt

'Tilde were always there when he needed them, and now there was only Carrie. He rang for the nurse and put on his most persuasive face as she entered his area.

"Mr. Thornedike, we are noticing some agitation from your monitor. It is most unwise for you to lie here conjuring up stress, and you know full well that is what you are doing!" This nurse was almost angry, Massey noted as he shrunk down under the sheets. His face wore a look not unlike a basset hound with the family dinner meat in his teeth. "You are so dead on right, ma'am, it scares me how good you are at what you do. I was lyin' here with the willies, thinkin' about my daughter who's missin' since last Saturday. I need to talk to a friend before I can settle down again... I promise I'll go straight to sleep soon as I speak to her for just a few minutes. You can talk to Mattie Bell first, 'cause she's with her right now at my house on Squires. Please, I just GOT to talk to her!"

He was so into his plea, tears welled in his eyes, a touch not missed by the yielding nurse. She smoothed his hair, crooning she would see to his request in a jiffy, and tiptoed out of the cubicle. "Well, I guess I ain't lost it yet!"... Massey gloated, tapping his fingers on the mattress. The nurse made a couple of calls, the second to Mattie Bell. "Will you please prepare the woman he wants to speak with, warning her to keep away from anything that might rile him up?" Mattie could do better than that. She agreed, put down the phone and went for Carrie.

\* \* \*

Toby was settled on the porch to lick his wounds after Linda, when he saw Mattie, looking around as if searching for someone. "What's up?" He went to her side as Aaron made them a trio. She was clearly struggling for words, mumbling, "Massey is begging to speak with Carrie, and the nurse is worried she might upset him." Mattie's expression told Toby she had reservations, and he suddenly got a good idea. "Mattie, how good are you with the Gullah dialect? Say we put something together, the nurse tells Massey he only has a minute, then sounding like Carrie, you rattle off what we decide will satisfy him. I don't think any of us WANTS those two to talk right now, not with the girl dropping bits of herself all around us here. Damn! I wish this was over!"

They liked it... even Aaron was for the charade, though it meant enduring Mattie's parroting his island's patois. They went back and forth for a spell, and Mattie went to the phone to connect with Massey. She was unsure of the farce, fearing discovery. After all, the man knew... had spoken closely with Mattie just last week, but he might have been too dazed to pick up on her voice this time. Will had gone to lie down in Franciene's room... said something about feeling weird. Toby went to check on him while Mattie was phoning, and found him up, wandering around touching things and looking at the girl-stuff as if trying to know something of his half-sister.

"Hey Toby, I'm okay. I thought if I hang out in here maybe she'll throw me another sign... I don't know, maybe it's all a bunch of hooey. Maybe what happened while I was asleep on the porch was only a nightmare" He sat on the bed, seeming to shrink down in the collar of his shirt as he talked on about fearing the day for all of them. "When we found her last Wednesday I knew she was part of me, you know? It isn't my fault, and it isn't hers, that our lives are so tangled up in the pasts of our parents." He took the bracelet from his pocket... the one meant for his mother and while he stared at it his broad and bony shoulders began to shake as he sobbed for the first time, in release.

Toby knelt at his knees and tried to comfort his young friend. "Yeah, Son, it's a tangle all right, but I have a feeling everybody's coming out of this, maybe today or tomorrow, free of the pain. I am still planning for us to go to Padgetts Island and the beach... soon as this is settled. How do you feel about that?" He had calmed a little, and nodded his approval. "I want to be sure my family is going to be good though, Toby, before we take off. If my dad can come on home, I'd like to wait for that. Do you think Mom wants to stay with him? Has she told you what she wants?"

Toby was stalled by that question. "No, but she's sure to tell you when she knows herself. She is completed with you back in her life... it shines on her. What about this Mattie thing with you?" Toby was desperate to get off of the subject that was an open sore to him, but Will shrugged and chuckled, doing the same dance. "Man, she's too rich for my blood... I mean, she's learned her stuff awhile back, and I'm still waiting for mine to march at me. We'll be friends, but I'm going to need some time away to process what has happened here. Are you scared, Toby? You know... afraid we'll get hurt or even die from what's getting close?"

Toby knew Will and the rest of them had the same fear, that power they could not fathom was pushing toward them with the intention of punishment, or worse... perhaps to wipe them away like chalk dust on a blackboard. There was no use dabbling in conjecture, so he patted him and made a lame joke. "One thing for sure, it'll be one hell of an adventure!" That caused a chuckle between them....comic relief is priceless. "You think we could make mention of it in the new guidebook? This place would be crawling with snoops and psychics in days, what you say?" They were leaving the room as Will looked steely-eyed at Toby, and whispered,

"Toby, it's about to hit. She whispered while I was holding the bracelet just now, and she said, 'You are not my brother... you are dead just like 'Tilde. She is waiting for you now, over there. Give the bracelet to your mother so she can wear it in her grave." He shivered and wrapped his long arms around himself in defense "I didn't process it until we got outside her room, like she got to decide when it sunk in. I want my mom to go away from here, Toby!" He raced down the stairs with his friend on his rear. In the kitchen, Mattie was prattling in Gullah to who had to be Massey. "Lawd chile, we been mos' timorous ova' heah! You near 'bout scared us to death! How' you doin', honey?" She was nodding and smiling at his words, answering when he stopped.

"Das mighty fine an' all, baby, but you ain' well yet! Yo' boy heah is hungry to see you agin, lak we all is, but I jes' got a minute to tell you dey done found out 'bout Francie. She' been down tuh dat Silba Springs place in Fla'dah, wif a gaggle o' chillun from school. I ain' spoke wid her myse'f, but Jesse tol' me dey jes' fine. I know, I know, she ought not tuh've lef' widout you knowin', but dey's fool chillun', and you knows 'bout dat, now don't 'cha?" Another pause, then she rushed goodbye, with a promise to see him later in the day. Aaron went to her with his arms outstretched. "Mattie girl, that was near to perfect! I thought my Auntie was right there with the phone in her hand! How do you think it went? I mean, did Massey sound at all suspicious?" Mattie said nothing for a moment, and smiled as she said, "He was so glad to hear ANYTHING from home, he was accepting without questions or hesitation. I hated to lie, but it will all be for good soon. Now we've got to get ready for the rest of it."

She took hugs and praise from all, then went to find Carrie. Toby would not have wanted to go on that errand with her for anything. She was going to tell her what she had done, in case she already knew and would feel deceived. It was already eleven o'clock... getting later, and scarier. When Mattie found Carrie she was in Clothilde's cottage, clearing out her closet. She didn't turn when Mattie entered the room, but spoke into the dark chiffonier. "I appreciate you comin', Mattie, but the time to come was before you mocked me so rude, and lied to my Massey on the phone.

She turned to face Mattie, and her expression was so harsh it was too much to look at. Mattie knew any explanation would be futile, so she helplessly put out her arms and whispered, "I'm sorry, Carrie, I'm sorry if I angered you. We did it to settle Massey and keep him in recovery." The clouded woman walked into Mattie's arms and let out a big sigh. "Honey, please forgive me...I'm so tired it is getting to my core, this devouring storm. The girl is here now, near to appearing to us. I have no knowledge of her intentions, partly because she has changed spiritual form so many times this past week and is near impossible to read. Aaron and the rest think I have joined her, but she wants nothing to do with such... in fact whoever she is has now moved back or beyond all she was before. What is to become of my poor Massey when he knows he has lost his baby?"

There was no answer, not from either of their sources. The sound from inside the half vacant wardrobe caused them to turn toward it. A bright light mass was forming into a shape... a human-like wraith, undulating and pulsing so intensely that it wouldn't give up enough hard edge so they could name it. Carrie, unafraid, stepped forward, reaching to welcome it while making soft crooning sounds.

"OOOOOOWWEEEE…MMMUUAAAHHH…
SSSHEMMBBAAAHH…SSSSEEEE-LLAAAA…" The specter
settled down as if listening and absorbing Carrie's incantations.
It developed into a more visible form… IT WAS CLOTHILDE
BRASWELL! The two old friends, one alive and one dead, embraced
and circled the room wrapped in each other's arms. "You are here to
help us, aren't you, Sister?" Mattie heard Carrie say the first words
as she backed away from their place in the room. She was accepting of the visitation, even glad for it, if it was to bring answers. She
held her breath waiting for the spirit to reply. In a voice not unlike a
scratchy, 1930's phonograph record being played with a dull needle,
she spoke. Mattie strained to hear her words.

"I could not help myself. I could not save my life. The young
one will remove whatever stands in her way, be it you, or you, the
mothers, and the sons of the mothers, or time itself. I fear she took up
some of my power when I died, before Aaron was clean enough from
drugs to receive it. There has been, and there is still going to be,
revenge taken for what the girl believes is the ruination of her place
here. She comes within these hours before midnight, and she will
find whoever she wants to find. I have seen Benjamin, Sister Carrie,
and he is at peace, but he wants to tell you and my Aaron to stand
as one in the danger. I will tell him you are doing this, and that you
send love. Get word to Palmland that God loves them. Massey will
be home for Father's Day. He has been sending to me all the time.
He is my other son… tell him that for me. I need to be gone. The
cooler will be opened very soon, the pony will run, and all will be
known. Oh! Here I go!"

The light was swept backward with a great Whoosh! and the
door of the armoire slammed shut. They had wanted to ask her so
many questions… needed clarification for her riddles, but they had
to be satisfied with what was given. Holding hands, they ran to the
big house to tell the others. Carrie was fretting. "She should'a waited
for Aaron! He would'a wanted to be there!" Mattie was full of questions but wanted to wait for the others. There had been so much
separate agenda, it would be best to stay close for the rest of it.

Topsy was still trotting and wheeling around in her paddock, snorting and squealing as if trying to speak. Carrie stopped in a line with the pony's stare and spoke to her. "You can come home, baby, we can help you if you embrace the love that's still deep inside of you." All her words did was infuriate the animal into an air pawing display. Carrie took Mattie's elbow and rushed her into the house where everyone had gathered around the kitchen table... all except Linda, who was taking a walk. Mattie and Carrie talked about the visitation with 'Tilde, Will related his Franciene events, and they shared their pony woes, before brainstorming to form a defense. It was a half hour past noon.

\* \* \*

After the call from Carrie, Massey relaxed and let his mind run back over the last tumultuous week... what he could recall of it. Franciene running off, his complete confusion when he discovered Aunt 'Tilde not on the boat with his girl, then Carrie finding her dead in her kitchen, and... WAIT! Franciene was coming home last Wednesday! He came for her at the landing, and she wasn't on the boat! She had called Tuesday night and said she was sorry for running off and would be home on the three o'clock ferry the next day! How could he be so confused? Calm down and go back, Massey... graduation weekend, Francie slipping away on her pony to catch the boat... LINDA SUE! She came back! He saw her, or thought he did, on the beach. The boy too... all grown, tall and wonderful! If he put it together, it seemed his life was in flux. Next stop... Metamorphosis!

He recalled seeing his daddy and his wife at the end of that tube leading to the bright light. His fear of the hereafter was now gone. It IS true what they say... once you have cheated death, everything gets clearer and more precious when life resumes. Massey vowed to let the tide take him from that moment, and his decision made him upgrade in seconds, from guarded to satisfactory. The monitor in the nurses' area gave proof, and it was unanimously touted miraculous.

# LAURELAND COTTAGE

It was obvious to Andrea, she was escaping reality... no one could judge her crazy or even hysterical after twenty-four hours in the mountains. She and Sonja were making the most of the coolness of the altitude and the rich, loamy fragrance in the forest on their walks with Cudgel, bounding ahead on familiar trails. Her daughter had exhausted her for hours with, "What if's," and she had patiently answered her squeaky entreaties positively, though not trusting her own words. She even considered trying to contact Strahan, desperate for a crumb of news, but her conviction to receive or place no calls unless one came from her son, ruled the day. They returned from a rock-hopping trip across the stream down to the ranger station to let them know they were in residence, to find the telephone ringing. They both rushed it, but Andrea picked it up, shouting, "Cliffie? Cliffie, is that you, darling? It's Mommie!"

It was Dan. Poor Dan, he was always out of step, somehow. "Dan Fuller, DON'T YOU CALL HERE! Don't call unless you have my son beside you! I TOLD Jesse no one was to call here except Cliff!" She would have hung up then, if Sonja hadn't taken the receiver. "Captain Fuller, this is Sonja Hartsell. Do you have any news of my brother? Is that why you are calling?" She glared at her mother when she tried to take the receiver. Dan had no plan when he called, but their sweet, fearful voices wrenched his heart. He let his big mouth run right off.

"Only news I got is that I'm on my way south, and if he's within a hunnert miles of where they found the car, I'm gonna find him for you! I can't do nothin' sittin' on my butt here... not for you all, nor my buddy Massey Thornedike. I plan to find your daddy and go from there. I got a friend with an air boat that ain't tied up in lawmen's red tape, and I can get your daddy and crisscross that floatin' mess better'n' any chopper. I just wanted to let you ladies know somebody at home cares about your trouble."

Dan hung up quietly, thanked Miss Ruby, who was wiping her eyes with her apron corner. "Lord, you sure are a darlin', Dan. Where in the world is that woman who's waitin' for you?" She squeezed his arm, to hear him whisper wickedly, "You keep lookin' so purty like you are, Ruby honey, and you'll find out it's YOU! Tell Jaime he's got the schedule whether he likes it or not, and the keys are in the jeep. I'm takin' the pickup. That snazzy jeep wears my ass out on the road! Tell him I'll call him soon's I get to Golden Gate. And you tell him I'll be checkin' as to whether he minds the schedule on the other side. OH! Ruddy said he will mate for you when you need him! Now you got to keep close touch with the other side… there's folks there who'll be needin' to cross on short notice!"

Ruby nodded to each point, so proud of her friend. He started to walk away, stopped, and said, "I'm on my way to tell Massey where I'll be. He would want to know." Ruby stopped him. "No, Dan, Massey does NOT need to know. He's dealin' with stayin' alive, right now. You just go do some good and bring it back." With that he was gone.

* * *

Jasper hadn't had much business Tuesday morning… thank goodness, He and Pansy were still worn out from the funeral and Massey's strange emergency. It seemed unnatural for such hubbub to occur, piled up like it was on their quiet Island, and they were not girded for it. Families took their issues up privately until they were forced to broaden their circle for support. Jasper was the one above all who got involved if word leaked about anything unusual. This few days had been his most taxing, he and Pansy had agreed to that as they started their day this morning.

Pansy was busy with her chickens and her garden as her husband waved on his way to the store. He guessed Jaime and Cissy were the third and fourth to come in, when they asked if anyone was waiting for the ferry. They had dropped Dan in Frenchport and dutifully filled his order to go back across, following the turnaround schedule. "No, but I 'spect somebody'll be along terrec'lly. They's some folks at Thornedike's I know is wantin' to cross sometime today. Why don' you call down to de house, an' see 'bout what they want?"

Jasper was well aware of the slackness of youth, and wanted to corral Jaime for the sake of his friends who needed to cross. He would offer his bateau, of course, but the ferry was the proper way for ladies to travel. Those ladies had been discomforted quite enough, and this jack-leg boy of his, with his silly gal was going to tend to business. Jaime balked. "Nah, you can just tell them I'll be in touch if they need a ride. They can call Ruby's and leave word, okay?"

Damn sorry white boy, Jasper thought to himself, but nodded with wise eyes boring into Jaime's, making the boy look at his feet. "I'll be tellin' your daddy 'bout 'dis, Jaime, you s'posed ta' be on the run ev'ry hour, an' you knows it! If there come a troublesome t'ing, an' you off sparkin' someplace, you'll be de blame fo' hahm e're it come." With a guilty wave, Jaime and Cissy backed out and were gone. Within minutes he was up Gnat Creek, pounding away, with Cissy's feet pressed into the overhead, while he pictured taking turns at Franciene and Mandy.

It was all over in three minutes flat. Cissy had to shake her head to return to now... she reordered her clothes and raked through her hair, unsure what had just happened. Jaime was at the controls, still breathing heavily from his wretched performance. He had only gotten partially into his fantasy, and still wanted it fulfilled. He looked back at Cissy, only slightly ashamed of his deception, and held his arm out for her. Poor girl, she rushed to him with relieved tears welling in her eyes. Good old Jaime Fuller wins again. Bully for him.

\* \* \*

There was nothing else for Dan to do but go. He had stocked the truck with what he expected to use, stopped for a bucket of chicken and some beers, and filled the truck with fuel and water. Then he realized he had forgotten something important. He turned in beside a pay phone and dialed Massey's house phone. Carrie answered with, "All right?" as usual. Dan simply greeted Carrie and asked to speak to Linda Sue. She came to the phone, and after "Hello's" were exchanged, Dan told her of his plans.

"Whatever you and your boy decide about Massey, it can't matter… not where his daughter and what's happened to her is concerned. The only hint we have is that Hartsell boy's car gettin' pulled out of the canal down there in Florida. Linda, I got to honor my word to my best friend, and I care about that poor boy's mama, since way back. I'm gonna go help that shitass husband of hers look for him, and maybe somethin' 'bout Francie will come out in the bargain."

She wasn't surprised that Dan would be so decent… it was just like him. Linda told him so, and he thanked her for that. "You all take care, and I'll try and let you know what I find out, soon as it happens. Tell your boy and the others, but don't tell Massey what I'm doin'… He don't need to know how to build this damn watch, he just wants to know what time it is! I'll see you soon, darlin'." And he hung up.

Linda found them on the dock, watching the swift current filling the small creek. She was wearing a soft yellow short skirt and a white tank, and she was about as pretty a sight as Toby could stand, knowing the luscious delights she was packing. He swallowed hard and patted the deck between them for her to sit. It was almost too peaceful… like before a storm…they could feel it. It was Will who spoke first. "Isn't it time to get this lady and Mattie off the Island, Toby? I want to tell Mom, right now, what's going on. It concerns her as much as any of us, don't you think?"

Toby wasn't expecting that, but agreed. "Yep, you're thinking right on. Linda, for the last week, your boy and I have been embroiled in something deeper and more frightening than we want you to know about. The situation has brought us together, as if for a joint purpose. Honey, you have a closer history with this family than us, but now we're evened out, faced with something not of this earth, and it winds around Franciene Thornedike. Will, you should give your mom the bracelet to wear right now. I don't know why, but it could be a charm to keep her safe. When 'Tilde came to Carrie and me in her bedroom, she told us to do it… I forgot that part. I want you to give it to her now, please."

When Will handed the bracelet to a stricken Linda, Toby took it and put it on her wrist before she could examine it. He patted it into place as one would a bandage on a child's knee and said nothing. She finally looked in Toby's eyes as she took Will's hand and said, "I will go if you and Will insist, but I believe I can help with Franciene if I stay. She has affection and a need for me as Carrie said, almost like the mother she never knew. I know you men want to protect us but the women are already deeply into this... too deep to walk away now. After all the years since I put my son with his grandfather have passed without us being together, I don't intend to leave him when he most needs me. I want you both to tell me the truth, as it happens, from now on if we are going to stand together. Do I have your promise... from both of you?" "God", Toby thought, "She could sure as hell have mine, and anything else she wants." He and Will both promised, hugged as a trio, more a family, and went to the house with their arms still around each other. Mattie, Aaron, and a darkening Carrie waited with news. Aaron and Mattie were down the steps coming toward them. Aaron told them what was up.

"Jasper just let us know Jaime will be reachable if we need a trip across in a hurry. He said to call him and he'll put it together. Not five minutes later, he called back and said Ruby told him Jaime just announced he and Cissy were going to Edisto overnight, and he, Jasper, would have to do the ferrying if any was done. He was hopping mad at Jaime, and said he was going to fuel his boat and tie it up on the floating dock to save time. Well, it appears his outboard has been de-commissioned. The fuel lines are full of sugar, and it's all froze up. He is trying to borrow another boat, but nobody's around much during the day if they have a way off."

A flurry of chills flowed through the group as they assessed their options. Aaron continued with the dismal situation. "Carrie said it's Franciene who did it... but she won't say how or why she thinks so. She wants us all here to face what she has coming to us. Toby, what do we do next?" Toby had a quick thought. "What if somebody... anybody, could bring the ferry over here? Aaron, you could call over and get somebody to bring the boat. Okay, it's going to take some time, but at least we will have a boat by three o'clock if we find somebody quick. I'll Call Miss Ruby right now!" He had nothing better to suggest, so he ran inside... came back in seconds. The phone's dead, man... and the radio too!" Carrie screamed, and it was almost a howl.

# CHAPTER
# THIRTY-SEVEN

Franciene paddled the canoe back to the beach, wrestled it up to the dunes, and covered it with driftwood and palm fronds. Finally, she staggered to Sandy's, and, sweaty swimsuit and all, dove into the shower. The cool water was hot as it left her body and went down the drain, taking what remained of the deed she had just done with it. She stripped off the sodden suit and washed her sunburned little body all over with Sandy's glycerin soap, finishing with a spritz of Florida Water, a limey, moisturizing after-bath astringent Sandy kept on hand. She dug around in her bag and found a pair of cutoffs and a tube top, dressed, and fell on the day bed in the living room, at the end of her endurance.

Sleep came as if she were a tiny child with nothing clouding her conscience worse than spitting beets at her nanny during lunch. It was going on one-thirty. Franciene spent her nap astride Topsy, galloping the beach with the sparkling surf beating time. It was a celebration dream... The marooned little girl would soon be free.

\* \* \*

God, it was hot in South Florida! Dan thanked his good judgment in not driving the jeep at least a dozen times as he drove toward the west coast. His truck wasn't as sexy as the CJ-7 Golden

Eagle, with its' wings spread across the hood, and those buckskin denim, high-backed seats, but it was air-conditioned, and the road was smoother beneath it. What the hell, Dan mumbled mentally, let the kid be the sport... he'll sure as shit score better with the help of a cool ride than his old man would. After five hours of non-stop driving, Dan stopped at a seafood shack south of Winter Haven. While his fish burger was grilling, he called Ruby for any news of Jaime, or Massey and Linda.

"Boy, I don't know WHAT'S goin' on! Your boy an' Cissy took off for Edisto earlier. Y'all's boat's here, an' Aaron's called about somebody bringin' it to Squires to stand by. I tol' him to see after Jasper's little boat since there ain't a soul here freed up to go, an' he said Jasper's outboard's been sugared! Damn! No word 'bout Massey, but I guess that's good. Looks like you're gonna be gone 'til tomorrow, don't it? 'You plannin' on skinnin' that boy of yours when you get back?"

He was planning just that. Before he rang off he had an idea, which he shared with Ruby. "Call over to the sheriff's office and see if anybody over there is gettin' off early enough this afternoon, and wants to make some extra cash. I'll pay half a hundred to get that boat across the sound today. You front me the money and I'll pay you back, and buy you supper Sunday evenin', anywhere you say."

"That's a deal, Daniel! How can I call you to wrap this up?" She was all a-twitter about the prospect of a date with Dan Fuller. He said he would call her after his lunch, and considered himself quite clever as he flipped the handset bar to make another call, this time to the Griffin's house. He delivered his plan to grateful Jasper, who couldn't wait to share the news. Ruby got lucky, finding a deputy about to clock out who would be happy to spend the afternoon back and to on the water for fifty bucks. Ruby gave him the spiel about the boat, where the keys were, what to check before he took off, and congratulated herself. Too soon, however, the consenting officer walked out of headquarters and right into the path of a UPS truck. He wouldn't be boating anywhere for a good while.

Franciene fitfully thrashed around on Sandy's day bed, then settled down again. No Barney Fife-Asshole was going to get in the way after all she had done. Her successful dispatch of the deputy settled her down to a deep sleep.

\* \* \*

If Toby had any clue what was in store he could prepare for his place in this day, but he had none. Oh, there was fear that was real... it was enough to gird him for something. SOMETHING! How was that to be enough? He had not been apprised of the inner truths, because Carrie chose to keep him ignorant, and he did not know why. He felt he was being regarded as a cornered pawn. Was Aaron his salvation? Who else among their number knew where they should turn now?

There was a force that could possibly destroy them all, here in this lovely place, but where was the key to the door they could escape from? He did not believe there was anyone else who knew, except Carrie. All of the people in this circle had their own reasons for being here... Toby was isolated in his state of no worthy consequence, other than his love for the two people he had plucked out of the air. Damn! Why didn't he just fucking disappear? He waited for the answer to his private prayer... got only the mantra that said, "STAY THE COURSE!"... from his own whirling head. Maybe those he cares for would come out into the light without him, but he didn't trust that thought. Instead, he would stick... in case they might need him.

It was getting on toward three o'clock, and still no boat from Frenchport. Will, Aaron, and Toby took the jeep to the store for an update. Now all of the Island's phones were useless, the sky was darkening, and they saw some cloud-to-ground lightning in the distance toward Savannah. Maybe it explained the dead radio and phones, but the boys were not buying it! Not one of them! Jasper came out to meet them, holding his arms out in a helpless gesture.

"I got no phone, an' there's no boat come heah yet! What you reckon's goin' on wid all dis mess? You all sho' needs a way to go 'cross don' you?" He was so sweet, with genuine concern for them all, and what he must know was a crisis, they were quickly comforted. Aaron clasped the older man's shoulder to say a lot with no words, and answered his query. "We shore do need a boat, Jasper! You checked, and your phone and radio are both out? You' got a VHF, AC-DC system to beat six bits in there. Is the electricity out? Have you got good battery power?"

Jasper was nodding as he spoke, "Yeah, I got lights okay, jes' no way to talk to nobody, nowhere! What about dem new fangled radio phones? I know Miss Sandy's got one she keeps for de school chillun, an' Miss Ruby's got one plugged in on her bar all da' time! If dere's anyt'ing you can talk in, it's one o' dem!" He was proud of his idea, and relished their response. "You know," Aaron said, "Sandy Calhoun's telephone line comes across from a different place than the river side of the Island. Her house just might have contact with Frenchport! I'll take you two back to Massey's so the ladies won't be alone, and go see for myself. If I can call Miss Ruby's, she can tell me our chances of a boat. Hell, I'll row across in Jasper's bateau if I have to. It wouldn't be the first time I did it, for a lot less of a reason!"

Hey, the Islanders know how to scramble, from generations of need... it was a good plan. Besides, it wasn't smart to be scattered about, not knowing what was up. Will and Toby were dropped off and Aaron slid out of the drive, scattering shell and sand as he went. Inside, there was a mood they had not left when they drove to the dock. Toby squeezed Linda's arm, but got no response... not even a glance. Mattie stood and spoke first. "Toby, Linda's upset about the horses. She is wondering why everybody else knew, except her, about Copper, and that Topsy may be hosting a spirit... possibly Franciene's."

Toby took the bracelet off her wrist, and... Linda stood, her fists clenched with anger. "That bracelet is MINE! I know how it came to be, and even though I might not have wanted it when Massey had it engraved for me, I had a right to know what was on it, and the rest of the story before this moment. Will, I'm not angry at anything you've done, but I guess I've just been through too much because of your father and what he meant to me, I am full of rage at being kept in the dark. And you, Toby! You knew a lot of this when you came to Waycross! What am I supposed to believe anymore? I'm going to talk to Carrie right now! She'll tell me!" She flung herself out the screen door. All the rest could do was stand there and hope Carrie didn't make it worse.

In fact, Carrie was about the business of trying to make it better for everyone. She had been at her tarot cards and her meditations since the visitation from 'Tilde, and the moment she spent with Topsy. The cards told her they could be in great danger, from the hour of five o'clock in the afternoon, to five the next morning. She had ventured on, not failing to refer to the Holy Bible, where she always found help and comfort, and the assurance that if demons are allowed in, they must be overpowered by the use of the stronger, Most Holy Power of God. In this advice Carrie found peace, and saw Franciene in a new light, as a victim instead of the predator, or their enemy. Just what Francie had orchestrated for her.

Linda gingerly tapped on the screen door, called out to Carrie, and was invited in. "I had to come see you, Carrie," she said, "What's with Franciene? Do you know?" She wasn't prepared for the answer she got. Carrie stood tall and straight, and said in a whisper, "She is here, child, she has made her presence known through my meditation. She warned me she will appear almost immediately, and then we will know all. You are safe, as I know it, but you and I are not alone here. My poor girl is a wrath unto herself, and those other than us are in danger. She has told me she will spare the two of us if we leave her to the others to do as she will. She means to destroy the others because she sees them as her enemies."

Linda moved closer to Carrie, as close as she dared, because there was a forming vortex of swirling mist making up between them. She tried to call to Carrie, but the roar was huge. "I want no harm to come to my son and my companions, Franciene!" Linda yelled into the fray. She felt the need to speak to the mass she could not fix on. "We must meet and come to a peace!" Hah! There was no reply... only a force that threw the two women into a corner of the room... unharmed, but chastened. Carrie helped Linda to her feet, breathless and worried. "She will not abide any interference, not from us...not from anyone." She became limp, as if helpless to do anything.

"My girl, she is not her own person now, only what has been commanded of her by her evil will. She is LOST! Oh, Dear Jesus! The baby is LOST! Linda, we must go save the others now! They have angered her! She sees them as chattel to be thrown away!" Linda stood firm... determined to communicate with the force. "Franciene Thornedike! If you are here, give Linda a sign!" She waited... The sign came in a flash. The bracelet she wore began to glow and heat, as if a blowtorch was trained on it. Linda shrieked and slapped at the searing thing on her wrist, until it clattered to the floor. Her arm was scorched and smoking for only a moment, then the wound vanished as if nothing had happened. Carrie took the bracelet up from the corner, handed it back to Linda, warning her, "She was reminding you of why she is angry, honey, it must be her insane jealousy of your boy... her daddy's only son. The time has come to arm ourselves and be ready for the coming night. I want us to gather at the church...all of us and Pansy and Jasper too. Let's go now... it's none too soon."

\* \* \*

Aaron pulled the jeep up beside Sandy's cottage, a foreboding thick as pluff-mud making him confused and most timorous. He took the key from its place, turned it in the lock and stepped inside. What he saw on the day bed caused him to scream... a scream tormented creatures make, or those entering the deepest Hell. It was Benjie... charred and smoking as if he had just been blown apart by the ignited scrap-iron moonshine. His lidless eyes rolled to look into Aaron's as he croaked out, "See What You Done?"

# THE EVERGLADES... AND DAN'S QUEST TO HELP AN OLD LOVE

Dan found the causeway leading to his buddy's place just before the late sun bathed in green and gold. It occurred to Dan that it was the prettiest time of the day, everywhere he had seen it so far. The causeway was of crushed shell and coral, cautiously built up higher than the grass. It came to be in the fifties, back when no agency existed to refuse permission to disturb such a bold strip of nature's nursery to the sea, for anything, much less a good old boy's retreat. At the end of two miles of approach, the thicket announcing Talbot Purchase's Conch-shack appeared. Dan had planned to surprise his friend, but since they hadn't seen one another since '77, for some Key West reunion bash, he had an edge of doubt about his luck finding Tally at home, or even alive.

Funny, somebody named "Tally Purchase", being terminally short of funds, but the man only had what he needed, and only needed what he had, as long as Dan knew him. When they were shrimp boat strikers as young men, jumping on boats from the Keys to the Gulf, the two had vowed to be around for each other forever, no matter what. It didn't matter if the pact was resurrected during many a drunken night, they kept their promise soberly intact. Now, Dan would use a piece of it for Tally's expert knowledge of the area, and the use of his air boat. The hammock he claimed years ago as his own was just west of the Preserve and the Indian Reservation, with not a neighbor for miles. It was perfect for the less than perfect man.

A black and tan hound came to greet Dan from a shady spot by the ruddy old cabin. There was a screened porch wrapping all around the square structure, its' whitewashed tin roof peaking with the standard exhaust fan as the only climate control. Dan could hear music coming from inside... John Hammond's blues, if his ears were correct. "Nothing changes, not really", he muttered, chuckling as he patted the dog's tome and went up the steps to Tally's open door. "Where's that old sumbitch I used to out-fish, fight, and fuck?" An impressive, embellished rebel yell was his answer, and in a moment they were rassling all over the rough porch floor. "What the hell you doin' down here in this heat, Bo? I can see you comin' when it's cold as a well- digger's ass up there, but it figures I ought to be droppin' in on you, hot and humid as is!"

Tally was babbling, so happy simply for the human company, the fact that it was his old friend, Danny Fuller was simply awesome. Dan followed him inside, regarding their matching widened girths, and the like attire, as usual. They had iced Blue Ribbon longnecks, two each, before the bullshit subsided, and he could answer Tally's question. They went out back to old rockers facing the wild wetland in twilight, and Dan told his pal what was going on. He got a good measure back. "I know a little bit of it... they think the boy met some kind of foul play a couple of days ago or so. I ain't talked to nobody since day 'fore yesterday... been a little down in the back with all this dampness. I don't know why a broke-down old bastard like me don't move to the desert. Shore would lighten up some of this misery. What's your part in this, bud, besides bein' from the same place? You must know the family real good, or maybe it's more. C'mon now... tell it!"

Tell what? Tell the whole twisted story, from St. Marys to Palmland, from Massey and Linda to Franciene and Will? He took a thoughtful pull on the beer, sat it on the table between them and squinted off into the sky, now losing its' spectacular fire to become simply purple, mauve, and blue, before darkness and those incredibly close stars peeked out. For now, a little bit of truth would have to do. He began.

"I know ev'rybody up there, you got to understand, and we go back, off 'n' on, since the sixties. The boy's mama and I were sort'a close for awhile one summer when she was stayin' at the beach with her fancy friends, but her family wasn't havin' it, seein' I was so gnarly an' poor, what they called, uncouth! She had a sort of arranged thing, an' a few years later, married the richest boy they could find for her. I had moved on too, so it didn' tear me up, in fact I was proud for her." Tally said nothing as Dan went on. "Well, when her boy Cliff turned up missin', and the police found the car in the canal and his shoe and all, I got to feelin' so damn sorry for that poor mama, I told her I would come down here an' try to find out somethin'. If you had'a known her when I did, boy you'd do the same thing!" He stopped there. It was enough to satisfy Tally, and no more. He went for two more beers and sighed as he sat back down, rocking slower than before, took a good third of the brew down before saying it.

"Dan, you an' me never lied to one another, 'cept about things other than the three "F's", so I'll tell you this. A fancy kid like him, in this heat, even if he had'a come up alive outta' the water, would'a lasted, if the gators hadn't found him, no more'n half a' day. Jesus! There's snakes of some fearsome types crawlin' all over this swamp, and with the bitin' flies, skeeters an' gnats, no drinkin' water, and him more than likely busted up some from the mess he'd got himself in when the car went over, well, I don't have to tell you. What is it you want to do to help? We can go to wherever the daddy is, and I can call my friend, the sheriff."

Dan was nodding to all of it, but had to back up a little about Strahan. He did NOT like the man, and was sure it was mutual. "How about we start with the police? Can you get some inside stuff, like places we could go lookin'? Could we take a ride in your air boat, just to crisscross where he may have gotten to if he'd been able to move around? We aren't even sure if he was alone or not. There's something else I haven't told you. Massey's girl Franciene is gone too, and he thinks she might have been with the Hartsell boy."

"OOOOWEEEE!" Tally whooped again, this time with a wicked twist." She must be about pluckin' age by now, I figure... How old? Sixteen? Seventeen? What I remember from pictures when she was little, she should be quite a little peach blossom by now!" It made Dan shudder anew, to think of all the possibles. It was at that point he clammed up about his friend's daughter. No use dirtying the water more than it was already. They sat on the porch for another hour, when Tally suggested they go toward the reservation and patronize the barbecue and fish fry shack near the gates. Dan was skeptical until Tally showed him a sample menu, and he felt his stomach growl pleadingly. That lunch burger had been processed hours ago. They found a clean table and were waiting on drinks in the dark room when someone called out Tally's name. Talk about coincidences... it was the sheriff himself.

His name was Delmar Porter, he was raised no more than fifty miles from where he now lived, and he was well qualified for what he did, both occupationally and mentally. A portly, but fit man ten years or so Dan and Tally's senior, he made quite a statement. Those Wellington boots housing his trouser cuffs and that gung-ho Marine belt buckle said it all. Delmar was happy to join the two half-drunk sports... out here near the reservation he was regarded as a bigot, giving little or no quarter to Indian customs and foibles. The place was now mostly an outdated landmark, since so few wanted to live their lives in such a backwater place. There were still some who welcomed the steady, predictable life, and they tolerated no harassment from such as, "Sheriff So-be-it". He was called this behind his back, alluding to his, "My way or the Highway" creed.

Their meal was mammy-slappin' delicious... and consumed before they opened the subject of the missing preppie. As it happened, the sheriff was as glad to meet Dan as Dan was to meet him... always a bonus to talk to an old friend of the family involved in his cases. He listened to Dan's guarded remarks, and said slowly, "You got to know we aren't treating this like a homicide, or even a misadventure yet. The kid was last seen on Saturday, just a few days ago. He might have accidentally let his car, and a beauty it once was... a collector's dream... slide into the canal while not paying attention, chickened out of telling his dad, and simply hitched a ride out of here... I know what MY daddy would have done to my ass if it was me. He's likely to be cooling his jets until his papa cools out himself. Why do you think the other way, Dan? What's made you get on the suspicious track?"

Dan was struck dumb. He wasn't about to spill the story he would not even tell Tally, to a strange law, and sure to be a skeptic. "It's just that the boy has always been level-headed, man, I mean, almost nerdy! You know, the little boy to the manor born, with no chance to take risks or grab life like we all got to, cause nobody was watchin' us!"

Each one of them, silently grateful NOT to have been a Cliffie Hartsell, while all that mischief was waiting out there to be done. Delmar was getting it, nodding wisely, as Tally offered, "See, just the act of drivin' off without tellin' anybody was as wild a thing as he ever done, accordin' to Dan, here. No, I got to agree, it looks real bad to me too." Dan got to the point at that moment. "Sheriff, I want to do some searching for myself, if Tally here'll take me out on his air boat. That way, I can go back and be able to tell that poor mother I really tried to find him." He was leaning in to the middle of the table, nearly nose to nose.

"And what IF? What if the Lord saw fit to let me find him? Why, that would be so fine, wouldn't it? Tell me, sir, would you please, is there any word from anywhere that could help us? Have you spoken to the father, Strahan Hartsell, yet? I'd just as soon not, myself, but I will if he knows anything we can use out there." Delmar nodded gravely, adding, "He's so griefed up, he's hardly able to put one foot before the other, an' he's been like that every time I seen him. His lawyer-friend told me he's hopin' he'll give up with this actin' out, and go home to his wife and daughter. They can't, none of 'em, make a move without him tellin' them what rubes and dummies they are. His own people are full o' fear of him, like he's got somethin' on 'em up home." Dan liked this man's opinion of good old Strahan. He was not quite done.

"Here's what I say... if the boy's gon' be found, he will, when the Lord above says so, and that's it!" The two agreed, just to be polite, but the plan was in place. They would set out at first light, before Strahan could find out about them and raise hell. Much as they would have liked to keep on partying, they paid the tab and left the place before eleven o'clock. As Tally was pulling his jeep out to the highway, Dan saw a figure by the road's edge, waving his arms. He was Seminole, of advanced age, and appeared to be distressed about something.

"It's old Hillis, from the reservation. I bet he's ticked about seein' Del here tonight. Hope he didn't know we were together. They all like me and trust my judgment in things, and I bet he would disapprove of that scene in there at the table. If you don't mind, I'm gonna' stop to see what he wants." Dan was glad... he never wanted to miss the chance to interact with wonderful old people like him. Sorry, Tally wasn't having it. "You stay here, buddy, I just don't want to put him on display, you know?"

As much as he wanted to get up close to the wonderful old Indian, his experiences with the Gullah fathers in Carolina, gave him understanding about their pride and elegance, and how many years they had been objects of the rudely curious. One time, back in the sixties, he had seen Jasper hit a white woman over her head, real hard, with an ear of corn when she asked him if he was from the famous "Blue Gum Tribe"! It was quite a moment, and she went away quietly, pulling kernels out of her hair. He strained to hear from the open side of the jeep, but it made very little difference, since the man was speaking a mixture of two languages, in excited modulation.

After about ten minutes, Tally came back and they were up to seventy before he spoke. "He said he has a secret and it could get him in big trouble with Sheriff Porter, but he wouldn't tell me what it is." Dan knew his old friend, and could feel him hedging, but said nothing. Tally went on. "I fear he's startin' to slip off-center a little, but tomorrow we can stop by the reservation from the water-side, and kind of look around a little." Dan wasn't all that curious, but agreed, still intrigued by the old man himself. He was a deep soul, and it showed, even from a distance. They were bushed, and when they got to bed, lights out came within minutes. The old dog lavished a slimy slurp on the side of Dan's face as he drifted off in the hammock on the porch, but he was too tired to wipe it off.

# CHAPTER THIRTY-EIGHT

Oh, if Strahan Hartsell knew that crude redneck slob, Dan Fuller, was messing in his affairs, he would have imploded on the spot. As it was, he couldn't have been more removed from "Purchaseland", and the visiting captain. The two days Strahan had been in the search area seemed more like two weeks, when he factored in the two long, late, and very wet evenings they spent in Naples. It was a ritual, no matter where the two friends were or what the scenario, and they paid their dues, come morning, without a word, but with a bloodymary or a brew to soften the claws of the thing that had a-hold of their necks.

That first bleary morning, when he had been roused with news that there may be a trail through the grass out there, they had raced to the tented operations center only to find a dozen muddy men, asleep or passed out in the shade. Jay was at once about interrogating the ones he could wake up, and Strahan had tried, and failed, to reach the two supposedly still tracking. It was becoming an infuriating failure, they both agreed, and the reward was withdrawn on the spot, with a growled retort. "My son is out there, eaten by gators, and you as you are, aren't worth the excrement he will become. I am telling you all to pick up your skanky asses and get out of here, before I see how sharp this machete is. Now, GIT!"

They did GIT, and glad they were to go. All of them were so covered with bites and scratches, even their hangovers were of no import. It had been a nice dream, perchance to find the kid in a couple of hours and grab the man's money, but it was just too much like work after the rum and tequila ran out.

Strahan faced his barrister so defeated, Jay wanted to cry for him. "Where IS he, Jay-Jay? It's gotten so I would be relieved to find his poor little remains, just to know." Jay clasped his hands, like a minister does after Sunday services, and said, "I know, boy, I know. What do we do now?" He silently prayed to God that Strahan would elect to go home, as much for himself as his friend. Not to be... not quite yet. "No, I am not beaten, not until this day ends. Come on! Grab a pair of those waders and a pistol. I'll bring this machete, and we're going to follow as far as there's a bent reed, you hear? I can't go back to my wife and daughter with nothing at all! Tell me something... who said children bring joy to our lives? I've never BEEN so sorrowful, not ever I can recall." The two soft-sided men girded up and drove to the place where the trail had last been left cold... about five miles west of Tally's Hammock. It was Tuesday morning.

* * *

Dan woke with the sun, dragged on his shorts and walked around the funky old house. It was hardly haute decor, but he liked what Tally had done. There was just enough around to identify the occupant, but not enough to clutter it up... a wall of old black and white, and sepia snapshots, some poorly enlarged, likely by some old drug store somewhere nearby. He could barely distinguish the features on most of them but kept looking anyway. Yep! He found himself and Tally, and there was old Massey too! They were, of course, in a fish-catch shot on Brown's Dock, Bimini, laughing at the hugeness of a Blue Marlin between them.

When he turned into the kitchen, there was Tally, scooping eggs onto their plates. Coffee was poured, and a pan of fried gator-tail was produced from the oven. "You slept real good," he said, laughing, "I could hear you out there." Dan was gingerly cutting into the big chunk of meat, laughing at himself. "I know I've had gator before, but it was a long time ago. You got me good this time!" It was to Tally's utter delight.

Skimming the reedy-green ocean that was Big Cypress Preserve, the fringe of the deeper glades was a thrill. If their quest wasn't so dismal, Dan would have felt like he was on holiday. It must be something to do this all the time. When he said as much, Tally chuckled, "You know yourself anything loses its' shine after a bit. I even recall bein' with a girl I thought I'd never get enough of, an' she went and ruined it by wantin' to do it, six... seven times a day. 'Guess you can choke on anythin'. This is fun if I don't HAVE to do it, but when I'm with a friend it's just fine too. We'll go back to where the canal goes up to the causeway, where the car was found, and have a look. I don't think that big crew would 'a missed anythin' close by, but we can start there."

Tally was still thinking about his old Indian friend's vague words of last night, but without being sure what they meant, kept the suspicions to himself. In about ten minutes they were curling through the canal, sort of slow, then fast, looking for breaks in the grasses. Dan was not hopeful, and asked, "Don't gators make paths through there, same as an animal or a person? Who's to say we won't run up on a nest of the sum-bitches?"

What a funny shit-ass he still is! Tally had never, not ever, found a friend who made him laugh so easily as this one. He could tell, as soon as he was with Dan, that it wouldn't be but a few minutes before he'd be weak with laughter at something. "You feared of wally-gators, Bo-Cap? They ain' gon' hurt YOU! They like sweet meat! Your ole' pickled carcass don't do nuthin' for them! "LOOK!" He was pointing as he stopped still in the water. "See that bank right there? It's sorta smoothed out and the reeds are bent and broke. Gators won't make such a mess as that. They seem to have tunnels in the grass...not all thrashed down. That's a place to start workin' our way into. You get up on the tower and here... take these glasses. You'll want to make three-sixties with the glasses, zig-zaggin' as I move along." Dan wasn't good on towers, but he went up, obediently making full turns, scanning up and down through the binoculars.

He saw nothing. The trail of flattened grass seemed to weave, then at a small creek it stopped and didn't pick up anywhere he could see. Dan yelled down to Tally, "Go back to the start of the trail again. I'm gettin' out."

They turned and after a minute stopped in the water. Dan hiked up his boots and stepped to the bank, using the reeds for support like jointed ski poles, as he wove back through the trail. He saw nothing of human presence, and was about to turn around when there WAS something there, wrapped around the base of a reed almost in the mud. It was a gold chain with a medal... like one you get in school for sports. Dan's heart lurched when he lifted it off and saw that it was from a Virginia school. Clifford had gone away someplace like that the last two years! It couldn't be anybody else's! The boat retraced, but after a closer look they saw nothing else. Tally was as mesmerized by the discovery as Dan, his next move in the direction of the reservation off Big Cypress. He made a wide arc, skipping gracefully by all possible obstructions. The bank of the Indian tract came in sight in less than the time it took them to get to the canal. Tally jumped ashore to tie up, motioning Dan to follow. He scrambled onto the bank and caught up with Tally, entering the trail between scrub palmetto thickets.

"It's a real stretch, goin' this far away from the canal where the boy disappeared, and it's likely the folks here DON'T know anything, but neither your friend Hartsell, nor those yokel cops would think to come here. I tell you, Dan, these folks has ways a' knowin' things you don't question. Last night, and now I'll tell you, the old man on the road told me he was helpin' a young 'white one' to go home, but he couldn't go 'til he could hop and fly. I don't know what the hell it meant, but it's worth a look-see. The Indians say things in riddles, I think sometimes, just to fuck you up for fun. Who knows, it might be a critter... a bird or a rabbit. He's an honest man, and he wanted me to know, THAT'S the hook! Why would I care about a critter bad enough to stop in the road to hear tell of it?"

Dan had nothing to say... he couldn't get around all of it yet. They came to a fenced home and barn, neat and viable. There were chickens and guineas and ducks, a couple of cows, and a fairly good looking, though aging sorrel mare. The house was larger than Tally's, and built up off the ground about fifteen feet. Underneath was parked an old truck, a motorcycle from the fifties, still shiny red, and a gaggle of parts for each. There was a fire burning under a black pot, making a pungent smoky smell they couldn't identify. The old man was stirring it slowly, lifting and dropping the contents, and singing to himself.

"Hey, Hillis! How' you doin' this mornin'?" Tally was waving as they approached, whispering to Dan not to speak. They stopped short, and the Indian came to them. "I'm boiling up poultices. Need many changes to make the healing march without a halt. Come, it will be good for you to see." They followed without a word until Dan hissed, "See WHAT? What IS this, Tal? I feel like I'm in a bad post-war movie! What are we doin' here?" Tally gripped Dan's arm, hissing back. "Don't do this! He is very aware! I want to get inside and see what he's about! Just do what I do, and shut UP!" Once inside, they followed Hillis through a spacious great room with a scattering of handcrafted cypress furniture covered with bright throws and a variety of animal hides. The look was too pure to be contrived. This old guy lived the life. He stopped at a rough wood door and motioned them to wait. When he appeared again and beckoned them, once inside the room, they were rendered speechless.

He was a mess... a swollen, ravaged mess, homespun poultices overlapping most of his naked body... and, Oh, God, Dan was distraught when he saw a heavily wrapped lower leg, missing the foot, immersed in a bowl, in a slurry of ice and water, with herbs and bark floating around in it. Dan dropped to his knees by Clifford Hartsell's side.

"Dear Jesus!" He thought crazily, his neck is swollen as big as his head!" He raised the boy's eyelids and was relieved to see that the pupils were reacting to light. He stood to face the caretaker. "Why didn't you tell anybody? How long has he been here? He needs to be in the trauma center RIGHT NOW! Tally, call the sheriff! Get somebody here before the kid dies!" The two men went out of the room with Tally prodding Dan to shush. "That man should NOT be dishonored for trying to save the boy's life! Dan! The boy would be GONE... a tasty gator dinner, if Hillis hadn't somehow brought him to his home! Get ahold of yourself and let's get more details first. I want to see how the poor kid IS, you know, check his vitals and see if he can hear us. Now, for God's sake, pull yourself together! If he was gonna' die under the old man's care, he'd already be dead!" Dan had to admit he was being sensible. Tally was EMT trained, and in moments, using a kit left with Hillis months back, he was stunned to find Cliff's condition, while critical, was stable... his injuries, though gross, not life threatening.

There was no fever, so no infection was indicated... a miracle when an amputation occurs in the unsterile wilds. It seemed to Tally that he had hit his neck or head, or been twisted about so that his neck was almost broken. God was with him...that would have killed him instantly. The foot was the most ghastly part of his misfortune. He obviously was freed from an alligator, after losing just his right foot. Dan tried to get him to react, saying his family name, his sister's name, Jesse's, all those he loved, but nothing appeared on his face... at least not until taking the boy's scarred hand, he had said one word. "Franciene."

Clifford lurched from the mattress, and fell stiffly back. His eyes flew open and stared in horror, his mouth made a huge "O", and he appeared to be trying to fight off something before his eyes. Hillis pushed them away, sat beside the boy, and with a soothing chant, calmed him back to a fretful sleep. Then he stood, taller than before.

"I ask YOU now to go!" He was pointing at Dan's chest. "Sir, please, I am a friend of his mother's, and I want him to be well," he was speaking slowly, without slang, to let the oldster take the words in. "The name I spoke is a girl who may have caused all this, and she is still missing. We are only trying to get the children back home again."

Whew, Dan didn't know he could say it that good. Even Tally was impressed. They went out to the great room to figure what was next. Tally asked Hillis about his doctoring methods, some in his native language, and Dan was going crazy to know what he was doing to the boy. Tally came to him and began to explain.

"The ways are strange... sort of magical and very, very old. I can't explain in words you can repeat to anyone, but I will tell you he is a living miracle, after what he's been through. Hillis knows he needs to be moved to a hospital, but the transfer must include HIS methods, to keep the boy from becomin' septic... ravaged by infection and rejection of what he's done so far. Dan, he says the stump MUST remain in a super cold state, like it is now, with those treatments in the basin, until he gets home! He won't back down! Here it is, buddy, for some reason man, I believe him."

Dan was half crazy with worry for Cliff, and didn't want to lose him now, after finding him alive. He was hell-bent to deliver him to his mother. "Okay, we can do that, and the old guy should go too, since he has kept him wantin' to live this long. All I want now is for us to get a chopper here and get him home. Can we do that?" His eyes were tearing up, and Hillis was touched by his caring. "The boy will live, and I will help to get him home. You have not spoken of his father, and I know he is here, from Purchase's words to me. We must tell him his son is found before we go. It is the right thing to do."

He had the kind of presence that you didn't bicker with, and although Dan detested Strahan, he knew the man was right. "I'll go call a chopper, Tally, if I can use your mobile, and I can get Strahan's mobile number from the sheriff. No need to have all the laws flockin' in here... I'll keep it quiet. He took the phone into the room with Clifford, hoping he would hear him getting a rescue effort going. After the chopper was secured, and before he got hold of Strahan, he took out Andrea's number, and dialed it. Andrea anxiously said "Hello!", and he rushed the sound of her voice calling her son's name, to his ear. He opened his eyes, his lips parted, and it came... beautiful music for Andrea... "Mom? MOM?"

The words were hoarsely emitted, and he said nothing else, but Dan got the phone to his mouth and sobbed, "I got him for you just like I promised, Andee, and he's comin' home to you today. Now you two ladies high tail it to the hospital, 'cause that's where we're headed in the chopper, you hear me, honey?" She heard him, and as he rang off he could hear her sobbing gratitude over and over. Now, Dan needed to call Strahan. It wouldn't be good, calling such a man to announce he had done his job for him, especially old Captain Dan, the loser man! He couldn't do it! Tally was helping pack the things they would need for the flight, but Dan called him away to do his dirty work. Tally, as usual, had a good plan.

"Okay, I'll call him, but I don't want him to find out what's gonna' happen, so he can't do nothin' to interfere! I'd like to get the lot of you on that bird an' outta' here before he comes, 'cause he'll want to do it his way, bein' like he is, and those law strings he pulls. Now, Hillis," he turned humbly to face his friend. "We thank you for saving the boy from death, but we've got one more favor to ask. If you all can leave me here to deal with Mr. Hartsell, can we count on you to stay the course, and not part from the boy until he is out of danger, even if it means you might come up on hard moments?"

The wise old man closed his eyes, took a breath, and spoke. "I have been prepared, Purchase my friend, to give my medicine to the white boy as long as it takes. It doesn't matter where we must be. There is more to do, and I will minister to him until he can stand before his mother and hold out his arms. He is a gift from our God Above, as he is now, and it is my appointed task to give him back whole again." The question could now be asked, and Dan wanted to know.

"Tell me sir, How DID you rescue Cliff? Why was he not eaten up by the big gators out there? I know about gators, and they don't just take a nibble and turn tail like that." The Indian nodded, "No, he would have taken the boy to his death, but I was paddling the canal and had my rifle with me. The gator's thrashing drew me near, and when I saw the boy, I shot the gator so he could escape. He had given up the fight for his life, but I startled him so, that even with his shock and pain he was able to stumble for quite a way in the grass. I paddled around and met him when he reached the other creek bank, and that is where he fell. I got him in my boat, and the rest is known. It sounds like a bragger's tale, but it is the truth." Of course it was. The chopper was about to land, and the team aboard would be bringing Cliff's gurney in, to begin the offense of transferring him without his father's presence.

"All we gotta' do is tell Strahan Hartsell we had no time to waste, and Cliff came first, don't you think?" Dan was getting more and more nervous. The rest of these people could go on their way, but he had to live right up underneath the Palmland power push. It couldn't be helped now. All he could do is remember why he did it, and how Andrea had sounded when he spoke to her at the mountain cabin, and he felt justified and proud. Besides, he knew Andee would want to personally thank this man who saved her son's life.

Dan took his first breath while there was nothing to do, and was overcome with emotion, when he thought of his own, pain-in-the-butt son, and what if it was him in that shape? That wasn't all... it was Massey, and what they might have to face about Franciene and her whereabouts, and her part in Clifford's tragedy. The copter crew, Hillis, and a sedated Cliff Hartsell, took off in minutes, and Tally was on the phone to Sheriff Porter as they watched the bird fly away north. It was nine forty-five.

* * *

It was getting way on into the afternoon, and Aaron was not back from Sandy's. Toby didn't mention concern to the others, but going to look for him was eating him up. The women, including Carrie, were almost frozen with fear of what was next. Will was pretending valor, making jokes and engaging them in storytelling as best he could. Carrie had asked Toby after Aaron left, if someone should have gone with him, and he now thought the same thing. She explained her worry. "He is out there with the edges of danger creepin' in, an' I don't know if he's one to be brought to task or not. I do know, the girl and those two boys were close as could be, and always tended one another. Those things don't change. We just got to trust Aaron's good sense, an' their affection for one another." Maybe saying it would make it so. They were silent for a few minutes, watching the clock move.

They couldn't be still. He turned to Will. "Will, boy, if you'll stay here with your mom and Mattie, Carrie and I will go see what's keeping that fellow." Hoping he sounded casual enough, Toby nodded to Carrie, who was perfectly in step with him. They took the Rover... An army tank sitting in the yard would be welcome this day, but it might as well be a Radio Flyer wagon, if the force tracking them was what they feared. They made little talk as they motored to the beach... Carrie seemed to be conversing with herself, nodding and shaking her head, plucking at the bright batik caftan she wore.

She came back for a moment, and turned to him. "Oh, Toby, what have we got into now? I wish we could go back to before... before 'Tilde died, and those two children ran off, and Massey had his attack, and Clifford... OH! CLIFFORD'S COMIN' HOME! He'll be back today! I only just now saw it! We got to tell the Hartsells! They' gonna' be so joyful! If the radio phone works, I'm callin' Jesse soon as we get there!" He couldn't believe how quickly she was so transformed, happy, smiling warmly, a smile that took charge of half of her big face. Toby wanted to believe her... something good happening for a change, but it was too alien to fathom.

What was she plugged into? How did stuff like that just POP out? They stopped at the teacher's house, behind the Jeep that had brought Aaron. Toby's heart was making his shirt pulse, and Carrie's eyes were as face-filling as her smile had been a minute ago. The door wasn't quite closed, and he pushed it to enter. The smell was unmistakable... something had burned in there, and not long before they came. Toby went to check the phone, of course it was dead, and when he returned to Carrie she was standing over the day bed... its spread was covered with slimy ash... and Aaron was not there.

"We have to leave this place, child, we must spend no more time in this evil air!" She put her palms together and raised them to the ceiling, and murmured, "Jesus, Dear Jesus, take away the bad thing comin'. Don't let it show itself to us, not like it did to poor Aaron." She hustled Toby out, stating they each would take a car, with strange resignation. He stood up to her, in a rare moment. "What if Aaron comes back for it? What if he's just walking the beach? I think I'll go see." He took just one striding step, before she stopped him.

"You don't want to go there, Toby." He shook off her hand and ran across the dune. One set of footprints, accompanied by marks he could not define, but guessed they were made from blunt sticks making holes and being dragged, led straight to the surf, then nothing. His mind spun to the conclusion. "Carrie! There are no other prints here! Aaron went into the ocean taking something with him! He must have come out down the beach! I have to go see!"

She would not try to stop him this time, but stood silent, while he tore down the beach as far as he could go, then passed her, going the other way to where the forest met the sea. He was without breath or words when he faced Carrie again. "He didn't come out of the water, Carrie." he said flatly. This she already knew. They walked to the cars, then just as Toby was about to back the jeep and pull out around the Rover, she raised her hand. He had expected it. "I will come in a little while, Toby. I need to see what is here." Toby wasn't afraid for her... it wasn't that, exactly. Maybe he wanted to see as well. "Let me stay too, please, Carrie." She was not to be moved. "No! You go back to tend to the others! I demand it!"

It was beginning...she had just told him. He put his hand up in salute, a gesture she returned as he drove away. If she could, Toby knew she would do all in her power to divert danger from the rest of them. He had doubted her for the last time. Those suspicions before were caused by her fierce devotion to Massey's child, because she WAS Massey's child. Whatever compelled her to dismiss him, Toby prayed she would be safe and back to them quickly. Toby's sort of prayer was needed badly, because Carrie was about to come face to face with what Franciene had become. The woman stood outside the house on the beach, breathing deeply and reaching even more deeply into her resources, to gird for what she knew was there.

The charming cottage, with its haint blue shutters and drift-wood stained siding, was pulsing with spiritual presence, as Carrie stepped to the door. She was not afraid... only overcome with sadness and a foreboding of the reality she had fought off so long. She entered, expecting anything... even the possibility of her death. Franciene knew what Carrie was about. After she had seen Aaron to the water, she had taken her own form, and decided to take a tub bath with all the attending luxuries Sandy had around the bathtub. She slipped out of Mandy's swimsuit, and stepped into the fragrant, steamy tub. The girl had never spent one single day outside of her own indulgence, and she wasn't going to abandon old ways now.

Her perfect little body found more than enough space to thrash and cavort in the vintage, oversized bathtub Sandy had searched for and found in Savannah. The candles she brought from the other rooms, even in the daytime, created the hedonistic effect she had created for herself since she was a tiny child. It was at the point when she was submerged, all but her face, when Carrie appeared in the doorway. The room-filling black woman stepped to the tub and, with a sweep of her arm, turned the water ice cold. Franciene, shocked to furious, sprang to her feet.

"What brings you, Aunt Carrie, darling?" Her voice was enticingly, but acidly sweet... like she was about to break into off-key song. She stepped from the tub like a fairy from a rose petal and began drying herself, with no hint of the rage she held. Carrie was scorningly silent, letting the girl strut and dress in slow motion, in a terry beach jacket she found behind the door. Franciene pushed past her old friend and flounced into the kitchen, where she opened a Dr. Pepper and sat at the table... waiting for an answer. Carrie followed her, calculating each move she made. When she finally spoke, she expected the words to croak out. What kind of thing had the child become? She finally asked, "Tell me what has become of you, and what you intend to do here today. Can you answer me, child? Those you have done bad things to... did they deserve to die, or be harmed? And… what about your daddy?"

That was the one! When Carrie mentioned Massey, Franciene seemed to bulge and bloat with evil, and released the pressure by screaming. A howl like a wolverine in a steel trap blew Carrie against the kitchen door. She tried to open it, but it was locked. All she could do was stand and take what was next. Franciene was no longer in charge of her delicate body. The howl was left in the air, and The Bitch spoke.

"QUESTIONS? YOU ASK ME QUESTIONS? All the years I wanted answers... My daddy had another life! He had another BABY! He GAVE that boy what was MINE... while I was a prisoner in that house, on this Island...and he never told me. It is not enough that I was kept from the world, and the world was kept from ME! Not even YOU could be on my side when I wanted freedom! I know you told Daddy to send 'Tilde with me! I should have shoved the rest of that dumpling down YOUR throat!"

Carrie felt herself crumbling inside with each word of recrimination from the wretched girl, devastated, as she came to know now, that they all were in harm's way. She formed words carefully, hoping to say something calming. "Francie, honey, we LOVE you! Your daddy has no other in his life more dear to him than you! He is near dyin', cause he feared you' gone for good, these last few days! He will surely die, when he knows what you' done, and what you are doing." Franciene's face contorted into a gory mask. She advanced on Carrie, grabbed her throat and slammed the big woman to the floor.

"HE caused this demon to go inside me, by making me weak, from lifelong rage and a dream of revenge, you dumb old Mammy! I should kill you now, but my plan has to be followed. Aaron is done... Mandy, Troy, Clifford, Aunt 'Tilde, and I count five more, before I can go to my daddy with who his only family is! Now, you get up and go tell my 'Baby Brother', that I will see him SOON."

Carrie, stunned more by the words than by Franciene's attack, lay still and silent, watching her scurrying around, gathering her things, then dressing in one of Sandy's long, clinging, voile dresses... a deep green watered print with covered buttons, fastened between her breasts and her thighs. Chills racked Carrie. This was not any dress Franciene would choose! Rather, she would scorn it as a "Granny Dress"! As she was going out the door, the thing turned back to her best friend and guardian, showing a tiny hint of the child so deep inside.

"I didn't mean to be bad, Aunt Carrie, don't tell Daddy it was me that hurt Aunt 'Tilde." With that, she gave a prissy little pout, and left. Carrie dissolved in grief for the children she loved, while lying there on Sandy's kitchen floor. When she was calm again, she got to her feet, checked the radio phone with little hope... finding it dead, she ran to the car to warn the others, speaking in whispers to whatever was listening, for help.

After she whirled away from Carrie and the confrontations with her and Aaron she had wanted to avoid, Franciene was back on the beach, gathering herself and her sluggish power for the next step. Damn! She didn't want to put Aaron in the ocean! He was going to ruin everything, and had to be gone. She stood looking out as if trying to see any sign of her old friend. He had been so horrified when she took Benjie's form and pointed that ruined finger at him. Maybe Benjie had done it! That's it! He took HER over, not the other way around!

She felt better. Aaron was not one of her targets anyway... neither was Carrie. She had her doubts about Jasper and Pansy, and if Jaime came back before she was done, and tried to mess with her, well, he had just better not!

# CHAPTER THIRTY-NINE

What she had not received, due to all the confusion, was that her long time suitor and his sweet little Cissy were hard at preparing for their wedding, in a little town where such no-wait ceremonies are still allowed. It was one nice thing happening in the midst of all the rest. Jaime wanted no more of the turmoil. If he was to be a man, and a good one, he believed he needed an anchor, and Cissy was ready to stick! She would keep him straight, By God! Besides, Franciene Thornedike would never have been his... that dream, that fantasy belonged right where it was and would forever be. Jaime had no way of knowing that Cissy actually saved his life... by begging him away to the Justice of the Peace. She looked every bit the bride... a soft white sun dress, a little lace veil... to a tee! Jaime stopped at a florist and came back with a nosegay of gardenias and pink rosebuds to Cissy's delight. Never mind that he was done up in a Murray Brothers fishing shirt with the sleeves rolled up, and no better than his best pair of faintly stained khakis... he was ready and willing to be her man... Happily Ever-AFTER!

\* \* \*

The rescue was complete, and Strahan still hadn't been apprised of the events of the morning. The fact of his switched-off phone was testament to his faith in positive results from the search. When he and Jay got back to the base camp from their fruitless trek, he stood silently looking out over the waving sea of grasses... there was nothing to do but nothing. It was nearly noon when the sheriff's car found them. The big man wasn't sure he could stand facing this broken father with his confession... that his son was probably home by now, in the hospital the man himself had built, being tended by a staff he had helped to pick, and he was one of the last to know. He was relieved that Mister Hartsell was not alone.

"How're you doin' this mornin', Sir?" Del asked as kindly as he could. Strahan only nodded, as Del continued, all in one sentence without taking a breath. "I'm mighty pleased to tell you your boy has been found alive, and we airlifted him home a bit ago, with the best paramedic crew just'a workin' on him, but there was no time to waste callin' for you all to have a say, as you can imagine."

There! That ought to take care of the first part. He waited for it to sink in, but was ill prepared for what came. Strahan turned to his friend, grabbed him in a hug with sobs convulsing him for about five seconds, then he turned back to the breathless man with all of the questions coming out in the same torrent Del had used.

"Tell me where he was, and what his condition is, if you don't mind, sheriff. I would appreciate any news you can give me, then I will follow as quickly as it can be arranged." He motioned silently to Jay-Jay, who hurried off to get the plane. Strahan was obviously in shock, Del caught the signs. He suggested they sit in the car with the AC on while he gave the amazing account. The tough old boy tried as hard as he could to be pragmatic and concise, but before the story was finished, both men were weeping. Jay was back to announce the waiting jet, and that they would be there first if they could leave right away. Mister Hartsell, being accustomed to being everywhere first, asked to be raced to Naples in the police unit, and was obliged by the relieved sheriff.

It went better than he thought it would, but Del would be tenuous for a stretch, since he had left out the part about Clifford's chomped-off right foot. It was a wise decision, because if the horror of his son being so maimed had been let loose, Strahan might have snapped. He needed to get back home with all his faculties, and the HELL out of the Glades.

* * *

The afternoon was plodding along on Squires, and at Thornedikes', all were numb with distress over Aaron's strange disappearance, but not one could admit out loud that he was drowned or otherwise dead. Carrie had not returned, but Toby was getting used to her strange movements. He wanted to spend some time alone with each of the others, and decided to start with Will. He and Mattie had been in an intimate huddle on the dock for a long time, so Toby didn't mind breaking in. Mattie kissed his cheek and patted Toby's arm as she went to the house. He took her place by his young friend. It was charmingly warm when he sat.

"What do you two think about this day, Will? I know you... you most likely think we're about to meet our own demons in Franciene's form, and you may damn well be right." Will looked at his hands, abashed that Toby had read this in him, and he nodded slowly. Toby moved on, already sure he would get nowhere. "You see, son, the fear I have is that she is going to come for you as the threat she sees you to be, and we will be unable to stop her. Carrie hasn't said so, but I'll bet she fears the same. You said before that you're staying, but I want you to think about taking the girls and driving as far from Frenchport, preferably west, then north, as you can get, in the next twelve hours, and let us have our turn at your sister. It might sap some of her strength and drive, if there are lesser subjects to come at. Your mom is in danger as the one who gave you life, even though Franciene seemed to take to her, back when they met. You think about what to do. I can not bear to risk your life and your mom's, considering those already gone. It is not going to happen, I swear to God! I'll give you a few minutes."

He left a stunned Will, went inside and still no Carrie... and, sad to see, no Aaron. The women were in Massey's study, looking quite lost. Toby wanted them gone so badly, he was ready to try anything. "Linda, honey, I think Will wants to get you two away from here and come back to help us, but I'm hoping you can convince him to go too. I'll catch up to you tomorrow, wherever you are, but tonight we need to deal with this thing without worrying about your safety." While Linda was considering his words, Mattie said, "Toby, you can't order, or even wish us gone! I am here for a purpose... to be at Carrie's side, and we can not draw Franciene out if her enemies aren't here. Carrie is at the Griffins. She called before you came in, to tell me not to go, and that she was about to pull all the ends together. Why on earth would we go? I hope I speak for Linda, but I want you to hear it from her."

Linda stood, and was firmly planted, even more so than in Waycross, when she let him have it, full bore. He knew he was already beaten... but she drove the last stake. "How can you expect me to go now? Maybe YOU are the one who should go, and leave this to those of us who have history here!" That one hurt so much, but Toby remained silent to let her finish. She began to pace... He could not let himself look at her intimately, in that soft dress, so he could stay focused.

She whirled to face him, and said, "I don't mind saying this in front of Mattie... I am close to being in love with you, Toby, and if we can survive this, and I can make sense of what Massey is to me now, and to my boy, there could be a chance for us, if you want it. No running away is possible for me, wherever I go. We will stay together, all of us, and I pray to God Aaron isn't dead, and comes out on the other side, whatever shape we all might be in. Will is committed to staying too... this is his family, more than any of us can claim!"

"Mom's right, Toby," Will said as he came in the room. "It's all of us together... right, Mom?" Once again, Toby felt small and stupid and alien, but the admission from Linda's heart was like a balloon under him, and he floated it to a place among them. Moving to her side, he put his hands on her shoulders and kissed her on her damp cheek with all the walls down. "I love you, Linda", he whispered only for her ears, and backed away to allow the quorum its power. They could pull the thing between them out of whatever rubble was to come, he prayed, and if not... No! He couldn't think that way, not with what they were facing. He needed the promise of her love, and Will's, to stand firm.

As he moved back, Toby was horrified to see a change come over Linda's dear face. She began to flash between her own features, and those of a woman he did not know. A young woman with chestnut hair and topaz eyes kept bouncing out, and then, as they stood and watched, she was reduced to an infant on the floor, naked and wailing. Mattie instinctively fell to her knees to scoop the baby up, but she found nothing there when her arms extended. Linda had reformed across the room, now with a look Toby could only interpret as demonic. His gut churned as he watched Linda's lovely body glide toward the desk, stopping in the center of the room to stomp her foot in a gesture of defiance.

She clenched her fists, crossed her arms over her chest, and spun around to regard each one, now frozen in place. Then she floated, barely an inch off the floor to stop beneath Massey's portrait. "We will see who counts... who really counts, won't we DADDY? Why did you think you could shove me back for that boy? Steal what was mine and give it to HIM! I will wipe them away with one sweep! I will leave no one but you and me! Why don't you come home and face me, after all the times I had to face YOU?"

The voice was not Linda's, but it was not a young girl's voice either. The sound she made was more like the sound of dry, burning leaves, hoarse and crumbly... the words chopped off and hissed together. They were in the presence of such evil, Toby could not look at their' faces, afraid their terror would exacerbate his own. The visage... the demon inside Linda swept again before them all and began to threaten each of them singularly.

She went to Mattie first, strutting and sneering, as she said, "Florence Nightingale, I presume? You believe your patchwork powers can stand against mine? I say, FUCK YOU! You and this... " She wheeled to Toby. "This faded, stringy STUD who thinks HE is the Great Protector? Another five years and he'll be eating baby food and watching old Tarzan movies!" She put her hand out, his darling Linda's hand, and shoved him with force much like that of a silverback gorilla. Toby ended up against the library shelves, his hand grabbing at anything for a weapon, but quickly slumped, beaten by the reality that it would be Linda Sue, not Franciene, who would suffer a counter attack.

The last one to be intimidated was Will... poor, gentle boy, who all his young life considered acceptance of his situation as the most positive tack to take, even though most would wallow in the anger and insecurity, rejection and abandonment can instill, was now being menaced by his mother… hosting his sister's disembodied soul! It was too ugly. Toby caught a glint in her eye. It was LINDA! She was fighting to take over to protect her son. But Franciene was too strong. She circled him sensuously, and with all the strength she could transfer, she lifted and held him, crazily, like a magician's illusion. Only this was real. Will was horizontally suspended over Linda's head, and she was chuckling up at him. Her laugh was dirty… the essence of evil. She let him down and was about to create another scene, when Carrie came into the room. "You STOP that right NOW!" she called out the same five words, in the same voice that Franciene had always known meant business.

Linda stopped… then mechanically began turning to face the woman in the doorway. She looked like a player in the jerky vignettes that mechanical Christmas windows display, as her face and body fought for dominance. Will lost it… he ran to the wet bar and was ill, choking and sobbing all at once. The voice began again, this time less rude, more appeasing. "I WOULD stop, Aunt Carrie, but I simply cannot! This INTRUSION has to be fixed! You are to let me alone while I take care of MY family affairs!"

Carrie wasn't having any of it. "You leave this good woman's body, and you leave it now, Franciene! She has done nothing to you, except try to love and help you. You have gone BAD, honey, and it might be mine and 'Tilde's doin'. We pulled you into our circle so's you'd have the GOOD powers… not this destructive kind. Leave her NOW, and go on back to what you were, and I'll try an' help you much as I can. Jasper and Pansy are waitin' for us at their house, so you can come on with me!"

Did Carrie really believe it would be that simple… that easy? Franciene was part of what a week could barely hold in its' bounds, and she was too self-centered to know or care that those in the room with her had filled the last seven days to the end of anymore tolerance because of her. She tossed the few thoughts she could muster around in her all too twisted brain, and only one villain surfaced. "Why isn't my Father here? Why is he hiding from me? I came back to settle with him, and he is gone! Is it another fishing trip? Is he off making another brother for me? Why, if I have the power, can I not find him?" She was almost crawling up Carrie, so close in her face was she, now slipping from Linda to her own form. It was a smooth, silken transfer, from fortyish Linda Sue, to seventeen Francie, without a blink. They all watched with horrified but fascinated attention. As soon as it was Franciene again, Will and Toby heard Linda crying softly behind them.

They ran to her as she said, "It was Diane and Baby Darrie, and they were HERE! They were both ALIVE, and we talked about what they were doing since they left the world so tragically. The little baby boy could speak! It was NOT a dream, I swear! He asked about YOU, Will... he couldn't have known about you unless they were Angels or something, don't you think?"

She was babbling between sobs, and they believed her. She thought she had seen her old friends for a moment when they were trying to fight her being possessed by Franciene, but it was the wicked girl who had summoned familiars to portray Linda's lost friends, in order to weaken her, so Franciene could possess her. Thank God she was shielded from any harm, by the forces for good. The two men held her between them, shielding her from the sight across the room. Carrie had literally grown in height, and loomed over the neophyte demon, shouting back the answers she sought.

"Stupid Suckling! Did you think I would have cleared a path to my dear Massey, so you could have stopped his poor, sickly heart for good? You could NOT have passed through ME, girl, not me and NOT 'Tilde! Now! What you are going to do is obey me, and get to the Griffin house! We will deal with you as if we were one!" She was formidable and as commanding as any force imaginable, but the girl, while lovely and delicate, stood up to her like an ugly version of equal. Will slipped his dazed mother out of the room, and Mattie and Toby, struck fearless in their resolve, went to flank Carrie. Mattie had already whispered Toby silent... to let HER speak to Carrie with her mind, so she could receive. Carrie was full of fear, but it was not in evidence as she repeated her command to Franciene. She felt them beside her, and Mattie was intent on what the brave woman would send to her.

The words filtered into Mattie's head in a steady, cadenced mantra. "Toby needs the book now... you need your love. The girl is not yet beaten back... We must see her gone. Jasper and Pansy, you and Will... and myself, we can save them, all but those we cannot reach. The BOOK... Toby needs the book! It will tell him, if he seeks the place where there are numbers and the circle with many sides. TELL HIM NOW!" Her eyes never closed as they had when she was sending before... her effort to disguise the directive. She had spoken to Franciene at the same moment the message was sent, quite impressive to Mattie, and another moment when she welcomed glimpses into her future, more senior powers.

Toby felt something tugging at his sleeve...it scared the beJesus out of him, until he saw it was Mattie's fingers. They moved slightly behind Carrie as she fiercely engaged Franciene. She whispered the need of the book and what to find, and he slipped back into the shadows the late afternoon painted beside the hall entrance. He had the book in his backpack in the pantry, and he raced on tiptoe to get it. GONE! It was not there!  He counted through the suspects... Carrie? No, SHE had asked him to get it! Linda? No way! He had not told her about the book... she had no knowledge of it at all. Will? Possibly out of curiosity, but he would have asked him about what he had read, Toby was sure of it.

Mattie might have taken it, thinking to protect him from too much knowledge. He stole back to the doorway and motioned to Mattie. She was nearly to him when Francie saw her. "Nursie! You stop there!" She swept over to Mattie while Toby tried to get between them. "YOU! I can stop you permanently if I want! I have only words for this Angel of Mercy!" She took Mattie away to the center of the room. "My Aunt Carrie thinks me bad... what do you think?"

Be careful, Mattie, Toby said silently. He and Carrie exchanged glances, and Will was clenching his fists and looking poised to spring, but they gave him head shakes in unison, and he stepped back. Franciene was looking up and down Mattie's body with smirking scorn. "You're sweet on my half-brother, aren't you, you BITCH? I'd bet you're older than he is by at least three or four years... WILL!"

She snapped at the boy, causing him to jump closer, as if ordered by a drill sergeant.

The awful girl cocked her head and sneered, "Want a peek into the future? This is how your little nurse will look when you hit forty!" As he gaped in horror, lovely Mattie started blowing out like a balloon, then as if pricked with a pin, she deflated into a shriveled bag, her hair, tousled mousy-gray wads of what resembled Spanish moss, her teeth, yellow and oversized between deeply creased lips, flaps of skin on her knees and elbows, the ravages of gravity. She looked at least eighty, instead of the age she would be when Will reached forty.

He screamed, "STOP!"... while falling toward the now decrepit Mattie, but was blocked by Franciene, standing in an impatient pose, tapping her sandaled foot on the rug over the offending safe. "Who do you think you are, boy?" She was shorter by half a head, but her menacing aura made her huge to the boy she hated so. Her ugliness had claimed pieces of his strength as she had hurled harm to those he loved, and he was tired... tired but not done. Toby meant to stand with him, and made a slight move but Carrie stopped him. "They have to do this between them, Toby, but if she overruns my block on her powers and would harm him, well, then we can go in. You see to Linda... you will find Mattie with her in the front hall, pretty as before."

"That wicked girl isn't able to buck me yet, but she is clever, and her youth makes her most threatening. I am going to call for Jasper and Pansy to come and join with me. Soon as Mattie's up again, send her to meet them. I can tell them what we will do as they walk to the house. Go on now, we' got no time. Another thing to count on, we got two on the other side standin' by... that's mother and son, and they won't let us down." Her tone was confident, but Toby saw fear in her telling eyes. It was hard for Toby to turn his eyes from Will and his demonic sister, as she walked slowly in a large circle around him, her arms out in a sarcastic, welcoming pose, but he managed it, and saw to Linda and Mattie, sitting on a love seat in the big hall. Toby sat down on the floor at their knees, trembling while taking a hand from each.

"Did she hurt you? Are you both okay? SHIT! I want to tear her apart! Aaron, and his mother... Clifford Hartsell, and God knows who else! She's to be blamed for her daddy's troubles too! You all need to leave here... you've GOT to go... while she's distracted. She's filled with rage and hate, and she could, in an instant, turn all of it on any of you! I'll ask Jasper soon as he comes, to get a boat here so you can get away!"

Toby feared someone would die on this day, and was damned if it would be one of the women, or Will. He knew it was foolhardy to think he had a particle of choice who she sought vengeance from, but he swore she wouldn't get at anyone he loved without a hell of a fight. After what the two women had endured, he prayed they would agree to leave the Island willingly, and right away. He was wrong. Nothing would shake the two women's determination to stay. Mattie slipped off down the driveway to meet the Griffins, who were nearly at the turn, while Linda gave him a comforting hug and went back where her boy was facing hell.

# FRENCHPORT HOSPITAL INCOMING

It was nearly three o'clock when Andrea and Sonja braked their car at the emergency entrance of Frenchport Hospital. Plagued after all the stress, with painfully stabbing middles and weak knees, they walked in, hand in hand, to be told the chopper had not arrived, but would be on the roof within minutes. They were directed to the waiting area to find Strahan and Jay-Jay, pacing together. Strahan ran and embraced them, at once full of questions, asking how they had learned the news. Andrea turned out of his arms and sat down in a straight chair, giving no answer.

Sonja remained, weeping in her daddy's shoulder, when they heard the helicopter over the building. They nearly collided rushing to the stairs, and when the group spilled out on the rooftop tarmac, Strahan was shocked to see Jesse, his own Jesse from Palmland, standing there waiting... a small cooler clutched to his chest.

Downstairs in CICU, Massey was experiencing some surreal sensations. While he expected to be foggy and groggy, the wakeful dreams were another story. He had not reported any of them to the staff, simply because he didn't want them to stop... maybe it was all about Franciene! After all, it was ALWAYS, ALL about Franciene, wasn't it? He drifted away to find his view one of his favorites... the beach at dawn... no, it was later. The sun had climbed, maybe near to noon. He felt himself floating twenty to thirty feet above the sand, moving from the point to the strand's center. There was someone down there. Massey was moving still closer, wondering if he would know the person. It was a man, and he was reclining on a graceful driftwood tree, reading a book. When Massey was directly overhead, the man stopped reading, closed the book, and looked up into his eyes as sure as Massey was a Thornedike. By God, it was Aaron Braswell! He waved and smiled, glad to see a friend, as if this happened every day. Massey returned the greeting, and it was over.

As he floated on down the deserted beach, the disembodied man was struck by a strange drawing in the smooth sand. It was a circle, but multi-sided, with wedges pointing to the center, to another many-sided circle with nothing in its center. There were some strange symbols in the diagram, and numbers scattered in a kind of of pattern... some inside, and some out of the spaces. "Somebody's been playin' a beach game I never saw before!" Massey mused. He anticipated the next event, as he lay in his narrow bed... maybe his girl would show herself. There was to be no "next time." Massey had no more visions like the one with Aaron. As if she was the sea fog herself, Carrie was between him and anything pertaining to the missing Franciene to keep him alive. Massey slept... and healing took a good hold on him.

# CHAPTER FORTY

Up on the hospital roof, the 'copter landed gingerly, with the frantic family kept at bay until the rotor was still and the staff could enter the building with their patient. Strahan surveyed the mish-mosh of attendees to his son on the gurney, and stormed over, ordering them to stop at once! The first person he came to was Dan Fuller. "What are YOU doing with MY son, Fuller?" Strahan Hartsell was enraged, and for a split-second, would have struck Dan a blow, if his wife and daughter hadn't run past him to catch up to Clifford, now nearly at the elevator. Hillis was on his left, his big brown hand protectively on the side rail of the gurney. An I.V. was dripping sustenance, and an EMT was bagging the semi-conscious boy when he had difficulty breathing.

Andee got to him first, and with all the dignity bred deep inside her, she maintained enough to refrain from touching her son. Instead, she asked the medics as to his condition. One lagged back to answer her. "We need time to evaluate him in ER, Ma'am. OH! Excuse me! Please let this man through. He has vital material with him." Andrea turned to look right into Jesse's poignant eyes.

"Let me by, Missy ma'am, I got precious cargo in he'ah." She let him by... for no other reason, than he had never asked anything of her... without the purest purpose. The group, all but Dan, disappeared when the doors closed. He was still circling with her husband, trying to escape his boorish tirade. Sonja was crying for her daddy to stop, when Andrea stepped between them. "Strahan! DO stop at once! This is NO time for airing differences, however petty. I want to thank Captain Fuller straightaway, since it was he who searched, found, and rescued our son. You and Sonja can meet me in the emergency room. Will that do?"

Her tone was the most deliberate her husband had ever heard from her ever before, and it shocked him into mute retreat. Sonja took her daddy's arm and walked him to the stairs, assuming her role as comforter. When Jay tried to ask him what was going on, Strahan seemed not to hear. He was unable to cope with anything resembling a catastrophe, and remained silent as the trio ran down the stairs to emergency, barely making it to see which way Cliff was taken, as his gurney and entourage disappeared into a green draped cubicle. Well, no lousy shower curtain would hold Strahan back from his boy, until today believed dead. He elbowed through to Cliff's side in time to see them haul the wrappings from his naked body, revealing the bluish, jagged stump where his right foot had been. In a second the father was on the floor, retching and useless.

It was Jay who took hold. He pulled Andrea back from the awful sight, held her while she wept, and ordered an attendant to see Sonja outside. Jay was seeing his best friends at hell's door. "Now, now, Darlin', we got to get a grip here. Poor Strahan's wore out, is all. We ain't slept a night since we left to find the boy. He didn't know nothin' 'til the chopper was on its' way here! Can you believe it? That sumbitch, Fuller, he took charge, over Cliffie's own daddy, and never said a word! What did he tell you on the roof? I saw him take you aside up there."

The last thing Andrea would do was speak against Dan, now and forever her hero. She only knew that Cliff had said the dear word, "Mom", a few hours ago on the cabin phone... her demand had been honored by Dan... No call until Cliff could call her himself! Her old friend had met her demand, and she would not forget it. She looked down at Jay, shorter by a head than she, and spoke carefully. "Jay-Jay, what does it matter now? I just want my son alive." She began to sob, "I want him home so we can love him back to life."

What could Jay do but shut up? Just then a doctor appeared. (It had been five minutes, but seemed an hour). He was grim but pleasant as he began. "Mrs. Hartsell? Is... Oh Dear!" He nearly tripped over Strahan, and motioned Jay to help lift the limp man to a couch in the hall. He was about to speak when Strahan sat up. They all turned toward the quizzical mumbling as the doctor began. "I'm relieved you have come around Mister Hartsell, we need to dash right along." He was from middle-eastern roots... tall, darkly elegant, and much more articulate than his conversant. He looked back and to between mother and father with perfect balance as he told them the most incredible news.

"Your son sustained what should have been a mortal wound. He was destined to expire from blood loss out in the mud alone, except for the Indian man who was with them when they arrived here. I have no way of comprehending how he managed to retrieve the boy, at least not yet... but be sure he saved his life. We have to speed into surgery, just as soon as you sign the papers, because by some miracle the boy's amputated foot is still viable and we want to attempt to reattach it." He saw their disbelieving faces and paused so they could take it in.

Strahan was on his feet at that point. "How can that BE? He was out in all that filthy muck, dragging what was left of his leg along..." Andrea swooned a little and Strahan collected himself, and spoke more delicately. "The septic conditions... the lapsed time... again, How in this WORLD?" He sputtered the last words, but the doctor was unfazed. "I only know whatever was done to both the stump and the severed appendage was miraculous and we have a chance to stand your son on two feet again. Here are the papers...SIGN! A nurse had slipped into the mix with a clipboard. They signed... of course.

Hillis and Jesse had been shown to a small staff lounge. The nurse knew there was something special going on between them, and wanted to help. The two old men, different only because of conditions of their birth, had little to say at first. They just sat. If their faces were studied, anthropologists would agree they could be related... perhaps closely. It was Jesse who broke the silence, speaking aloud to himself.

"I went out to the freezer to get some chickens so's Suzanne could make 'em all some soup. We got word the family was all comin' home, and she know how dey all sets great sto' by her dumplin' stew, when nuthin' else'll do, no matter if it be hotter 'n' hades outside. Bless me, when I opened de lid, they was dis wee li'l white cooler, like for a boat trip, jes' sittin' up on top o' de chicken box. Dey was a note a' layin' on it. I was most timorous 'bout readin' sumthin' not fo' me, but I did, cause I was tol' to. It say, "Carrie sends this to Clifford. Go FAST, Jesse. Go to the hospital roof, NOW!" Jesse was highly animated and emotional, as he spoke, in sharp contrast with Hillis. The inward peace of the Seminole finally touched a chord, and Jesse settled into calm. When Hillis spoke it was a cut above a whisper, but it filled the small place like a roar.

"Your work was of The Great God, my friend... way, way higher than any kind of work those who think themselves Holy Men. This shows us His Power, and what His Love for us can do. I did my job... you, Jesse, did yours. We are almost finished. The last task we have is to lead those who love Clifford to right. I needed to meet you... it is good to know you will be near the boy." His wise old eyes brightened, and he asked, "Did your Suzanne 'make that chicken and dumpling soup? My stomach is as empty as a drum!" They stood and smiled, their two similar noses nearly touching as they shook hands. Jesse led his new friend out to the big Bentley, and they motored out of the parking lot.

Back inside, Dan believed himself to be pretty much odd-man-out. "Par for the course!"... He smirked, as he headed for the doors to the street. His jeep was still down at Tally's, and he didn't have a ride to the marina. About to start walking the mile-plus to the docks, he was hailed from a lowered, tinted window. It was Hillis. "DAN FULLER! CAPTAIN DAN! Where are you going now?" He had awareness of Dan's predicament and suggested Jesse stop. All it took was a nod between them, to invite the solitary captain to join them for dinner. Dan would be taking his first Bentley ride... something he couldn't pass on. Besides, old Hillis at the dinner table with him, and Jesse too... seemed like the best company he could ask for. He thought about Massey as they rode along but elected not to phone him with the news, not yet. It was bizarre, Cliff in the same building with Massey, and neither of them knew. What in God's name had happened to Franciene?

She was having herself a time, that's what! A good time that Carrie was about to spoil. Franciene still had Will transfixed and helpless in the center of the study. She was jabbing him with her fingernail as she made point after point. "You are NOT a Thornedike, do you hear? Your name is Will Parrish! There is no mention of your birth in my daddy's records, and those stocks are NOT going to YOU! I'm the one who had to stay prisoner in this house all my life, and I will NOT be cheated out of what's mine!"

She was still wearing the dress from Sandy's house, but now it was held together by just four buttons at her waist. Her long brown legs seemed to go up to her shoulders, and her heaving, taut little breasts were all but exposed. Her hair, in a demure baggy bun when she appeared, had fallen below her shoulders in tousled ringlets. Anyone just entering the room would have thought the two were dancing, or at play, and would have regarded them as stunningly beautiful... these golden children.

Toby found it painful looking at her, in sharp contrast to what others might first see. Even so, it was becoming more clear by the minute that Franciene was playing with them all like felines play with their prey... before the kill. Carrie was poised in front of the desk, a symbolic buffer between the danger and her Massey. Toby stealthily slipped through the shadows around the edge of the room to her side, and whispered, "What do you think she will do to him, Carrie? We can't just stand here while she destroys him!" The circling stopped short. Francie had heard or sensed the exchange. Will, still frozen, tried to turn to where they were standing but found he couldn't move his head. Franciene suddenly stopped at the edge of the rug. Her wicked expression changed from angry to quizzical, as Toby realized she could NOT step off of the rug's edge! He glanced at Carrie again... she, so intent on her spell she hadn't known he had spoken to her.

The woman was at war with Franciene's powers, striving to protect Will, and it was working! Franciene flipped the mean face back on and hissed a sneer at Carrie, just as Mattie entered with the Griffins. Pansy went to Carrie's side without fear, and Jasper strode right into the place where Will was trapped. Taking his arm, he walked the boy nearly to the corner of the room, and forcefully swept the rug away from the floor. It was marked in a circle as large as the rug, a many sided circle full of geometric angles, symbols, and numbers.

"How did THAT get there?" Toby wondered silently. He had known for days that the powers they were surrounded by were of a kind he pooh-poohed as foolish superstition, but moments before Jasper's move Toby almost tripped on the edge of that rug with his big feet, and the pine planking under it was exposed unmarked. However the markings got there, it was scaring the hell out of the problem child. She turned around at the instant of Jasper's gesture, and let out a scream one would expect from Circe herself.

Jasper went back to the center of the circle, to stand at what appeared to be the lid of a safe. It was round like its' painted border, the same multi-sided design as the outer circle. Jasper was daring Franciene to approach the center! She watched, mute, as he knelt and opened the safe... reached in and brought forth an envelope. He turned and held it out to her, causing Franciene to hiss and recoil. She knew what was inside. Those shares of stock with the bearer name changed on each one. She could only guess how they got back in the safe. Clothilde, Carrie and their little helpers running around, had materialized them back from where she took them, and they did it for HIM! They were all about stealing her place in the family for Will Parrish! She had to stop them... but just how?

Their power against her was collected...overlapping...and too strong for her to stand against as she was. It was clear to Carrie that the girl was losing a little ground. Carrie spoke. "You cannot do evil and not pay, child. Those pieces of paper aren't worth all this. Why couldn't you come to know there was room for both of you in this home? We're not going to allow your ugliness to smear any more blood on these good people OR your father's name."

All of them...Jasper and Pansy, Mattie and Linda, Will and Carrie... and Toby, were now evenly spaced around the edge of the circle... silent and still. Toby was aware of something new... in that instant he felt newly POWERFUL! The beautiful, lean, and strong figure that was Jasper still held out the folder... strong and determined. Franciene gave it all she had left. She pushed her hair away from her face and turned to him. Her voice was different... clearer and more mature.

"Do you think it's only about a little bit of FUCKING MONEY?" Carrie winced at the word, forever a lady with tender ears. She and Pansy touched hands, and were joined by the vivid manifestation of 'Tilde. Toby knew it was she, and was struck by how much Aaron resembled his mother... facially, and in her movements. The tiny woman swooped to stand in Franciene's space, and began to give her the answer to her question. "This never HAS been about possessions, you miserable girl. All of us here are your victims... even you. I am gone from the earth, this is so... but I was the one who was most ready. That's why you will fail! You took good and replaced it with bad, lived in love, and now are hateful.

They all know how I died, Franciene... I told them, one by one. Yes, Aaron knows." She waited for that to sink in. Franciene recoiled, but snapped back, "No matter, Auntie, dear...He's dead too! I thought you would know." She took a few steps that were pitiful attempts at strutting, but stopped and shrunk when Clothilde answered. "Yes, I would know if my son had crossed over. That is why I know he is still HERE."

She waved her thin arm toward the hall, and Aaron stood there, sandy and salty, but certainly alive, and he was clutching the book to his chest. All who saw, had to steel themselves against moving to embrace him, but the silent order for stillness was heavy in the room. All except for Franciene, who was imploding before all of their eyes. Her body convulsed, as she gathered up one last wave of strength, letting her sail over the circle, and out the door. Aaron was first behind her as she ran to the barn. The others stopped on the porch and let him continue alone.

It was his fight first... it was HIS mother she had murdered. Toby picked up the book Aaron dropped on the hall floor and opened it. The place depicted the same circle they had been visited by in the study. He took the open book to the love seat, turned on the lamp, and began to read. Aaron ran as fast as he could after her. Somewhat impeded by his soggy jeans and shirt, he still was able to catch up as Franciene jumped from the paddock fence to her pony's back. He dove for her from the other side of the fence, nearly missing, but was able to swing behind her and hang on until he was centered on Topsy's rump.

They cleared the top of the gate by inches, the pony making her ritual eastward arc, and then she stretched out... grabbing for more speed. Aaron yelled in Franciene's ear through all that flying hair, to turn the pony and stop, but he knew better. Her tawny thighs were locked around the mare's flanks and her hands buried deep in her mane. Just like old days... Aaron and Francie were going to the beach... one more time.

It was near to sunset. The beach was the place for sunrises, the river side of the Island offered up the most perfect sunset views... clean air, still waters, and peace. Over the deserted beach, slashes of ambient light and colors from the west were doing their best to give the ocean side of Squires its usual finest hour. Two riders on one fiery pony slashed the scene at its' peak, barely pausing before crashing into the surf. Aaron had ceased trying to make them stop, concentrating on staying astride. If he had gone off, it would have been fatal, given the pony's speed.

Aaron hoped to overpower Franciene as they slowed in the churning surf, but Topsy was swimming so strongly they were soon beyond the breakers in deep water, capping white from the now gusty, onshore wind. He could only guess how Topsy was being driven away from shore by powers beyond her own. Franciene was determined to use her pony to drown him for sure this time. As for time... there WAS no more. Aaron once again yelled to the frenzied girl, and then he strong-armed her off of Topsy's back. Franciene was grabbing for Topsy's tail... her mane... anything she could reach, but Aaron was all over her. If he had to die, he would see this thing that was once his dear friend, now the soul of evil, to her end with him. They fought as if of the same strength, first one was pushed under, then the other, swallowing brine in tandem. There was no need for words as they battled to live, their wild eyes spoke between the blows.

Topsy was treading water around the scene as if a spectator at a duel, which in truth she was, but she was also waiting for her cue.

* * *

The dreams began again. Massey was sleeping soundly, gaining strength toward wellness with each brief nap. This one would be different... his image of Aaron replaced by one of Aunt Clothilde and Aunt Carrie, dressed like it was Easter Sunday morning, and garnished with his traditional gift of purple violet corsages. Behind them, more hazy forms gathered. He saw them clearer, as if they were slipping from a fog. First, Pansy and Jasper... it was good to see them again. Next, Dan, his buddy, with Linda and Will, his lady-love and their own recovered son... and last, his wife, Frances, flanked by his parents, and everyone looking beautiful, just beautiful.

They were smiling and looking very content. Then, on perfect cue, they began to hum the melody, "Swing Low, Sweet Chariot," ever so softly. Frances came to him, as close as she could without getting on the bed, and whispered, "Massey, darlin', don't you be worried about anything. Everything is going to be ALL RIGHT."

Frances retreated, and Carrie, with 'Tilde beside her, came close. "My honey-chile, we love you, and we'll be with you through this... me here all the day, and Aunt 'Tilde 'biding while you sleep. That's a promise from us you can count on, 'cause you' goin' to be like our own child as long as you live and beyond." They were gone, back in the fog that instant, and he saw Dan waving and giving the thumbs up, as Will and Linda Sue approached the bed.

Massey tried to speak, but was unable to make a sound. He wanted to ask why Franciene wasn't there if all those he loved and who loved him were assembled for support. Linda leaned over close, kissed the air between their mouths, and said softly, "I never wanted us to be parted, Massey, and if my heart rules I still don't. Whatever you need from me to survive this crisis, you will have, I promise you." She retreated as Will replaced her. He felt the boy's ease and sincerity as he said, "Papa, I'm so sorry about all this. I just want you to get well real soon, so I can be the son you wanted and didn't have. And you have to believe me, I don't blame any-body for me not having a family, not Mom, not you... not anybody." He too, kissed the air above his daddy's cheek and was gone.

"What IS this? Am I about to die?" Although still in the dream state, Massey's fears were mounting and so was his blood pressure. His "visitors", disappeared when the nurse breezed in, reproachfully adjusting the intravenous drip and taking Massey's clammy wrist for a pulse check. "My Dear, you are upsetting yourself far too much about something! I'm close to sedating you, and I know you hate that!" She recorded his vitals and stood looking down at his face, trying to read his thoughts.

"I just had a damn nightmare, is all, Honey. No, I won't take any of those drool makin' chokers you want to shove down my gul-let, and that's a fact. I'll watch a little TV, and see if that settles me down, what about it?" He finished off the last suggestion with a broad wink, and made as if to grab her. His charm was boundless, and he knew it. Maybe the nurse was right... he shouldn't exagger-ate the visitations simply to combat his loneliness. Why didn't a one of those people mention his girl? What was missing here? And why were they all hovering and clucking over him that way? He sighed, slapped the sheets in frustration, and flipped through the channels until he found an old film about Spain, and bullfighting, and Ava Gardner... a perfect getaway for sundown.

* * *

Sundown on Squires Island Beach... usually idyllic, but this eve-ning there was a life or death struggle with no one to see or stop it except a frightened pony, circling them beyond the waves. It was Aaron who took the upper hand, driven to unchecked rage as he again saw his mother's shriveling little body in that poor wooden box. He shoved Franciene's forehead down, then down deeper. She fought to the surface once more, before he took her arm and twisted until she upended to avoid the pain.

He felt the arm crack, but it did not stop him. She would die now, for her deeds. Her head was still pointing toward the bottom when he gave her butt one last mighty shove with his foot, and then she was gone. He waited a minute, then two. It was still... too still for there to be any life in her. Aaron reached for the pony's back to climb aboard. Something shot out of the water like it had been catapulted from the bottom. It was the blue and green dress... the strawberry blonde hair...but it seemed strangely not to be Franciene!

Both Aaron and the pony grew still... stone still. The wide-eyed girl wiped her hair from her eyes, saw them, and swiftly swam to the pony's flank. Aaron was ready to knee her under her chin when he got a good look at his target.

IT TRULY WASN'T FRANCIENE! He wrapped his long arms around her waist and hauled her up on Topsy's back like a sack of corn, went to the pony's head and held onto her mane as he pointed her toward the beach. When they were on shore the girl slipped from the horse's back to face Aaron. "How did this happen? Where is Franciene? One minute we were paddling the canoe, and now I'm here! Hey! Where did I get this awful dress? I had on a pink sun suit! And who are YOU? Please, tell me I'm not going crazy!"

Aaron told her she was not going crazy... and that everything would be alright now. He was sure of the power that had placed this poor girl back in her life, but not at all sure who had wielded that power.

Perhaps it was just as simple as this....IT WAS THE POWER OF GOD!

Down deep as if weighted, a slim and lovely but very dead girl hung face down in the darkening surf, her hair fanning out like an angel's diadem. The pink and white, two-piece sun suit, now a murky blue-purple in the piercing rays from the last glow of the day, and her broken arm hanging by nothing but tender tissue. Franciene had come home.

This is the Interruption of the Story... Not the END

# EPILOGUE

*According to Toby Howell*
**JUNE - 1982**

It was fitting and proper to get in touch after a year. Enough time had gone by for hurts to heal, maybe to reflect, and start to make sense of what that week had been to them, each one apart, and together. I took myself to Padgett's as I vowed I would, but not with Will in tow. He wanted to stay and see his family through the stages they were all sure to face. I would not have expected less from this enigmatic youngster. I am proud to busting of they way he is growing up.

I wasn't alone at the beach, but it wasn't anybody sweet-smelling and soft-sided. Captain Dan had been at loose ends, what with the crises, both Massey's and ours, and Jaime and Cissy eloping, I told him to follow me to the beach house. The Hartsells delivered a brand new, marine-yellow Jeep with a huge Carolina blue bow around it to the Harbor, as a thank you gift for Dan getting their boy home, so one day not long after, he was a sight to see roaring up the driveway to the beach house.

The Hartsells even had the old Jeep trucked back home to Frenchport from Tally's for him, and with nothing pressing we spent the entire time either drunk or half-drunk, between the beach and Nevilles. It was providential for Dan, because he and sassy Shirley hit it off in five minutes that first visit. I think he'll have her in his pocket as long as he wants her there... they both seem to like the situation just fine. By the way, his married children are blissful... and pregnant...with twins. Captain Dan a grandpa? It fits him like a glove.

As for Linda Sue, she got covered up with Thornedike matters, so I made my retreat as unobtrusive and shallow as possible. If I had forced myself on the scene and stayed, seeming to hang on like a lion with a haunch of fresh kill just beyond its claws, what would it have proven... that I can out-maneuver a convalescing man who recently lost his beloved daughter under horrible, obscene circumstances? No. After merely surviving that week, all of us, we felt it was time for miles to come between us for resolution. If Linda and I are to be in this life together, it will happen at the appointed time, after her issues are put to rest.

It helped a little that the lady was a sobbing mess when I said goodbye. I was basking in being cried after, but I want her to WANT ME... not need me to lean on. We are too strong, each alone, to cleave to a need for each other from some silly weakness. I know as this part of our story winds down, that I do truly love and want Linda Sue, even after the tumultuous times we had together. Adversity, they say, breeds character. I believe it filters out falsity, and allows the perfect center to shine. She shines so bright... well, never mind.

Will is going to be making some hard, grown-man choices for himself soon, and he hinted that we will strike out together once again, at least for awhile, as soon as Massey is renewed. Hey! If I had Carrie Treacle in my corner my whole life like Massey Thornedike, I'd be Champion of this World!

Carrie, wonderful, enigmatic woman she is, will be a part of what I do from now on. The deep powers she possesses saved lives and restored sanity to those who believed themselves unable to repair the damage done by so much fear and uncertainty. She was in charge, even before it all happened, when she expressed trepidation about Franciene's week of un-chaperoned graduation fun. She suspected the girl was up to something bigger and more harmful. Her visions of the week's outcome caused her to intercede to save her "adopted family".

When she "saw" the image of Franciene's body washed up on the riverbank after Toby and Will found her and covered her with palmetto fronds, she could not allow it to remain there for Massey to know. She was certain when the terrible truth was discovered by someone on the Island, he would be told in minutes, so she sent her back into the river, near to where that detached arm was found in the Tomochichi shrimp boat's net-spill during that impossible week.

Only a select few of Francie's neighbors could have known about her evil powers, and how they intensified after she dispatched 'Tilde with the poisoned dumpling. They loved her as a sweet and innocent daughter of Squires, so while she was off, about her exodus with the two boys, they figured she had finally slipped the over-protective grasp of her daddy, with something close to their blessing.

Everyone except Carrie, the Griffins, and finally Aaron, when his mother's spirit came to him with how she died, were oblivious to the truth. Those who had knowledge, realized it was much too serious and terminal a possession, and when that became obvious, she was already too lost. She had to die, so the others could live, and that is what drove Carrie to action.

In the end, it was Carrie who saved Cliff and Mandy, and it was Aaron who gave what had become of poor little Franciene, the Eternal Peace she needed. It can be said here, that there is a lot of this going on in the world whether or not we can see, or know of it... it is called, Triumph of Good Over Evil!

Back to this before I am done... there is no one but Will who can be my travelling companion. We have a lot of things to teach each other. His Dad will understand, if I know his breed, that a boy only comes to manhood when he can choose his way, and it turns out to be the right way. Massey has grown up too, I think, along with his boy... [might be because of him]. It had to be the toughest moment of his life, when he learned his little girl was gone. The decision was made by all who love Massey, to spare him the darkest details only those who were there could know, so he bore a mourning period without knowing her worst deeds. Anyway, Will and Mattie are still quite the item, and that's good!

Aaron. Nothing new to say about THIS fine young man, except he is just that. I didn't know him when he was deep into the drugs. He managed the feat of coming clean within hours after his mother's death... a miracle of nature that puts rehab to shame, and sheds the light of hope on him. There are excuses and explanations for everything, but I know as sure as my name is Tobias, that Aaron Braswell is blessed, and saved for something huge. He is re-ordering his mother's house to suit himself, and is enrolling this fall in Beaufort at a small school that instructs in art pertaining to nature. He will do well. Both his Mamas will see to it, one during the day, and the other all through the night.

Now about Mandy... I only met her that terrible evening when Aaron rode into the yard with her, all wet and shocky, and never saw her after the next morning when we sent her off to Frenchport with Jasper. She said she was going home to Lighthouse Point, lickety-split, as soon as she could find her car, and that she would try to make amends with her Mom and Dad. Then she said she was going to take advantage of an opportunity few are given. Wonder if she knows how much that really means... to all of us.

Miss Ruby will be where she is until she no longer can, but I want to say on her behalf, and the behalf of all those stalwarts we, who come and go, never regard for long. I WILL REMEMBER THIS ONE! She has touched those around her, to their betterment, as long as she has been there. God Bless Miss Ruby's Good Heart! I wish her a long, healthy and happy life.

No worries after Jasper and Pansy. They are, and will remain, the stalwart Mother and Father of Squires Island. I will be looking forward to a warm reunion with them when I return to Squires Island... Yes, I said "WHEN"!

There must be mention of the Palmland contingent, with Clifford Hartsell most central to this tale. His re-patriation was consuming, and life-changing for all, and would be Palmland's claim to fame for years to come.

Cliff's amputation saga was one for the books... although much was not documented due to medical incongruity. It was said to be not possible that a severed foot, under those awful conditions, could be successfully re-attached, but here it was... his foot FIT! By God, it fit as if a puzzle piece... and the necessary connectors magically connected! Nerves, arteries, veins, bones and the muscles, tendons, ligaments, cartridge, even all the tissue fragments were there on the stump, healthy and waiting for their prodigal foot's return. Cliff has been spared any memory of the reason he was found in the mud that day, so he was satisfied with the story that he lost control of the car while Franciene and he were arguing, and she had likely panicked and hitch-hiked away after the car sank in the creek, believing him dead, with no word to anyone.

Hillis had a nice meal that big day, and soon after asked to be put on his way home. It was no task for Jesse to phone the hospital where he knew his boss was, and within a half-hour, The Great Hillis, descendant of a mighty Seminole Chief, long dead, was south bound for home in a chartered jet with a handsome cash reward from Strahan Hartsell.

What I know about the senior Hartsells, or their very sheltered girl-child, I could put in a thimble, but they are still there... still mega-rich, and still snooty as ever. Let us go to better, more promising places... Like Padgetts Island.

Our personal reunion, Linda, Will's, and mine, will have to wait... We unanimously agreed we need to continue patching up our lives before impulsively casting half-healed souls together, whatever the hell that means. Anyway, I'm here at The Beach, and I will remain here, reflecting on the most amazing, unforgettable seven days of my life. I sure hope none of those Boykins try to heave me out of here before I'm good and ready to go. Besides, I am building and installing new shutters all around the house, and taking my time, as a gift to Katie's family. Not a bad exchange. I Love You, Katie Darlin'!

Yours truly, Tobias Howell, esq.